RENEGADE IMMORTALITY

RENEGADE IMMORTALITY

Christopher Clay

Renegade Immortality

Brown Books Publishing Group
Dallas, TX/New York, NY
www.BrownBooks.com
(972) 381-0009

A New Era in Publishing®

Publisher's Cataloging-In-Publication Data

Names: Clay, Christopher, 1985- author.
Title: Renegade immortality / Christopher Clay.
Description: Dallas, TX ; New York, NY : Brown Books Publishing Group, [2024]
Identifiers: ISBN: 978-1-61254-665-0 | LCCN: 2023949761
Subjects: LCSH: Special operations (Military science)--Fiction. | Grief--Fiction. | Siblings--Fiction. | Kidnapping--Fiction. | Research--Peru--Fiction. | LCGFT: Action and adventure fiction. Thrillers (Fiction) | BISAC: FICTION / Action & Adventure. | FICTION / Thrillers / Military. | FICTION / Magical Realism.
Classification: LCC: PS3603.L3864 R46 2024 | DDC: 813/.6--dc23

ISBN 978-1-61254-665-0
LCCN 2023949761

Printed in the United States
10 9 8 7 6 5 4 3 2 1

For more information or to contact the author, please go to www.ChristopherClayAuthor.com.

I dedicate this book to my mom, an outlaw of the highest order.
A true Renegade. You were right, it takes all kinds.

Prologue

Caucasus Mountains

Eighteen Months Ago

Within the thin walls of a shanty structure, silence fell upon the four men gathered around a small table. A single light fixture, hung from the ceiling, swayed back and forth like a pendulum. Inside the makeshift safe house, the four figures intently studied a topographic map of the target area. Light spilled around the chilled room ever so gently as the wind forced the structure's walls to lightly succumb to the moving air. With each pass of the light, each man's puzzled face was put on display.

Cody Willis had stood with his muscular arms folded across his chest before his hand came up to rub the short beard on his chin. At six-foot-even and 185 pounds, he had the build of a triathlete. It was obvious to any onlooker he worked very hard to maintain a balance of speed, power, and endurance. His dirty blond hair stuck out the back of his hat, curling at the end.

To his right was Val Grayson, team leader and the most experienced man in the room. Only an inch taller than Cody, he was ten years his senior and built like an Olympic swimmer. Even in his late forties, his broad shoulders and defined chest could be seen through his Crye combat shirt. He pushed his gray hair back and watched his team intently with his icy blue eyes.

Frank Pierce, third-in-command, stood with his hands stuffed in the kangaroo pocket of his hoodie and looked at the maps and surveillance pictures they had taken. At six-foot-four, he was the tallest member of the team and often joked he was, by far, the strongest.

Completing the team of rebels with a cause was Tom Lorry. Though he was the junior man on Renegade, he was not inexperienced by any means, and despite being the shortest at five-foot-ten, he was also the largest. His shoulders looked as though they'd been surgically removed and replaced with bowling balls, his heavily muscled arms making an extra-large shirt look like it was too small.

Tom was the first to break the silence. "What if we're looking at this thing all backward?"

He paused for a few moments, looking up from the map with raised eyebrows, trying to read each man's face.

"What if we do a quick hit on the house and snatch him there instead of trying to find the perfect spot to do a vehicle interdiction? We've already done the recce on the house and know more about it than we do about his sporadic travel routes," he said, using the military vernacular for reconnaissance.

Val Grayson let out a pondering hum, contemplating the change without taking his eyes from the map.

"Okay, talk us through it," Frank Pierce piped up. When he spoke, he spoke with confidence, looking directly at Tom to show his mate his full support.

Tom started up again. "Well we know he uses different routes of travel to avoid this exact thing from happening. On top of that, his protective detail ain't too bad, so it's gonna be a lot harder to get the vehicles to stop and not raise suspicion. If his detail is worth their salt, they're gonna be put on edge and just haul ass outta there; however"—Tom pointed back at the grid that contained the house—"if we hit the house where he feels safe and his security is comfortable, surprise may give us the upper hand."

Cody Willis let the discussion unfold before him. He'd remained silent through the exchange of plans between his teammates, but felt as though he needed to interject soon. He never wanted to stifle free thinking within the team—it was one of their prominent strengths. He thought Tom posed a good argument against taking the vehicles on the road, but also wasn't exactly eager to go straight inside the lion's den, so to speak. They hadn't been able to get inside this man's house, so they had little idea what the layout looked like.

On one hand, it would be nearly impossible to predict exactly what the security team would do on the road. On the other, if we take direct action on the house, the fight would be taking place inside a house and CQB is always a risk. Then again, at least everyone would be contained. All of these thoughts and more went through Cody's head in an instant. He stood there, silently weighing their options.

Val cut in. "Okay, so we *quietly* ghost the outside patrols, access the house, snatch him up, and hightail it outta there? Cody, how many guys is he supposed to have with him?"

"Last count was five: three outside on roving patrol, two inside at any given time. But that was a week ago when we first got in country. Things could've changed."

Val considered the options, his eyes darting over all the maps and then around the room at each team member in turn. "Alright, let's make it happen. I want Tom and Frank on long guns. Once the rovers are gone, Cody and I will take the house, free flow through, take out the two inside—assuming there wasn't some last-minute change—and then we'll grab this dirtbag. After he's under control, we take a vehicle on-site while y'all provide overwatch and exfil back to the trucks . . . one each. Y'all good with that?"

Val looked at each man independently, waiting for the various responses.

"You know it."

"'Bout time."

"Let's do it."

Val looked at Frank. "I need you on overwatch with the SR-25 in case things get spicy. I'd rather you be on the gas gun and not some bolt action."

"Val, I thought we talked about this. He has a name. It's Big Boss," Frank joked.

"You can name your rifle Mary Poppins if you want, just do what I ask, will ya?" Val replied with an eyeroll.

The team chuckled as they collected their body armor, radios, medical gear, and other assorted kits. They all finished with their respective last-minute equipment checks and headed out of the door to load their equipment into their trucks. Cody moved close to Val on the way out and nudged his shoulder with his own.

"Mary Poppins . . . It's got a nice ring to it, don't ya think?" Cody said with a laugh.

"Don't encourage him. This mission is a big deal for us. If we get this guy, it's a huge payout for us. You saw the bounty on him; I need y'all at the top of your game," Val replied.

"I've been keepin' an eye on the guys. They're ready to roll. Eager, but not overly so."

"Sounds like you've got a handle on things then. Let's knock out a few last-minute things before we head out. I gotta call Chop and let him know we're all set to execute."

"Okay, Boss, sounds good. You cool if I use the other SAT phone real quick? I need to call the girls."

Val nodded and walked to a secluded area to make his call while Cody did the same.

After securing the backup satellite phone, Cody felt excitement brewing as he dialed the numbers. A wide smile spread across his face as he thumbed the button to start the call. Cody's fingers tapped nervously waiting for the connection. He heard the series of beeps telling him something was happening when he heard his daughter Elena's voice.

"Daddy!" she exclaimed.

"Hi, baby girl!" Cody replied, a smile nearly splitting his face in two. He couldn't help it. Elena always seemed to have that effect on him.

"Where are you, Daddy?" Elena asked.

"Well, honey, I'm very far away right now, but I should be home soon."

"How soon? Like tonight?" the three-year-old asked.

"No, honey, not tonight. Maybe two or three more days. Are you doing good? Where's Mom?"

"Aww, I wanted to see you tonight. Mom is right here. You can talk to her."

The phone shuffled a bit and then sounded as though it was passed through a mosh pit as Elena ran away to the next most exciting thing. "Here, Mommy! It's Daddy!" he heard Elena say as the phone exchanged hands. Cody had spent the last three weeks away from home, and after hearing his daughter's voice, it really sunk in how much he'd missed her. How much he missed both of them.

"Hey, babe," Cody's wife, Jenny, said.

"Hey, love. You girls doing okay?" Cody asked.

There was a beat of hesitation on the other side. "Yeah, we're getting by," she finally replied.

"What's wrong? Something sounds off with your voice."

"No, it's nothing. We can talk about it when you get back," she said quietly.

Cody didn't have the heart to tell her the operation they were conducting was high risk and there was a chance they might not get to have that conversation if they waited. He had to find a way to gently pull the information out of her and fix the problem here and now. That was his job in its simplest form. Fix the problem.

"Oh, come on, I haven't had a chance to talk to you guys in a few days. Gimme something to work with here, babe."

He heard a sigh escape her from the other end. "Well, that's exactly it, Cody. We haven't heard from you in three days. Your daughter has been asking about you nonstop, and I don't know what to tell her. 'Sorry, Elena, Daddy is too busy catching and shooting bad guys to call us right now.'"

Cody frowned. "That sounds good to me. And it's the truth, so what's the problem?"

"That *is* the problem, Cody."

A silence hung in the air. Neither said a word.

"Like I said, I wanted to talk about this when you got home. Look, I don't want this hanging over you while you're out there. I know how dangerous distractions can be when you're working. Forget I said anything. We'll talk when you get home, okay?"

"C'mon, Jenny, that's not fair. You know I don't think of you or Elena like that. Like some sort of interference. You two are my world. You're what brings me home, what gives me a reason to fight."

"We know you love us, but at least when you were a cop, we saw you more than once or twice a month. That's all."

"Yeah, well, we've picked up a few more contracts in the last couple years, and it's making a difference, babe. We're able to do things and go places the military can only dream of. Plus we get to make some more money. I want you girls to be comfortable, and the money here is *way* better than anything I'd make at the department."

Another sigh. "It's not about the money, Cody. Things have changed in the last few years since we have Elena now. You can't run around playing John McClane, doing cool guy stuff all the time anymore. Your daughter needs you. *I* need you."

Cody's heart sank. "Are you asking me to choose between ProCorp and the two of you?"

"Listen, I know you love your job, but something has to change. I'm sorry to spring this on you while you're out there . . . somewhere. Please don't let it get inside your head. Be careful."

"I always am. You know that," he replied.

"I do. Listen, we'll be driving back from my mom's later tonight." There was a pause. "Just remember that I love you," Jenny said.

Cody closed his eyes and pictured his wife, realizing how much he missed her. "I love you more. Give Elena a big hug for me, alright? Tell her I love her. I gotta go."

"I will. Bye, Cody," Jenny said. Her voice was shaky, like she was fighting back tears.

Cody thumbed the button to end the call and stood staring at the Caucasus Mountains' moon. The chill in the air hit his face, sending a shiver down his spine. Or was that the realization that either his dream job or his marriage was about to end? He couldn't exactly be sure and chose instead to focus on the mission just like Jenny said. Keep his head in the game so that he could go home and get this all sorted out.

A little ways away, each man had dressed differently according to his own preference—donning the latest high-performance outdoor gear to help protect them from the elements at this altitude. All were the norm for such a scenario as the one they were presented with tonight: locating the whereabouts of a suspected mid-level financier of terrorist activities. Similarly, each man wore cutting-edge, lightweight body armor in their plate carriers—which held their spare ammunition, batteries, personal communications equipment, and escape and evasion necessities.

Their Ops-Core helmets hung dual-tube night vision goggles off the front. Val was the only exception in that he preferred the Ground Panoramic Night Vision Goggle, or GPNVG, with its four tubes instead of the standard two which gave him a wider field of view, and thus, more situational awareness.

They loaded their gear inside two separate, nondescript four-wheel-drive trucks and drove to their designated rendezvous point just a mile from the target house. They'd been conducting low visibility, or low viz, surveillance on their target for about two weeks and had found some weaknesses in his security team. Once Positive Identification, or PID, had been confirmed, Val sent the intel up the chain, which was returned with a snatch-and-grab order. They quickly began their recce of both the moneyman's security and his comings and goings, which eventually led the four-man team to where they stood tonight.

The trucks were staged off the road and concealed with nearby foliage and netting to camouflage them from innocents driving by. Cody, Val, Frank, and Tom ensured their weapons were loaded and checked their radios for function. They patrolled through the thick forest of the Caucasus Mountains, their night vision goggles illuminating the way. Thanks to a light rain, the various branches and foliage were damp, softening their steps and making detection difficult. None of them spoke as they moved, each cueing off one another and closing the distance to their target.

Eventually, they came upon a house—or, more appropriately, a mountainside estate. The house was estimated to be 3,800 square feet, contained three floors, and had only one access road to the main highway. Val, through the glow of his white phosphor goggles, was the first to see the estate as he crested a hill.

Val keyed the push-to-talk on his plate carrier. "All elements, this is Actual. I have eyes on the target building."

He heard the replies through his helmet-attached hearing protection.

"Zero Three copies," he said. "Zero Four copies. Zero Two enroute."

All of the operators gathered around Val, kneeling on one knee as he began issuing orders.

"Frank and Tom, why don't y'all set up on the north side over by the large boulders. Should provide some decent cover while Zero Two and I descend down this hill and wait at the far edge of the creek to the west. There's some decent concealment in the woods for us."

Cody chimed in, "I agree, but how about one of us stays near the creek and the other take a position on the south-west side to maintain eyes on the backside of the house? Last thing we want is someone sneakin' out the back while we ain't looking."

Val gave a quick glance to the large house and said, "Good idea. Frank, you bring Bubo with ya."

Nicknamed after the mechanized owl from *Clash of the Titans*, Bubo was a modified DJI Mavic Pro II wrapped in a MultiCam Black skin; it gave their team an undeniable edge. Bubo allowed its user to identify any heat source on target utilizing the latest FLIR thermal optics in the lenses. Additionally, the internal motors were, as Tom put it, "stealthified" since they were nearly silent at fifty feet above the ground and beyond.

"Of course, never leave home without him," Frank replied, taking off his backpack to set up the drone.

The team sat in relative silence and watched the house, hoping for any irregularities or roaming patrols while Frank finished his preparations and start-up routine.

Frank launched the mini drone and circled the house.

"Drone is up, clear to move."

"Copy. Zero One and Zero Two moving," Cody replied.

Cody and Val moved south down the hillside, being careful not to silhouette themselves against the night sky.

The two-man team split up when Val reached his position on the west side of the structure. "This is Actual. I'm set on red," he said to the rest of the team, referencing his side of the house.

"Copy, Actual. Bubo is flying high and looking good. I got eyes on two of the three rovers. I think the third is underneath the overhang of the balcony. Don't wanna risk being compromised by getting Bubo too low."

"Roger. On it," Cody replied.

Frank continued his aerial assessment of the house and its surroundings while looking at the iPad mini he used to control the drone. Tom lay prone an arm's length away to provide cover.

Staring at the screen, Frank whispered ominously to himself, "The field mouse is fast, but the owl sees at night."

Tom, momentarily distracted, looked at Frank and asked, "Dude, was that a Ricky Bobby quote?"

"Kinda creepy, ain't it?" Frank chuckled without taking his eyes off the screen, completing the line. Tom smiled to himself and returned to the scope of his rifle, shaking his head. Cody reached his position 150 meters away from Val and advised the team he was in position.

"Good call on the third goon. He's sitting right underneath the balcony taking a smoke break," Val said into the boom mic.

Frank looked at Tom. "Am I good or what?"

"Or what," Tom replied, still scanning the front of the house through his riflescope.

Val activated the PEQ-15 infrared IR laser on his earth toned HK416. Though invisible to the naked eye, the IR laser and illuminator allowed the operator to illuminate and engage targets while wearing night vision. Luckily for Renegade, these bodyguards were not so well equipped.

Val aimed it at the center mass of the closest patrol, who was walking left to right from Val's view, and keyed his radio. "Alright, boys. Pick a target, and let's try to make this as clean as possible."

He released the push-to-talk and saw the dazzle of Cody's IR laser from his position, which was aimed at the backside of the house. He then saw another laser activate on his left, with Tom signaling he was on target.

Val could just barely see Tom's stationary guard at the front of the house but had complete trust in his teammate's ability to hit his target under these conditions. Val closely watched the stride of his target. Judging the speed of the guard's walk, he placed the laser just in front of the man, maintaining an inch or so off his chest as he moved to Val's right, around the west side of the house.

Cody saw Val's target was moving and keyed his radio. "Tom, on you. Actual and I are set."

Tom held his Horus reticle at the top of his target's head, accounting for bullet drop. He thumbed the safety selector to fire and, ever so slightly, let his right index finger touch the single-stage three-and-a-half-pound trigger.

Time seemed to slow momentarily. Suddenly, from a distance of about 450 meters, a very soft pop was heard by Cody and Val, causing them to engage simultaneously with one round each. In just about three-quarters of a second, three shots were fired, but only two were audible.

Each man's suppressor certainly did its job, masking the flash and supersonic crack of the bullets. The guard in the front of the house dropped like a puppet whose strings had been cut. Val's target took half a step before falling forward on his face, and Cody's target slumped backward in the chair where he had enjoyed his final cigarette.

Frank kept his eyes locked on the iPad screen and panned the drone's camera around the north side of the house. He continued to fly the drone in a semicircle around the house from one hundred feet above until the scan was complete.

"Targets are down . . . Break . . . Clear to move to phase-line green," he advised Cody and Val via the radio.

"Roger. Moving," Val replied quickly.

Val and Cody moved cautiously, but quickly, to the west side of the house while Frank and Tom provided overwatch and sniper cover from their position. The dim lights inside the estate were just bright enough to white out the night vision goggles as they closed the distance. Cody and Val reached their designated point, holding cover on the exits.

"We gotta do something about these lights before we make entry," Cody said.

"Way ahead of you, little brother. I spotted the control box on my side as we were setting up. I'm gonna cut the hard line to the power. We gotta move quick though, 'cause once it's cut, they'll know somethin's up."

Cody held security on the rear corner of the house and radioed Frank, letting him know their intentions and that he should ultimately expect the blackout. Val moved quickly to the exterior control panel and pulled his rucksack from his back.

He tore open the zipper quickly and selected a pair of bolt cutters that had telescopic handles. This allowed him to reduce the size of the bolt cutters while they were not in use, but once deployed, they gave him leverage for the more difficult cuts. Val placed the sharp edge of the tool on the cable and hesitated for just a moment before using his push-to-talk.

"All elements, this is Actual. I have control. Goin' black in three . . . two . . ."

Before he got to one, he released his push-to-talk and then cut the line.

Immediately the entire house went pitch black. Cody's NVGs were instantly relieved of the overpowering illumination from inside the house. He could see the entire layout of the first floor. He didn't see any movement but could hear hushed voices coming from inside.

No more than a second after the house went dark, he felt a strong hand on his left shoulder giving him a squeeze. It was Val letting him know he was ready to move. Without a moment's hesitation, he glided around the back patio furniture under the overhang and walked directly to the door. His weapon was aimed directly into the large room through the open glass doors.

He approached the door and stopped about four feet from it while Val moved from behind him to check the handle. Luckily it was still unlocked, most likely from Cody's guard. Discovering the handle moved freely, Val looked directly at Cody who was already prepared to engage any lethal threat on the other side. Cody waved his rifle barrel up, then down, signaling to Val he was prepared for the door to open. Val opened the door quietly, and as soon as there was enough room for him to fit, Cody rushed in to cover his sector of fire.

The two-man assault team could see the whole floor plan clearly; no threats were spotted throughout it. They continued to clear around obstacles and furniture as Cody made his way to the first-floor staircase. Val completed his clear and moved to accompany him.

Val moved purposefully with the grace and speed only born from experience. Both Renegades could hear at least one voice coming from the staircase. They moved with skilled precision up the stairs, each covering their respective areas and taking special precautions not to trip on the stairs as they moved. As Cody reached the top, he saw a man in the kitchen, armed with a pistol on his hip, hands frantically searching for a light switch.

No immediate threat, Cody said to himself.

It appeared as though the man might have been looking for a snack when the lights went black. Beyond him, on the other side of the room, another set of stairs led to the third and final layout of the room. Cody activated his IR laser and held it on the man's upper chest while Val made it up the last few stairs quietly.

Cody and Val, having worked together for as long as they had, were comfortable enough to move around each other in complete silence, each one cueing off the other's movement. Cody sidestepped to his right, keeping his laser on the guard until Val got into position. He saw Val's laser ignite and immediately moved his attention to the second set of stairs. He could hear a man calling something out in a foreign language from upstairs. Cody could only assume it was the fifth and final guard calling out to his associate on their floor. He froze in place for just a moment, listening intently to the voice. To his side, Val still held steady on the kitchen man who had made his way to a different part of the wall and was still desperately attempting to find the light switch; his back still turned to his two unknown assaulters.

Val slowly slung his rifle to his front, letting it rest on his Crye plate carrier, which allowed him the use of both his hands. In the blink of an eye, he grabbed the man in a deep and unbreakable rear-naked choke, cutting off his supply of oxygen. The man thrashed his legs, his hands clawing at Val's arms, desperate to break free from the unseen terror.

Cody remained motionless as he watched the stairs through his night vision. The scuffle sounded unbearably loud in the dark since sound, at this point, was the only sense able to provide any information. The fifth guard yelled out to his partner again, but only muted gags and an unmistakable sound of a table being knocked over were his response. He descended the steps slowly which was a mistake on his part. Cody first saw the man's feet as he came down the staircase, then the barrel of an AK-47 assault rifle.

Cody took one step to the right to get a clearer shot just as the man readied his weapon. The IR laser centered directly on the man's chest, and Cody fired four shots in rapid succession. The first three hit the guard directly in the chest, with the fourth striking him on the right shoulder. His lifeless body crumpled down the remaining stairs.

The kitchen man had succumbed to the choke, and Val released the unconscious body, letting it slide to the hardwood floor. He regained control of his HK416 and rushed to the staircase. He saw a large pool of blood spreading from the guard who lay motionless in a heap at the bottom of the stairs.

Cody squeezed his shoulder, giving him the signal. The two began the sequence again, this time clearing the staircase to the third floor. At the top, the two men could see two closed doors on the far side, one lit with a faint glow around the frame. Val flashed his IR laser on the door, signaling Cody to check this one first.

Both men detected the unmistakable odor of marijuana coming from the door as they approached. Cody and Val set up on opposite sides of the frame. Val reached for the knob. His gloved hand carefully turned the handle, hoping whoever was inside wouldn't hear the rattle. It was locked. Val shook his head. Cody motioned with his leg to kick the door in. Val nodded in agreement and prepared himself for the breach, aiming his rifle directly at what lay beyond. Cody faced away from the door and mule-kicked the handle side with everything he had. The door exploded inward; Val went through not a second later.

The men located their target who was, mere moments ago, enjoying his blunt and bubble bath. Candles were even lit on the stylish decorative counter completing his ambience of rejuvenation. The man nearly jumped out of his skin when Val burst through the door. In the man's defense, Val probably did look like a space-traveling, four-eyed alien through the faint glow of the candles. It was clear why the target was seemingly unaware the lights had been cut: he was wearing some type of face cream with cucumbers placed over his eyes.

Val kept his weapon trained on the man, saying only, "Get up. Some people wanna talk to you."

Val pulled the naked man from the bathtub, water splashing everywhere. Cody was confident Val could handle the pampered man by himself, so he took the opportunity to radio Frank and Tom who had been waiting patiently for an update. "This is Zero Two. I pass Goldmine. I say again, Goldmine. Prepare for extract."

Frank took one more pass around the house and peered over at the only road leading out. He saw no moving vehicles and no outward sign of a disturbance. He recalled Bubo to him while Tom scanned the perimeter of the house. Bubo flew directly overhead and descended into Frank's grasp. He quickly secured the UAV in his bag and returned to his beloved SR-25 to help Tom cover Val and Cody's extraction.

Val had grabbed an expensive-looking bathrobe for their target, throwing it over him before pulling a small black bag from his pocket and placing it over the man's head. The man offered no resistance, likely out of sheer fear. His hands were soon secured by heavy-duty flex cuffs. Both Cody and Val grabbed him by an arm and led him forcefully down the stairs to the second floor.

They approached the front door of the house and looked for anything out of place through the windows. Val only saw the lifeless body of the guard eliminated by Tom.

Val keyed the radio. "Breaking exterior, front door."

"Roger. Front door," Frank replied via radio.

Cody shoved open the door and quickly regained his control of the prisoner who was now yelling something unintelligible to the men as they moved. They chose the luxury SUV parked out front and opened the back-left door in which Cody stuffed their prisoner inside like he was throwing a bag of dog food in the backseat. He pushed the man to the far side of the car, giving himself enough room to sit beside him. After pulling a small syringe from the shoulder pocket of his combat shirt, Cody pulled the top and drove the needle into the financier's thigh, pushing the plunger down with his thumb, administering a powerful sedative.

Val jumped into the driver's seat and found the keys in the visor. With a turn of the key, the vehicle came to life.

"All good back here," said Cody. "Let's bounce."

Val shifted the transmission into drive and sped away. Frank and Tom followed their movements from the front door to the car. Once they saw the Cadillac moving, they broke down their position without saying a word, preparing themselves for the hike back to their staged vehicles.

Two hours later they were all sitting together in the safe house with a heavily sedated terrorist financier. Cody, Frank, and Tom unpacked their gear and prepared for departure while Val was busy on his satellite phone, arranging the pickup for their capture. Once the logistics were set, he walked in the safe house and plopped down in a wooden chair, letting out a satisfied sigh.

"And another bites the dust, eh, Boss?" Tom said as he carefully broke down and packed his weapons into the impact-resistant case.

"Yeah, just gotta wait on the transport dudes and then this dirt bag is officially someone else's problem. Anybody gotta use the SAT phone while I take a piss?"

Cody looked up from his bags and checked the time. It was already dark back home on the other side of the world, which meant Jenny and Elena were just getting ready for bed. He'd been able to stay on task while out in the field. Though after they returned with their target, he couldn't stop thinking about the phone call with Jenny.

Her words kept ringing through his head. He carefully weighed the pros and cons of each option. If he left Renegade, what would he do? There was no way he was going back to the police department in Austin. Where would he go that wasn't doing the exact same thing just for someone else? Besides, what was he really qualified to do anymore?

Hello, I'm Cody Willis. I work for ProCorp. I've spent the better part of a decade hunting and killing some of the most dangerous men on the planet.

No, his mind was made up.

Cody loved his family, but Jenny was as independent as they come. She didn't *need* Cody to make it in this world. Elena would eventually understand. Her daddy fought bad guys and kept them where they needed to be: either fearfully hiding deep inside some distant cave or dead in the ground.

No. Cody was staying with Renegade, with ProCorp. It's where he belonged.

He said, "Yeah, I gotta call home real quick and check on the girls."

Val handed the phone over to Cody. He dialed the number and heard two rings before it connected. An unfamiliar male voice answered his wife's phone.

"Cody? Where are you?"

"Who the hell is this?" Cody's stomach suddenly knotted up. Something was wrong.

"It's JP. Where are you?" Cody's heart sank, and he immediately felt sick after recognizing JP's voice. He was an old friend from his former police department.

"What's goin' on? Where's Jen? Elena? Are they okay?"

Every Renegade stopped what they were doing, hearing the panic in Cody's voice as he stood motionless, his grip tightening on the phone. His friend's voice cracked as raw emotion seeped through. Barely able to say the words, JP managed to finally get something out.

"You need to come home right now."

"Tell me what happened," Cody said loudly, trying to speak over the ringing in his ears.

"Cody, where are you? Are you with some people? You're not alone, are you?"

"JP, *wher*e are Jenny and Elena?"

There was a long stretch of silence. Right before Cody was going to start shouting, JP spoke. "Cody, I'm so sorry. They're gone. Both of them. They're . . . they're dead."

JP kept talking, asking where Cody was and asking who was around him, but Cody was no longer listening. His blood had turned to ice. The satellite phone slipped from Cody's hand and crashed onto the floor, breaking into as many fragments as his heart.

1

Austin, Texas

Present Day

"Gentlemen, as you can see from my research, I am very optimistic about the samples and architecture we found last year."

The fit woman in her late twenties turned her back and walked a few steps forward to the large sixty-inch LED TV screen attached to the wall. With an outstretched arm, she pointed to a small gray square on an enlarged, black-and-white aerial-satellite photo to pinpoint the exact location. However, little attention was being paid to the screen. Instead, most eyes were taking in her backside.

"I believe this helps add some credibility about ancient civilizations before us and how they're linked internationally. Specifically, the link, of course, being giants."

She caught a few eye rolls as she turned around, but continued nonetheless.

"Although I'm sure you're skeptical of my conclusions, I feel confident there is proof out there waiting to be found. With your financial help, we can prove these theories true." She spoke with enthusiasm that the rest of the room didn't seem to share. The woman, Tessa Willis, was an archaeologist who specialized in ancient civilizations, more specifically

Nephilim—giants throughout the biblical texts first mentioned in Genesis's chapter 6.

This particular presentation of Tessa's suggested the ancient race of giants actually existed before civilization began. The stories of this ancient race remain in culture today, as Tessa had always pointed out, although they were largely depicted as myth. However, their existence did help link all world cultures since the beginning of time due to the influence of these giants stretching worldwide. Even more intriguing, every culture had stories—or at the very least even myths of giants—at some point in their history. And Tessa knew myths had to start from something.

Many of her peers in the archaeology communities thought she was wasting her time and was way off course, as they believed evolution was the obvious answer. Some even thought a race of ancient aliens could be at the helm. While their claims certainly seemed convincing, she just couldn't bring herself to believe them.

Nevertheless, she collected her data and studied ancient texts, which led her down what she felt certainly was the correct path. Initially, she came upon the stories of the Nephilim as a small kid in Sunday school. However, it wasn't until she grew older that she realized their stories were sprinkled throughout not just a few times, but in the entirety of the Old Testament.

Even later in college, she had discovered extra biblical texts such as the books of Jasher, Enoch, Jubilees, and the Book of Giants while researching historical sites and internet theories for a term paper. These books did not make it into the bible as people know it now, but these books were actually referenced by many of the prophets and characters in the bible itself. The more she uncovered, the more Tessa's curiosity grew.

What she found intrigued her to a degree that could not be dismissed. She discovered there were numerous historical documentations that wrote about heavenly beings—some even calling them angels—coming down from above and sleeping with human women across nearly every known culture in the world.

These angels, called Watchers, became corrupted, and when they took human women for their own and mated with them, it resulted in the creating of their hybrid offspring called Nephilim. The Watchers, in turn, taught them the secrets of the stars, how to make weapons, and how to wage war. Eventually, they enslaved mankind, using them for hard labor to achieve their own ends.

Nearly every culture of the ancient world has a similar story, most of which had no way of cross-pollinating as the sheer distance between them would have been too great for a human to travel at the time. Tess couldn't help but scoff at the idea that it was all just coincidence.

Across these cultures, the so-called Nephilim had common characteristics. These certain qualities included red hair, six fingers and toes, double rows of teeth, elongated skulls, and access to advanced and forbidden knowledge that seemed to bridge the gap between science and sorcery. The most common similarity of all, however, was their lust for blood and the insatiable desire for violence.

Tessa had a strong belief that these are whom some ancient cultures worshipped as their deities and they had orchestrated the construction of several megalithic structures worldwide. She believed in part that these hybrids proclaimed themselves as rulers over mankind and subdued them by reason or force—likely the latter, based on the historical narrative she'd uncovered.

The more she studied this forgotten history, the more she realized that the Darwinism theory refused to accept this and often even worked to disprove it. She'd found articles from the late 1800s where large bones were discovered, only to be loaned to the Smithsonian for display and never seen again. Tessa couldn't help her intrigue. Something about it reminded her of the old TV shows she watched as a kid that would whisper of conspiracies. To her, that feeling of desperation and excitement in wanting to know the truth had never gone away, even after all these years. It was this excitement that gave her the drive to prove her theories true and is what had led her to this room of potential investors, hoping to fund the digs and studies she wished to pursue.

Tessa could see the eyes of the testosterone-filled conference room drift from her legs to her face. She'd been talking for nearly twenty minutes about her findings and theories, but their eyes only gravitated toward her in a way that said they were most interested in her body instead of her theories. This was far from what she had set out to do with this presentation. Having just turned thirty, she took her fitness seriously, especially when she was on the cusp of going on a major expedition, and her toned, athletic build proved it. But their gawking was not going to keep her from her goal.

A Texan by birth, she was a little short-fused, and she was the type to never hold back what she really thought. She couldn't help herself. "So that's how it's gonna be?" Tessa said to the room of men.

She panned back and forth, trying to lock eyes with as many of them as possible. Their gaze shifted back to the neat gray folders in front of them as they shifted uncomfortably in their seats. They knew they'd been caught.

"I came here to discuss my theories with you, but if your only focus is my ass and not what I have to say, then we're done here."

And with that, they were, indeed, done. One by one, the suits exited the room without so much as a second glance or nod of thanks for her time. When the last man exited the room, she allowed her shoulders to droop a little and released a huff of air. She felt foolish for letting her emotions and temper get the best of her, but she wanted to be known for her discoveries, not a tight ass.

Tessa gathered all but the last neat gray folder, which sat untouched at the far end of the large, ovate conference table. Until that moment, she hadn't noticed the man standing at the back of the room. He leaned against the wall with his arms crossed and gazed at her intently. Returning the stare momentarily, she felt an eerie vibe from him. She continued to put her folders away.

He continued to stare. Tessa did her best to pay him no mind, until finally she'd had enough. She turned quickly to put him in his place, or so she thought.

"Listen, if you're about to ask me out or something like that, forget it. I came here to give a presentation."

"And yet you didn't finish," he replied softly.

Tessa looked at the man, dressed in a sharp, perfectly fitted Armani suit. Not quite twice her age, he had thick, stylishly combed hair and wore a hint of what Tessa assumed to be expensive cologne, but not one that was too strong. There was an air of privilege and arrogance that radiated from his persona, making Tessa slightly uncomfortable but not in danger. Attempting to defuse the situation, the man buttoned his suit jacket and extended his hand.

"I'm Bartholomew Cox, but please, call me Bart. I represent a company who is very interested in your theories. I'd really like to hear the rest of your presentation, Ms. Willis."

Tessa raised an eyebrow and assumed where this was going.

"Oh, sure . . . I'd bet you'd love to hear what I have to say over some drinks and dinner right?" she said, irritated. "Maybe a late night cocktail at your place or hotel room?"

"I like your fervor, but I'm afraid you're quite misguided at my intentions. Although you are impressively attractive, Ms. Willis, I'm much more interested in what you believe about giants—Nephilim, if you will. You see . . . over the course of time I—or more accurately, my company—has uncovered similar findings, suggesting this belief merits scientifically accurate explanations. We've come to the same conclusion as you, that giants roamed the earth thousands of years ago and had unique abilities or, at the very least, access to technology we no longer possess."

The man cleared his throat and then began to speak in a lower tone, emphasizing his serious demeanor.

"My company is discreetly seeking out these Nephilim remains to rediscover what they knew and perhaps what technology they had access to. From what I've gathered in the last twenty minutes, I think you're on the brink of a discovery and could use some help. How's your Enochian?"

The archaeologist was stunned, and her facial expression showed it. Her eyes were squinted, looking directly at Bart, trying to gauge whether or not he was serious. After a moment or two of them locking eyes with one another, Tessa finally spoke. She hadn't mentioned anything in her presentation about the Enochian language, but she'd spent plenty of time researching it. Often referred to as "the language of the angels," Tessa felt as though Enochian held some special link as opposed to the critics who dismissed it as a joke.

"What do you mean, 'help'? Are you saying you're interested in investing in my research and digs?"

"Not exactly. What I am saying is I believe your overall theories are mostly correct, but you're focused on the wrong places. In particular your studies and theories in Bolivia; they're only partly correct. Based on some areas we've uncovered in the last few months, we know we're close to a major breakthrough, but I don't have the right people . . . yet. That's where you come in."

Tessa took a seat on the table, doing her best not to show her excitement, although she never had a good poker face.

"I want to put you at the head of my research team. All expenses paid. And the position comes with a handsome salary," Bart said.

She wanted to maintain an outward portrayal of skepticism, but was failing miserably.

"What findings? What areas? Why did you ask about Enochian?"

"Like I said, my company has been conducting discreet research for some time. Our path has led us to a remote area in the Amazon rainforest—Peru to be exact. We've found something very interesting, which I'm sure you'd like to see. But alas, it's for company eyes only. The only thing preventing you from being a part of this discovery is your acceptance of my offer."

"How much are you offering?"

"Name your price," he said, not flinching a muscle.

Bart, maintaining his gaze upon her, tilted his head down slightly as he stared into her eyes. He knew the hooks were in now, even if she did not.

"Everything is already in place, but the catch is I'd need you on-site and ready to work in no more than ten days. Is that possible?"

"Uh, yeah, I mean . . . I can make that work, but you never answered my question about Enochian."

"Nor did you answer mine." He paused for effect before continuing. "Good, then it's settled," Bart said with a clap of his hands. "I'll arrange for your equipment and transportation to Peru. No need to worry about visas or your passport. You'll be flying privately."

Bart provided her a business card with his contact information and promptly left her alone in the conference room. Tessa Willis sank further down in one of the chairs, took a deep breath, and exhaled loudly.

"What just happened?" she said to herself.

Her mind raced about the details that would require her attention prior to departure. Pondering what to do with her apartment, her car, and the other various things tying her down, she looked at the business card in her hand. The card was simple yet elegant and only read, North Spear, Bart Cox, with his number marked clearly on the other side.

Bart walked down the stairs, fishing for his phone in his tailored jacket. He pulled the device from his pocket as his personal bodyguard moved ahead of him to get the door, ensuring Mr. Cox didn't have to touch the handle. He knew how much his boss hated touching the same things as the common, everyday person. He held the door as Bart didn't so much as look up from his screen while searching for the right contact.

Standing outside, Bart held the phone to his ear, counting the rings until it connected while the bodyguard keyed a small hidden radio in his sleeve, signaling their driver to pick them up. After the fifth ring, the smartphone connected. The young-sounding woman on the other end asked what extension he was trying to reach.

Bart couldn't help himself and instinctively wondered how attractive the secretary was and if he could still bed her like in his younger days. Back then it was easy, but now as he grew older, it was a little more difficult. Sure, he had the money and power to flash around, but at the end of the day, Bart knew he was slowly losing his touch. He pushed the thought aside, replying to the woman.

"Mr. Adams, please," he said succinctly.

"One moment, Mr. Cox. Please hold."

Bart was usually the one putting people on hold; he hated having to wait. He had to refrain himself from bouncing on the balls of his feet impatiently. If everything went according to plan, this could be his chance. His opportunity to rise above the middle class curse he was born into. Sure, the other members of Legion would still view him as "one of those," but he'd make them understand. He'd make them see who he really was underneath. He was royalty, same as them—they just didn't know it yet. Soon enough, they would. This would put him one step closer to the top.

Bart heard the line click as it connected.

"I hope you have good news," Mr. Adams stated matter-of-factly.

"I do, sir. When we last spoke, I assured you I'd find a way inside. I'm happy to report I've found a woman with a special skillset that shows very high promise," Bart replied, unable to keep the pride out of his voice.

"'Shows promise'? I want certainty. *Results.* Don't let your ambitions cloud your judgment, Cox," Adams said with a tone of aristocracy.

Bart could feel the disdain leaking through the phone, but it only fueled him more. He wanted so badly to snap back. To everyone else, *he* snapped the orders, *he* made the demands. But instead, Bart choked back his snappy reply and chose the path of diplomacy. He wasn't much of a frontal-assault type of man anyway. He preferred to take care of his business in the dark.

"Yes, sir. I understand. I will report back when I have something more substantial. I won't fail—"

The line disconnected before he could get out the last word. He looked to Al, his bodyguard, to see if he'd observed the encounter. Luckily, he was too busy doing his job to notice the embarrassment. Bart played it off nicely, pretending to end the conversation with a "Thank you, sir. That's much appreciated. I'll be in touch" as though he'd received high praise. As his car rolled to the curb, he waited for Al to open his door before climbing in. He sat in the backseat, offended—though he wouldn't dare show it. Above all else, Bart craved power. To be in charge. He looked out the window as his driver and Al took their positions in the front seat.

Without turning to look at them, he ordered, "Take me to my hotel, and get me some female company for the evening. Blonde. I like blondes. The higher the price, the better."

"Yes, sir," Al said with a nod.

2

Wheels screeched on poorly paved asphalt as Cody struggled to regain control of the car. Rain fell from the night sky and pounded the windows, roof, and hood of the vehicle with an intensity he was sure would break the glass.

"Please, not again!" Cody screamed, his enraged tears fueled by helplessness and frustration welling in his eyes. He struggled to control the vehicle that seemed to have a mind of its own as the steering wheel veered left and right without pattern. It seemed no matter what he tried, the car was destined to carry out its own path.

It was getting closer, the part he hated the most. Soon, pain erupted in his head, neck, and left shoulder. Then everything went black. It was over finally . . . although, it wasn't. It never was. He felt cold, but there was something else too. His thought process slowed like it was trudging through waist-high mud. He tried to assign the correct words, to identify the sensations that felt so familiar—like a fever. It was hard to make sense of surroundings where nothing quite seemed like reality.

"Get me outta here! Please stop!" His words echoed in his head. Time seemed to slow to a snail's version of crawling. He tried moving his hands, but they were firmly locked to the steering wheel.

He panned his view to look right, seeing Jenny and Elena screaming at him in agony, begging for his help. Though he felt none of their pain himself, seeing his beloved girls in anguish was worse than any physical torment he'd ever experienced.

Seeing their faces, he shouted back, "I can't hear you, baby!" but no audible sound escaped his lips.

He looked around as best he could and still heard nothing. Looking back in their direction, tears streamed up their foreheads and into their hairline. Their bodies rotated like hands on a clock. Elena's hair was sticking straight up as if it held an electric charge. Her gaze shifted from him to something he couldn't see, then back to him. He strained his ears to hear her, or hell, just hear anything.

What does she keep looking at? Cody thought.

Suddenly, Cody Willis's lucid dream came to an end as he leaped out of bed, snatched his Glock 19 from the nightstand, and threw himself to the nearest corner of the bedroom. Finally released from the nightly occurrence, he activated the weapon-mounted light and scanned the room, yielding the same results as the night before: emptiness, darkness, and a room devoid of life.

He pulled the pistol in close once he realized there was no physical threat. His conscious mind began to catch up, realizing his body was simply reacting, once again, to the all too familiar nightmare. He was slick with sweat, and his hands were shaking so hard he almost dropped his gun.

Cody finally lowered the pistol, his knees weak from the adrenaline rush. He still felt like he was nearly about to faint. His sight swayed and dipped in uneven patches and sunspots appeared everywhere as his eyes drifted once more around the room. Stumbling forward in the early morning darkness, Cody fumbled with his empty hand to grasp the closest bedpost for stability. Panting hard like a worked dog, Cody went through his standardized countdown procedure to ground himself as he crawled back into bed.

"Six walls, five windows, four corners, three doors, two guns, one man."

He repeated it to himself. "Six walls, five windows, four corners, three doors, two guns, one man." Once more. "Six walls, five windows, four corners, three doors, two guns, one man . . ."

Suddenly, Cody's watch beeped and pulled him back to the real world. After the dream, it seemed the sandman had kicked him to the curb for the night. Laying there, listening to the alarm chirp and vibrate, he blankly stared up at the ceiling, the reminder of reality settling in. The reminder of his loss.

Nearly every night since their death, Cody had the same nightmare. There were occasional variations, but not often. Despite it being more-or-less the same, it hadn't gotten any easier to manage.

He'd learned they were killed in a horrific car crash. Some intoxicated college-aged idiot thinking only of himself. This wasn't entirely dissimilar from Cody. Or so Cody thought.

Every morning since he'd returned from that fateful night, there was nothing but silence. No more pans clanging in the kitchen from Jenny making breakfast. No more pitter-patter of little feet trying to sneak in and see if he was awake.

Nothing.

He watched the ceiling fan as it rotated effortlessly to produce the clean, crisp morning air that dried his sweat-soaked body. Inhaling through his nose and dramatically exhaling through his mouth, Cody thought, *I wonder what other people think about when they first wake up in the morning?*

His soul desperately yearned for the soft touch of his wife's hand across his shoulder. Just the thought of it caused the memories to come flooding back and make his eyes well up. Cody pulled his left arm up and into his blurred vision to wipe away the tears. He blinked his sight back into focus and checked the time. He wasn't surprised to see he must have been up at least for half the night. After attempting to bring his right hand up to deactivate the alarm, he realized with a jolt his hand felt unusually heavy.

"What the—"

Cody cut his sentence short while sitting up in bed and propping himself with an elbow, looking at the pistol still clutched in his hand.

Had he just slept the past few hours holding his pistol? *Well, that can't be safe.*

He swung his legs and feet out to the plush carpet floor and laid the pistol back on the nightstand before killing the alarm. Cody flicked on the bedside light after a minute or two of sitting in the dark while rubbing the back of his neck. Taking into consideration the aches and pains throughout his body, it was definitely time to get out of bed and start the day.

Cody crossed his arms and lifted them, stretching toward the ceiling. He felt his muscles pull, tendons stretch, and bones pop and crack back into all the usual places. When he lowered them, he could feel the loss of definition and weight all over his body since the nightmares started. They had really done a number on him, mentally and physically.

Cody grabbed his phone and swiped to unlock the screen. He scrolled through a multitude of custom playlists until he found the one his heart desired. Moments later, the speakers placed throughout the condominium shredded the silence of his solitude and filled the air with the sound of drums, heavy guitar, and a soothing melody of female vocal harmonies.

Not quite refreshed from the four hours of sleep, Cody walked to the kitchen and instinctively fired up his instant coffee maker and tossed in a K-Cup with a double dose of caffeine. As the coffee brewed into his cup, he thought briefly of the upcoming day's events, which included a hastily planned celebration party for his sister who had landed some big deal and was hired to head up a project out of the country. She hadn't explained the situation in much detail but was adamant she wanted to see him at the event.

He had reluctantly agreed to attend and quickly ran through scenarios and his preplanned replies to the myriad of questions she would undoubtedly ask about how he's been doing since "the accident," as she called it. It wasn't an accident—not in Cody's mind. It was his fault. He chose himself over his family, and now they were gone forever. The guilt washed over him again like a tidal wave.

As the coffee maker spit its last remaining ounces into the cup, the sound drew his attention back to the world around him, relieving him from thinking about the bombardment of questions as well as his own personal guilt. Cody doctored his coffee in the way he had since he was a rookie cop: filling a tablespoon with honey and stirring it into the rich, dark Arabica coffee. As of late, he felt like he didn't have much to look forward to, but coffee was one part of his morning routine that he could never ignore.

Cody leaned on the counter for what seemed like eons. The smell of his wife's perfume he'd purchased on her last Mother's Day filled his nostrils, but deep inside, he knew it wasn't real. Though he knew it was just a memory, he still felt her absence heavily. He longed to be with her, to see her—even just one last time. A slight buzzing sound snatched Cody's attention to his vibrating phone on the counter. He pulled up the smartphone and saw a text from Frank Pierce.

Hey man, just checking on ya.
You gonna make it today or what?

He knew the questions about this afternoon's BBQ would be here sooner than expected, but he still wasn't expecting them quite this fast.

Frank was Cody's "little brother." Though they were not related by birth, they'd shared enough history and knew each other well enough that one could easily mistake them for being so. They'd met years earlier working with each other in close proximity and found that they did it well. Cody saw something in Frank that not many other people saw—at least, not initially. He was the one that pushed Frank to the top of his capabilities, which Cody always knew he had. Cody trusted Frank with his life and had done so many times since they'd met.

Cody considered ignoring the message, but thought better of it and texted back: *Yeah man, of course.*

Cody downed the dregs of his coffee and changed into a pair of running shorts and athletic shoes. Grabbing an old, leathery notebook that had seen better days (the front of which read Pain for Time) he removed the rubber band holding it closed and opened it up to where he left off the day before. He found today's workout session, consisting of back squats, front squats, and deadlifts. Cody closed his eyes briefly with a heavy sigh.

"Guess it's gonna be one of those days."

After the brutal PT session he was sure would cripple him for life, Cody prepared for the rest of the day. Or as much as he felt he could, that is. He changed into a clean set of clothes and began stuffing his pockets with his daily essentials, going through a nonverbal checklist with himself to make sure he didn't forget anything necessary.

Glock 19, check. Handheld light, check. Bench-made folder, check. Keys, check. Wallet and phone, check and check.

He secured the striker-fired pistol in a Kydex appendix-inside-the-waistband holster and positioned it inside his waistband. Pulling the pistol from the holster in a swift motion, he pointed it directly across the room at a VTAC target pinned to the wall. He mentally envisioned himself pressing the trigger straight back as he aligned the Aimpoint ACRO P-2 red dot on the target's left eye socket.

Cody brought the weapon close to his chest and pulled the slide back just enough to verify the chamber was loaded, then checked to make sure the magazine was loaded to capacity. Satisfied, he deliberately and carefully returned the pistol to its molded-plastic home.

Although Cody lived alone and knew his everyday carry like the back of his hand, he completed this procedure no matter what before he left the house. As he completed his routine, he once again began mentally rehearsing the preplanned responses, but his thoughts drifted to Elena, his daughter.

The thought made him cringe with a sudden and brief flash of inward anger. He knew he shouldn't go down this road but couldn't stop his mind from wandering. The thought of his daughter, however, reminded him suddenly of something he had bought for Tessa. Cody grabbed it from a backpack inside the closet before walking out of the apartment and to his truck.

Climbing into the driver's seat, his mind continued to drift, recalling memories he didn't exactly want to remember right then. It hurt too much to do so. He felt his palms become clammy, and his fingers felt cold. It was as if his own blood were freezing. Soon, his heart began to race.

"What the hell is going on with me?" he whispered to himself.

His phone vibrated in the console, giving him a much-needed distraction. Cody realized he hadn't even turned the truck on yet. He inserted the key and fired up the engine, then reached down and picked up the phone. Frank had texted again.

En route see ya in a few mikes . . . out

Would Frank recognize immediately how much of a mess he'd become? Was it that obvious? Cody wondered if Val was going to be there, but figured he'd find out soon enough. He put the Toyota pickup in reverse, backed out of his parking spot, and drove the familiar route to Tessa's house.

3

Cody travelled down the highway, catching himself thinking about Val and how the boys were doing. Val was like a big brother to Cody in the same way Cody was to Frank. He thought back to the circumstances, years ago, that led to their meeting and, ultimately, their friendship.

Val was just over ten years older than Cody. Initially Val mentored Cody while he was still a police officer with a major agency in Central Texas. He'd first taken notice of Cody during an After Action Report at a statewide training conference. Attendees included members of the military special-operations circles and law enforcement. Val had been a member of the army's premier Special Mission Unit, often abbreviated to SMU and pronounced "smoo." He was impressed with both Cody's attention to detail and his tactical competency as Cody recalled his experiences as a first responder to an active shooter event that had gained significant media attention.

As it turns out, talking about it was what Cody needed to finally allow himself to admit he had ultimately found himself frustrated with his career in law enforcement. He had grown sick of always reacting to deadly incidents and wished he could prevent them instead.

During the various training events, Val introduced himself and quickly befriended him. Over a period of many months, Val quietly assessed Cody from the shadows. One day over lunch, Cody explained these frustrations to his newfound mentor, and Val saw the opportunity to make his pitch.

"I dunno, man. I'm just sick and tired of always going to these messed-up situations where the damage is already done. I just wish there was something I could do to get rid of really bad dudes like this once and for all."

"Funny you mention that. I'm putting together a team and could use your skills," Val said.

Cody peered over their food at him. "What kind of team? I thought you were in the consulting business?" Cody inquired.

Val leaned in, hands folded on the table. "I work for a company called ProCorp. Well, a division of ProCorp actually. It's called Applied Sciences. I've been asked to find, train, and field a team of my own. I want to bring you in as my second-in-command. My 2IC, if you will. We'd run a team of our own how we want, when we want. About four to six guys total."

"Run a team doing what?" Cody asked, his eyes locked on Val's.

"Filling contracts, both government and private. Could be anything from kill/capture to executive protection to training firearms handling. They hire us when the government can't get directly involved. We choose whatever contracts we want to bid for."

"Does it pay well? I can't leave my family high and dry to play John Rambo, ya know?"

"The people in these circles pay big money for hard skills like the ones you and I have. But like I said, we pick and choose when we'll be gone. We have complete autonomy. How about this, I'll match your current salary plus 10 percent, full benefits included. It will come with certain, uh, perks, including but not limited to training opportunities, travel, and maybe ending a few of those so-called really bad dudes."

After a long discussion with his wife, Cody readily agreed and took the offer.

Over the next year or so, they trained and worked hard together, with Val teaching him the finer points of gunfighting, close-quarters battle

(CQB), low-visibility surveillance, and good old-fashioned manhunting. Over time, Cody recruited Frank, filling the third position. Tom had come highly recommended by some of Val's contacts and was soon brought into the fold. Before they knew it, they had their team. Val, having a strong affinity for Warren Zevon, appropriately named his group Renegade.

For a while, everything was good. The money started flowing in, and everyone seemed content. But Cody was not aware of how addicted to the lifestyle he'd become. It was his identity. He *was* Renegade 02. At least, he used to be.

Cody came back to the present and felt the need to talk to Val. It had been over a year since they were all together, the night when Cody's choices had finally come to a head. What would he even say to him? Was there anything he could say?

As he thought about Val and the boys while cruising along the highway, he realized he had missed his exit and let out a defeated sigh. He'd taken the exit to Renegade Ranch by mistake, their physical branch location of Applied Sciences Group. He quickly turned his rig around at the earliest opportunity and corrected course back to the party.

After getting back on the right track, he attempted to clear his head and began to focus on the task at hand. *Mission objective number one: survive the BBQ and don't stick out like a sore thumb.*

In the past, blending in had been easy for Cody; it was a learned skill perfected over time. Like most things, that was then, and this is now, and he was well out of practice. As he neared the street where Tessa lived, Cody started reciting his carefully planned replies out loud.

"Oh yeah, I'm fine really. No, seriously . . . it just takes time, but I'm hanging in there.

"You ain't gotta worry about me, I'm not one to give up easily . . ."

He practiced controlling his facial expression and added the sheepish grin for good effect.

Cody's fingers slid on the steering wheel as it passed through his grip. He turned onto Tessa's street and could see the line of cars next to the sidewalk in the distance. His heart rate quickened its pace, and he instinctively began combat breathing, inhaling for four seconds, holding four more seconds, and finally exhaling for another four. Cody had used this technique to his advantage before, but now it seemed to fail him as his anxiety grew with every second.

He found a suitable parking spot across the street, three houses down. He parked his truck, inhaled deeply through his nose, and exhaled out his mouth. Cody stared himself down in the rearview mirror, talking aloud to his reflection.

"Okay, man, showtime. Keep it together."

Exiting his vehicle, he could hear the children playing and screaming in the backyard. The muscles in his neck and back instantly tensed.

Relax, he told himself.

Cody closed his eyes for a moment and wished Jen was with him. Just a simple touch of her hand on his shoulder or the way she held his hand was enough to silence the madness. There was a stillness about her that balanced him out. Now he was out of control. Emotionally, spiritually, and all but physically. He was all alone, with one exception.

Cody still had Tessa. With a small smile that only the thought of Tessa could bring out, he realized she must be waiting for him in her house just across the street. He pulled his shirt down over the Austrian-made pistol, making sure it remained concealed, and looked both directions down the street, checking for Val's truck. He didn't see it. Unless he was driving something else, he was not here.

Cody began his stroll across the yard while allowing his mind to run multiple scenarios of conversations that were inevitably going to take place. The walk from his truck to the front door seemed to pass in the blink of an eye. By the time he reached the porch, he'd forgotten every half-practiced line. He considered knocking but figured with all the chaos inside that no one would hear him anyway, so he let himself in.

Chaos was not the appropriate word to describe what he was met with as the door opened. Pandemonium, perhaps? No less than six kids ranging four to ten years old ran amuck, chasing each other, playing some game he didn't understand, and screaming at the top of their lungs. His heart ached to see his girls again, and he remembered with a lurch that his daughter once ran with this crowd of familiar kids.

Like a flock of seagulls swarming to fetch bits of bread tossed at the pier, Cody watched some parents chase their kids in an attempt to get them to settle down. He observed other adults he didn't recognize surrounding the kitchen island, socializing with one another. They all sported alcoholic beverages of some kind, either beer, wine, or something of the sort.

Cody looked around nervously, searching for someone, anyone, he knew personally so he could start up some meaningless conversation to blend in. Cody thought this was beginning to feel like work. Well, at least how work used to be. Through the kitchen, Cody could see a few more kids and, of course, more adult supervision in the backyard. He made his way outside to get the lay of the land and see who was there.

He walked out onto the back patio and could smell the intoxicating aroma of barbecued meat. Momentarily distracted, the smell almost drew him in completely when he felt a strong grip on his left shoulder. A hard object poked him uncomfortably in the back, feeling suspiciously like the barrel of a gun. Cody was just about to proceed with his next course of action of disarming the potential assailant when he heard a familiar voice.

"Gimme all your money, old man," the voice whispered in his ear.

Cody knew exactly who it was and played along, slowly putting his hands up to his shoulders in a position of surrender. He turned around and saw Frank's familiar face grinning back at him, a beer bottle turned fake gun clutched in his hand.

"Dude, you're losing it. I've been eyeing you since you came through the front door."

"Oh whatever! I felt your rookie ass eyeing me the whole time," Cody replied, shoving Frank's arm playfully.

"That's exactly what I'd say if I had just been ambushed by someone I trained."

"Just remember, Frank, I taught you everything you know, not everything *I* know."

"Uh-huh, well, I *know* for a fact it's damn good to see you."

Frank pulled Cody in, wrapped his arms around Cody's frame, and picked him up. The hug was so tight Cody felt his back pop—twice. Cody had always imagined that Frank's bear hugs were exactly what it felt like if a grizzly actually got its paws wrapped around you.

Cody returned the hug immediately and felt the anxiety begin to disappear, even if just for a moment.

"Nah, man. It's damn good to see *you*!" Cody said, laughing as Frank finally put him down. "Who's a guy gotta kill to get a Coke around here, huh?"

"Check the YETI. Stocked it just for you," Frank replied and pointed over to the cooler in the corner of the porch.

"Just for me, huh? Should I hold my breath for a jalapeño margarita?"

"You certainly could, but you'd probably pass out, though I did throw a little something in there you might like."

Cody walked over, opened the sticker-covered cooler, and quickly saw Frank wasn't lying. It was stocked with ice-cold Coca-Cola and a six pack of spicy Ranch Water. Cody peered over his shoulder at Frank with a grin, amused his little brother remembered his social drinks of choice.

"Spicy Ranch Water?" Cody asked.

"I consider myself too much of a man to make something like that for you. Figured it was the next best thing, so you'll have to live with the Ranch Water," Frank said with his charming smile.

Cody laughed at the dig. It was common knowledge that jalapeño margaritas were to Cody Willis what shaken-and-not-stirred vodka martinis were to James Bond. They had become his signature drink.

Cody and Frank stood outside on the patio, catching up for a minute or two when Cody asked, "Where's Tessa? You seen her?" He couldn't help but look around nervously.

"Yeah, I saw her a few minutes ago. She's around here somewhere," Frank replied, scanning the crowd of faces.

Cody wondered if Frank could detect his anxiety. His hand twitched rapidly, fingers lightly tapping the side of his leg. He didn't even realize he was doing it, but Frank's careful gaze caught a glimpse of the panic, causing him to raise an eyebrow. He must have decided it best not to point it out as he didn't say anything.

"So man, how are the boys doing? Y'all got anything lined up, or just doing the training gig lately?" Cody asked, trying to appear nonchalant.

"We're good . . . for the most part. Val is . . . well, ya know Val, doing his thing and trying to get us into something like always, but stuff falls through at the last minute. Tom is same-old Tom, and to be honest, he really misses you—even if he doesn't say it to you directly."

Frank paused to retrieve a Blue Moon, his personal favorite, from the cooler.

"We're making do without you, but it ain't the same. They're tied up on some short-notice request at the moment, and I, my friend, am staring down the barrel of some much-needed time off."

Frank finished his sentence with a full smile and popped the top of his beer and applied a chunk of orange. He really did look happier than Cody had seen him in a while. He thought it was about time Frank used his vacation days. It was well deserved as far as Cody was concerned.

"Yeah man, I miss y'all too," Cody said, rubbing the back of his neck. "I was hoping Val might make it out so we could talk. Been awhile, you know. Think he'll show? You know if Tessa invited him?"

"Uh yeah, about that . . . I don't think he's convinced you're up to it, that's all. I think he figured he would give you some space first. But he told me to pass along his congrats to Tessa, of course."

"He say anything else about me?"

"Nope," Frank replied, taking a swig.

Cody thought about it for a second and realized he'd just have to let Val work things out, too, for the time being. Frank saw Cody carefully reflecting on his words and asked, "So, man, how are you *really*? You good?"

"Oh yeah, I'm fine. Really. No, seriously. It just takes time, but I'm hanging in there." He did his best to pass off as believable.

Immediately Frank looked down at Cody over the frame of his sunglasses and shot him a look that clearly said, "Bullshit." Cody should have known better than to try something like that on Frank.

"Really, bro? You gonna use some BS line like that on *me*? I bet you already had those lines preplanned, huh?"

Cody was embarrassed that he had just lied to one of his best friends. He turned away to avoid eye contact. "Honestly then?" Cody questioned.

"Yeah, honestly. What else?"

Cody took a deep breath and thought carefully about what he wanted to say. Honesty was always the best policy, with the problem being it was rarely easy. But how much was too much? He contemplated for another moment. He had taken the easy road before, and he was done with easy. Besides, what chance did he have getting back in Renegade? After what happened? Nearly none at all.

"The dreams are . . . How do I say this? Intense and unbelievably real. Sometimes they're the same scenario. Other times they come out different. I'm still seeing their faces every night, and I'm waking up in sweat-soaked clothes. The guilt is eating me alive, man. I'm not sleeping well. Maybe four or five hours a night. Some days more, other days less. It's under control, but it's always present. Always there."

Frank looked at him carefully. "Have you ever talked to anyone about this? A counselor or anything?"

Frank knew the answer, but he asked anyway. Cody shot him a look like he was crazy and ignored the question.

"That's what I thought. Ya know, man, you should—"

Frank was interrupted by a female voice calling out to both him and Cody. They turned to see Tessa, sporting a wide smile, walking in their direction.

Whew. Saved by my kid sister, Cody thought.

"Well look what the cat dragged in! I'm so happy to see y'all," she said, wrapping up Cody in a warm hug and then turning to give Frank the same. "Where's Val? Is he here?" Tessa asked, looking around the backyard after pulling away from Frank.

"Sorry, chica. He had a . . . a work . . . thing. But he wanted me to tell you he's super proud of you and congrats," Frank said.

Tessa felt the tension in the air, realizing she walked into something uncomfortable. But this had never stopped her. She looked at Cody.

"Oh, y'all still aren't talking?"

Cody shrugged.

"It's been over a year already. You guys need to work this out. You're worse than a bunch of college sorority girls."

"Don't look at me. I'm all for it! If we got Cody back, I would happily dump all that administrative bullshit back on him. Tom and

I are tired of filling that role. Besides, we ain't much good at it," Frank replied.

"Yeah, yeah, yeah. Anyway, enough about the damn past. Tell us what's been going on. Quite a turnout you got going here, Tess. You finally land the deal of a lifetime or what?" Cody asked her.

It didn't take a body language expert to know that she was practically brimming with excitement. "Uh, yeah!" she said sarcastically.

"So tell us all about it," Cody said, prodding her.

"Well, you know I've been working on these archaeological theories and trying to get funding, right?" she explained. "So out of nowhere, some dude named Bart says his company is super interested in my work. At first, I thought he was screwing with me, then this joker pulls out his checkbook, looked me in the eye, and basically says, 'How much is it gonna cost to get you in Peru leading my team right away?' I was speechless. I mean, what am I supposed to say? I really feel like this is my chance!"

Tessa was nearly glowing as she retold the story from a few days earlier. She went on to explain how the company, North Spear, wanted to bring her in immediately to head their team. Apparently Tessa hadn't been exaggerating the man's insistence that money was no object. It really seemed like this company had deep enough pockets to make the project happen, thus the BBQ celebration and sudden soon-to-be departure.

Cody, however, couldn't let go of the cop at heart. Although he tried his best to appear nothing but pleased, he felt himself becoming cautiously suspicious while she talked. He listened intently, trying to think if he'd ever heard of North Spear. Nothing came to mind, though the world of academia wasn't really in his wheelhouse. After a few minutes of listening to her explanation of the presentation gone awry, he couldn't help but interrupt.

"Hang on a minute. I want to make sure I get this straight. So you're telling me you called out all these bigwig assholes to their faces—classic Tessa Willis, by the way—they get offended, and then they leave and this *one* guy stays behind and says he's willing to pay for you and a team to start diggin' in South America?" he asked.

If looks could kill, Tessa's would've killed Cody and burned his remains.

"Uh, yeah, that's what I just explained over the last two minutes," she stated.

"Let me start off on the right foot, or at least try to. I'm super proud of you, you know that, but doesn't this all seem a little bit odd? You've been looking for funding for like, what, two years?"

"Exactly my point, Cody. That's why I'm so excited."

"Just seems a little too good to be true is all. I mean, have you even heard of this company? What's it called again?"

"North Spear," she said, mostly through her teeth.

"Listen, sis, all I'm saying is what if they're not who they say they are?"

"Ah jeez, Cody, here we go again with the paranoia shit. Look, the team is already in Peru. All they're doing is paying me to go down there for a year and lead the dig. Come on, Cody. I thought you'd be supportive after all this time."

"I am, I am. It's just—"

"Just what?" she interrupted.

Cody realized he struck a nerve and decided to back off. What Tessa didn't realize was her absence would leave a hole in her brother, a hole he couldn't really afford. "I guess I'm just sad I'm losing you too. That's all."

Cody could feel Tessa's own guilt start to build. He could see the look of realization that he might truly go off the deep end if she wasn't here to help in some way. This was going a way he hadn't intended; the last thing he wanted to do was stifle her dreams.

"Cody . . ." she started.

"No, no," Cody said, stopping her. "Like I said, I'm *happy* for you . . ." He didn't know how to convey what it was that he was feeling. He needed her to understand. Luckily Frank rushed in to save the day.

"Yeah, we're both happy for ya, Tessa, and you know what? I have a feeling everything is going to be just fine. We're at a party. Let's enjoy ourselves, shall we? After all, these Blue Moons don't drink themselves," he said.

Fortunately the three were able to move on for the time being and continued to catch up while the BBQ celebration continued on around them. The crowd came and went as Tessa would leave momentarily to entertain her guests and return to catch up with her brother and his teammate. As the party drew to a close, it became just the three of them.

Tessa sat down with a plop on her back patio furniture next to Cody and gave him a big hug. Cody smiled and pulled out an object from his pocket.

"Hey, listen, I know you think I'm paranoid more often than not, but in my experience, I just call it being prepared. I want you to take this with you. I was going to give it to you at some point anyway, but now I especially want you to take it. It's an Iridium satellite phone. You can use anywhere in the world. I've already got my number programmed. This is for emergencies only."

Tessa sighed loudly enough to showcase her disapproval and glanced at Frank. Frank held up his hands as if to say, "Not my idea."

"Fine, I'll take it with me if it will bring you a little peace of mind. The North Spear reps told me there wouldn't be much contact with people outside the dig because of connectivity and the possibility of leaks, but what they don't know won't hurt them, I guess."

"Thanks. I hope you never have to use it," Cody said.

He couldn't help but wonder what she meant by "possibility of leaks." Why would a scientific dig be worried about leaks? None of it really made sense to him, but her work was always confusing. He wasn't sure he could get behind the idea of giants walking around either. The whole Nephilim idea made him uncomfortable.

Frank lifted his arm and checked his watch; Cody did the same out of habit. With a deep breath and sad look on his face, Frank stood from his chair.

"Well guys, I guess it's that time. I gotta get going. Got an early morning ahead of me. Tessa, I'm super proud of you and hope it all works out."

"I really appreciate you showing up. It was really good seeing you again. Don't be a stranger."

Tessa stood with him and gave him a kiss on the cheek, surprising both Frank and Cody. She'd never done that before. Cody noticed that Frank blushed slightly, although if Cody pointed it out, he figured Frank would chalk it up to the booze. Meanwhile, Cody couldn't help but wonder if that was really the case.

"Don't worry, I won't," Frank replied and went about his way.

After Frank was out of earshot, Cody stood and looked at his sister.

"What was that about? You got the hots for Frank now?"

"'Course not. It's just I . . . well, I don't know. It just felt . . . natural?"

"Natural?"

"Oh stop, it was harmless. We've been friends for years."

Cody wasn't sure how he felt about that. Not so much in that he disapproved, just that he didn't want her to end up like him if anything ever happened to Frank in the field. Tessa wasn't ignorant about the dangers of what they did, but perhaps she didn't know exactly how dangerous it could be.

"Uh-huh, well, don't go falling in love or anything with my best friend. He's mine, and I'm not giving him up. You're always trying to take my stuff," he said, giving her a slight shove.

Tessa just chuckled and put her arms out to give her big brother a hug. He did the same. Both knew it would be a while before they saw each other again. Cody let go of his sister and looked into her eyes.

"Be careful out there. I know you can handle yourself, but I don't know what I'd do if anything happened to you. You're all I got now."

"I'm a Willis," she replied. "I got this."

4

Cody awoke in a panic like most nights, still sweat-soaked because of the nightmares that plagued his memories. He glanced over at the clock which read 04:30 a.m. He laid in his bed, fully awake from the all-too-real nightmares. Oddly enough, tonight the nightmares focused on Tessa. He tried to remember it, but only a few small details remained.

Trying to calm himself down, Cody recalled the details of Elena's face, the color of her eyes, the distinct smell of her hair, the softness of her skin, and the way she cried out for him. His memory soon transitioned to images of his wife. Her long dark hair tossed gently by the wind, how she would walked past him. When the anxiety would rise, he would think of his family, which then brought about the guilt. It was always a dangerous cycle.

Thinking even about Jenny's voice made his eyes well up, and he began to cry. It was soft at first, as though he was afraid someone would hear him, then turned to deep, soul-tearing sobs. Minutes later, he decided to do something he had not done in a long time. He prayed.

Wiping the tears from his eyes, Cody tried to pull himself together as he looked at the ceiling toward the heavens. "Lord, I know I haven't talked to You in a long time, but I can't keep living like this. Please help me. I guess . . . I guess that's all I got for now. Please don't forget me."

It felt awkward for him, like trying to talk to someone he didn't know. Even worse, he felt almost foolish, as though he was trying to talk to someone who didn't care to listen.

He rolled out of bed and began his daily routine. He stretched his crossed arms out above him and felt his muscles stretch and bones pop, providing some relief to his high-mileage, thirty-five-year-old body. He walked into the kitchen and fired up some dark roast coffee.

He sipped the hot, dark liquid carefully and thumbed through his Pain for Time journal. Today's punishment consisted of mostly upper body exercises, pull-ups, bench presses, barbell complexes, and so on. He prepared for the workout as he gathered his things.

After the gym, he showered, changed his clothes, and hopped into his Tacoma. It was still early as he watched the usual crowd of people stir on the roadways from the parking lot.

Sitting in his truck, his mind wandered to Tessa. It had been a couple days since the party, and she'd be leaving sometime today. He thought about Frank and figured he'd be up by now. Cody checked his watch thinking to himself, *Ah screw it. If he ain't up yet, he should be.*

He pulled his phone from his pocket and typed out a text message.

Hey little brother, wanna do lunch today?

I got some time to burn this afternoon.

After the text was sent, he forced his mind to the present and started his truck. He needed to make a stop at his storage unit to pick up some work necessities.

A short fifteen-minute drive later, he arrived at the storage facility and punched the code to drive in. After the death of Jen and Elena, he couldn't stand to be in his old house. It was filled with too many memories and reminders of what used to be. He'd since moved into an inexpensive apartment with just enough space for him and his things. In an effort to maintain a low profile, he kept all his work-related items stored safely in an air-conditioned storage unit, which looked less like a typical storage unit and more like a scaled-down version of Bruce Wayne's bat cave.

Cody parked his truck and accessed the secured building. He walked to the appropriate aisle and unlocked the disc lock to his unit. Purely out of habit, he checked both his left and right before opening the door. He didn't want any nosy people getting too interested in what he had stored away. It was a large ten-by-twenty square-foot unit that housed the majority of his weapons and equipment.

On both sides of the unit stood storage racks, six feet high and approximately six-and-a-half-feet long. Each rack contained three levels. Sitting on the racks were several large deployment bags—heavy-duty, luggage-type ones containing various pieces of equipment. Each were prepacked for different environments or missions, and they had an embroidered Velcro patch that read R-02, which was Cody's callsign within Renegade.

He slid the door partially closed behind him. The smell of dusty nylon and gun oil filled his nostrils. Here, he felt at home. Perhaps that was because it reminded him of Renegade Ranch. If this storage company hadn't run such a tight ship, he'd strongly consider stringing a hammock and just living here.

In the middle of the unit against the far wall sat his safe. Secured inside was his collection of firearms, which remained ready for professional use. Cody opened the safe and carefully selected today's rifle. Cody knew today's events required live fire and some force-on-force scenarios. He had been using a BCM Recce 14 recently, but after seeing Frank, nostalgia set in. He decided on his tried-and-true Hodge Defense AR-15 with a 12.5-inch barrel. The rifle had remained largely untouched since Val had told him it was best he left Renegade for a while.

He pulled the weapon from the safe, checked to make sure the chamber was empty, extended the stock, and aimed at a nearby wall. He indexed the T-2 red-dot optic at a small target taped to the wall and pulled the crisp four-and-a-half-pound Geissele trigger until he heard an audible click. Next, he checked the battery compartment of his infrared laser, happy that he'd remembered to remove it before stowing the rifle away. He replaced the battery in the laser and did the same for the ultrapowerful Modlite weapon light. Satisfied, he took a glance at his weapon, realizing how much he missed it.

"Been awhile hasn't it, ol' girl?" he asked softly.

He collapsed the stock and started to stow it in the bag when suddenly he realized he used the exact same pistol, rifle, and kit bag on his last operation. He couldn't help it. His mind drifted back to that very night. After both his girls had died, he'd done his best to hold it together at work. After the initial grieving period, he'd convinced Val he was good enough to work in the field. Renegade had been tasked with another Applied Sciences team named Nemo to track down and surveil a suspected child trafficker. A few days into the operation, Cody had positively identified him while watching a safehouse their target was known to use.

Val had been in the driver's seat, Cody in the passenger's. Sitting there in that car, he thought about the night when he found out his wife and daughter were recklessly killed and how he had no power to stop it. He had heard JP's voice as if from underwater while his heart begin to race and all the images suddenly began to surface. Then he thought of all the children who were forced to do horrible things because of human depravity. He thought of all the parents, like him, who would never see their children again.

Cody could hear Val in the driver's seat trying to get his attention. Val must have seen his second-in-command locked onto his target like a rabid dog, but he couldn't get through. Before Val could react, Cody had bolted out of the nondescript car, pistol in hand, and strode right up to his target. Both teams had strict orders to observe and report only. All of that went right out the window when Cody drew down and emptied the entire nineteen-round magazine straight into the European human trafficker.

Feeling like he was reliving their deaths all over again, Cody had felt his hands begin to shake, the palms of his hands turned hot, and he had begun to sweat. He'd always figured the symptoms of PTSD would come for him sooner or later, but he never thought his own family would be the catalyst. He could hear Val yelling behind him but couldn't fathom any of the words. Instead, he just stared down at the splayed body of his target, satisfied he had hit his mark.

Jen and Elena's deaths had pulled a thread that had unraveled his life like a poorly sewn shirt. Val, Frank, and Tom could see the toll it had taken and the guilt he put on himself for not being there. Secretly they all knew he was on a downward spiral but didn't intervene fast enough to prevent Cody from sealing his fate.

After Val had suggested Cody leave for awhile, he had no idea where to go or what to do. Fortunately for Cody, Val had more than a few contacts in the industry and had worked a deal with an old friend at a privately owned range, who let Cody teach some flat-range shooting and CQB classes to law enforcement. Cody knew it was for the best, but that didn't make it feel any better. Not only did he lose his wife and daughter, but he had now lost his three best friends.

Back in the storage unit, he shook himself out of his memories. He finished packing his gear for a day at the shoot house and loaded his equipment in the bed of his Tacoma. When he looked down at his phone, he realized Frank had texted him back.

Yeah, man I'm down. Let's do
Lucky's BBQ

He must have missed it while he was sucked into the darkness of memory lane. He shook off the negative thoughts to the best of his ability and focused on the task ahead: teaching free flow CQB and threshold evaluation of a corner-fed room to a bunch of sheriff deputies with very minimal training from a small county. But it was no small task. Cody certainly had his work cut out for him.

Meanwhile on a small private jet, Tessa sat across from Bart on their way to an exclusive airport in Peru. Tessa looked around the lavish aircraft and was astonished at the luxury. She caught Bart looking at her with a smile.

"I'm glad to see you're impressed with our travel arrangements," he said as he reclined in the leather chair, clearly proud of himself.

"That obvious, huh? It's just that I've never flown in a private jet, and I knew they were fancy, but wow . . . Y'all really went all out for a no-name archaeologist to lead your 'secret' dig." Tessa sipped on her champagne. "Which begs the question, when am I gonna get to see something actually related to giants or their connection to Enochian?"

Amused, Bart pulled out a briefcase from beside his leather chair. He carefully opened it, pulled out a manila folder, and casually handed it to her. "Now that you're on the company payroll, I see no harm in giving you access to company information.

"These are aerial photographs of the site we've uncovered and some of the artifacts the team has found thus far. Please, take a look and tell me what you see," he said, watching her every reaction.

Tessa put down her glass and thumbed through the photographs. She saw one in particular that piqued her interest.

"What the hell is this?" she asked.

Bart smiled from ear to ear, knowing he'd picked the right person for the job.

"That, young lady, is the million-dollar question, or rather multimillion-dollar question, and one of the reasons you're going to be leading the team."

Tessa looked at the picture, trying to make sense of it, but she could only see the rough shape of a rectangular object. Her mind raced with possibilities of what it could be as she peered up from the picture and locked eyes with Bart with a quizzical look, waiting for him to explain.

He finally did once he knew the torture of waiting was as much as she could bear.

"As best as we can tell so far, it's a burial site of some sort. Possibly a tomb or something, we think. My specialists—soon to be your specialists—believe it's made from some type of metallic alloy they can't identify, and our ground-penetrating sonar can't break through it. It has ancient writing or language no one can make sense of thus far, though admittedly it is fairly damaged. We're pretty sure it's Enochian, so that's where you come in."

"What do you mean 'they can't identify it'? And, I'm sorry, did you say we're attempting to answer a *multi*million-dollar question?" she asked as Bart studied her curiously for a moment before replying.

"You are perceptive, not that I'm surprised. But to answer your question, this particular alloy is believed to be a compound that can't be recreated by any metallurgist. At least not with current technology. The particular elements have been bonded in a way that defies our current understanding of science. I myself have not seen it up close, as I've been busy looking for someone like you to help us out." It was a good thing Bart was a good liar.

In fact, Bart was the first North Spear executive on-site and knew exactly what it was that he saw, but Bart also recognized the need for a specialist on hand. It didn't hurt that this particular one in front of him was easy on the eyes, but he wasn't going to let that misdirect his intended path. Bart knew language was the key.

Tessa silently stared at the picture while Bart watched every flinch in her face, every squint of her eyes.

This is the one who will catapult my ascension up the ladder, he thought to himself. Her accomplishments would be the final step he needed to make him worthy.

She took a deep breath and exhaled loudly, knowing full well that her work was cut out for her. Needless to say, she was beyond excited. She felt as though she was in *Charlie and the Chocolate Factory* and had just been handed the golden ticket.

Tessa studied the picture for several minutes before finally saying, "So you're telling me North Spear has found an Egyptian-style sarcophagus in the heart of the Amazonian jungle, inside an ancient temple, made of an alloy that can't be recreated, with what you believe is Enochian text written on it? Am I understanding this correctly?"

Bart, looking upward, recalled the question line by line, concentrating on the facts before he nodded ever so slowly in affirmation. Tessa slumped back in her seat, picture still in hand, as if she'd just finished Thanksgiving dinner and couldn't take another bite.

"No wonder you said multimillion-dollar question. This discovery could change history. Could change . . . everything."

"You ready for the best part?" he asked in a serious tone, meeting her eyes once more.

"Go on . . ." she said, sitting upright and securing her full attention.

"This 'sarcophagus' is forty feet long, approximately ten-to-twelve feet wide, and six feet tall. Quite simply, Ms. Willis, I believe we have found a Nephilim burial site with an intact endoskeleton inside. The lack of damage on the outside leads us to believe the remains inside are untouched."

"Shut up!" she blurted instinctively.

Tessa's mouth dropped open, unsure of what she'd just heard. She had searched for signs of proof of this very thing for the majority of her adult life and had always come up short. Now she was flying thirty thousand feet above the earth, heading directly toward the very thing that had eluded her until now.

Bart chuckled softly, amused at her reaction and at her partial disbelief. He sipped his expensive whiskey, crossed his leg over his knee, and gazed out the window to his left, watching the clouds.

"I assure you, Ms. Willis, I'm not screwing with you. I've been searching for Nephilim remains and artifacts for a long time. This is serious business to me," he turned back to face her, "and nothing will get in my way," he said.

Bart took another sip and turned back to the clouds, watching them pass by, lost in his own thoughts. Tessa felt the intensity of his words and sensed something deeper but chose not to dig.

She shifted her attention back to the pictures and continued to study them. She pulled her computer from her backpack along with several of her notebooks that contained many years' worth of her research and findings. She flipped through the pages, looking for commonalities with other drawings or discoveries she'd come across.

She was just thinking of such potential similarities that could make an affirmative link to other found artifacts when she was struck with a thought. Tessa, not being able to help herself, peeled her focus away from her work and looked up at Bart. "What is North Spear anyway?" she asked. "And why is this so important to you and your company?"

"Well, Ms. Willis—"

Bart's eyes shifted to hers before Tessa interrupted. "Please, call me Tessa. My mother was Ms. Willis. Well, Mrs."

"Well, Tessa," he emphasized, "North Spear is not my company. I have been chosen to represent the company on their behalf for this endeavor. We believe this discovery can indeed change the world, and our pursuit of it will not cease."

"Uh-huh." Tessa peered at him. "So why would a company with resources as deep as yours believe the Nephilim existed in the first place? Who actually owns the company?"

Bart looked at Tessa with a grin as he paused to take another sip, "If I were you, Tessa, I wouldn't worry about who's paying the bill so long as you get to make the discovery of a lifetime. If I got to live my dream and change the world, the ends would certainly justify the means."

Tessa thought about Bart's statement. Perhaps he was right; she probably wouldn't get a chance like this ever again. She pushed internal warnings aside and nodded in agreement.

"You make a good point, Bart. I guess I should go with the flow so long as the river is moving."

"There's nothing to worry about, Tessa. We'll take care of everything," Bart replied as he brough the glass to his lips once more.

5

The door inside the scarcely furnished room burst open as heavily muscled men poured in, alternating left and right. Their rifles pointed toward their respective areas of responsibility. Cody heard the safeties snap from "safe" to "fire." He watched as the men identified their targets and squeezed their triggers just as their red dot settled.

Each gun went click as they simulated firing a bullet. After "engaging" their respective cardboard targets, each man continued to scan his sector as instructed. Satisfied, they remained in their position of dominance within the room for a few moments before lowering their weapons. Cody stood from his seated position in the middle of the room. He was surrounded by cardboard targets with pictures of both threats and nonthreats: some held weapons while others held cell phones or beer bottles. The idea was that each sheriff's deputy needed to quickly discern the bad guy from the good.

Cody knew the exact layout including where each target resided. He had instructed each man to use his weapon-mounted light while he was scanning as a form of nonverbal communication to the others. Then all members could see who was still scanning and who was not. More importantly Cody paid close attention to when the deputies made the conscious decision to engage. He observed the third man in the room had been a little too hasty in his processing time. The man had aimed at a nonthreat directly over Cody's shoulder when the safety came off and the hammer fell. This was not the first time the mistake had happened.

"Alright, guys, bring it in," Cody said, waving at them.

He could tell this small-town part-time SWAT team was close. They worked well together, and while they weren't as smooth or seamless as his boys in Renegade were, these twenty-something-year-olds could certainly get the job done. All they needed was a little polishing.

"Check it out. You guys did a good job on that. But there are some things we need to clean up. Rick . . . dude, come on. You're killing me. How long have you been a cop?"

"'Bout two years now," he replied.

"Okay, in the two years you've been on the job, do you think the citizens you protect expect you to shoot the right people if they need to be shot while simultaneously saving the people who need to be saved?"

"Well, uh, yeah. Of course they do."

"Then why did you shoot that no-shoot over my left shoulder?"

The deputy's cheeks flushed. He knew he'd messed up but had hoped no one had seen it. Failure was embarrassing, most of all in front of your friends whose lives depend on your performance. That fact was not lost on Cody. That's why he was here, teaching this class, so others wouldn't make the same mistakes.

"I don't really know," Rick replied.

"You're outrunning your headlights, Rick. You're making decisions faster than you can process the available information. I don't care how long it takes you to figure it out: scan and assess your target, *then* decide whether or not he or she needs to get tuned up. No one cares how fast you shoot when you shoot the wrong people. You can do better than that. The *citizens* you swore to protect deserve better than that. Don't they?" The room nodded in response.

Though initially gut punched by being called out in front of his peers, Cody could see that the rookie cop knew Cody was right. There was a fire that smoldered. Finally, something had gotten through to him. Cody wondered if he himself would have listened if the shoe were on the other foot.

"Alright, boys, head back up front, grab some more ammo, jam a couple mags at most and let's do it again. I'll rearrange some targets and watch the team from the catwalk. Remember, just do the next right thing. Cover your sectors of fire, make your points of domination, assess the room, and shoot the people who need to be shot. It's that simple."

Cody stood on the catwalk and pulled his eyes from the deputies to glance at his watch. It was closing in on lunchtime, and he didn't want to be late.

He watched them intently as they took the final room. Individually, each officer flowed into the room, guns at the ready while Cody took mental snapshots of their points of domination so he could coach them on their performance. The audible pops of the Simunition paint bullets could be heard as they systematically assessed good guy from bad guy. After successfully neutralizing the threats, they each called out, "Clear," slung their weapons, and looked up toward the catwalk, waiting for Cody's input.

"*Much* better this time around, fellas. Much better," he said nodding in approval. "Alright, it's lunchtime, and I'd say you earned a decent one today. Be back in an hour and a half."

The deputies turned away, poking fun at each other and socializing amongst themselves while Cody made his way down the catwalk and toward the parking lot. After firing up his truck, he navigated his way to Frank's favorite barbecue joint, Lucky's BBQ; he knew the route by heart.

Seeing Frank at Tessa's celebration party had brought back a myriad of familiar feelings that only the comforts of an old friendship could bring. He had momentarily forgotten the pain or at least had been able to put it aside while they talked about guns, old hunting trips, and memories of way back when.

Today, though, he knew it was time to divulge what was really going on behind closed doors. Cody knew he'd never be able to open up to some therapist sitting in a chair with a legal pad writing down a bunch of psycho-babble nonsense. On the other hand, however, he also knew he couldn't keep everything bottled up. It was practically overflowing already, and it was only a matter of time before it erupted and caused him to have a major meltdown. The guilt was beginning to eat him alive.

Considering what exactly he was going to tell Frank, Cody finally settled on just telling him everything. *At least it'll all be out in the open.* After all, if he couldn't trust Frank, who could he? He forced himself to recall the dream from last night, remembering how different it was somehow from the previous ones. He struggled to make sense of it.

The context remained the same: helpless, unable to react, unable to move, unable to do . . . well, anything; only now it was Tessa rather than Elena or Jen who was the victim. He feared the trauma was getting the best of him, taking hold like a wave that refused to let him go to the surface for a breath. He feared it would eventually drown him in sorrow.

He knew this was the final straw, that maybe Tessa was right, and that he was always paranoid. Whether or not Frank would agree with her, he wasn't sure. But Cody figured small steps were better than no steps and that opening up to Frank was a solid first one. There was one thing he knew for sure: he couldn't keep it locked inside forever; it would certainly eat him alive.

He pulled into a parking spot that allowed him to maintain a view of the truck from inside the restaurant. He saw Frank's Ford Explorer parked in a stall and knew he was already inside waiting for him. Cody parked and sat there for a minute, collecting his thoughts.

"This is the right thing. You have to tell him what's going on. No more secrets," he said to himself. He took a deep breath before he pulled the door handle and made his way inside.

He walked into the lobby and started speaking to the hostess when he saw Frank waving his hand from the booth. Cody made his way over and plopped down across the table. He sat with a sigh and looked up to see Frank smiling at him in his happy-go-lucky way, but this time with a hint of worry.

"Well, ain't this a treat! I get to see you twice in a week after not having seen you in months. What's up?" Frank asked.

Cody decided on omitting everything he had practiced on the ride over. "Nothing really, just wanted to see ya, bro."

Frank tilted his head down and looked at Cody from the top of his eyes.

"What? I just wanted to see how you and the boys were doing. Seriously! I swear."

"The guys are fine. They're working on something with the FBI. Special request from a friend of Val's. Kinda hush hush, ya know? If word got out that they were using paramilitary contractors stateside and not local LE, the media would go wild, so don't go telling anybody."

"You know me, I'm going straight to Fox 7 after this." Cody chuckled before continuing. "That's good, man. I'm glad they're staying busy."

"What about you, Cody? You staying busy?" Frank inquired.

"Trying to, but I'm . . ." Cody trailed off, not knowing where to even begin. "I'm at the end of my rope here, dude. I feel like I don't have anyone to go to. After losing the girls and then getting booted from Renegade . . . you know, after smoking that piece-of-shit dirtbag trafficker. I'm lost, man. Totally lost. You were right, and I'm starting to think Tessa is too. It's all my fault," Cody finished quietly.

"Woah. Hold up. What're you talking about, Cody? What's your fault?" Frank asked, leaning in.

"Everything," Cody croaked. "If I had just realized what I was doing, maybe I would have changed. That night we did the financier op in the Caucasus Mountains, the last time I talked with the girls, Jen told me it was time to hold up my end of the bargain. It was time to talk about leaving ProCorp. I told her we'd talk about it when we got back, but the truth was I had already made up my mind."

Cody looked down at the table, unable to make eye contact with his friend and instead found himself playing with his silicone wedding band. His subconscious instantly tried to distract him by wondering why he still even wore the thing. He finally looked up, tears welling in his eyes, the pain ready to explode from just beneath the surface.

"I'd already decided that I would stay with Renegade. I thought the girls didn't need me as much as I needed this job. We had agreed early on that I would only do a few contracts with ProCorp and move on to something more stable . . . and less dangerous, but I just couldn't walk away. If I had left like I told her I would, then maybe I would've been there. Maybe I could have prevented the accident. Maybe it was my selfishness that killed them." He felt like he was finally falling off the edge of something that he had been struggling hard to stay balanced on top of before. He couldn't stop the emotions that came with the freefall. He broke down sobbing.

"Cody, you can't hold yourself responsible for that. It was a freak car wreck. You understand that, right?"

"No. It was the consequence of my choice. Don't you see? I chose myself over them, and now I'm paying the price. I mentioned the dreams to you at Tessa's."

Cody paused, making eye contact, searching for the right words.

"I see them, Frank. Every. Single. Night. I see Jen and Elena. I'm haunted by the memory of how I failed them. I have these dreams where something is going wrong—very, *very* wrong. A car wreck, a house fire, find her dead floating in a pool. Every single night. They all end the same way, with me able to do absolutely nothing. Both of them . . . dead."

Cody's tears ran down his face, unsure if he could go on. He heard Frank's voice, calm and cool like a flowing river.

"It's okay, dude. I'm listening."

Cody nodded and wiped the tears from his face, searching for the composure to continue.

"I've been dealing with it as best as I know how, but something's different now. Last night, the dreams shifted to Tessa. I'm waking up to visions of her being raped and left for dead, being tortured and . . . and I just can't take it anymore. I need some help, and I don't know what to do."

Frank looked at Cody with no small amount of guilt of his own. Shame flooded his face for having missed the signs, for not being present when he was needed the most. If expressions were anything, he looked like he felt a fraction of the similar type of guilt Cody felt, not being present to do something, anything, for his family and the people he cared about.

Cody felt the weight on his shoulders lighten, as if his confession shared the load and lessened it. Tears ran down his cheeks into his stubble. The waitress came by the table, but Frank waved her off politely and gave her a wink for added measure. He stretched out his arm, put his hand on Cody's shoulder, and squeezed.

"You know there's some decent places nowadays that help vets and cops . . . and people like us. They specialize in first responders dealing with this kind of thing. Have you looked into it?"

"No, I haven't. You're honestly the first person to hear about this. I didn't want anyone to know how bad it's been. How bad *I* am. Please keep this between us."

In that moment, Frank realized Cody was falling deeper into despair since his departure from the team rather than getting better. Cody's mistakes after his family were taken from him had not only taken away his role as Renegade 02 but taken his mission, his purpose, and his self-proclaimed identity. Now, he was totally lost. A piece of driftwood left to the mercy of the ocean. Frank knew he needed a lifeline.

"Don't worry, man. I ain't gonna tell anyone if you don't want me to."

Cody looked up from the table and stared into Frank's eyes with a seriousness Frank had not seen in some time.

"I know. That's why I'm coming to you, so I can take care of this the right way. These dreams are tormenting me, dude. I can feel it in the depths of my soul. Something is coming. Something I can't explain, but it's coming. You think you can help me?"

"You better believe I'm gonna try," Frank replied without a moment's hesitation.

6

Tessa rode beside Bart in the backseat of an expensive Land Rover on their way to the North Spear site. From a bird's-eye view, their vehicle was sandwiched between two other Land Rovers that were escorts. She took in all the beauty of Peru, with its majestic mountains in the distance and lush, green tropical rainforests. She couldn't remember the last time she saw this much green anywhere. She was a long way from home, that much was certain.

Along the way, Bart explained he'd named the site Azazel after an infamous Watcher Angel who was known to teach man horrific things. The meaning of the name was not lost on Tessa, though she thought it was a bit much. She began to realize Bart had a flair for the theatrical.

Prior to landing, he'd warned her the drive to Azazel would be somewhat lengthy and a little arduous since they had to pass through the mountains and into the rainforest.

Azazel had remained hidden for centuries under the thick canopy before being discovered less than six months ago. North Spear had quickly caught wind of the discovery and immediately sent a scouting team to check it out. Within just three weeks of the discovery, nearly two hundred North Spear employees were in the country setting up for a full excavation.

Roughly 25 percent of the contractors were private security directly from North Spear, including the driver, front passenger, and the other two Land Rovers traveling as their escorts. Tessa thought it odd as she'd never seen these many security personnel on a site like this, and definitely not this well-equipped. These men carried assault rifles, radios with earpieces—the whole nine yards.

On the outside, they looked like Cody and his buddies, but their eyes weren't the same. Cody, Frank, Tom, and especially Val had a look in their eyes that said, "I'm the most dangerous man in the room." These guys just looked like guys who spent a lot of time walking around trying to look tough. Tessa couldn't help but ask. She leaned to Bart.

"What's with all the muscle? We fighting off an invasion or something?"

"Don't worry about it too much. We received some reports of narco-terrorism activity and just want to ensure the safety of all our employees. I'm sorry if they make you uncomfortable."

The thought of armed extremists certainly did. She began to think Cody may have been right about his worries, especially if North Spear felt strong enough about it to dedicate so many G.I. Joes. Her mind drifted back to work as they passed the beautiful mountainscapes with lush greens and skies so blue that it looked as if pollution was a fairy tale. The thought of working on her dream dig made her giddy.

She desperately tried to keep a calm, collected demeanor, especially around Bart, but she knew her true colors showed from time to time. She focused her attention on the work ahead, deciding she should at least know her team.

"So how many actual archaeologists will I be working with?"

"Just you. We have other scientists who are experts in other fields though and about thirty others—fifteen locals we hired for logistical situations and the same who are sensitive-item-recovery specialists. They all know you're the expert here and fully understand you're in charge."

"Am I gonna have to deal with them siding on the ancient alien theory, or are they of the same historical background like me?"

"Rest assured, Tessa, they are all of the same belief that we have uncovered a Nephilim burial location and possibly more. Though I suppose if Nephilim existed, then angels existed, and if angels existed, then technically they *are* a type of extraterrestrial by definition. They *are* alien if they're not from this world."

Tessa thought about this for a moment. "That's certainly an interesting observation, Mr. Cox. But I have to say, I'm surprised you were able to find scientists in other fields with similar theories. Where did you find them? I mean everyone in my community thinks I'm crazy. They think I've been chasing Sunday School stories this whole time. It's nearly impossible to be taken seriously when you challenge the status quo of academia."

"You'd be surprised honestly at how small the world really is. It's kinda like fishing, I suppose. You just have to look in the right spots. Three team members are scientific theologians. They are Christian in faith, but quite scientifically minded. You see, they want to prove scientifically that God exists and believe they can do just that. We also have one geologist and a metallurgist who just came aboard before you. All are respected in their fields. I recognized I needed an expert in Nephilim archaeology, and you most certainly fit the bill."

"Bart, what made you choose me? I mean, I'm not even that well respected in my field. It just doesn't make sense is all. I'm super grateful for the opportunity, believe me. But with all the resources available to North Spear and you guys end up choosing me? I guess I'm just trying to figure out why. I want to know exactly what you need from me here."

"Let me be clear," Bart said, fidgeting with his sunglasses. "I've travelled the overwhelming majority of this earth for the better part of fifteen years. I've recruited, hired, and fired several thousands of people. I'm a scary judge of talent and, truthfully, I've been keeping tabs on you and your research for about a year now. Are you at the bottom of the totem pole? Yes . . . for now. But you have a drive not found in most people, and you have the tenacity to see it through. If everything goes according to plan, what we uncover at Azazel will skyrocket your career. *That* I guarantee you. North Spear has a way of being very influential."

Tessa detected a hint of malice in Bart's voice, somewhere between a boasting and a warning. After everything she'd seen in the last week, starting with their first meeting, she sensed an ulterior motive within Bart but couldn't put her finger on it. He'd done nothing but come through on everything he'd promised; however, something still didn't feel right. Perhaps it was because she hadn't spent much time around his white-collar type.

Despite her internal feelings about Bart, the more time she spent around him, the more she became accustomed to him. He had a certain way of making your skin crawl and then making you feel like nothing was wrong after a few mere words from his silver tongue. Although it was hard for her to overlook his occasional pompous attitude, she figured it came with the territory.

She checked her watch and realized the drive would continue for at least another hour. Tessa turned back to the window and took in the amazement of Peru and the awesome, powerful landscapes contained within its borders.

7

An hour had passed since Cody arrived at the restaurant and bared the heavy reveal of his dreams and pain to Frank. They ordered lunch platters of barbecue and spent the rest of their meal talking back and forth about different programs that dealt with lost loved ones. The feeling of guilt that saturated Cody's soul for not being home when his wife and daughter needed him most was becoming overbearing—something Frank could now see very clearly.

After their meal, Cody and Frank sat at the table in complete silence, a mountain of barbecue crushed, and sauce-stained white paper plates between the two of them. It wasn't an awkward silence, but more so a shared love of the quiet, a love of not needing to fill the air with pointless words.

Over the hustle and bustle of the rest of the restaurant's occupants, Frank tossed back the last few ounces of the amber beer in his glass. Cody rustled his shoulders back and forth, setting himself a little lower in his chair, and pushed the bill of his hat up at nearly a forty-five-degree angle—a subconscious movement that always signified he was full. The young brunette waitress strolled by and lightly placed the check on the table, bestowing them a pleasant smile.

"No rush, boys. Take your time, and when you're ready, I can check y'all out up at the front."

Cody and Frank both shot her a smile and nodded as she strolled away. The two men locked eyes, each of them shooting glances towards the small leather-bound book that contained the check. Cody held Frank's cold stare, simultaneously pushing himself back up in his chair slowly. Frank slowly but deliberately moved the stack of empty plates and glasses to the far side of the table.

"Don't even think about it," Cody said in a low, serious voice, tension and chill hanging heavy in his tone.

"I don't think you're that fast anymore, I mean, you are getting old," Frank replied, the smallest corner of the right side of his mouth hinting at a smile.

"The only thing getting old around here is you trying to buy me lunch," Cody said.

The two men leaned forward, muscles tensing, eyes locked in a competition of predictable outcomes. Under the table, Frank slid his foot forward until he found a leg of Cody's chair. Following the chair leg up, he located the support rod connecting the two front legs and braced the toe of his shoe firmly against it, waiting for the right moment.

A smirk appeared on Cody's face as he already knew the outcome. He set his phone down on the tabletop with his left hand, freeing it up, and cautiously gripped the tablecloth with his right without Frank seeing. Suspense filled the air, background noise became a void of deafening heartbeats. Frank's foot tensed, and an explosion of energy shoved Cody back from the table. Simultaneously, Frank shot a bulky arm out, swiping at where the book lay.

To Cody's surprise, he flew backward, but it didn't matter. He had been clutching the tablecloth so tightly that when he was shoved backward, the cloth came with him. The contents of the table shifted just enough so that the book moved out of Frank's immediate reach. With the speed of a cobra, Cody slapped his hand on top of it and pulled it toward himself.

"Dammit!" Frank pounded the table with a hammer fist.

The two men exploded into laughter now that the showdown for the check was over. After a few moments passed and the laughter died out, Cody couldn't help but search his memory for the last time he had laughed so hard.

He also couldn't remember the last time he had actually sat down and spent any time with his little brother-in-arms. Cody's face must have dropped a bit because Frank gave him a puzzled look.

"What?" Frank asked.

"Nothin', man. I'm just trying to remember the last time . . ." Cody trailed off.

"The last time what?" Frank persisted.

Cody looked at him for a second and said with a smirk, "Trying to remember the last time you beat me to the check, if there's ever been a time."

Frank released a huff of air as if he were insulted but chuckled at the banter.

"Come on, old timer. We better get you back to the home before the orderlies put out an APB."

"Better watch it with that old-timer talk. I'll still punch you in the face with your own fist."

Frank worked his way out of the booth-style seat, looked over his shoulder, and stuck his tongue out at Cody. The two of them walked toward the front kiosk to pay the bill, but the waitress was nowhere in sight.

"Figures," Cody huffed.

"Hang on, I see her," Frank said, spotting the young lady in the lobby. "I'll send her over here. I gotta pee though, so don't leave me."

With that, Frank strode over to the waitress and informed her that they were ready to pay. He dug into his pocket and pulled a money clip filled with cash, retrieved a fresh twenty-dollar bill, and handed it to her, but she shook her head.

"Oh, I'm sorry, sir. We have to take payment at the front register."

"Oh, this isn't for our bill actually," Frank protested. "This is just to say thank you for giving my brother and I a little extra space and time when he walked in," he said, holding out the crisp bill.

"Oh, of course, but you don't need to do this," she said, shaking her head side to side. Frank stood motionless with his arm still holding the money. Realizing he wasn't taking no for an answer, she gave a faint shy smile and accepted the money.

"Well, thank you. Is . . . is your friend okay?" she asked quizzically, peering over at Cody, who Frank saw still stood by the front kiosk but luckily wasn't paying them any attention.

Frank paused for a moment to actually think about it. He had blindly assured Cody that everything was going to be fine but hadn't really stopped to think if he thought it true. So much had transpired in Cody's life within the past eighteen months that Frank, in truth, was surprised he still functioned like a human being. Of course, Cody has always been one tough bastard.

Frank felt a pulse of hope ignited like a match in utter darkness. As he looked back at the waitress, he sported a smile that started just out of the corner of his mouth. "He will be," Frank replied, and she nodded.

Both men walked through the parking lot to their trucks. As they did, Cody realized the time of companionship he got with Frank had helped and actually opening up like that to someone made Cody feel somewhat better. It had been a while since he'd had anyone to confide in, making him wonder why he'd waited so long. But there was one last burning question in Cody's mind. He wasn't even sure if he should ask it. Perhaps because he was truly afraid of the answer.

"Honestly, do you think I'm crazy?" Cody asked.

"Crazy? No," Frank said firmly, leaning against his truck. "I think you need a purpose. You need something that makes you want to live life again. Maybe we could get you some help, and if you start getting better, I could even talk to Val about you coming back. Get ya on your feet and back in the field."

Cody's response to that came quick. "No. I can't come back."

"Why do you say that?"

"Well for one, Val won't let me. Two, I chose that life for selfish purposes once before, and I'm scared I'll do it again. What if I can't handle the pressure? I'm not the same man I was before. I'm not Renegade 02 anymore."

Frank thought about his response carefully. The skin between his eyebrows creased in concentration. "You may not be actively filling the role, but trust me, Cody, you're the only Renegade 02 there ever was or will be. Think about it. If you weren't, Val would've replaced you by now. He may not say it, but he wants you back. As for the other stuff, I'm here to help you with *anything* you need."

"Thanks, Frank. You don't know what that means to me. Thanks for lunch. Really."

"You paid!" Frank said with a laugh.

"I didn't mean the bill," Cody said, walking toward his own vehicle before he turned back to Frank once more.

"You said *anything*?" Cody asked, eyebrow raised.

"Anything," Frank replied with a wink. "You know that."

Cody paused and nodded. "Thanks, brother. I really appreciate it."

8

After almost a full twenty-four hours of travel by both air and car, Tessa's dream was about to become a reality. The North Spear driver carefully navigated through what Tessa could tell was a recently cleared trail through the rainforest. She was thankful for the constant flow of air-conditioning during the drive. Tessa rolled down the window once they got inside the rainforest and was hit with a blast of humidity and heat. She took in a few breaths of fresh, but humid, South American air. She felt as though she was breathing water vapor from a humidifier and decided to partake in some more AC while she could.

For the rest of the drive, the young archaeologist looked out the window nervously like a child arriving at Disneyland for the first time, even though the only thing visible was dense foliage. Her heart began beating quicker. She could sense they were getting close when Bart interrupted the silence and confirmed her suspicions.

"Tessa Willis, welcome to Azazel," he said, his eyes locked on the sight looming before them.

Tessa shifted her body to get a better look. The first thing she noticed was an immensely impressive waterfall that refused to let her attention stray. Standing at least a hundred feet tall, it sounded like a rushing freight train even from the backseat of the Land Rover. To the right of the waterfall, a pair of warrior angels that were carefully carved into the stone of the hillside guarded an entrance into the earth. They stood nearly the entire height of the waterfall and had clearly seen their share of hard times over the centuries. Tessa noticed they were robed with cloaks that covered their heads and their wings were folded behind them. They held their swords by the hilt, tips of the blades touching the ground.

Roots had nearly grown completely over the entrance into what Tessa could only assume was a cave of sorts. Trying to recall everything that Bart had told her about the newfound discovery, she could see where the foliage around the entrance had been recently cut down, revealing the ancient artistic structure. Her mouth was wide open as she stared at the site before her and then back again at Bart in the seat next to her. It was more beautiful than she could have imagined.

"You gotta be kidding me," she said, directing the statement to Bart.

"Trust me, I'm not. There's more. *Lots* more. But what do you think so far?" he asked.

Tessa hopped out of the Rover as soon as it came to a stop. The heat and humidity were now an afterthought as she continued to stare at the majestic stone angels. She pondered his question for a moment before replying.

"It's incredible," she replied breathlessly, eyes still locked on the heavenly guardians watching over their post.

"The architecture though," she continued. "It doesn't fit this part of the world. I've never seen anything quite like this in South American culture. Some of the features look reminiscent of the Middle East, yet some of the detail work looks Asian?"

Bart shrugged his shoulders, giving her the impression that he knew nothing. He took pride in his ability to lie and often used it to his advantage. In fact, he knew exactly what the architecture meant but didn't like to play all his cards at once. Bart was confident she'd put all the pieces together soon enough.

Her mind began to race thinking of a reasonable explanation. Was it possible this site predated anything she'd seen thus far? She came to the realization she was standing face-to-face with a structure built before Mayans or Aztecs or any other ancient civilization ever recorded. Tessa scanned her surroundings, taking it all in as best she could.

The waterfall was deafening the closer she ventured. Thousands of gallons were constantly falling into the large pool of water that collected at the base, which then flowed out into the rainforest. She could see a recently built bridge reaching from one bank of the creek to the other, allowing pedestrian access. The canopy of the rainforest was so thick it nearly blocked the sun—except for the space directly above the waterfall. The force of the raging water refused to let anything grow around it.

"Please, allow me to show you around. We still have lots to go over," Bart said as he motioned the way toward the bridge.

Tessa continued looking around, suddenly realizing she didn't see any work crews or dig teams. *Where the hell is everyone*? she wondered.

The North Spear contractors popped their doors and promptly exited the vehicles. They all moved with purpose and without hesitation. She grabbed her backpack from the back of the Land Rover and followed Bart across the small pedestrian bridge, careful not to trip and fall into the stream below.

The oppressive heat quickly began to attack her as sweat beaded around her forehead, arms, and back. The salty liquid rolled down her shoulder blades and underarms until she felt sticky with it. Although no one had ever accused Tessa Willis of being a girly girl, she didn't exactly relish the thought that she would have to live in these conditions for the next year.

She rolled up her sleeves on her lightweight hiking shirt and was happy for the vents in the back that took some of the heat off her body. She looked around and was surprised to see Bart didn't seem the least bit bothered by the conditions, but she could, however, clearly see the sweat breaking on his face. Bart was also wearing clothes befitting the rainforest, but naturally of a much more expensive material.

Perhaps he's tougher than he looks, she thought to herself.

Bart made no effort to roll his sleeves or make himself more comfortable. She couldn't seem to take her eyes off the site during the short hike. She realized they'd have to get in the water if they were going inside and gave them a quizzical look. Without hesitation, Bart walked past her and jumped into the shin-deep water. *Well, he's certainly not afraid to get dirty.*

"The boys and I have decided you should do the honors. Especially since it's your first time at Azazel," Bart said, yelling to be heard over the water.

Tessa wasn't sure what they were talking about and jumped into the water regardless. She did her best not to fall face first. After sloshing through the water, she joined Bart, who was standing on the steps looking up at the stone archway carved directly out of the mountain. He, too, was always impressed but would never admit it.

Tessa felt like an ant standing underneath the entrance. She wondered if the size was constructed so large for specific purpose, because otherwise, she could not see why anyone would waste the man power, hours, and trouble of making such a monument. Much to her surprise, the entrance was a dead end after only ten feet in. She could see a small inscription on the smooth wall and peered closer to get a better look.

The inscription was about the size of an index card, and after a few seconds, Tessa realized it was written in an ancient language she actually recognized. It was Enochian. The language was recorded by Englishman John Dee in the late sixteenth century who had claimed that he and his colleague had the language revealed to them by Enochian angels. Many scholars and linguists argued Dee had made the whole thing up, but here, right in front of her face, was the evidence. Evidence carved into solid rock thousands of years before Dee ever existed. She took a few steps back to look at the stone angels again. Luckily, she'd brought along her journals containing the alleged angelic alphabet.

Were they Watchers? she pondered.

She quickly turned to look back at Bart, his gaze watching her every move. Sliding her backpack off her shoulders, she pulled the journal out and ardently flipped its pages until she found her diagram of symbols and translations. Oddly enough, she'd seen this exact arrangement elsewhere in her studies.

"We've all taken bets on what it actually says. So, expert, what's it say? We're all dying to know."

She ignored the question and continued her search, her mind drawn to ancient Egypt. She flipped the pages in one of her books and found the picture she knew held the connection she was looking for. Tessa held the book up to the hieroglyphic-like inscription on the solid rock. It was a perfect match. She whispered the text to herself.

"Death is only the beginning."

It was an ancient Egyptian proverb, a belief that death was merely the next step to something more. As she stepped away from the text, she found herself smiling. She understood what this meant. Those who had studied the Nephilim understood their influence on the ancient Egyptian culture and religion. For Tessa, this was but another link, another piece of evidence to show just how far the influence of the Nephilim had spanned. Her heart raced, momentarily wondering if she was in a dream.

"Well? What's it say, hotshot?" Bart asked.

"It's an old Egyptian proverb that says, 'Death is only the beginning'," she said, turning back to him.

"Interesting," was all he said in turn, his gaze still clearly on her.

"How so?" Tessa asked. "Interesting" didn't quite seem to cover the fascination she felt at this reveal. Did he understand? Did he truly know the scope of what this meant?

"Let's just say there's a lot more where that came from."

Tessa frowned and looked around. "Where? It's a dead end. There's nowhere else to go."

"Put your hand on the inscription and push," he said, beckoning his head to the inscription behind her and wiping the sweat from his forehead. "I'm melting out here in this heat. Come on. Let's go."

She looked at Bart, partially annoyed and partially befuddled. He urged her along, clearly becoming frustrated, no doubt due to the jungle humidity.

"Humor me," he said with a hint of impatience after she hadn't moved.

She placed her right hand on the ancient writing and pushed, unsure what to expect. To her amazement, she saw the stone wall swung inward like a door, but only a few inches.

Tessa put her hand on the inscription again and pushed with more force. The rock wall separated into a perfectly concealed and precision-fit entrance layered in the wall's surface. She pushed the door fully open and was amazed at the craftsmanship and skill required to achieve such a feat. The massive stone door was a hidden access to what looked to be a forgotten tunnel.

Tessa Willis looked up in sheer awe and saw the door stood at least fifty feet tall and about twenty-five feet wide. She couldn't see any hinges but knew its construction was a work of art. Nothing like this had been preserved in such pristine condition. She walked into the concealed cavern that sported an expertly crafted set of stone steps. The first thing she noticed was the temperature change. Inside the cave, the climate shifted almost instantly to a reasonable seventy degrees. Now she understood why Bart was in such a rush to get inside; the climate inside the cave was certainly much more comfortable.

Walking down the first set of stone steps, she couldn't believe her eyes. Tessa stopped, turned around, and looked at Bart for some type of explanation. She tried to speak but only managed a few mumblings. "What . . . how . . . uh . . ."

"Like I said, you haven't seen *anything* yet. Keep going."

One thing Tessa couldn't argue at this point was Bart had definitely come through on his promises. She carefully continued to navigate down the cavern's winding tunnel.

As Tessa made her way through the cave, it only took a few twists and turns before she knew she would be lost down there without Bart and his personal-security-detail's guidance. She suddenly found herself grateful for their instruction, even though they weren't exactly the friendliest of types so far. Instead of speaking, they silently pointed their flashlight in the direction they wanted her to go. Sullen and hostile seemed like better words to describe them.

The deeper they went, the tunnel continued to split off in more and more different paths every ten feet. "This place is a damn maze," she said to herself. After a series of gentle turns, she stopped and turned back to face them, and ensuring she was still going the right way.

She raised her arms as if to say, "What next?" None of them said a word, just beckoning with their lights to keep going. Just as she was becoming nervous, she heard sounds up ahead.

Bart slipped past her, waving his hand and urging her to follow. Tessa fell in line right behind him to see that the cave opened up into a massive cavern foyer easily the size of a warehouse. One hundred feet above her head stalactites hung from the ceiling like rocky icicles threatening to drop at any moment.

All around her, she could see the hustle and bustle of people working determinately. But doing what? She didn't know. They all seemed to have their specific purpose in the resolved way they navigated the commotion, and they looked resolute in doing it. English, Spanish, and several other languages sounded around her echoing in the vast cavern hall, causing her to wonder how far globally this operation spanned.

Her eyes drifted back to the turmoil surrounding her. Tessa could see the various tunnels and entrances leading even deeper into the cave, winding into what looked like pitch-dark blackness. Suddenly the scene hit her like a lightning strike. Generator-powered work lights cast their illumination to one side in particular, giving her a clear look at her new worksite. She was staring at a megalithic temple carved directly into the rock. There were obvious signs of water damage caused by thousands of years of erosion or perhaps a massive global flood. The sheer excitement of it all was causing butterflies to flurry in her stomach.

Looking to the temple ruins, she saw two prominent, intricately designed support columns sculpted out of the cave's walls. Next to the columns stood a figure on either side of the entrance that led into the temple. The figures stood twenty feet tall. Each held a spear in one hand and a shield in the other. The rocky temple entrance was covered in thick moss and looked like it had seen better times.

"Lara Croft, eat your heart out," she mumbled to herself.

At the top of the Azazel temple with a staircase leading up to its entrance, she could see a stone face with large teeth carved intricately into the apex. Tessa observed the face, which hosted flames inside hollowed-out areas that glowed yellow and red, displaying an open mouth and fiery flaming eyes.

The architecture designs were similar to what she saw outside: an amalgamation of ancient South American, Asian, and Middle Eastern features. Her mind ran a million miles an hour, a multitude of questions rushing through her head like water through a fire hose. Large equipment boxes scattered the cavern floor outside the temple; people sat around them in camping chairs and dedicated cabin tents that housed what looked to be both the workers and scientists. Bart reached out with his hand and placed it on Tessa's shoulder. She turned around instinctively with her eyes wide and mouth open.

"Well, are you impressed yet?" Bart asked. "Did you really think I was going to go through the trouble of bringing you out here to show you a waterfall?"

Tessa was speechless. She couldn't help but turn back around to take in the view of the temple and the cave. It was almost overwhelming. One of the security detail members walked up and handed Bart a crisp twenty-dollar bill.

"You called it, sir. She's speechless."

"Take her to the tents and introduce her to her team for me," Bart said, pocketing the money.

The security consultant nodded and walked to Tessa who was still standing frozen in amazement.

"Excuse me, Ms. Willis. I'm Al, short for Albert," he said politely. "I'm the head of security here at Azazel. It's pretty amazing the first time you see it, isn't it?"

"I don't think it'll ever stop being amazing," Tessa replied. Al smiled graciously and nodded like he understood.

"Ma'am, I am going to introduce you to your team and show you where you will call home for the foreseeable future. After that we'll need to start the security brief."

"What? A brief?" she asked.

"Don't worry. It's just a bunch of boring information about the dos and don'ts around Azazel. We'll also need you to submit all electronics to our tech department for screening purposes. No one but Mr. Cox is allowed a phone while on-site. We can't take any chances of our work reaching the outside. Operational security is of the utmost importance. I'm sure you understand."

Tessa nodded her head but thought it strange they'd confiscate *all* electronics. Suddenly she remembered the satellite phone her brother all but forced her to take along.

"You need all this right now?" she asked with what she hoped seemed like innocence.

"No, please excuse my manners. Of course it can wait till later, but we do need it done by the end of the day."

Tessa considered giving up the SAT phone, but something inside her told her it was best to stow it away just in case. She thought about what Bart had said about the cartel action in the area. With this thought in her head, she decided then and there she would hide it. After all, how else would she let anyone know she needed help in case of an emergency?

She smiled at Al. "Of course. I understand. I really had no idea it was this extravagant. All I was shown were some pictures of a tomb. Bart never said anything about all *this*. I'm still in shock, I think."

Albert grinned at her. "One thing about Mr. Cox, he likes to keep a few surprises up his sleeve.

"May I introduce you to your team?" he continued. "They're this way by the tents and equipment."

The archaeologist gathered herself and did her best to regain her composure. "Yes, of course. I'm anxious to meet them and get started soon."

She turned to say thank you to Bart but saw he was preoccupied with what looked like a satellite phone twenty yards away and decided it was best not to interrupt him. He turned and made eye contact with her, to which Tessa waved and mouthed the word "Thanks." Bart smiled in return and gave her a wink. She followed Al to the tents while Bart made his way outside the cave and back into the humidity of the jungle. Waiting for his satellite phone to connect, he instinctively looked upward at the sky as though he could see the signal circling just above the canopy. Patiently he stood, listening to the waterfall mask the sounds of the wild. Bart watched as a flock of birds flew overhead.

Glancing back down, he saw the screen showed that it had finally connected. He thumbed the button to make the call. After a series of clicks, he heard his boss's voice.

"What?" he said as though Bart had called at an inopportune moment.

"Yes, sir. I have the archaeologist on-site now." Bart listened intently to the phone.

"It's about time. How soon till you get it open?" the voice asked.

Bart hesitated for just a moment. "That part is still undetermined, sir, but this one can definitely decipher the ancient Enochian. I'll have an answer for you soon—"

"Cox, we both know how important this is, and I can't afford for you to screw it up. This girl better not fail," he stated in no uncertain terms.

"I understand, sir. I feel confident we'll find a way," Bart replied, trying his best to sound collected on the phone.

The cold voice spoke again, and Bart listened intently. "I want inside that tomb, Bart. No exceptions. Keep me in the loop in near real time."

"Yes, sir, of course. As soon as I know something, you'll know something. I've never let you down before, and I don't plan to start now, not when we're so close—"

"Just *make* this happen," his boss seethed into the phone. "Got it?!"

Bart nodded profusely, despite that his boss wasn't able to see him. "Perfectly clear, Mr. Adams. Please let the other chair members know how much I appreciate this opportunity."

The line disconnected before he had complete the sentence, but Bart completed it anyway. He hung up the phone, slipped it in his pocket, and turned to look at the temple. He became lost in thought as his face turned into a deep scowl. He knew this was his chance. If he was to ascend the ladder in North Spear, if he was to secure his future . . . this would be the milestone where it happened. Bart needed this to succeed as much as his superiors did. No . . . he needed it *more*. After all, *they* were already set for life. His eyes squinted as his mind drifted to the next step in his carefully planned chain of events.

9

Even after working at Azazel for two weeks, Tessa was still perplexed at the problem she had in front of her. From the relative comfort of her hotel room, she lied awake, staring at the ceiling, mulling it all over and almost hoping that if she stared hard enough, the answer would simply show up in writing on the ceiling. Sprawled around her, her journals lay opened and bookmarked while her textbooks were scattered about her worktable nearby. Nearly everything was littered with handwritten notes.

Initially, her main concern centered around living inside a cave. However, she soon was pleasantly surprised to learn that North Spear had spared no expense, housing all of the outside talent in a five-star hotel. After all, most were accustomed to living in comfortable, convenient places where their every need was only a simple phone call away. In the Amazonian rainforest, however, that was far from the case. The unfortunate part was the fact they had to commute at least an hour each day just in one direction. But between living far or living in the cave, Tessa definitely preferred this.

After the security brief, her concerns had been mostly alleviated when Al explained in detail that they had enough security to protect the site twenty-four hours a day. It was obvious North Spear wanted to keep the site private and exclusive in order to stake their claim. With this, it also quickly became clear to Tessa she had never worked on anything like this before in her life, and she had to admit, the magnitude of it was slightly daunting. On the one hand, the nuances of things she couldn't fully comprehend such as the severity of the security made her uncomfortable. While she didn't know what dangers warranted this extent of privacy and protection, she certainly didn't want to find out what level of danger they might be faced with without them. She tried not to think about it too much.

On the day of her arrival, she hadn't been able to get enough of the site and had explored as much of the temple as she could. Some of the team members were kind enough to show her around, using its various catacombs and labyrinths that were dug deep inside the earth. The level of detail in the stonework was impressive to say the least.

After a few hours of exploration, she hadn't been able to help herself and returned to see the sarcophagus. Al, her guide for the time being, obliged. He had politely escorted her through the twisting tunnels until she stood before the massive rectangular tomb. She knew right away that she had found the object of her newfound obsession. It was bigger than she had imagined, and the pictures Bart had showed her on the plane hadn't done it any justice. She could see that the intricate Enochian markings and language carved into the side had been heavily damaged over the centuries. When Bart had later joined them and informed Tessa of her task to decipher and translate the markings, Tessa had tried to explain it would be difficult given the extent of the damage, but he didn't seem to listen. He went on to explain that it was believed the ancient text was a set of instructions and the secret to open the tomb was simply just waiting to be found. Tessa tried to share his enthusiasm, although in her head, she was already busy at work problem solving ways around the impairment.

The room's walls were covered in glyphs—ancient pictures telling a story of what had been buried—and sealed away inside the massive tomb. The team had seen nothing like it in their individual experiences and had, thus far, been unsuccessful in opening the sarcophagus even with their range of equipment.

According to Tessa, the images on the wall documented a great war. Though the Enochian text didn't appear to line up with the glyphs, this was likely the first documentation of the reign of the Nephilim over mankind in the area, as well as their eventual downfall. It was heavily damaged, but with a careful hand, she found she could understand the context: a war between giants and men. The glyphs and carved images depicted the giant rulers traveling across a great body of water. Upon arrival in the new land, they were regarded as divine beings by the local tribes. The Nephilim appeared benevolent at first, helping these tribes by teaching them skills to enhance their livelihood, including the working of metals as well as how to manipulate ores to build tools and weapons. Their influence began to spread across the continent just as they had done in the Middle East. They were regarded as heroes.

As Tessa had worked at deciphering the glyphs and writings, she found herself quickly enveloped in the story. Right before her very eyes was a previously untold account of how simple tribes had started their civilizations, modeling them after the ancient so-called Fallen Ones. Once the Nephilim had reached a point where their control was all but assured, the tribes came to worship the hybrid creatures like gods.

Using their advanced understanding of creation, the Nephilim offered not just their expertise but their genetic code. Promising longer lifespans and access to knowledge beyond their understanding in exchange for the transhumanistic upgrade and teachings, the giants were to take for themselves the fairest of the women. The tribal leaders agreed. And that's where the turning point became clear.

Unfortunately, due to the centuries of water exposure, it was difficult for Tessa to tell what happened exactly, but one thing was evident: the Nephilim began doing something their fully human followers could not abide.

Some of the tribes refused to give their daughters over to the advanced hybrid race. In response, the Nephilim simply took them without asking, displaying their true ability of dominance. Those that rebelled against the Nephilim were quickly conquered, their chieftains sacrificed alive to their angelic ancestors. Tessa wrote down everything she could and did her best to copy what she saw despite her lack of drawing ability. Some of it almost made her sick.

Typically, the Nephilim would hold some sort of ritual before they bit the head off of the rebel chief, drinking his blood like they were quenching themselves with water. Things only continued to worsen as other glyphs depicted experimentation of genetic manipulation, resulting in ghastly, unnatural creatures similar to those of myth. The lines were drawn. Open war had begun across ancient South America.

Two distinct tribes of human were clear: those who glorified, worshipped, and served the giants, and those who fought against them at all costs. Unfortunately for Tessa, several large portions at this part of her findings were lost due to the extent of the damage to both the Enochian text and the carved images. According to the story written along the walls of the tomb chamber, or at least what Tessa could decipher of it, the giants had fallen one by one as the size and strength of the tribes grew. The last known survivor, the Last Son of Anak, was finally defeated and buried right there in the ancient temple that was once used as a place of worship. Tessa had gazed upon his tomb, desperately wishing she could find the answer on how to open it. But even the nameplate carved into his tomb had been damaged beyond recognition.

Although the ancient language written along the sarcophagus itself was believed to contain the directions on how to open the massive casket, Tessa lacked the necessary portions, which made it nearly impossible for her as far as she was concerned. Several times during her studies she couldn't help but notice that these portions almost seemed as though they were removed intentionally, but she couldn't be sure.

Thus, Tessa lay awake inside her room, surrounded by her books and notes, searching incessantly for an answer or solution that might help her in some way. Tessa knew uncovering this Nephilim skeleton was the key to ensuring her success, yet somewhere deep down inside, she felt . . . she couldn't describe it. But she knew she desperately needed the validation of seeing the monster bones for herself, with her very own eyes. And, more than anything, she wanted to prove to both her former colleagues and to herself, that she was right all along. They *did* exist.

However, she couldn't help feeling as though something dark and infinitely sinister rested inside that tomb and that it was just waiting for the moment it'd be unleashed. She was not superstitious by nature and cast the thought from her mind when it entered, but still it lingered when all was quiet.

Her alarm rang out, signaling it was time to get back to work. She stood from her queen-sized bed and gathered her journals. At the very least, she'd have the long drive to Azazel to continue her thoughts.

After navigating the waterfall and retracing the now-instinctive route through the cave complex, Tessa saw some of her team already stirring just outside the temple. Luckily, she'd made some friendships rather quickly and her team had welcomed her openly. She gave them a polite wave as she glanced around the rest of her surroundings. As soon as she saw the mess tent, she realized she'd forgotten to grab some coffee. Tessa had been so distracted as of late that the thought of eating or drinking had completely eluded her. Knowing she would soon need the caffeine, she made her way over and inhaled the smell of bacon, eggs, and hot coffee that filled the air inside the tent walls. Her stomach growled.

She looked around for anyone familiar. She saw the North Spear security team filling their bellies and laughing about what she could only imagine was an obscene joke. Truth be told, friendships outside her own team were nonexistent. In fact, most of those outside it disgusted her. It hadn't taken long for her to see that the security were not true professionals. Instead, they were merely boys that were well armed rather than the men they thought themselves to be.

A couple of them looked her way with a flirtatious grin. One winked, thinking he actually had a chance. She rolled her eyes and continued her search. She saw across the room Jake Reynolds, the lead theologian scientist and her trusted confidant. Jake had become something like a father figure to her over the last couple of weeks. He gave her a feeling of wholesomeness that made her feel at home—something she was especially grateful for now. She found him to be very kind and had never heard him say a mean word to anyone.

Tessa did not open up to many people right off the bat, but for some unknown reason, she found herself doing that very thing with Jake. They talked as easily as two long-term acquaintances would. A man in his late fifties, he'd become a Christian after a near-death experience in his twenties. In his thirties, he began searching for physical evidence of historical biblical events and artifacts. He often talked endearingly about his family, which consisted of his wife and two teenage boys; in return, she would tell him about her own. Tessa mentioned both her parents had passed sooner than expected, leaving Cody and Tessa with only each other.

Her talks with Jake as time went on were calming compared to her conversations with Bart. Though lately, Tessa had sensed there was something bothering Jake. Despite her asking him almost every time they crossed paths, that seemed like one subject Jake didn't seem eager to share with her just yet. Instead, he would glance at who was around them and then shake his head as if to say, "Later." Tessa was determined to get him alone one of these days.

But it seemed that today was not one of those days. Sitting across from Jake was none other than Bart himself. Tessa was surprised to see Bart so early in the morning. He didn't usually arrive until just before lunch and never stayed more than a few hours.

Something's up, Tessa thought. *I'll bet he wants an update.*

Bart normally let them work in peace, but he was quickly becoming impatient. Tessa assumed that since she could decipher the Enochian language Bart must have thought she was going to have the tomb open after having seen it a few times, but she and her team knew the truth. These things take time. They were dealing with an ancient civilization that, in many ways, was more advanced than their own, even by present-day standards.

Both men were deep in conversation, occasionally blowing on their hot cups of coffee in between sips. She knew Bart would ask her about the tomb and her progress, but she didn't know what to say. Tessa could sense his restlessness growing each time they met.

The simple fact of the matter was she wasn't any closer to opening it than she was the day she arrived at Azazel. Despite her best efforts, she couldn't find anything from her findings on-site, and none of her other research or books offered any help. New discoveries within the temple itself were commonplace as the exploration team continued mapping its interior, but nothing had progressed with the tomb. Quite frankly it would take multiple teams of archaeologists and linguists *years* to translate all of the Enochian text to English. Bart was foolish to think a team of five could get it done in a couple of weeks.

She walked through the food line and offered a kind smile to the servers. After getting her plate of hot food ready to go, she made her way to the coffee pot and poured a large cup. Turning from the beverage table she saw Bart, elbows on the table, coffee cup in both hands, eyes fixed directly on Tessa. She knew he was waiting for her to sit down and provide him with her progress.

She took a deep breath and walked toward them, preparing herself for what was likely to end up becoming an ass chewing. She arrived at the table, set her tray down beside Jake, and sat across from Bart. Jake turned his head in her direction as he heard someone walking up.

"Mornin', Tessa. You've looked better. You sleep okay?" Jake asked.

"Wow, thanks for the level of honesty there, Jake," she said, taking a slow sip of the hot drink. "As a matter of fact, I did not. Didn't expect something so candid from you so early though."

Bart remained silent and took a sip of coffee. His eyes hadn't left Tessa since the beverage table.

"Oh, uh . . . sorry, Tess. That's not what I meant," Jake stuttered.

"Relax, it's fine," she said with a grin and picked up her fork to dig in the food. "I'm just messing with ya. I'm just worn out, that's all. I've gone through damn close to every book I have and haven't found anything like what we've discovered. I'm trying to document everything we come across, but we're in uncharted territory and frankly, I don't know which way to go. We're literally uncovering forgotten history."

As she finished the sentence, her gaze drifted towards Bart. The North Spear executive set his cup down on the table softly and interlocked his fingers.

Oh shit, here it comes. I'm fired, Tessa thought.

She couldn't help but feel like Bart was staring into her soul, burning a hole right through her head with his eyes. If she *thought* he was growing impatient before, she certainly knew it now. She couldn't blame him.

Bart finally spoke. His words were concise and calculated. "I'm sure with your expertise, Ms. Willis, you and your team will find a way."

That's not what I expected.

He continued after a brief pause. "Hopefully sooner rather than later."

Tessa took the meaning as she'd be fired or replaced if she didn't. However, there was a certain emptiness in Bart's eyes she couldn't quite decipher. Devoid of emotion, more specifically empathy, they revealed a truth he didn't want exposed.

"Well, I can assure you, it's not from lack of trying," Tessa finally settled on.

Bart considered it a moment and nodded his head in agreement. Jake jumped in, sensing the tension built in Tessa. Having spent the last two weeks with her, he'd become more than accustomed to her body language and personality quirks.

"Don't beat yourself up, kid. You've been working harder than anyone," he said, giving her a playful nudge. "It seems the Nephilim, or whoever built that thing, were smarter than us and didn't want anyone to get back inside. Maybe we aren't supposed to see what's inside of that tomb? Considering every piece of historical myth or legend of these guys tells us that they were pretty frickin' bad. One constant theme across all cultures was how violent and oppressive they were. The bible was pretty clear that God didn't want them around anymore. You know what I mean? He floods the world to get rid of them, then later directs King David to seek them out and destroy their descendants, the Rephaim, all the way down to the very last one. Even their livestock. I mean if that's not a statement in itself, what is?"

Bart shook his head in disagreement. "Dr. Reynolds, please. I respect your beliefs, but let's not be superstitious."

"We need to tread carefully here, Bart. This is beyond superstition now. The facts are we are having this conversation in an ancient Nephilim temple and talking about opening up a tomb that could contain the very remains of one right inside. I'm going to go out on a limb here and suggest something we should consider. What if it's empty? What if it's not a sarcophagus but something more like a resurrection chamber?"

"Are you saying you think that's some sort of stasis chamber?" Bart asked.

"I'm saying we know they were highly advanced, highly intelligent, and literally born out of evil disobedience to God. Who knows what they're truly capable of creating."

"Listen, I understand this isn't easy for either of you. Anything worth doing is not going to be. If it was easy, everyone would do it. But the chair members of North Spear have invested a large amount of money into this and won't accept anything other than seeing a return on their investment. Simply put, we can't afford to fail here. I'm sure you won't mind if I stop by after breakfast to take a look myself?"

Tessa and Jake looked at each other curiously and shrugged their shoulders. It seemed odd to them he was asking, but Bart had a knack for being polite. It was always easier to catch flies with honey than with vinegar.

"Of course, this is your operation," she replied.

Tessa, Jake, and Bart continued eating their breakfast with the subject changing from work to life in general. Jake spoke about his family and how he missed them, always looking for an opportunity to brag about how smart or talented both of his boys had become. Tessa didn't mind. She found it endearing. It was clear how much he loved them. But during the conversation, Tessa couldn't help but notice Bart's mind was elsewhere. It wasn't hard to notice. At least for Tessa. After all, both Willis siblings were keen observers. It paid dividends for Cody as a police officer and for Tessa in her work as an archaeologist having to look for the smallest detail. Nevertheless, she saw something being worked over in Bart's mind but couldn't quite put her finger on it.

Only having known Bart for a couple of weeks now, she'd become more comfortable with his mysterious nature. Despite this, she couldn't help the tiny voice in her subconscious that told her to beware. She had mostly ignored the feeling, pushing it aside as best she could and disregarding it, wondering if her brother's paranoia had been rubbed off on her. The thought of her brother caused Tessa's mind to wander. As Jake continued on about his family, Tessa thought of Cody.

She wondered how he was doing and if he was holding up okay, hoping Frank was taking care of him. Tessa subconsciously formed a smile she couldn't hold back at the thought of her brother's partner in crime. She kicked back the last of her coffee and stood from the table.

"Alright, boys, I'll see ya down there. I'm gonna grab some material from my tent."

Jake and Bart both looked up and nodded in her direction, acknowledging her departure. Tessa walked to the trash cans, tossed her paper plate, placed her tray on the stack of dirty trays, and made her way out the tent.

10

Bart finished the remainder of his coffee and said his goodbye to Jake. He needed to make a phone call and get a few things settled before making the trip into the temple. Leaving his coffee cup on the table for the staff to clean up, Bart stood. An air of privilege was unmistakable as he walked out of the mess tent and away from any would-be eavesdroppers.

Pulling the small satellite phone from his pocket when he was outside the cave, he searched his contact list until he found the number he needed. Bart was a man of power and influence, but he certainly wasn't born into it. He'd acquired what he had over a long career of meeting the right people, working his way into a position of authority, and stepping on a few necks to get there. One thing was certain: when Bart got his first taste of power, he knew he would do just about anything to get as much as he possibly could—no matter the cost.

The man he was calling, however, had had the opposite upbringing. He was born into power and had influence Bart could only dream about. Secretly, Bart feared the man despite only having met him face-to-face once. Mr. Adams, in the simplest of forms, was a frightening employer. Although handler was a more appropriate term.

Bart tapped the SAT phone and held the device to his ear. Waiting for the line to connect and start ringing, he realized his face had become flush and he was apprehensive about the conversation to come. He took a deep breath in through his nose and let it out of his mouth to help clear his mind. Just as the last of his oxygen exited his lungs, the line connected.

"You had better be calling to tell me it's open," Mr. Adams's stern voice said.

Bart quickly inhaled, rushing to answer. "Not yet, sir, but we're making progress. The team tells me they think they've figured it out, but they're just working a few things to make sure we can remove the specimen intact," Bart lied, fighting to keep his voice steady.

The voice on the other line went silent, but Bart could hear his breathing through the long-distance connection.

"My patience is wearing thin. Need I remind you what's at stake?"

"No, sir, it has been made clear."

"Good. Get it done. Do not call me again unless you are standing above the specimen looking at it with your own eyes. I want what is *inside*."

Bart knew the feeling. Bart himself wanted a way inside Adams's world, although he would never wish this aloud. The entombed Nephilim inside the sarcophagus was the only way to ensure that would happen.

"Yes, sir, I understand."

"I sincerely hope so, Cox. I will not hesitate to replace you."

The line went dead as soon as the last word was spoken.

Bart closed his eyes and winced, his grip tightening around the phone. He was running out of time, and for the first time in a long time, he was unsure of what to do. This was his chance to move up the ladder, but it seemed the ladder was tilting dangerously from under him. He'd put all his faith in Tessa Willis. Now he was starting to wonder if this had been the right choice to make.

Bart knew Mr. Adams was a man of his word. If he sent a replacement, that would be it. Bart could kiss his future goodbye.

No, that couldn't happen, it *wasn't* going to happen. Not after everything he'd done to get here.

He turned back inside the cave.

The tomb alone was an archaeological marvel, guaranteed to be studied for years to come.

Tessa had noticed Bart's entrance but remained hard at work transcribing the Enochian to one of her books. Luckily she had made a good deal of progress in the past couple of weeks, but she could only hope it was enough for the time being. The idea of being at the tip of the spear on such a project exhilarated her, though she wanted to know why Bart was in such a rush. Despite what he had said about returning investments, it had not made any sense to her *why* he needed to get it open. There seemed to be something more than simply money at stake.

What is he not telling me?

Desperately she searched every waking minute to find a way to open it, but clearly Tessa and her team of experts were missing something vital. She knew the secret was close, but just couldn't quite figure it out just yet. Doubt had begun to set in.

The tomb itself was perfectly rectangular with precision-crafted right angles at every corner. Ladders were propped up along the tomb with large, thick towels that protected it from further damage. On the top of the tomb was another intricately detailed carving, but no one had a clue what it meant since they couldn't yet find anything in their books or previous research to help. Grooves had been cut that looked suspiciously similar to topographical lines on a map. Directly in the center on top was about a six-foot-by-four-foot area, completely smooth and untouched. It looked like a spot flat and perfect enough for an air mattress or something of similar size.

Along the outside were grooves crafted around it like a frame that spread out in a snaking flowing riverbed. Tessa had never seen anything like it in her studies and couldn't make sense of it. She knew Bart held high hopes she would immediately recognize it, but she had no idea, despite her best efforts. Tessa walked toward Jake.

"Well, any luck since yesterday?"

Jake sighed heavily. "Nope. I'm beginning to think it's all one piece and isn't actually a tomb, but more of a monument. The lines are so precise I can't see how the top could actually move at all!"

Tessa considered his statement for a moment. "Have we figured out how they made the . . . uh . . . the alloy? Is that what we're calling it? I mean seriously, how can such an ancient culture make something so advanced?"

Jake's head hung in disappointment, which gave Tessa her answer. She honestly hadn't expected one, but figured she'd ask anyway. Jake called over the team's geologist, Kurt Bennett, and metallurgist, Amanda Edwards. Kurt pulled himself away from his work and walked toward them.

"Hey, Tess, how was breakfast? Decided to get an early start and lost track of time, but wanted to know if it was worth it or not?" he asked.

"Bad move, Kurt. Today was bacon day, and the eggs were on point."

"*Why*?!" Kurt yelled out as he threw his hands on his face dramatically. Tessa grinned at his theatrics.

"I totally forgot!" Kurt said, dragging his hands away. "So much for 'the early bird gets the worm,' huh?"

Tessa couldn't resist poking at him. "If you keep skipping meals, you'll end up eating worms."

Everyone chuckled and looked toward Amanda as she joined the group.

"I told him the same thing, Tessa, but he doesn't listen to anyone. He'll learn someday."

Kurt was middle aged and somewhat portly. His hair was thinning on top, which he refused to acknowledge, and instead chose to comb what little hair he had all the way over his scalp. Everyone on the team agreed not to bring it up.

Amanda was in her late twenties. Coming from Georgia, she, too, had a southern drawl, which comforted Tessa when she spoke. Relatively new in her career, she was appreciative to be using her skills on such an important task. Both she and Kurt had been working tirelessly to help the team in whatever ways they could.

The team had only been on-site for two weeks prior to Tessa's arrival, but they were able to discern at least what elements the tomb was made of. Much to their amazement, the metallurgic makeup consisted of 96 percent iron, 2.6 percent chlorine, and 0.74 percent sulfur with no carbon.

Amanda wouldn't have believed the findings if she hadn't tested it herself. One point she really drove home to the team was that this type of metal couldn't be recreated under current atmospheric conditions, suggesting it was very old and most likely created before the fabled worldwide flood.

Jake, however, was able to jump in and offer an explanation. The scholars in his field had documented how the atmosphere was compressed to nearly twice its current density and contained no ultraviolet radiation.

Due to its construction, everything in the temple pointed to prehistoric Nephilim origin. The question now was *how* old. Early tests suggested it was anywhere from ten thousand to twenty thousand years old. Tessa remained hopeful the temple would reveal its own secrets in time and she would be the one to soon discover the lost information hidden somewhere just inside the temple complex. However, she was stressed out of her mind at the complications she faced in doing so. She felt like she was close to the finish line, but couldn't get past the last hurdle.

After Bart strode into the atrium, he spoke with her team, listening intently to what they'd discovered in the last few days.

All in all, it didn't amount to much. The team had not discovered the secret to the tomb as of yet, and Tessa Willis was assuming all the blame. After all, she was the head of it, wasn't she? She wondered if Bart could tell she was cracking at the seams. Surely Bart would understand the limits to human capacities and would also understand that even the brightest of minds need time to let ideas and thoughts incubate. She watched as he conducted his walk around the tomb and had quick discussions with members of the team about its makeup and theories of how it was constructed. Eventually he left them to their own devices and turned his attention toward Tessa.

"Tessa, would you give me a minute of your time, please?" he asked politely.

Tessa turned from her colleagues and agreed.

They pulled away from the members of her team. "What's up, Bart? If you're about to tell me the importance of getting this thing open, save your breath. I'm harder on myself than you know."

"Well, that's exactly what I want to talk about. I would agree you're harder on yourself than anyone else could be, and that's why I want to reiterate why this project is very important. Not just for you and I or what it will do for our careers, but for future generations. The research from this operation will live on past both of us for decades to come."

What the hell does that mean? she thought.

"Okay? So what is it you're trying to say?" she asked, trying to keep the suspicion out of her voice.

"What I'm trying to say, is that I don't think you understand what will happen if you can't open that tomb. Everything I've worked for over the last twenty years has come down to this project. The people above me—the ones who *own* North Spear—have paid a lot of money to ensure this thing gets opened and that the recovered specimen remains intact."

"Specimen of what though, Bart? We don't even know what's inside. What are we going to do if it's empty like Jake was saying earlier?" When he didn't immediately answer, Tessa's eyes narrowed slightly. "What aren't you telling me?" she finally asked.

"Let's take a walk, shall we?" he said, arm extended toward the exit.

When she didn't move, Bart placed his hand firmly on her shoulder. His hand squeezed ever so slightly, making Tessa feel all the more uncomfortable. His touch was firm and intimidating. They walked silently out of the main burial room and through the hallway deeper into the temple.

"Let me be absolutely clear: the mere discovery of an ancient biblical giant is just the tip of the iceberg here, Tessa. North Spear has their hands in just about every scientific field you can imagine. There's big money in science. History, archaeology, physics," Bart paused. "Genetics," he stated slowly. "Pharmacology."

Tessa wondered what the latter two had to do with ancient giants.

"Do you really not see what we can accomplish once we have him in our possession? So many questions will be answered. So many possibilities will be right at our fingertips. Everything we've worked so hard for is right inside that tomb, and all we have to do is unlock it. And when we unlock it, some of the greatest potential the world has ever seen will be in our grasp. A potential that has been lost to us for too long," Bart said, his heart beginning to race in excitement.

"Hang on a second. Are you saying what I think you're saying?"

"Tessa, the specimen's DNA holds the secrets to the stars, to genetic manipulation. It's part *angel*, for Christ's sake. Those bones are more valuable than any precious metal or natural resource on the planet. With the genetic code, we could do so much good, Tessa. With our advancements in the understanding of genetic manipulation, we could effectively end disease and double—even triple—our own lifetimes. The possibilities are endless.

"We can transcend the human condition. We can become something better. Who knows? Perhaps we could even stop aging altogether. Stay exactly at your current age but with the knowledge of three lifetimes. Isn't that appealing to you? It certainly is to me."

Bart finally slowed down, breathing heavily. It seemed like he had been wanting to say this for a long time indeed.

He gauged her reaction carefully, which Tessa was doing her best to keep as blank as possible until she could gather her thoughts. "The secrets to the future can be found in the past," Bart said quietly, leaning in toward her. "If you fail, I fail. And that can't happen."

Tessa didn't know what to say. His words felt like a threat, but Tessa understood without a doubt he was serious. She found herself forcing a smile to hide the ominous feeling his words left in her mind.

"I'm working as hard and as fast I can, Mr. Cox. I don't know what to tell you other than my team and I are doing our best," she said carefully. She couldn't help but continue, needing him also to understand the weight of what he had just said but with all of the negative aspects she couldn't help but foresee. "I want to open this tomb as bad as you, but perhaps Jake is right. Do you really think North Spear should be trying to manipulate the DNA of bloodthirsty totalitarian giants? Let alone introducing it to mankind? Again, I might add," Tessa replied, her nails digging into her hands in attempts to stop them from shaking in fear.

"I need you to get this tomb open. Your team needs you to get this tomb open. North Spear needs this tomb open. Tessa, *the world* needs this tomb open. It's for the betterment of the species," he said, straightening up.

Perhaps he did understand the gravity of it. Perhaps he just truly believed the ends justified the means.

Bart must have seen the fear in her eyes as he released his grip on her shoulder. He hoped he'd gotten his point across. Based on the fact that he could see her hands shaking, he had. He offered her a brief, unauthentic smile before he left her in the temple without another word.

11

Tessa sat on her bed, finishing the remainder of her room-service dinner. She barely got any work done after her conversation with Bart. His words echoed in her head until she couldn't think of anything else.

What the hell did I get myself into? she thought.

Unable to make sense of it, her thoughts ran wild.

Is Bart serious? Is that what they plan to do with it? Use it to study genetic manipulation? Surely they understand there is no way of knowing the effect it can have until generations after it's introduced. And those effects could be beyond *disastrous.*

Tessa stood and walked to the mini-fridge. She needed something to take the edge off and found what she needed. Grabbing the small liquor bottles, she hastily unscrewed one of the lids and downed the first bottle without a second thought.

The alcohol dulled her senses, allowing her to shift focus. She grabbed her notes and journals, hoping that maybe this time she'd discover some clue or secret she'd missed before. Although she didn't find what she was looking for, something else caught her eye.

It was a key piece of translation she'd been working on the last couple of days. It had been written on the tomb on top of one of the ends.

DEATH IS BUT THE DOORWAY TO NEW LIFE.
WE LIVE TODAY. WE SHALL LIVE AGAIN.
IN MANY FORMS WE SHALL RETURN.

She recognized it from ancient Egypt, like many of the other discoveries in the temple, but something about this particular translation and what Bart had said clung to her mind.

After reading the words aloud, she felt a cold chill. She needed to tell Jake about this. Something wasn't right, and she couldn't keep it a secret. She glanced at the clock on her phone one last time, which read 01:32 a.m.

It was later than she had expected. There was no way he'd be awake at this hour. She sent him a text, urging him to come by her room first thing in the morning before setting the device down on the nightstand.

She closed her books and laid her head back on the pillow. As she stared at the ceiling, Tessa felt her eyes getting heavier with every passing second. The day had taken its toll, and she was ready for it to be over. She turned out the lamplight and pulled the blankets tightly around her, eyes closed.

Instantly, she was transported. Tessa was standing in front of the temple, but it looked . . . different. There was no damage. In fact, it looked brand new and freshly constructed. Standing outside she could see a ceremony of sorts starting to form. Torches lit the way inside while members of an ancient tribe were escorting one individual up to the entrance. It was a woman. She was young, pretty, and walked with full confidence.

They were speaking a language Tessa had never heard. Three men stood on each side of her, keeping in close proximity as they made their way. The woman was beautifully dressed in what Tessa could only describe as some type of wedding garments that were highly decorative and layered with both beads and flowers.

She thought about calling out to them but didn't want to disturb them. They passed right by her. Somehow she knew they couldn't see her.

Her curiosity was not able to be contained; she followed them directly into the temple.

She was amazed at how different it looked without all the centuries of decay and distortion. Tessa even recognized specific rooms she'd documented or catalogued in the previous weeks as she followed the crowd of seven to a room she'd not seen before. The escort stopped at the entrance, and the woman took a bow before entering. She glanced back, seemingly at Tessa, which caused her heart rate to spike.

Can she see me? she thought to herself.

Tessa could see tears quietly streaming down the woman's face, but the young woman turned to face forward and continued willingly into the room. Tessa followed hesitantly but was determined to see what was going on.

She looked around when she entered and saw that the room was lined with men and women who stood along the walls and were chanting something unintelligible. All were dressed in ceremonially tribal headdresses and outfits. An overwhelming stench filled her nose. It was like a dead skunk left in the Texas heat for weeks on end. Her eyes traveled to the sight before her. In the center of the room right before her very eyes was a forty-foot-tall Nephilim giant sitting upon a stone throne.

Just the mere sight of him terrified Tessa to the core. His matted red hair hung down to his shoulders and shone with an iridescence she'd never seen before. His beard was thick, intricately braided, and hid any potential facial expression. His body was intricately muscled, the likes of which a body builder would have died to replicate. Massive hands lay upon the arm rests where Tessa counted six fingers on each hand. His nails were yellow, as long as swords, and filed to a point.

Tessa's body stood frozen in fear.

In front of the four-story giant was a stone bed. The woman slowly walked to the bed and laid down on her back. The men circling the room began chanting louder, their bodies convulsing. Suddenly it all became clear. The chief of this tribe was offering his daughter to the Nephilim.

Suddenly a blinding light consumed everything. Tessa tried closing her eyes, but it didn't make any difference. The light pierced everything.

There was no escaping it. From the light she heard a voice, the fear in her heart evaporating as though melted by the intensity of the light itself.

"Be not afraid, child," he said, calm and strong.

Tessa dropped to her knees, unable to see the angel.

"Stand, daughter of Eve. I am not worthy of worship. I am created as you are, and I have come to deliver a message."

"What message? What is this?" she asked, unable to escape the glaring light.

"A message from the Most High. You are embarked on a journey you do not understand. I have been sent to provide instructions and direction. Open your eyes, and I will show you."

Apprehensively, Tessa opened her eyes to see the angelic being. His appearance was not as she expected. Fire surrounded his body as though he was engulfed with a flame of a thousand colors. He wore armor that appeared alive, constantly shifting in shape around his shining skin. The armor retracted from his head to reveal long blond hair and piercing blue eyes sharper than any sword a man could forge. He held out his arm to show her something, but she only saw the previous scene of the sacrifice suspended in time, as though the angel had pressed pause with a cosmic remote.

"Do you know what you see?" the angel continued.

"A chief offering his daughter to wed a Nephilim," she replied, surprised to hear her voice. It was sturdier than she thought it would be.

"Yes, offered in marriage, but in actuality, it was a sacrifice. The offspring of the Fallen are partaking in a ritual they believe will allow them longer life. Due to their hybrid lineage, they enjoyed a lifespan longer than men, yet they still craved more.

"The woman will die. Her blood will be drained from her body for the benefit of the so called Man of Renown you see before you."

Tessa looked over at the woman whose suspended tears still fell down her cheeks. She couldn't be older than sixteen.

"Their fathers, my kin, taught them blood contains the wellspring of life," the angel continued. "Their fathers were present when He laid the cornerstone of the Earth, and we were present when He breathed life into man. We rejoiced together. Sadly, you were deceived in the garden by the serpent, the Dragon. The prophecy foretold the debt would be paid and the battle won by the Seed of Woman. My kin were tempted by the beauty of women, and they, too, chose sin.

"The offspring of the Fallen were used as a weapon against your kind. To prevent the coming of the Son of Man. If they could contaminate all of mankind, they would prevent their own destruction. Despite all their efforts, there remained one man, Noah, who was still blameless in his generations during the great cleansing of the world.

"Here the hybrid is paying homage to the old ways. He honors his ancestors who chose to rebel against the Holy One. Those are the ones you call Watchers. You see, there is power in the blood, carried over into the Unseen Realm. They seek to make the world in their image. Against the will of the Most High."

"How? What do you mean?" she asked despite her fear of the response.

"He will take the woman for himself," the angel answered. "The chief will sacrifice his only daughter to the Nephilim in exchange for knowledge and protection. He condemns his daughter to certain death and does not yet understand he freely gives up his dominion and authority on earth given to him by the Most High."

"Authority and dominion?" Tessa asked. The piercing light was causing her eyes to water, and she held up a hand to shield her face from its warmth.

"Yes," the angel said. Its voice seemed to echo with the tone of many. "All men and women are sons and daughters that have been created to have authority and dominion over the earth. No one can take it away, but it can be *given* away. The tribes have been deceived to give up what is theirs, and in doing so, they ensured their own destruction. That is the mission of the Nephilim. To deceive, dominate, conquer, and enslave. If they were to return, certain destruction would befall mankind. The time has not yet come, and the Most High forbids it."

The angel's intense gaze pierced her own. "You have been tasked with thwarting their return."

"What? What can I do to stop this? There's no way!" Tessa exclaimed. Why *her*? What was she supposed to do?

"Your employer seeks to bring the Nephilim bloodline back. This is why they want your help. You hold the secret to giving them what they need to succeed."

The angel's words had suddenly made everything so clear. If North Spear did uncover and extract a Nephilim DNA sample, it was only a matter of time before their spread got out of control. Their DNA would pollute the human race, reigniting a malicious, bloodthirsty agenda. They would again take hold of the world. They would return.

"What do I do? How do I stop this?" Tessa begged. The light only seemed to glow brighter, and Tessa was forced to close her eyes.

When it seemed the light had faded, she opened them. She looked around, but the angel had disappeared. There was knocking sound in the distance. Tessa couldn't see the source. Instead all she saw was the suspended scene before her. The terrifying sight of the Nephilim, his fiery eyes, yellow fingernails, and six fingers caused her body to quake in fear.

The knocking sound continued again.

The angelic voice returned although he didn't reappear. "Make the call, daughter of Eve. Make the call."

Tessa awoke hours before her alarm with a fervor she'd never felt before.

What was that? Is this really happening? Make what call, to who?

She heard the knock at the door once more. *Jake!*

Tessa remembered the text from late last night. She ran to the peephole and verified it was him. He looked worried as she opened the door quickly to greet him.

"Hey, what's going on? Did you find something?" he asked.

"Yeah, I think I did, but I don't know if I should have."

"What are you talking about?"

She ushered him inside, closing the door quickly behind him after ensuring no one else was with him.

"Well, yesterday, Bart pulled me aside, right? And he mentioned how North Spear already has plans for what's inside that tomb. Jake, they're planning to collect the DNA from the Nephilim inside, assuming there is one."

Jake frowned and shook his head in confusion. "Collect it for what, Tessa? Did he say?"

"Not directly. He talked about putting an end to disease and living forever."

"What? That seems really weird."

"Right? It was very awkward to say the least, but there's more. Last night I was going over my translations and came across something you need to see."

She retrieved her book from the nightstand and displayed it to Jake, whose eyes went wide.

"You know, Tessa, it's clearly stated and documented in second-temple Jewish literature that the disembodied spirits of the Nephilim were cursed to roam the earth when their physical bodies were destroyed. Their spirits became the demons we know today. Searching for hosts to inhabit. I couldn't think of a more suitable host than someone who has been 'upgraded' with actual Nephilim DNA, can you?"

Tessa took a deep breath. "That's not all, Jake. I had a dream," Tessa said, her eyes drifting off in a thousand-yard stare, remembering the petrified face of the young woman, frozen in fear moments before her slaughter.

"What kind of dream? About what?" he asked.

"I . . . I don't know how to explain it. I was given a message. I saw the temple. Not as it is now, but as it was when . . . when he was there."

"Who?" Jake asked, confused.

It would be a miracle if he believed her after this.

"An angel came to me in a dream," Tessa said slowly.

She needed to keep calm and collected if she didn't want him thinking she was downright losing it. Jake might be her most trusted confidant here, but that wouldn't stop him from thinking she had simply one too many sleepless nights if she didn't tread carefully. "He showed me the giant that's buried in the tomb. We can't let them open it, Jake."

"Well, I mean we can't exactly open it even if we wanted to right now, remember?" he replied, eyebrows raised.

"Good point. Never thought I'd be glad about that." She sighed, sitting down on the end of her bed. Would that be the game plan? Simply not trying to get the tomb open and seeing how long it would hold them off? Would that be enough? No . . . surely not. What if someone else other than Tessa figured out how to open it? What then?

Jake was rubbing the back of his neck nervously.

"You believe me, right?" Tessa asked, suddenly staring at him intently.

"Of course I do, Tess. It's just . . . this is a lot to take in, that's all. Look, why don't I grab some stuff from my room, and I'll be right back. We can figure out a game plan then. Okay?"

She nodded. Jake gave her an encouraging smile, and with a comforting last pat on the shoulder, he stepped promptly out of the room, leaving Tessa to her thoughts.

The more she thought about it, the more she wondered if this was an ordinary dream. Maybe she *had* had too many sleepless nights. Tessa sat on the edge of her bed, her head held in her hands, unsure of what to do. Something was definitely *off* during her last conversation with Bart. That's the best way she could describe it. Tessa knew he had been hiding something, but she never thought it would have been this.

I'm done. I can't do this anymore, she thought.

She hopped into the shower and changed into a fresh set of clothes. She had just started to pack her belongings in her suitcase when she heard a knock at the door. Breaking her train of thought, she rushed to open the door for Jake, eager for his gentle presence.

But instead it was Bart standing at her door, pacing impatiently side to side. She stifled her unexpected gasp and hoped it wasn't too obvious. He looked troubled, but definitely not as troubled as Tessa felt in the moment. She contemplated slamming the door closed, but she was a Willis. She'd been taught to face her fears head-on.

"Everything alright?" Bart asked. "Looks like you either had an early morning or late night."

"Early morning. What can I do for ya?" she asked, the fear crackling through her voice.

It didn't go unnoticed. Bart stared at her for a moment. "I was hoping you'd give me a minute of your time?"

"Uh okay, sure. I got some stuff to talk about too."

Tessa opened the door, stepping aside to allow Bart entry into the suite. He nodded in thanks and glanced over to see she was already dressed for the day. The scent of her body wash and shampoo hung in the air as he walked past her and sat down on the couch. The young archaeologist closed the door gently, suddenly realizing her hands were trembling.

This is not a coincidence, she thought.

Now she was scared but couldn't articulate why.

Hesitantly she made her way to the couch opposite of Bart and sat down, doing her best to maintain her cool. She felt like Bart was looking right through her and feared his reaction when he heard what she had to say, causing her to wonder if she should even say it at all. She tried not to glance at the half-packed suitcase that lay in the corner of the room.

Bart cleared his throat and began the moment she sat down. "I wanted to apologize for my pugnacious behavior yesterday. You see, Ms. Willis, my employers do not tolerate failure. The stakes have never been higher for me, and I tend to get caught up in it all. I'm counting on you, and I want you to know I've decided to give you a handsome bonus in the event you get the tomb open. A $250,000 bonus, to be exact."

Tessa's eyes widened at the dollar signs, but her mind was already made up. He waited for a bigger reaction, but none came. Instead he saw something different in her eyes. Familiar in the way a woman looks at a soon-to-be ex when a breakup is just over the horizon. He shifted uncomfortably in his seat, waiting for a response.

"Wow, Bart... That's really generous," Tessa replied somewhat warily.

"You don't seem very impressed," Bart quipped.

Ignoring this, Tessa sat up so that she was sat on the edge of her seat. "Bart, I need to ask you something." Her voice slightly cracked out of fear. *You can do this, Tessa.*

"Go on," Bart said, unsure of where this was going.

"Why is this expedition so important to you? What is this *research* going toward?" Tessa asked, staring at him.

Completely blindsided, Bart knew he couldn't tell her the truth, but she had caught him off guard—something he never expected. *Which lie do I tell her?* Bart shifted again, crossing his legs the other direction, and steadying his gaze as he attempted to figure out what had just happened in such a short time.

"Well, this is unexpected. Why do you ask?" Bart asked quizzically.

To hell with it. "Because I don't believe you've been honest with me," Tessa blurted out.

"Mm-hmm. And what makes you think that?" Bart asked, wondering what tactic to play.

"Let's call it a woman's intuition," she said with a hint of aggression in her voice.

"I see," he said, and to Tessa's surprise, he smiled. But there was no warmth behind it. "I've been in business a long time, Tessa. And to me that smells like bullshit."

Taken aback, Tessa could tell Bart was now taking the offensive. She knew it wouldn't be long before he lost his cool, but hopefully by that time, she'd at least be long free of this and well out of here.

Better to just bite the bullet. "The truth is, Bart, I want out. I don't know exactly what your end goal is, but I want no part of it," Tessa firmly stated.

Though Bart made perceivable change in his body language, the shift was undeniable. Something even a blind man could see. Bart's last hope and real chance of success was backing out on him—something he couldn't afford and most definitely wouldn't tolerate. After several seconds of staring into Tessa's eyes, he spoke.

"I can certainly say this, Ms. Willis, you're full of surprises. I didn't take you for a quitter." His tone was quiet, calm, and calculated. But on the inside, his blood felt like it was made of lava.

"Say what you want, Bart, but it is what it is. I'm sorry," Tessa said, feeling anything but. She was frankly just relieved. She thought this would be more difficult and was surprised at how easy Bart seemed to be taking the news.

"Me too," Bart feigned, reaching for his cell phone in his pocket. "I'll get your travel arrangements set up immediately, as I assume you want to leave as soon as possible."

"That's not necessary. You've gone through a lot to get me out here. I'll book a ticket to leave today," Tessa said, trying to soften the blow.

Bart looked up from his phone and held up his hand, doing his best to remain calm.

"Please, it's the least I could do. Why don't you go start packing your stuff, and I'll have you at the airport within the next few hours," he said calmly.

Tessa nodded in agreement and walked to her room, hoping he hadn't noticed the hastily packed suitcase in the corner. She picked it up and started packing in her belongings in a tidier fashion, now feeling calmer than she had a few hours ago. Even though he was taking this pretty well, she didn't need him to know how quickly she had wanted out or how freaked out she had been. She started packing her clothes, books, and work journals for the journey home. She grabbed her canvas backpack, and as she did, the SAT phone from Cody slipped out onto the bed. Instinctively she looked up through the cracked door leading into the living room of her suite. She saw Bart pacing and talking quietly, glancing every so often toward her. Tessa felt a tinge of fear.

She thought back to the dream, the encounter with the angel and his words about making the call. Looking down at the phone, she had no idea who to call or what to say. Leaving the phone on the bed she continued packing and heard Bart say in a hushed tone, "Okay good. Yes, the suite. Don't make a scene," before hanging up and slipping the phone into his slacks.

Okay, now I'm really scared.

Don't make a scene? Am I making something out of nothing?

She took a deep breath. No, she wasn't. Her instincts told her differently and she knew now she needed to listen to them. She called out to Bart. "Everything okay?" she asked.

"Yes, just getting everything settled," Bart replied.

She continued packing her clothes and heard a knock on the door. She desperately hoped it was Jake. The young archaeologist hurried to the living room to answer it, but Bart had already beat her to it. His hand on the knob, he turned to look at her before opening it.

"I've got it. You finish with your stuff."

Suspicious but trying not to give herself away, she nodded in agreement and walked back to her bedroom, leaving the door open a little wider this time. She looked down at the phone on the bed, grabbed it and slipped it into her back pocket. Glancing back toward Bart, she saw him talking with Al and a few other North Spear security guys who wore puzzled looks. Bart was speaking to Al within whispering distance, but she couldn't quite make out what he was telling him. Tessa saw Al's eyes widen as he glanced toward where she was standing in the bedroom.

Something was definitely up, and she tried not to all-out run to the bathroom but hastened to get there, shutting the door quickly behind her. Her mind hadn't stopped racing about the angelic encounter and "making the call."

For the first time in her life, she felt real danger. The only person she could think to call in a time like this was her brother, but what could he do? He was thousands of miles away.

I'm freaking out, she thought.

Breathe, Tessa. Breathe.

Tessa dialed his number while sitting on the side of the tub. Though weak, the phone eventually connected. But all she could hear was static. Eventually she thought she caught Cody's crackling voice, but she could only make out about every third word of his. Doing her best to give him something he could use, she spoke quietly but hurriedly, trying to say as many key words as she could. North Spear, dig site, Peru. She repeated the words again, hoping desperately that at least something was getting through. But based on the sound of Cody's frustration, she wasn't sure if anything was. She tried not to consider it a bad sign that she heard him cussing, presumably at the phone and not her.

Not knowing if anything she said was getting through, she said the only thing she could remember that would definitely get her point across: the family code phrase. "Green lightning, Cody."

It had been something her parents, Cody, and her had come up with long ago. It was a phrase to just those in their inner-family circle so that they knew who could be trusted. It meant safety if you had someone around you that knew it. But it also meant danger—a way to convey to those same people that you were uncomfortable. That you were scared. That you were in danger. It had been something she had rarely used, but she had never been more grateful for it until now.

Repeating it several times in hopes he would be able to pick it up, the door to the bathroom swung open quietly. She looked up, scared out of her mind, to see Bart standing in the doorway. His face held no real expression, like a shell of a human being completely devoid of emotion.

Tessa's trembling hands dropped to her lap while her thumb hit the button to end the call. She didn't know what to say or what to do.

Am I about to die? Please, God, I don't want to die.

Bart spoke. "I really wish you hadn't done that. Who did you call?"

"No one. What's going on? Are you going to kill me?" Tessa asked softly, tears welling up in her eyes.

Bart couldn't help but smirk, letting out a huff of amusement. He liked this, the feeling of power over another person. In fact, he loved it. Making someone feel about two inches tall made him feel ten feet tall.

"No, Ms. Willis. At least not yet. You still have work to do, remember?"

12

The darkness engulfed Cody, surrounding him in an unending sea of black. A single light source pierced the abyss, illuminating his sister from a distance. He knew instantly it was a nightmare.

There she is again, Cody thought.

Though lucid, he had no control over the dream or its outcome, sometimes not even his own actions. He could see her clearly, but he couldn't get to her. Tessa aimlessly walked slowly toward him, her head hung low, hair concealing her face from sight. She continued walking, though she never seemed to move any closer.

He reached out for her but to no avail. His arms felt heavy as though they were weighted. He tried calling out, but no sound emerged—only silence. Nothing could be heard but thunder on the horizon.

Arcs of vibrant electricity ripped through the sinister black sky, exposing dark, moisture-heavy clouds . . . and something else.

Something distant. Something big.

Cody strained his eyes to focus, but the storm suddenly grew in both its intensity and violence. Heavy rain began to fall. Rain pounded the earth around him like it did so many times before. He and Tessa both were drenched, and water ran from the tips of their fingers like sink faucets. Still, she kept walking but never closed the distance. He looked all around but couldn't see anything other than her.

Something felt different. He'd experienced this nightmare before. He recalled the feelings of intense loneliness and fear he had before. The fear remained, but this time he was not alone. He felt a presence with him. No. He felt *several* presences surrounding him, outside his view. The strange-colored neon lightning shot over the sky again, illuminating a figure behind Tessa. Cody could hear something. It was faint, but somehow familiar.

The outline was massive, shaped like a man but disproportionate. Its legs were overly thick, and its torso was long. Cody couldn't make out much more through the darkness and had no way of telling how big it actually was. He continued looking up, the rain stinging his face, as he struggled to see its features in the dark.

"What are you?" he yelled at it, straining to be heard over the downpour.

The giant outstretched his arm, holding it parallel with the ground as thunder boomed overhead; the ground shook with the vibration. Its fingers stretched wide. Its hand was huge. Tessa had been at least one-hundred feet away, but now, in the blink of an eye, she was just a few inches from Cody, suspended by the giant's grasp like a puppet.

Her head still hung low, and her arm shot from her side and held parallel to the ground in a similar fashion as the giant. Her fingers stretched wide. Immediately, the rain stopped, hanging in the air as though gravity had paused momentarily. Cody scanned the area, looking at the large water droplets that hung in the air. All sound had faded. No rain, no thunder, nothing. Then he heard that familiar sound again: a buzzing followed by high pitched echoes.

A rumbling sound came from under Cody, or around him—he couldn't define the origin, but the earth began shaking. At the same time, Tessa's body contorted. As moonlight encompassed both brother and sister, Cody could see her more clearly now. Her hand stretched, reaching for her brother.

Thunder cracked overhead, and bolts of green lightning lit the dark sky. The deep rumble grew in pitch and morphed unmistakably into a foreign language he could not understand. Tessa kept her head down and began to translate.

"You have suffered so," Tessa said, sounding mechanical, like a robot. "Your loss has damaged your soul, gnashed your spirits, and changed the foundation of your true self."

What the hell is this? he thought.

He squinted the water out of his eyes and tried moving, but he felt tied by invisible restraints, his bones locked in place. Cody knew the monster behind her had control over him in that moment.

"Your guilt consumes you like we were consumed," his sister said. The giant's foreign language echoed simultaneously.

Water began to rise quickly, first to Cody's knees, then to his chest until all of his energy was put toward keeping his head above it. He fought to stay above the surface even as he was forced to take in gulps of water.

"You seek redemption. Enter the jungle, and you may find it, though you will surely die."

Cody closed his eyes, wishing it would end.

The giant suddenly made a sweeping motion toward the sky, as did Tessa. Above Cody, the clouds parted, darkness lifted, and an image appeared in the night sky. He was looking at a poorly paved asphalt road with which he was all too familiar. He closed his eyes, knowing what came next but felt the terror consume him nonetheless.

Cody gritted his teeth and forced himself to look back at the sky, look back at what he deserved to see every night for the rest of his life for not being home when his family needed him most. He could see his wife, Jenny, driving along, paying no attention to the only other car on the road.

It was getting closer, the part he hated most. The college kid's sedan swerved back and forth before violently careening across the median. Cody tried to look away, but he could feel the creature forcing his head, even his eyes in place to watch the horrific scene yet again. He watched as the car plunged into the ditch, hit a culvert, and then launched into the air as it flipped. It was headed straight for Jenny and Elena.

Cody blinked, and the scene changed. He was sitting next to Elena moments before impact. Elena seemed to have know he was there as she looked at him with that precious smile. Her gaze shifted from Cody as the oncoming car hit them in slow motion. The force of the impact sent them directly into a telephone pole that cut the car in half, separating Elena and Jenny from himself. Cody's cry of warning died on his lips, knowing there was nothing he could do.

He turned his head, unable to watch anymore as he found himself back in the enveloping water, tears beading off his nose and chin. He cried deep and hard from his torment. His teeth gritted against each other while his blood ran cold inside his body. He looked up not at his sister, but to the distance behind her.

"GOD HELP ME!" Cody cried out with everything he had.

His voice pierced the night like the crack of a rifle. The water retreated as quickly as it rose. In the distance, Cody heard the deafening roar of a lion. The waters dried around him as the sun began to rise, silhouetting a mountain in the distance. Atop the mountain he could see a lion's body contrasted starkly against the morning sky. He saw the faint glimmer of a key around his neck before the lion ran down the opposite side out of view.

Cody's eyes snapped open. He was breathing heavily. He threw himself out of bed, tumbling off the foot of it before slamming down on the floor hard enough to knock the wind out of himself. He laid on the floor, holding his knees to his chest, trying to control his breathing.

In the midst of his cries and desperate gasps for air, he heard it again: that familiar sound. As if someone had flipped a switch, he stopped crying immediately and listened intently.

Beep. Beep.

There it is again! It was faint but definitely audible. The buzzing was quickly followed by a sequence of high-pitched echoes. Wiping his face hastily from his tears and sweat, he sat up but remained on the floor and cocked his head sideways to listen better.

"The SAT phone!" Cody yelled.

He sprang to his feet and ran out of his bedroom as he followed the ringing sound down the hallway toward the kitchen. The ringing stopped, as did Cody.

C'mon, c'mon, ring again dammit!

He placed a hand on each wall of the narrow hallway where he had paused. The intensity of the nightmare had played tricks on his senses. It all seemed so real he was having a hard time focusing. The phone rang again. It was close, but still muffled. He proceeded down the hall quickly until he came to the coat closet just before the kitchen.

The ringing had stopped. He paused, waiting for the next set. The noise shrilly rang out again.

"The closet!" he said aloud.

Cody whipped the door open so fast he had forgotten to move his body out of the way and slammed the bottom corner of the door against the inside of his foot. He cursed in pain.

Falling to his knees he dug through the closet until he found his go bag. He clutched each side of the bag and ripped it open, the zippers giving way. He turned the duffle inside out, spewing its contents out into the hallway and quickly sorted through the gear until the phone clanked onto the tile floor.

Cody picked it up, pulled the antenna to the side, and looked at the caller ID. The small screen glowed bright in the dark and hurt Cody's eyes to look at it, but the programmed name was unmistakable: Sis.

He tapped the send button to take the call and pressed the phone hard against his ear.

"Tessa!?" Cody said loudly but heard no reply.

He pulled the phone away to see the call status; it was connected. He held the phone up again but only heard the crackle of static.

"Tessa!" Cody shouted again, his voice echoing off the walls around him. Through the phone came a distant and quiet female voice saying, "C . . . dy?" before static filled the phone again.

"Can you hear me?" Cody yelled.

Feeling helpless he slapped the side of the phone a few times (as if that had ever helped him before). He readjusted the antenna and held the phone to his ear again.

"Ody? I nee . . . elp." The broken words were hard to make out, but he knew it was her. He would recognize her voice anywhere.

"Tessa! Where are you? Tell me where you are! I can't hear you!"

Cody was beginning to panic. His heart raced and sweat ran down his face for the second time that day.

The voice came back, "I'm . . . orth spe . . . ite Azazel . . . elp . . . een light . . . dy—".

"What?!" Cody, now full-on frantic, twisted the antenna again and listened harder like his life depended on it. Which it seemed like hers did. The static cleared for perhaps just a millisecond.

That was all it took. Cody heard all he needed to as the voice came back online.

"Green lighting, Cody."

The line then went dead with static; Cody's blood went cold as ice. He pulled the phone away from his head and looked at the call status: DISCONNECTED.

"No!" Cody yelled again. He hit the recall button on the dial pad, but nothing would go through. Cody set the phone on the ground in front of him and stood up, his right shoulder braced against the cold wall. He had heard it, the code phrase his family used when they were kids to signify danger. Green lightning. It was made very clear to both of the Willis kids it was only to be used in dire emergencies. It seemed there was one now.

Cody thought of his dream, about Tessa, and how she had needed his help.

He looked down at the SAT phone one last time before he walked away, leaving his ripped bag and contents lying in the hallway. He wiped away the sweat from his face. Not able to control himself, Cody spun around and exploded with rage, grasping the open closet door in both hands. His grip released, hands moving in fury as he punched the cheap, hollow door and slammed it back into its frame. It caved easily from his powerful blows. Once his fists made a hole, he transitioned to kicks.

He screamed uncontrollably as the door splintered into a few large pieces. Thousands of smaller chunks of wood bounced off every surface around him. Covered in splinters and wood particles, he slumped against the wall, taking long, meaningful breaths as best as he could.

He thought for a few minutes, then pushed off the surface and walked toward his bedroom. He knew what had to happen next. This was no accident. The dream, seeing Tessa, seeing that fucking thing controlling her like a puppet—this was no coincidence.

He entered his room and walked to his nightstand where his smart phone was charging. Scooping up the phone, Cody pulled the power cable and punched the icon for Favorites. He reserved that for his family—both chosen and blood. Only four names were displayed. He waited while it rang a few times before he heard Frank's voice come over the line. It was thick with sleep and grogginess.

"Hey, man." Frank paused briefly and then continued when Cody didn't say anything. "You okay? What's up?"

"How fast can you get to my place?" Cody asked after a deep breath.

There was a few seconds of pause. Frank must have heard the trouble in Cody's voice. Cody pulled the phone away from his ear and the screen illuminated. The time read 03:07 a.m. A few seconds of dead space passed between the two men before Frank finally broke the silence. "I'm on my way."

Cody ended the call, opened his closet, and began grabbing clothes for the trip.

13

For the first time in a long time, Cody's actions were laser-focused. He no longer experienced the sense of wandering or emptiness that had cursed him for the last eighteen months. He had a purpose, and a mission, in front of him. He was going to do for his sister what he couldn't do for his wife and daughter. He was going to save her.

He continued stuffing his clothes by the handful into his go bags when he heard a knock at the door. Hyper vigilant and purely out of instinct, Cody grabbed his Glock 19 from the nightstand. He glided silently through the apartment, mindful of his footing, not making a single sound, the pistol at the ready in front of him.

At the door, he held the four-inch barrel level with the peephole, prepared to shoot anybody or anything that caused him potential harm from the other side. He carefully peeked through the fisheye lens and saw Frank waiting impatiently on the other side. Cody yanked the door open in a hurry, grabbed Frank by the arm, and rushed him inside.

"Hey, man, glad you made it here so fast. Look, some shit has gone down, and I gotta bounce outta the country. Tessa is in trouble. She needs our help."

Cody was speaking fast and excited in a way Frank hadn't expected at this hour.

"Whoa whoa whoa," he said rubbing his eyes and trying to make sense of what was going on. "Just . . . hold up a minute. What's going on with Tessa? Help? What kind of help and whaddya mean 'bounce outta the country'?" he asked. Confusion was etched clearly on his face.

Cody stopped throwing his clothes into go bags and took a deep breath. "Yes, exactly. Listen man, I know this sounds weird, but hear me out."

"Hold on, I'm going to need some coffee before we get knee deep into this," Frank said, rubbing his eyes, hoping that would help.

Cody walked quickly to the kitchen while Frank, still not fully awake, took a seat at the island counter. Cody put down the pistol on the counter and turned on the coffee maker. He wasn't sure where to begin, so he figured it was best to start at the beginning.

"Alright man, I know this is gonna sound crazy, and I really appreciate you coming over here so early, but I had a dream earlier."

"Okay . . ." Frank's voice already hinted suspicion. Though he didn't make a sound after that, Cody could see Frank already drawing his own conclusions about the seriousness of the situation.

"You know I've been having these dreams with all kinds of bad shit and that I just can't shake the thought of something happening," Cody started, pouring some coffee into two mugs. "I feel like . . . like these dreams are my punishment or something. You know, a passed judgment for not being around when the girls needed me. Anyway, things are different now. The dreams. For the last few weeks, they've been about Tessa. Ever since she left, I've been dreaming that she's in some sort of trouble, and tonight I have this wild-ass dream where I can't get to her, can't help her, and she's being controlled by some big-ass . . . thing. Like a puppet on strings."

Cody handed a mug to his friend, who looked grateful for the caffeine.

Frank took a deep sip of his drink and then cut in, "How do you mean 'thing'? Like a person, creature, or monster or what?"

"Yes. Honestly man, I don't know. There was this storm, like a flood and lightning—green lightning, all around us. Then it spoke to me about losing my family and *wham*! Back into the dream about Elena. It was almost like it was showing me where I've failed and telling me I'm gonna fail again."

"Okay, before you go any further, lemme get this straight," Frank said, putting his hand up to stop him. "And forgive me if I'm being too forward here. You had a nightmare, like you've been having for months, except this time it was about your sister, and because of this chronic-nightmare situation, you want to go to Peru to rescue Tessa from some . . . thing. Some unknown threat. That sound about right?

Cody, unphased by Frank's view of what he knew to be true, continued.

"Yes and no. Hang on a minute; I'm getting there.

"In the dream I kept hearing this sound, and when I finally came to, I realize it's my SAT phone ringing. So I grab it from the go bag in the closet."

Cody pointed to the closet and Frank saw the disaster scattered about the floor. The door lay in pieces, and several of the contents of the go bag were scattered around the floor. Frank stared at the shattered door in deep concern.

"Tessa called me, Frank. From Peru. The connection was weak, but she was calling for help."

"What makes you think she's calling for help? How do you know she's not just calling to check in?" Frank asked curiously, turning to look back at Cody.

The hair on Cody's arms stood straight up. Covered in goosebumps, he replied, "Because she used the code phrase: green lightning. It was our family safe phrase when we were kids. I'm telling you, man, I heard it clear as fucking day. She needs me, and I need you. We need you."

With those last three words, it seemed to click in Frank's head. He must have realized Cody hadn't called to talk about the trauma or the dream because he sat up straight in his chair, setting his coffee mug on the granite countertop with a clank. Now, Cody could tell Frank knew what he was asking for. Backup.

"Okay, hold it right there. Are you saying what I think you're saying?"

"What I'm saying, Frank, is that I'm going down there, and I'm gonna save my sister."

Cody's eyes were fixed on Frank's, refusing to break contact. Cody wanted to make sure he got his point across. Frank threw his hands up and slapped them down on the counter.

"Holy shit, Cody, have you lost your mind? You can't just make up missions, bro. One, you're not operational; two, this ain't sanctioned; and three, you don't know if she's really in trouble! How the hell are you even gonna get down there with guns and kit?! I mean, I'm assuming you ain't going empty handed."

Cody fully understood and mostly expected Frank's reaction. He calmly replied in an even and low tone. "You're right. I'm not operational. This is unsanctioned, but I'm telling you right fucking now Tessa is most definitely in danger, and this is for real. I know you probably think I'm losing my mind or already have, but either way, I'm going down there. I'm calling in favors as soon as my shit is packed."

Frank took in Cody's words, the reality of the situation setting in. He let out a concerned sigh, knowing there was likely no way to talk him down.

"What're you gonna do when Val finds out, hmm? You know this is gonna blow *any* chance you have of ever coming back to Renegade! He's gonna have your ass and then some."

Cody was ready for that one too. "He told me once, 'You know Renegade ain't just a callsign. It's an ethos.' As far as I see it, that's practically authorization right there. Besides, what's he gonna do? Kick me out of ProCorp?"

"Do you even hear yourself right now?!" Frank said, nearly yelling.

"What choice do I have, Frank? Tell me," Cody asked, doing his best to keep his calm demeanor.

Frank and Cody sat in silence, staring at each other for what seemed like an eternity before Cody walked back to his bedroom and resumed packing his clothes. He considered the environment he'd encounter in Peru and packed clothes he thought would be best suited for what he'd face, from civilian hiking apparel to full-on combat uniforms.

When he went to go bring a packed bag to the living room, he saw Frank standing in the kitchen, watching him. Cody realized how crazy this all sounded, but he knew it to be the honest truth.

"Look, I know this sounds crazy, but I'm 100 percent certain she called the code word."

Cody took a deep breath and laid his last card on the table. "Frank, if everything we've ever done together has meant anything at all to you, please help me. I need you on this," he pleaded, his voice heavy with desperation.

Frank took in the words. He could almost hear Val inside his head, telling him how bad of an idea this was. He knew deep down Cody couldn't pull off a half-assed mission by himself. Frank looked at his closest friend, knowing full well there was no way out of this other than through. They'd spilled blood together, and he knew somehow they'd weather this storm together as well.

Frank heaved a deep sigh. "Well shit, I better come along so you don't get your old ass killed trying to cross the road or something stupid. Besides, you weren't really any good without me anyhow." Cody grinned at him. "Where do you suggest we start?" Frank asked.

"Let's start with some digital maps and pulling any open-source intel from the company she's working for. Surely they gotta have something on the web. I'll finish packing and start working the logistics of flying."

"I've got the maps and open source. I can grab them from the ranch along with some surveillance and recce kits. We'll need to grab some clothes and stuff for the trip, too, and then I'm gonna have to sign some stuff out along with my guns." Frank sighed. "You know Val is literally going to kill us, right?"

14

Within the hour, Cody and Frank parted ways to work on their individual tasks prior to leaving. Cody flew down the highway well over the speed limit, careful to watch for familiar speed traps. Having been a former cop, his previous knowledge and skills came in handy in more than a few ways.

Pulling up to his storage unit, he knew he needed to grab the remainder of his kit before securing some transportation. Though still dark, first light wasn't far off.

He jumped out of his Tacoma the moment the transmission had been shoved into park. He thumbed through his keyring, looking for the correct key. The dim lighting was not helpful. After finding the correct key for the disc lock, he pulled the door upward, giving him access to his one-man ready room. Moving with purpose, he silently thanked his incessant need for organization in a time like this.

First he went to the racks stacked neatly against the wall and grabbed the large, gray deployment bag. Cody pulled it from the rack and plopped it on the floor, unzipping the top to see if there was anything left over from a previous mission. From it he pulled his MultiCam Mayflower UW Gen IV chest rig. Sifting through the general-purpose pockets and abdominal medical pouch, he made sure the spare batteries and trauma supplies hadn't expired or been used somewhere else. Satisfied, he dropped the chest rig back into the bag and grabbed his small assault pack off a hook. It held additional support items such as a full-blown trauma kit, escape-and-evasion survival kit, meds, water filtration/purification system, and a couple small dry bags.

Cody threw the pack in the deployment bag and grabbed ten magazines from his workbench drawer, tossing them alongside the rest of his kit. He walked to the wall and pulled his custom Mayflower APC plate carrier from the hook. The plate carrier allowed him to wear ballistic protection on his back and chest in the event of a gun fight, whereas his chest rig offered no ballistic protection and only carried his essential fighting gear like spare ammunition and communications equipment.

Next, he punched in the code for the safe. The button's beeps filled the air. Cody opened the heavy door and turned on the small LED light. The bright diode came to life, illuminating a neatly organized assortment of lethal options. Wishing he could take them all, he knew he'd be limited to only one or two mission-specific rifles and one pistol.

Cody stood in front of the safe with crossed arms, running through the most-likely scenarios he might encounter. Wanting something compact and quiet, he settled on the SIG Sauer MCX-SPEAR LT 300 BLK rifle with a nine-inch barrel, outfitted with a SureFire SOCOM 300 SPS suppressor, ATPIAL laser device, and Aimpoint Micro T2. Coupled with subsonic ammunition, the gun's normal firing signature would be greatly reduced and make detection very difficult, though the effective range was limited with the subsonic ammo.

With the mindset of two is one and one is none, he grabbed his old faithful: his Hodge Defense Mod 2. Even with a suppressor of its own, the Hodge was much louder than the MCX but offered more range and higher velocity. Besides, his Hodge was an old companion who'd been on nearly every mission with him. Frankly, he just didn't want to leave it at home.

He cleared both weapons, collapsed the stocks, and laid them gently in his bag. He grabbed his Volund Atlas belt that held all of his emergency reloads for both rifle and pistol from the top of the safe and stuffed his Glock 19 with X300 pistol light and red-dot sight into the Safariland holster.

Last, he grabbed his Ops-Core FAST SF ballistic helmet and PVS-31 night-vision goggles. He looked down at his kit and ran through his pre-deployment checklist, trying to remember if there was anything else he would need. Cody took a moment to give some credence to the fact that it had been a while since he'd done this. There was a familiarity he couldn't deny, but he also knew he was rusty. He noticed a slight shake had developed in his hands.

Pull it together, Cody. Your sister needs you.

He glanced at his watch.

The time read 06:12 a.m., and he figured he better get moving on the next step and secure some transportation. This next step would surely be the highest risk. Cody planned to reach out to a local ProCorp-paid pilot. In the event he used him, word would certainly get back to Val fairly quickly and the clock would start to countdown to what was actually going on.

Screw it.

Cody pulled his phone from the pocket of his lightweight hiking pants and scrolled through his contacts. He found the one he was looking for and texted one simple word.

Up?

Cody knew they'd need a discreet way to get into Peru quickly, and the quickest way to travel was flying. He knew only one pilot who often worked for Renegade and had even used him several times in the past.

Everyone called him Dirty Mike, and to Cody's knowledge, no one in Renegade knew his real name. Not even Val. What Cody did know about Dirty Mike was that he was an experienced, former military fixed-wing pilot who was extremely well educated and scary smart, but you'd never guess it by his appearance or the way he talked.

At first glance Dirty Mike was just another five-foot, four-inch, heavyset, deep South redneck who liked his chewing tobacco and sweet tea. No one would ever guess he could hold his own in a conversation about quantum physics and spacetime-continuum theory. That is unless you indulged him.

Cody had become friends with him over the years travelling to and from various assignments and hoped he'd be able to come through on such short notice. After all, he owed the Renegade a favor.

Cody felt the phone vibrate in reply. He glanced to check it.

Course I am. Sup?

Cody figured it was best to speak over the phone as opposed to writing in text. Another skill he'd developed during his time in law enforcement was the gift of gab. He learned early on as a young police officer that bullshitting your way into and out of conversations was priceless.

Cody tapped the number to call, and his phone began to ring. He mentally prepared himself for the next step, which would almost certainly ruin any chance of returning to Renegade—let alone ProCorp. He heard the line connect and took a deep breath to gather his senses as he heard the familiar deep-southern redneck's voice.

"Ain't heard from you in a bit. How you been? You back with Val?" Mike inquired.

"Yep. Been back a couple weeks now and I finally got my first gig. Val wants Frank and I to go check some shit out in Peru. Low-level reconnaissance stuff. You know how it is. Word on the street is you're still flying despite your old age and the FAA revoking all your licenses."

"Like I ever gave a rip about them," he replied.

"That's what I like to hear, Mike. Per usual, we got some hardware coming with us. Can you still get us in discreetly? As in, completely around customs?"

Cody heard rustling on the other end that sounded like Mike switching ears and the telltale sound of tobacco being spit into a cup. Cody hoped Mike wouldn't ask too many questions and catch wind of the deception, which would make this mission dead before it really began. But what other options did he have?

"You know I can, or you wouldn't be callin'. Say, how come Val ain't callin' giving me the heads up?" Mike asked. "He usually arranges this kinda stuff."

Cody quickly replied, "Well, since I'm back in the saddle, I asked to take the gig from start to finish. Just to grease the wheels, ya know? It's been about a year and a half, and I wanna show I still got it."

"Hmm, year and a half, huh? I heard about your family. I ain't got the words." There was a pause. "How much hardware anyway? You know I got weight limits that can't be ignored."

"You know me, Mike, I like to be prepared. Never hurts to have stuff and not need it, but it does hurt to need stuff and not have it. How about we get you in the gym and lose a few extra pounds so I can bring another case or two of ammo?"

"Mm-hmm. Yeah, I seem to remember you being a trigger-happy son of a bitch," Mike said in reply, but Cody could practically hear the grin in his voice.

"Mike, you know I like it when you talk dirty to me. Don't stop there," Cody quipped, silently letting out a held breath. If Mike was making jokes, that was a very good sign.

"You know I'm supposed to be on vacation, right? The old lady's got me doing stuff all up and down this house. You're gonna owe me big time for this, Cody. I'm talking big, like Franklin BBQ big."

"You got a deal. How soon can we fly? It's just Frank and I plus our crap," Cody said back.

"I'll have the plane fueled for you boys in, oh, I dunno . . . three hours? That enough time for y'all to finish tying up loose ends around town?"

Cody heard Mike's wife in the background asking where he was going in three hours. A smile crept across his face at the thought of a crusty old black-ops underground pilot being fretted about by his wife. Behind every tough old man there was an even tougher old woman. The smile quickly faded however at the reminder of his own wife, Jen. He pictured her dark black hair reflecting the morning sun as she stood in the kitchen.

Shaking away the scene along with the remorse and guilt, Cody forced his thoughts to get back into the game. "Honestly, Mike, I know this is pretty short notice, but we need to get moving fast. We're hot on the trail of something and need to get moving sooner rather than later. Can you do an hour and a half? Frank is grabbing some stuff from the ranch now, so I'll check with him to make sure he's good to go."

Mike huffed in disagreement. "Boy, you know as much about flying as I do about gunfightin'. You ever heard of preflight checks? That shit takes time, and I sure as hell ain't leaving that runway without doing it the way it's supposed to get done. I can do two hours and that's it," Mike retaliated, drawing the proverbial line.

Cody looked up to the early morning sky where the sun was beginning to crest on the horizon. He said a quiet thank-you prayer. "Y'know, Mike, that'll do. And this will cover that time you left me and Val on the runway getting chased by ISIS," he replied graciously to the retired pilot.

Mike snorted in protest. "I told y'all on the radio I was leaving in a hurry. Besides, it all worked out, didn't it?"

"You did un-ass the area in a hurry, that's for sure."

"Better than taking a bullet in the ass cheek. I'm serious about the BBQ, Cody. I better be getting some damn Franklin's on this kinda timeline. I don't care how long you have to wait in line. See you boys in a couple hours."

Cody heard the line disconnect before he could say goodbye. He looked down at his phone and went back to work loading magazines and checking to make sure he didn't leave anything necessary behind. When he reached his truck, he grabbed his SAT phone from the passenger seat and put it firmly in his back pocket. Until he found Tessa, he wasn't going to let that phone out of his reach.

Fifteen miles away, Frank pulled his Ford Explorer into the parking lot of Renegade Ranch and turned off the engine. He took a deep breath and carefully thought about the ramifications of what he was about to do. On the one hand, he was about to check out equipment that was strictly for operations and not personal use. Doing so would get him into serious hot water with his dream job. On the other hand, his best friend, his "big brother," utterly needed him. And if Cody was right, so did Tessa. Frank tortured himself with the thought of Tessa needing a rescue and him sitting around back in the States, not lifting a finger.

The very idea of Tessa being in actual danger was enough to outweigh the risks for Frank. He'd never had a reason to doubt Cody's instincts before, and if it was enough for Cody to feel this strong about breaking all the rules, it was enough for Frank. After all, they didn't get the name Renegade for nothing.

He strolled through the parking lot and pulled open the glass doors leading into the reception area. He looked at the clock on the wall behind the desk which read 06:15 a.m. He knew he'd have to work fast because Lucy, Renegade's receptionist and operational support manager, would be coming in no later than 06:30 a.m.

Lucy worked for Renegade in a multitude of roles. She served as the team's logistical support, administrative staff member, and financial manager of team assets such as weapons, vehicles, and equipment. She knew the ins and outs of Renegade better than anyone and had been with the team since its inception.

Frank knew he was in over his head if he thought he'd be able to pull one over on her, so he figured it was best to avoid her altogether. The way Frank saw it, what she didn't know wouldn't hurt her.

He walked past Lucy's desk and held his RFID access card close to the reader until it sounded with a beep, watching as the red light turned green. After pushing the magnetically secured door open, he walked through the hallway past the gym and into the intel room. He swiped the access card again and opened the door, then turned to his desk and took a seat in the roll-around chair.

Pulling open the top drawer, he retrieved his laptop with the preloaded digital-mapping software. With the laptop in hand, he simply needed to download offline available maps to any digital device like a phone, tablet, or handheld GPS. Frank pushed himself off the chair and moved quickly down the hallway to the team room. When he got there, the familiar sight of the large open space with metal cage lockers along the wall and the single wooden table in the center of the room greeted him.

Frank reached into his pocket and pulled his keyring out, selecting the one for his specific cage. He stood in front of his personal cage, a chain-linked, six-by-six-foot area that contained all his operational gear, inserted the key, and turned the lock.

Once opened, he wasted no time. He grabbed his deployment bag, immediately tore open the top zipper, and started selecting his mission-essential items. This was more difficult than the usual missions where they'd had more time and intel about the situation. Luckily he remembered Tessa telling him a few weeks back she was going to be working in the rainforest, so he wanted something lightweight and scalable so that it would fit just about any mission profile.

He finally settled on his Spiritus System chest rig and Crye Precision JPC plate carrier. Similar to Cody's train of thought, this allowed him to wear the plate carrier for extra protection and allowed the chest rig to be worn either in conjunction with the plate carrier or separate altogether.

Frank picked up the large deployment bag and set it on the open table. Knowing he and Cody would need some surveillance kit, he opened the community locker and grabbed the logbook hanging from the rack. With a messy scrawl, he signed out his favorite surveillance drone, Bubo, a custom drone complete with FLIR imager and night-visions lenses.

Next, Frank grabbed a pair of MPU 5 radios, which would allow them to set up their own mobile ad hoc network at their operational destination. Though he didn't anticipate being separated from Cody all that much, it would be nice for them to communicate effectively in the event they were—assuming they were able to stay within the defined limits of the mobile network.

Frank wasn't sure if any of their surveillance activities would require low-visibility capabilities, so he grabbed a couple sets of in-the-ear tubes and push-to-talk options to plug into their helmet-mounted ear protection.

All Frank needed now was his personal guns and ammo to match. He locked the community cage behind him and swiped the access card to get access to the arms room next door. Frank knew he was running short on time if he was going to avoid Lucy. The time read 06:25 a.m., and he still needed to load all the kit into his personal SUV outside.

He opened his personal weapons locker and quickly grabbed a single rifle and pistol. Based on past experience with Cody, he assumed his big brother would choose something close to intermediate range, so he thought it best to fill the gap and go for something with a little bit more reach.

Frank snatched his Geissele Super Duty eighteen-inch special-purpose rifle (SPR) from its resting place. Giving him a little more scale and velocity at extended ranges, Frank had the rifle outfitted with a 2X12 Nightforce scope, offset iron sights, PEQ-15 laser/illuminator, and

SureFire suppressor to match. He rested the rifle against the wall and picked up his night-fighting pistol, a M&P CORE with Trijicon red-dot sight, match-grade threaded barrel, and infrared weaponlight.

He grabbed magazines and ammo as fast as he could, doing his best to beat the clock. Checking his watch, he saw the time read 06:30 a.m. He was out of time. He heard the door to the team room open and knew exactly who it was without even turning.

Dammit!

He continued to grab his hard rifle case with custom foam cutout specifically for his guns and laid it open on the floor. A familiar voice broke the silence.

"Whatcha doin' here so early, young man? Thought you were supposed to be on vacation," Lucy's casual voice asked.

Lucy had popped her head around the door frame and was now looking down at Frank kneeling over his guns and case. Frank did his best to look nonchalant but knew it wasn't gonna get him very far. He refused to make eye contact. He tried to play it off as best as he could.

"Ah, nuthin'. I talked to Cody yesterday, and he asked if I would come help him out with some students down at the shoot house. Been awhile since we got to run-and-gun together, so I said 'Why not?'" he said, shrugging his shoulders.

Lucy squinted her eyes as she watched Frank toss some of his preloaded magazines and a case of 77 grain bonded-match ammunition into his deployment bag.

"Uh-huh," she said shortly. It didn't take a genius to know she didn't believe him. "You need *that* much match ammo and your eighteen-inch rifle? At the shoot house? Why don't you just pack the range ammo and a smaller gun?" Her fingers tapped against the door frame expectantly.

Luckily, Frank's back was toward Lucy as he scrunched his face like he was in pain, knowing he'd already screwed up by mentioning Cody. He had underestimated how much she knew about the details of their equipment. Frank thought as quickly as he could and countered as best as possible.

"Well, Cody and I are just walking the local cops through some stuff at the shoot house, and he ran his mouth about me being a badass at six hundred yards. You know me, Lucy, I can't let some podunk deputy outshoot me, so I figured I'd bring the heat. Can't back down from a challenge."

He finally stood up straight and did his best to make eye contact. Frank could tell Lucy still wasn't buying it. At least, not entirely. She paused momentarily and turned her head back toward the bench in the team room, eyeballing his deployment bag complete with his plate carrier, chest rig, and pistol belt.

"I see . . . You need armor *and* a chest rig for that?" she asked, probing him.

The young Renegade realized he was digging himself into a hole and needed to find a way to dig himself out and quick.

"If what Cody is telling me about these guys is true, I'm definitely gonna want some armor while I'm in that shoot house. Even on the catwalk," he said as he flashed his signature smile and a joking laugh.

She cracked a smile to one side of her mouth. Frank hoped that even if she didn't fully believe him that she believed him just enough to let it go and not push it any further.

She shrugged. "Okay, fair enough. Hey, how's Cody doing anyway? I've been meaning to call and check on him but didn't want to mess with anything that's just starting to heal."

Frank nodded in agreement, "Yeah, he's handling it the best way he knows how."

She peered at him. "Frank, just do me a favor. Let him know if he needs anything, all he has to do is ask, okay?"

Frank could hear the genuine concern in her voice and knew she meant it. He didn't want to, but he couldn't help but wonder if he could use that to his advantage.

"Actually, Lucy, there is something. I told him I'd buy a scope off him and it ain't exactly cheap. I don't have time to get to the bank before I head to the shoot house 'cause class starts at seven sharp. Can you sign out $2,000 to me from the safe? I'll pay it back first chance I get."

Frank held his breath waiting for her reply. He knew they would need some expendable cash for things like vehicles, low-rent hotels, on-site supplies, and food while they were in Peru. Without spending their own money right away, this was the fastest way to get currency in hand. Much to his surprise, Lucy straightened up and nodded.

"Of course. I know you're good for it. And besides, I'm the one who makes your checks. I mean, well, it's all digital nowadays anyway. If you forget, I just won't pay you," she said nonchalantly.

"Thanks, you're the best," he said, letting his breath out.

"I know. I'll put it in your kit bag while you finish up here. Don't forget your helmet while you're in the shoot house. Now hurry up or you're gonna be late," she said over her shoulder as she walked out. Frank heard the door to the team room open and close, and took a dramatically deep breath while he glanced around at his gear.

"We are so fucked," he said to himself.

15

Cody had arrived at the small private airport and parked his truck away from everyone else's vehicles, eager to get moving. He checked his watch again for the third time in twenty minutes. He opened the door and moved to the back of the Tacoma, unlatching the tailgate.

With a slight hop he plopped down on the makeshift seat and dug his phone from his pocket. It was now almost 07:30 a.m. Cody hated the idea of burning bridges with the team, but he'd learned from Val over the years that desperate times call for desperate measures. He sent a text to Frank asking his location using police shorthand.

Twenty?

He was just starting to wonder if Frank had gotten caught in traffic, or worse, gotten caught by Lucy, when he heard a vehicle pull into the parking lot. He turned to see Frank's Explorer heading his direction.

Cody hopped off the tailgate and pulled the front tail of his plaid Columbia shirt over the grip of his Glock 19, making sure it remained concealed. The aggressively textured pistol grip tended to snag the fabric and outline the firearm.

He watched as Frank pulled into the parking spot next to Cody's truck, facing the same direction and looking not too confident. The silver SUV came to a stop, and the engine quickly died. Frank's tall frame stepped out of the driver seat. His face looked solemn.

Cody understood what he was asking of Frank; he knew the risks were through the roof and this would likely make him PNG, a persona non grata, meaning there was no chance of ever coming back if he was excommunicated from the group and told to leave. Cody wanted to make sure the totality of the situation wasn't lost on him.

"Hey man, I know I'm asking a lot. Please believe me, I wouldn't ask at *all* if I wasn't absolutely sure Tessa needed us. I can't do this alone." Cody paused. "But I would if I had to. You're the best man I know, and trust me, we're doing the right thing—even if it doesn't feel like it right now."

Frank nodded. "I do trust you. I'll follow you into hell to get her back if need be. Tessa ain't my blood, but truth be told," he shrugged and had the decency to look a little apprehensive, "we've been talking a little since you've been gone. Nothing really serious. Just some texts here and there."

Cody nodded, taking it in. "Oh, so that's what that kiss on the cheek was all about at her going-away party."

"I mean, it's not like we're a couple or anything. We just like to talk to one another, that's all," Frank replied quickly.

Cody didn't want to let him off the hook that easily, so he nudged his shoulder playfully and raised his eyebrows. "Frank, are you telling me you have the hots for my sister?"

Frank's eyes widened a bit, trying to think of something a little more reflective of what he felt for Tessa. After all, this was her brother he was talking to. But finally, he shrugged. "You know what? Pretty much."

And Cody laughed. It felt nice, talking to his friend about something so . . . normal.

"Look, I was gonna talk to you about it if things started to progress," Frank said, "but you should probably know that I'm doing this just as much for her as I am for you. If you really feel like she's in trouble, I want to do what I can to help."

"Okay, this is the first thing we're going to sort out when we get back. For now, let's get back on mission."

"Fair enough. I was able to snag some recce stuff and Bubo. I got us some comms, cash, and a whole bunch of bullets."

"Good. I talked with Mike, and he should be here any minute to let us in the hangar. Just waiting on the text."

Cody looked at his watch for what seemed like the hundredth time, mentally doing the math since he'd received the call from Tessa. It had been a little over four hours. He tried not to think about the span of things that could have happened in that short time frame.

"I suppose that gives us a little time to start reaching out to old contacts and do some mission planning. I've got a few people in South America, but I don't think they're in Peru. Just a few former cop buddies who went federal with the DEA and whatnot. You got anybody? Or are we gonna have to hit the ground and figure it out on the fly?" Cody asked.

Frank thought about the question while he rubbed his fingers through his beard like he was wiping something away from his mouth. Cody suddenly saw his eyes light up, and Frank snapped his fingers.

"You know what? I do know someone. I totally forgot about her, but we did an op last year after you left. I met her in Mexico while she visiting or something. Her name is Juanita, and she's from Peru. She said I made an impression on her 'cause I reminded her of her son who died in the Peruvian military. Lemme see if I still have her number. Grab my laptop outta the passenger seat, will you? I didn't have time to check open source."

Frank pulled the key fob from the pocket and unlocked the door while Cody walked around and retrieved the laptop. By the time he had powered the computer up, Frank was scrolling through his phone and found who he was looking for. He saw Frank pull the phone to his ear and could hear the line ringing.

Cody laid the laptop down on the tailgate. He was immediately greeted by the login screen and looked at Frank, who was still waiting for an answer. Cody made a motion with his hands like he was typing and pointed to the computer. Frank held the phone between his shoulder and cheek and punched in the password.

Cody hadn't been in the game for a while, but he knew the drill. His first task was to find out everything the internet could tell him about

North Spear and start downloading offline, available maps to their phones and GPS devices. Google had just come up when he heard Frank enthusiastically talking in Spanish.

"*Buenos días*, Mamá Juanita. *¿Qué pasa?*"

Frank stepped out of earshot of Cody as he began searching for anything useful on North Spear. Google didn't tell him much other than that the company appeared well financed. Cody could tell their website was professionally created and claimed to be leading the industry in both technology and medical development. A few brief videos showed several scientists from the Foundation of Regenerative Health working with stem-cell research and biology. But as hard as he looked, he couldn't find anything that mentioned archaeology.

What the hell is regenerative medicine? What does that have to do with archaeology?

Cody clicked to bring Google back up and decided to try another route when a vibration on his leg stopped him in his tracks. It was Mike. His text told him the plane was ready and that he'd come around the side of the hangars to let them in the gate.

He quickly snapped the laptop closed and whistled at Frank, who turned and saw Cody making a circular motion with his hand in the air, signaling it was time to spin up. Frank closed the distance to Cody and their vehicles. Just as Frank was within five feet of Cody, he heard him closing the conversation.

"*Sí, señora*. I know, I know. Okay, sounds good. Be there soon."

Frank thumbed the red icon on his screen, ending the call. Cody started grabbing his bags from the bed of the truck while Frank, after grabbing the laptop, moved to the Explorer and opened the liftgate.

"Well, what's the word? You get anything set up?"

Franked hoisted the assault pack to his back and cinched the shoulder straps down tight as he talked.

"As a matter of fact, I did. She was a little butt hurt I hadn't called to check on her, so I got an earful about that, but she said her nephew runs some sorta hotel in Iquitos. She lives there, too, and it isn't too far from the Amazon. It's a small city near the river, and she's tied in locally. Juanita can point us in the right direction once we get there."

Cody finally pulled his deployment bag from the bed of the truck and began hoisting it toward the fence. Frank followed behind, pulling his own kit and rifle case.

Cody said over his shoulder, "Good deal. Nice work, man. Sounds like we'll be up and running in no time. I'd like to secure some wheels and start scouting the area within a couple hours of landing. We still need to upload the devices with the mapping software, but we can do that on the plane. You good with that?"

Frank looked at Cody as they came to a halt at the gate. He set his rigid rifle case down.

"You think you're pushing this a little hard? It's at least maybe half a day's trip to anywhere in Peru—"

"And that's exactly why I don't want to waste any time," Cody shot back immediately. "We're behind the power curve by four hours, travel included. That puts us at wheels down nearly twenty-four hours after the call. You know as well as I do if we don't hit the ground running and start pulling threads, we're going to lose her."

Frank turned away and thought about the timeline. He knew Cody was right, although he hated to think what that meant about their odds. He heard footsteps nearby and saw Mike's short, stocky frame through the gate, walking in their direction.

"Yeah, I guess you're right," Frank said, looking back at Cody. "I just want to make sure we both get a little rest so we don't start making mistakes. It is only the two of us, so there ain't exactly any room for error, ya know?"

"I know. I have no idea what we're up against," Cody said, rubbing a hand exasperatedly against his face. "I don't know if her dig site got attacked by locals or Narcos or God knows what." He hated to think about the unknowns.

Both Renegades heard a beep, then a click at the gate a second before it swung open. On the other side, Dirty Mike stood at five feet, four inches with reddish-blond hair shaved down nearly to his skin on the sides and only a half-inch long on top. He was holding the gate open with his frame, dressed in a Hawaiian shirt that was unbuttoned all the way to the top of his stomach.

He wore a thick goatee and if you looked closely enough, you could see small specks of fine-cut Grizzly chewing tobacco stuck inside. Mike's preferred travel attire consisted of cargo shorts and cheap athletic shoes with Velcro straps. To complete the package, he never left home without his .357 Magnum revolver secured in his brown leather shoulder holster. Good ol' Dirty Mike didn't look a bit different since the last time Cody saw him nearly two years before. In fact, Cody could've sworn he was wearing the exact same shirt.

"*Well*, ain't you a sight for sore eyes. You don't look any worse for wear, I suppose, and I see the Woodsman is still following you around everywhere," Mike said gruffly, nodding in Frank's direction. "C'mon, les' go. Startin' to get hot out here."

Both Cody and Frank smiled and slapped him on the shoulder as they walked through the gate and past their pilot. He tried to shy away from both young men, but was unsuccessful. Mike never did like physical contact. Anytime the operators from Renegade travelled via Dirty Mike Airlines, they made it a point to close the distance.

Cody replied, "It's good to see ya too, Mike. Where we at this time around?"

Mike pointed three hangars down and walked beside them as he asked, "Please tell me you know where we're going? I ain't gonna be flyin' all over Peru lookin' for a place to land."

Cody did his best to lie through his teeth. "Don't worry, we got everything planned out down to a T. How close can you get us to Iquitos?" Frank had shot a look of disbelief at Cody when he said they had it all planned out. He put his game face back on before Mike could see.

Luckily, Mike hadn't noticed and kept his usual pace, the shiny nickel-plated revolver swinging side to side as he walked. He replied after a few seconds of thinking.

"Prolly not as close as you want, but I know a guy who runs a makeshift runway that ain't far, and he owes me a favor."

"Mike, when you gonna get rid of that wheel gun and get something a little more practical?" Frank asked, eyeballing the revolver. Mike looked over, slightly offended.

"And get one of dem plastic toy guns you boys are always talking about?" He shook his head side to side. "Nah, I like my guns simple, effective, and not jammin' up on me."

Cody couldn't help but interject. "You're telling me you can fly massive, fixed-wing aircrafts with literally millions of parts, but you won't trust a modern pistol because you think it will jam?"

"Exactly," Mike said firmly, turning his attention to Cody. Frank and Cody looked at each other over him and busted out in laughter, relieving some pressure from Cody's anxieties if only for a moment.

They arrived at the hangar and looked up Mike's plane: a simple-yet-expensive cargo plane that Mike had managed to pay off contracting with ProCorp. He was kept on a retainer, financed using ProCorp funds, so the team kinda thought of him as an air Uber of sorts. Mike was insanely protective of his plane and had told Cody a number of times, "If bullets start flying, I'm taking off with or without you." Something that, once upon a time, he and Val had learned was absolutely true.

Cody and Frank started loading their various bags onto the plane while Mike checked the vehicle over one last time. Once the initial checks were complete, Mike climbed into the cockpit and started his routine, flipping switches and turning dials that all looked the same to Frank and Cody. The two younger men made themselves as comfortable as possible and started pulling their devices out, laying them out neatly so they could get to work.

Frank pulled the laptop from his backpack and turned on airplane mode, knowing Mike would chew his ass if he didn't. The predownloaded mapping software application came up after a few clicks, and Frank began checking the area around Iquitos and further north into the rainforest. He began selecting areas of interest to download on their phones and smaller wrist-mounted GPS devices.

Cody sat a bit farther down with his kit bag opened it up, and dug through his backpack, trying to find his Garmin GPS. Tucked into a pocket inside his assault pack, he checked the batteries. Cody leaned over and handed the GPS and his phone to Frank so that he could install the necessary software, which he started uploading to each device right away. Both men heard Mike call out from the cockpit.

"Alright, ladies, we're moving to the tarmac, and we'll be wheels-up in a few. Turn off all that fancy techno shit y'all like to play with. You can turn it on when we're at altitude."

With that, Frank closed out the application and turned off the rest of the devices. Cody pulled his SAT phone from his back pocket and considered turning it off momentarily, then thought better of it. Mike would just have to take it up with him personally—assuming he ever found out. Knowing a long flight was ahead of them, Cody knew they needed to rest. After all, neither of them had slept much, and both were up well before the sun.

He looked at Frank. "We should get some sleep while we can. Once we get to Peru, it's game on. A couple hours of rack time might do us some good."

Frank's eyes were heavy and welcomed the suggestion.

"Yeah, sounds good to me," Frank replied, yawning. "Let's start the mission planning when we get up. I'm toasted." Frank put in his earbuds, leaned back in his seat, and was out in less than two minutes.

Cody lay awake for a few minutes, knowing he needed to recharge his batteries but also feared the return of the dreams. For the second time since the death of his daughter, he closed his eyes and prayed silently.

"Lord, I know I've screwed up and made some awful mistakes. I accept that, but please help Frank and I rescue my sister and get her home safely. Tell my little girl I love her, and I pray Your will be done, on Earth as it is in Heaven. Amen."

The exhaustion overcame him as his breathing deepened and his muscles relaxed.

16

Tessa sat across from Bart in her suite, the fear of the unknown ever present. He'd transformed right in front of her eyes. The day before, he was the well-dressed businessman who'd hired her to take lead on an archaeological expedition. Today, he was something else entirely.

"Ms. Willis, let's stop with the games already. There is still so much left to accomplish. Who did you call, and what did you say?" When Tessa didn't reply, Bart exhaled a deep sigh and rubbed his eyes.

"What the hell do you want from me, Bart?" Tessa finally asked.

The man exploded from his seated position on the couch with a speed Tessa didn't know he possessed. His face turned bright red, and veins protruded from his neck.

"I want you to open the damn tomb! We had a deal, and you haven't fulfilled your end of it!" Bart screamed at the top of his lungs.

Tessa shrunk back in her seat, afraid for her life. She sat there, unable to reply. It had become abundantly clear she had gotten herself into something way over her head.

Seeing Tessa's vulnerability empowered him. Bart thrived on such a thing. Making people feel beneath him made him feel strong. He usually preferred to do so subtly, but he had come to find that this was so much more satisfying. Bart adjusted his expensive suit jacket and centered his tie before taking a seat back on the couch.

"See what you made me do? I hate losing my temper, but when you act like this, what else am I supposed to do? Huh? How else am I supposed to get your attention?"

The irritation in his voice was clear.

Tessa remained silent, still frozen on the couch almost as if the idea of her moving would set him off again. She refused to give Bart the satisfaction of crying, though the tears in her eyes were threatening to spill.

Bart rubbed his temples in circles, trying to remain calm, though failing. He took a deep breath and exhaled dramatically, standing once more.

"I want you to consider the ramifications of what's at stake. Not just for me or for yourself, but for the world, Tessa. We are working on a project that will change human history—existence even. Paradigms will shift, narratives will change, textbooks will be edited. Our work here will live on through the centuries.

"Speaking of living on, how would you like to be the person who discovered the cure to cancer, or even the cure to death itself? You can make the world a better place. Once we have this Nephilim's body in our possession," Bart paused for effect, "the possibilities are endless."

Tessa remembered the dream. One more piece of the puzzle settled into place. She fixedly looked at Bart, who had become lost in his own ambition. The dots she had been collecting for weeks began to connect.

This whole expedition had little to do with scientific archaeological discovery as she had been told. It was now clear Tessa had been misled by the well-dressed but unbalanced North Spear executive standing in front of her. North Spear wanted the body of the hybrid giant inside the tomb not as evidence of their existence but to replicate, dissect, manipulate, and eventually reproduce.

A defiance rose up within her, the smallest of sparks ready to ignite the raging fire.

The angel was right. Just like before, they're using our own selfish desires against us, she thought.

"You know, Bart, you think you're doing the world some service by getting this tomb open, but you're not. You think you know what you're dealing with, but you have no idea," she blurted out before she could stop herself.

"Me?" he asked incredulously, turning sharply. "*I* have no idea what I'm dealing with? Tessa, you have just entered a world it has taken me years to navigate, and you have the nerve to tell *me* I don't know what I'm doing. The people I work for do *not* accept failure. You and I are as replaceable as the person who changes the sheets in this hotel room. To them, neither of us are special."

"This is far bigger than you or me or the people you work for, Bart. You're playing with cosmic entities neither one of us can fully comprehend. The consequences of this would literally be on a biblical scale. The *entire* world was flooded to wipe these guys out. It's not just Christianity or Judaism either. Every culture across the globe has record of these guys, and none of them exactly paint these things in a good manner. We can't afford to bring them back in *any* capacity."

Bart said nothing, his face betraying no expression. Had he spoke, he would have openly mocked her naivety, but he knew that would only serve to embolden her position. Honestly, he didn't care if what she said was true or not. It didn't matter to him if the Nephilim were tyrannical, bloodthirsty abominations of God's creation. Bart craved power, these guys had it, and so would he once the tomb was open.

Tessa sat motionless on the couch, her hands carefully held in her lap and her eyes locked with Bart's.

"I can see this is going nowhere, so let's all take a little recess, shall we?" he said carefully. "I need to make a phone call to my superiors and let them know the situation. I doubt it will be favorable for you."

There was a knock at the door. Surprised, Bart looked at Al, who stood in the corner of the room and who Tessa had almost forgotten was there. Bart beckoned for Al to open it. When Al did, he cracked the door to see Jake Reynolds.

"Uh, hey Al. I was here to see Tessa, she . . . um, she texted me last night about something, and it seemed really important. Is she here?"

Al looked back toward Bart, unsure of how to proceed. Bart waved his hand as if to shoo him away.

"Yeah, sorry, she's not available to talk right now. You'll have to come back later," Al said firmly and he moved to shut the door.

The impact of Bart's last words rang in Tessa's head. She had to do something. She wasn't sure if Jake could help at all, but she stood a better chance with his help than staying silent.

"Jake!" she yelled out desperately.

His name had barely left her lips before Bart rushed over to shut her up, cupping his hand over her mouth. She hadn't even had the chance to yell for help, but it didn't matter. The damage had been done.

"Tessa?" Jake yelled back. He must have heard the panic in her voice because he tried to force his way into the room, pushing against the closing door. Unfortunately for him, Al's size and strength far outmatched his own. Not to mention Jake was at least ten years his senior. Al held the door for a moment or two until he released his resistance and pulled Jake into the room. Easier to contain the problem than to leave it in the hallway and pretend it didn't exist.

For all his troubles, Jake was rewarded by a hefty right cross from Al. Jake fell to the ground with a thud. He was stunned long enough for Al and another North Spear contractor to bind his hands with flex cuffs. Tessa fought Bart's hands off her face and ran to Jake. Immediately, she was intercepted by one of the security members and was also restrained.

Bart took a moment to look around, pushing his tousled hair back, hoping to maintain his put-together appearance. It was clear to everyone things were devolving fast.

"This is getting out of hand. I think it's best for everyone if we take a few minutes to collect our thoughts. Al, may I speak with you outside for a moment?" he asked.

Al gave a knowing look to his subordinates, pointing at his own eyes with two fingers and then back at Tessa and Jake. His team knew they needed to watch them carefully.

"Sir?" Al asked after stepping out into the hallway with Bart.

"I need you to keep a lid on this," Bart replied. "No one other than me comes or goes. Keep them in here until I say otherwise. I have to make a call. I cannot afford this right now, not when I'm so close. Keep them both working on whatever material they have here."

"I know things got a little tense in there pretty quick, but I mean, are we really going to hold them prisoner in this hotel room?"

"Do you remember how I found you? Huh?" Bart asked, peering carefully into Al's face. "Well?"

"Yes, sir," Al answered. He couldn't help his face from flooding with shame.

"If it weren't for me, you'd still be a drunk piece of shit lying in the streets of Phuket. I gave you purpose. I pulled you from the gutter," Bart said, jabbing a finger into Al's chest. "You swore to me that you'd stand by my side. Now is the time to make good on it."

"Understood, sir," Al replied.

"Good."

Bart walked to the end of the hallway and tapped the screen on his phone as Al stepped back inside the room. Bart knew nothing good would come from this call, but he also knew it was necessary. He just hoped Mr. Adams was in a good mood. The phone rang with its digital tone. The voice on the other end answered promptly and alert.

"You have it open?" the voice asked insistently.

"No, we have an additional problem. The girl, Tessa . . . she's refusing to work any further on opening the tomb. But she's the only one that can translate the Enochian," Bart said matter-of-factly, getting right to business.

"What do you mean 'refused'?" the voice inquired. There was a deadly air to it.

"She wanted to leave. She is now aware that this isn't an option. I have a lid on containment; however, she did make a phone call. And . . ." He hesitated. "Another team member, one of the scientists, has stuck his nose into it as well. I'll update you when I know more," Bart said, attempting to fill his voice with confidence. There was a beat of silence.

"I'm sending your replacement, Joshua Michaels. He'll be there tomorrow or the day after," the voice replied.

Bart's stomach dropped. "Sir, that's not necessary—"

"*I* decide what is necessary, Bart. Not you."

Bart's phone beeped as the line disconnected. He leaned his head against the wall and couldn't help but slam a fist into it. He pondered his next step. Whatever it would be, he refused for this to be over.

17

The excavation crew had arrived at Azazel a little earlier than usual. Mr. Cox had made it very clear to them they needed to keep pushing deeper and further into the temple. He wanted the entire place mapped and catalogued. Manuel, the foreman, knew these things take time, but Mr. Cox had neither the patience, nor did he have the knowledge that if they started moving substantial pieces of stone inside a cave, the pieces could very well bring the place down on top of everyone.

And it appeared that that's exactly what had happened thousands of years ago to the very passage the team had been recently working to uncover. An ornately covered doorway had been blocked by several immense boulders, almost like they had been placed on purpose. Perhaps hidden behind these barriers were ancient treasures such as gold coins or jewelry that had been long lost to the ages. Manuel would be lying if he said the thought of taking one or two for himself if they'd found any hadn't crossed his mind. After all, why not? It was him and his team that was doing all the work anyway. Why shouldn't he take it? These American historians and scientists would never know the difference anyway. He was just beginning to ponder what he would spend his fictional fortune on when he heard some of the crew talking excitedly.

He pushed through the crowd that had gathered in the temple's tunnel to see several men scrambling to push and pull the basketball-sized rocks out of the way.

They had nearly broken through.

Just minutes later, the doorway was cleared enough for a grown man to crawl through. Manuel was, of course, the first in. His heart pounded at the idea of what could be on the other side. One of the workers handed him a flashlight through the gaping hole. He shined the light into the rest of the space, which spanned far deeper than he could see. Both sides of the walls were lined with what looked to be tombs while the ceiling towered above his head at what he estimated to be forty feet. He stood in awe as more of his crew made their way into the new chamber, their lights filling the recesses his could not.

Together they carefully walked between the two rows of the tomb-shaped structures, which were perfectly aligned and consistent with the size of an average person. Between each tomb, a statue of a warrior had been carved carefully into the wall and seemed to peer at them as if skeptical of the crew's forced entry. As he walked amongst them, the foreman observed each tomb itself was intricately carved with symbols from a language none understood. He noticed the pictographs were on all four sides, each tomb different from the last, perhaps telling the exploits of the one inside.

The top of each tomb, however, were all the same.

They all contained a series of swirls and grooves in a stylistic design. He traced the grooves with his fingers, causing him to shudder, though he didn't know why. The two members of his crew were much the same, looking hesitantly at the stone warriors emerging from the walls. Several of the structures were damaged. Protruding pieces like arms or weapons were broken off and laid next to the body in shambles.

One of Manuel's men stood face-to-face with a particular headless warrior, closely inspecting the detail of the hand-carved artifact. The worker took off his hard hat in order to gaze up at the warrior more closely. Even though the statue was headless, he still had the impression it was looking at him. As he backed away from it, what the man failed to notice was the matching stone head lying in wait directly behind his feet. As he tripped over it and fell backward, he tried to catch himself, though even the most graceful of men would have been unsuccessful. His head hit the corner of the tomb with an audible thunk. The useless hard hat rolled away from his grasp.

The foreman rushed to him, gently cupping his head and making sure his head stayed in line with the spine. Head injuries are notorious for bleeding profusely, and this was no exception.

"Don't move," Manuel told the bleeding man firmly, holding his other hand to the injury to staunch the flow of blood while he yelled for help to those outside the newfound chamber.

Manuel knelt beside his employee, reassuring him until the medic team forced their way in. When they finally did, the foreman gently stood up to get out of their way, his loyal worker's blood still running from his fingertips. In his haste to make way for the medics, Manuel didn't notice as it carelessly dripped down to the ground. The droplets of blood began to run down the grooves and seep slowly but steadily into the tomb. During the shuffle of the hasty evacuation, Manuel did not hear the sound of the stone sarcophagus as its lid opened an inch.

18

The flight to Peru was largely uneventful, which—considering the alternative—the men were grateful for. Both Cody and Frank had gotten a couple hours of sleep and woke only to compile what open-source intelligence they could gather prior to landing. As Frank pored over digital maps, both topographical and satellite, to familiarize himself with the geography, Cody couldn't help but realize how well he slept despite the current circumstances. No nightmares, no terrors. Just solid, peaceful sleep.

Neither operator could find anything useful on North Spear from the internet aside from a website that appeared intentionally vague. There was nothing that left a footprint in South America or even a thread for them to pull. They quickly ascertained they'd have to rely on local human intelligence, or HUMINT as it was called in their circle. In Cody's past life as a cop, they called it community-oriented policing.

Dirty Mike had made some calls while they were in the air and arranged for landing at a designated makeshift airport. While it was short on the finer things like a paved runway, it made up for it by staying discreet. Cartels had used it extensively, and for the right price, any pilot brave enough to try could too.

The first thing they noticed after they landed was the humidity, which clung to their skin and refused to let go. Through several years of experience, they were wise enough to dress appropriately, with lightweight, breathable clothing that was designed originally for adventurers and hikers.

Neither one of them expected to blend in exactly with the locals, but at least they'd be comfortable and hopefully look like tourists who were planning on some simple, innocent outdoor activities. Once they hoisted the rest of their gear out of the plane, Cody and Frank said their thanks to Mike who was departing after a refuel and quick bite to eat.

Cody always wondered how that man managed to stay awake for so long. Maybe flying reenergized him. Some part of Cody figured that since Mike was a pilot, the only place he was truly happy was in the air. This type of passion for their respective fields was something Cody understood.

Frank had managed to get in touch with Juanita shortly after they landed, and he told Cody she was sending her nephew to pick them up. She had warned Frank it wouldn't be quick, and she was right. Luckily it was night when they arrived so there weren't many people around. The last thing they wanted was to draw any unnecessary attention, so if they did have to stand suspiciously outside, doing it away from prying eyes and not getting baked by the sun seemed like a good place to start.

Frank strategically placed a few of his softer bags around on the runway and plopped onto them. Cody had already done the same, his back propped up by one of his own.

"How long you think we have until Val finds out we're in South America?" Cody asked.

"Well, let's see," Frank said sighing and looking at his watch. "Today is Thursday. He's supposed to be getting ready for the ProCorp semiannual meeting this weekend. So I dunno. A couple of days maybe?"

"Oh yeah, I almost forgot about those. ProCorp lodge. What a place," Cody said, stretching his hands behind his head.

"After Val finds out about this, guess I'll never make it back there." Cody tried not to squirm with guilt at this, but Frank didn't seem to notice.

"What's it like anyway?" Frank asked.

Cody thought about downplaying it but decided better on it. Frank could always see right through him anyway. "Honestly, I'd be lying if I said it wasn't one of the coolest places I've ever been. The lodge is an old log cabin. And when I say log cabin, I'm talking like the size of a mansion. Makes you feel like you're back in the old west, man. You know Longbow, the guy who runs ProCorp, I guess the place has been in his family for a while. After he got out of the military and started up Applied Sciences, he turned it into a lodge for the team leaders and 2ICs."

Frank and gave a low whistle. "Sounds like a cool place."

"Backs right up against the mountain, has a sweet water feature in the backyard. Even has an underground, private soundproof range."

Frank could see Cody recalling all the details in his mind's eye. The longing was written all over his face.

"I know you miss it. I'm sorry . . ."

He thought about saying the rest of his sentence, "that you'll probably never see it again," but he decided against it.

Cody just shrugged. "It's not about me anymore. Getting my sister back is more important than visiting some lodge in the mountains."

Frank nodded his agreement before straightening up. "Hey, looks like we got company headed this way," he said.

Cody glanced over his shoulder to see a plume of dirt coming directly for them. Frank pulled the curved bill of his ball cap further down over his face to block the late afternoon sun while trying to positively ID the incoming vehicle.

"What are the chances this is some cartel lieutenant upset because a couple of gringos used his runway?" Frank asked.

"With our luck? Better than average," Cody replied.

The rusted single-cab vehicle came to an ungraceful and jerky stop that gave Cody uneasy suspicions. He stood up quickly, his fingers subconsciously wrapping around the roughly textured grip on his concealed pistol. Without hesitation, the driver door flew open. Cody pulled his Glock from his holster and held it at the ready. The driver stepped out with one foot and immediately, the truck lurched forward, forcing him back inside the cab to take it out of gear. It was clear the driver wasn't really sure what he was doing.

When the dust settled, out popped a young man—boy, really. He was no older than eighteen. He did not appear armed, giving Cody a sense of relief, but his grip on his weapon didn't lessen any.

"I got this," Frank said as he slowly rose from his nest of assault bags and packs before turning to the newcomer.

"Hey! Haven't you learned how to drive yet?" Frank yelled at him, shielding his eyes with his hat and squinting from the harsh headlights.

"Mr. Franks!" the young boy shouted in excitement.

The boy ran over to Frank and wrapped his arms around his waist, catching him a little off balance and almost causing them to fall over.

But Frank just gave a wide grin and patted Fernando appreciatively on the back. Cody came to the realization that he had absolutely no idea what was going on. *Who is this kid?* Surely Frank would have said something about an illegitimate love child in South America.

Frank looked up and noticed Cody's look of bewilderment. He gave Cody a palm of understanding and a reassuring nod at the situation.

"C'mon, Fren, help us get loaded up," Frank said to the kid.

"No problemo!" the boy declared, snapping to attention and giving Frank a mocking salute. Frank hunched forward quickly with his arms out as if to grab Fren, but the boy just laughed again and leapt out of reach, making his way over to the first bag. Systematically and with a purpose, he began loading the gear bags into the truck.

"Who the hell is this kid?" Cody muttered to Frank.

"It's Juanita's nephew, Fren, short for Fernando. He's our ride. C'mon, help us load the kit."

Cody had been expecting someone a little older and more experienced to help them out. Definitely not a wide-eyed, grinning kid like this. But beggars can't be choosers, so without another word, Cody got to work as well loading his various bags into the rusty old truck. He did, however, keep his Vertx concealed-carry bag handy since it held his SIG MCX neatly inside.

Never know when a compact rifle might come in handy. It was best to keep it in arms reach as opposed to having to dig to find it—or so Cody thought.

The former Renegade found Frank and Fernando sitting in the cab, all but filling it up.

"And just where do I fit in this picture?" Cody asked with a pointed look.

Frank poked his head out of the passenger-side door and, with a thumb, pointed to the truck bed filled with their gear. Fernando had the decency to give him an abashed smile. Cody's shoulders dropped, realizing his fate. He hopped in the bed of the truck, and off they headed back toward town.

It was obvious Fernando didn't receive visitors regularly. His smile went from ear to ear with excitement. Frank sat in the passenger seat, and soon he wished he had taken Cody's seat. Fren shot wild and excited glances at Frank and Cody between every other word and only so often turned back to watch the road.

"Juanita no say you coming!" Fren shouted over the whining engine and wind.

"Believe me, Fren," Frank began but paused when a large gust of wind whipped through the cab. Frank held his words until it died down. "I didn't know I was coming either."

Fren's expression looked very perplexed as he tried to understand how someone could both end up some place and not known how they had ended up there. Fren knew if he lived the amount of adventures Frank did, he would do his best to remember his journeys for all of them.

Meanwhile, Cody sat quietly in the back of the truck for the duration of the ride. Despite his original apprehension, he'd nearly forgotten how much he liked riding in the bed. It took just a few minutes for him to feel the certain freedom that went along with it as the air blew through his long, shaggy hair.

After a none-too-pleasant bump, he was brought back to the reality that he was in a sovereign country trying to rescue his sister. Despite the fear of the stakes at hand, he couldn't deny that being operational again gave him no small measure of fulfillment—sanctioned or not.

After nearly two full hours of driving, the trio arrived. Cody and Frank were clearly exhausted; if Fernando was from the late ride, he didn't show it. The small truck came to a sudden and jerky stop once again. Juanita stood in the doorway of a small but colorful house, leaning against the frame. Fernando was sure to take the truck out of gear this time, with the parking brake fully engaged. He had made sure not to repeat his mistake at the airfield in front of his aunt.

Frank wrestled his way out of the dented, rusty truck and found Cody already out of the bed, dusting himself off. Frank waved his hand in greeting toward Juanita who disappeared back inside her home, no doubt preparing to welcome in her new guests.

A few minutes later, they sat in Juanita's house that was just outside of town. It was a small place, less than a thousand square feet. It was obvious one of the ways she had prepared for the boys arrival was with plenty of food. Juanita was under no illusions as to what they actually did for work, but she was polite enough not to ask any real questions or dig any deeper than she needed to.

Luckily, both Juanita and her Fernando spoke English well enough to be understood, so the four of them sat around her small, wooden kitchen table to discuss the matter at hand.

"Juanita, thank you so much for taking us in and helping out my brother and I," Cody started, but her eyebrows knitted together in confusion.

Looking like she was processing the words, she quickly looked at Frank and then back at Cody.

"*Hermano*?" she asked.

"*Sí, hermanito*," Cody replied, suddenly aware of his lack of Spanish practice.

Frank chuckled. Cody smiled back at Juanita, who shrugged and didn't press.

"Frank not so little, ya know," Fernando chimed in.

Everyone laughed at the most definitely true statement. Frank was by far the tallest and largest person in the room. The oversized American took a large bite of rice and barely swallowed before speaking directly to Juanita.

"Mamá Juanita, what can you tell us about the area? We're looking for a . . . friend . . . and don't know much about her company. They goes by the name of North Spear, or *Lanza del norte*. They're supposed to be looking for something in the jungle not too far from here. Heard anything about it?"

Juanita thought carefully for a minute but eventually shook her head no. Frank considered another approach. "Is there anything weird going on in the jungle lately, say, within the last year or couple of months?"

Juanita's eyes lit up before she spoke. "Oh *mijo*, the jungle can be scary place. There are uh, *los espíritus*, you know?"

Frank and Cody considered her words, both leaning in. Cody's Spanish wasn't great, but he knew enough to understand her context and knew that she was talking about spirits or ghosts.

Cody shot a curious look at Frank, who returned a similar expression. Frank asked, "What do you mean, *los espíritus*? *¿Dónde*?"

Juanita laughed. "They in no one place, *mijo*, but everywhere. I tell you a story. When I was a *niñita*, I would run off to play in the jungle with *mis amigas*. One day I came across a house out in the jungle, all by itself. I told my papi, and he told me never to go there again. He said the *Ángel de la muerte* was out there, and he would take us if we did not stay away."

Cody thought about what she said for a moment before something clicked in his head, loosening a piece of information stored somewhere deep inside. "Juanita, please forgive me for asking," he inquired, and she nodded at him to continue, "but how old are you? When did this happen?"

Thinking about the question for a moment, she frowned. "*No lo sé, Señor Cody. Tengo sesenta y cinco años.*"

Cody did the math in his head, and the lightbulb suddenly flickered on. Frank could practically see it happen. "I can see the wheels turnin' a mile a minute, bro. Spill it."

Cody remained silent for a moment, thinking through the possibilities. "Dude, how well do you know World War II history?"

Frank shrugged his shoulders. "Uh, I dunno. Good as anyone else, I suppose. I mean, I *passed* history, so I know we fought the Nazis and then we won." He frowned. "Why? What are you thinking?"

Cody took a deep breath, preparing himself to explain. "Well, several Nazi party members fled Germany before we defeated the Axis powers in Europe. Some of the Nazis were infamous for what they did to the Jews in concentration camps."

Fernando and Juanita were peering from one to the other like they were watching a tennis match, struggling to understand exactly what the Americans were now speaking hurriedly about.

Cody paused, giving Frank the opportunity to ask, "What does this have to do with us or Peru?"

"Well, one of the more, let's say, well-known Nazi scientists fled to Argentina in the late forties, and again to Paraguay ten years later. He ended up in Brazil around 1960-something. Of course, the Mossad was all over that shit and tried to round him up. He allegedly drowned off the coast of Brazil in 1979."

Cody took another breath as the dots continued to connect themselves inside his head.

"Thing is, he was under surveillance off and on for the better part of a decade during the sixties. He moved around so much, and since Brazil is just east of here, I'm thinking maybe he had some sort of hideout here in Peru while he was evading the Mossad. Juanita's sixty-five, and the timeline adds up to be too damn close for coincidence."

Frank let it all sink in while did his best to translate to Juanita and Fernando. After he relayed what he could, he turned back to Cody. "Okay, but no offense, Cody, how the hell did you get from Juanita's lovely sounding childhood here"—Juanita nodded her head appreciatively in agreement—"to literal *Nazis*?"

Cody couldn't help the small slip of a smile before dropping the last bit of connective tissue. "His name was Dr. Josef Mengele, but he earned the nickname the Angel of Death. Translated into Spanish—"

"¡*Ángel de la muerte*!" both men spoke simultaneously.

Frank sat back in his chair, running his fingers through his long hair. "Holy shit, bro. How the hell did you remember that?"

Cody shrugged. "You might have *passed* history, but I majorly aced that shit. Bunch of useless facts rolling around up there," he said, tapping a finger to his head.

"Not so useless this time around," Frank replied.

Frank enjoyed reading up on military history as much as the next guy . . . as long as that next guy wasn't Cody, it seemed.

Cody continued. "Something clicked when Juanita was talking about angels and death. Add in South America and voilà. Speaking of which, you know Tessa's archaeology centers around biblical stuff, right? With a lot of angel emphasis too. How likely you think something like this is involved?"

Frank shrugged his shoulders again. "Beats me, but if it's the only thing we have to go on, then it's all we got for now." He turned back to Mamá Juanita. "Do you remember where this house was? Can you show me on the map?"

He pulled out his iPad and accessed his mapping application. He zoomed in on Peru and their current location and slid the smart device over to Juanita. She carefully looked at the map, trying to figure out how to navigate the software. After a moment or two, and with some help from Frank, she finally pointed to an area that seemed familiar to her from what she could remember.

At the very least, now they had something to go on as opposed to just running around searching for a needle in a haystack. Add in looking for it blind and that would more accurately reflect how Cody had felt just a few mere hours ago about their chances. But now, Cody felt a sense of hope rise up in him. Frank was right. It was *something*.

"Well, we've got our first thread to pull, but how we gonna pull it? That's at least fifteen miles from here. Through dense jungle, no less," Cody said, studying the area Juanita had pointed out.

"Leave that to me," Frank said, flashing his signature smile. He pulled out a small pouch from his backpack sitting on the floor next to the table. From the pouch he selected four $100 bills and looked to Fernando.

"Yo man, can you get us an old beat up four-by-four truck with this?" Frank asked.

Fernando's eyes went wide as he saw the pouch full of money. He didn't normally see people carrying that much American currency. He stuttered a little in reply.

"Uh, *sí*. I have it by *mañana*. You stay at my place tonight. Mamá Juanita insists. Isn't that right?"

The woman nodded. "It's no far from here."

Frank looked over at Cody and again flashed his signature smile as if to say, "Told you so."

After Cody and Frank expressed their thanks for Juanita's hospitality, they loaded back into Fernando's truck for the ride to his place.

Fernando owned, operated, and lived in his own hotel just outside of Iquitos. *Strange feat for a kid,* Cody thought as they pulled up. The hotel probably wouldn't have gotten a favorable rating on Yelp, but it fit Cody and Frank's needs perfectly. It stood at just two stories and had only ten rooms total, not including Fernando's personal room. The town of Iquitos lay only a few hundred yards away. The main road connected the two. It was small and, at the very least, out of the way as most travelers and tourists preferred to stay closer to something more densely populated with more attractions which, for Cody and Frank, suited them just fine. Just outside, the dense jungle loomed.

Fernando pulled his truck behind the hotel to park. The three men hopped out. Cody and Frank checked their surroundings carefully for any prying eyes that might see them carrying their equipment. After an initial scan, they moved their kit inside quickly. Fernando showed them to their rooms; both were on the first floor. Fernando had selected adjoining rooms for them, which was much appreciated in Cody's eyes. The closer he and Frank stuck together, the better. Once the equipment and bags were all inside one of the rooms, Fernando stuck out his hand toward Frank waiting for him to take it in return.

"That ain't gonna do, boy." Frank slapped his hand away and instead grabbed him around the midsection in a bear hug. Afterward, Frank slipped a couple bills into Fernando's shirt pocket. Confused, Fren looked down and pulled out the crisp currency. Before he could refuse or say anything, Frank winked at him and said, "For your troubles." Fernando looked at him with wide eyes before wrapping Frank in another hug as the boy's eyes welled up with tears.

"You good man, Frank," was all the boy could get out.

Fernando left the operators to do as they pleased. Cody had already begun setting up one room as a makeshift Tactical Operations Center, or TOC. He immediately closed the blinds and started pulling out their comms equipment, weapons, and assorted mission-critical gear to arrange it. *Just like old times.*

He pulled out the necessary electrical adapters to keep the radios charged or at least on a trickle charge so they'd be ready for the following day. Frank joined in, knowing the routine, and set up his individual kit. Pulling out his chest rig and ammo, he started loading magazines and stuffing them in their designated spots. He took another look at the map and saw it wasn't going to be an easy trek through the jungle. Hopefully Fren came through with the truck as promised; otherwise, their bodies would pay the price.

As for the adjoining room, they set it up for sleeping. Any piece of furniture that wasn't needed in the TOC got shoved into the sleeping room and out of the way. They'd have to share a queen-sized bed, which wouldn't be an easy task given Frank's large size, but at least there was a bed this time around. Satisfied, they each took a seat on one of the chairs in the equipment room and looked at each other.

"How you holdin' up?" Frank asked. He could see the worry in his brother's eyes.

Cody rubbed his eyes and then scratched his head absentmindedly. "I dunno, man. Better than expected, I suppose. I just can't believe this is happening. You know as well as I do. We better get on her trail quick or. . ." The rest of his sentence went unsaid but hung over them threateningly.

Frank took a heavy breath and nodded in agreement.

"Yeah, I know. We'll find her. It's what we do. Maybe we'll get lucky and run into her while we're driving through town."

Cody shot him a sarcastic look and quipped, "Don't count on it."

"For once I hope you're wrong, Cody. But if she is out there in harm's way, I want you to know I'd d*o anything* to try and save her. You know that, right?"

The gravity of what he had said clung to Cody's skin like perspiration. *Anything.* "I hope it doesn't come to that. For either of us. I owe you everything for this, man. Thank you."

Cody stood up and held out his fist for a fist bump, but Frank swatted his hand away and instead stood and wrapped him in a brother's embrace.

"You're damn right you do. Let's get some rack. We got a long day ahead of us."

19

Tom Lorry loved his job, except for days like this. Since coming to Renegade a few years prior, he'd always hoped there was something out there just like it, minus a few things here and there. After having spent the better part of a decade serving in the Ranger Regimental Reconnaissance Company, or RRRC, he knew there was more out there. After all, he'd seen just how far the spectrum could go when it came to covert action units. And as a ranger, he and his peers had always thought the Unit, as in the army's premier Special Mission Unit, nicknamed Delta Force, had been that very place.

It wasn't until years later he learned there were other places even more desirable. Places like ProCorp Applied Sciences. They had all the same funding and access to all the same training but without all the restrictions the military had to abide by. From his or any other action-oriented man's perspective, it was perfect. Except for those few things here and there. And one of those things was that he was still required to take care of paperwork.

It seemed as though he'd never escape it. Sure, Tom was the lowest man on the totem pole at Renegade and with that kind of role, usually he had to deal with the crap the more senior guys either didn't have to deal with or simply didn't want to. But knowing this didn't make it any better. Not that anyone made a big deal about seniority in Renegade, but Tom was a soldier's soldier. He knew his role.

Since Cody had left, everyone felt the impact. Tom had still been relatively new to the team when Cody was still around, so he didn't always see the innerworkings or some of the things for which he was responsible. But when Val had split all of Cody's duties between the three of them after Cody left, Tom suddenly knew the weight of Cody's previous role in a way he hadn't before. Losing a quarter of your team really made an impact, and Tom certainly felt it on days like today.

In the past, Cody had handled all of the inventory for the weapons, equipment, and vehicles used by Renegade. He'd been with Val since the beginning so he knew where everything was and where it came from, where it went when they got rid of it, and where they sold it off to. No matter what the "it" was. Val had assigned this to Tom in Cody's absence, saying he was hoping it would bring him up to speed faster. Tom knew better though but was too much of a soldier to say no.

He knew he was never going to know the things about Renegade Ranch that Cody knew, but saying no to a former Delta legend like Val Grayson was not an option—even if it was just silly paperwork. Tom had heard about Val all the way back when he was in the Rangers at the height of the Global War on Terror.

When he decided to leave the army, it had been his command sergeant major, or CSM, that had introduced them. Tom's CSM had been in the same platoon with Val back when they were in the same squadron in Delta. He'd heard Val was looking for good guys that would be a good fit for the role, and Tom was just about a perfect one—with the exception that Tom did not find himself well-suited to administrative tasks like inventory. He'd much rather be out in the shop working on his heavily modified RAZR UTV, shooting on the range, or lifting in the gym. Anything, really.

Nevertheless, it had to be done. Val needed it for the upcoming semiannual ProCorp meeting, and their numbers needed to be up to spec. He would be leaving before the day's end and wanted to make sure his team leader had the numbers good to go. Although the teams of ProCorp Applied Sciences division certainly enjoyed their sense of autonomy compared to military units, they still needed to account for their resources, expenditures, and issued equipment.

It was no small thing to outfit a private army comprised of some of the most lethal men the United States had ever produced. The owner of ProCorp, Longbow, ran a tight ship in that regard. Each team leader was allowed to run his team his own way, but they were far from invincible.

ProCorp held sensitive contracts across the globe and carried out blacker-than-black missions for both the government and private clients. Longbow and his second-in-command, Hedgehog, made it very clear they could not afford to have the spotlight shine on them. If the wrong people caught wind of what they did, the whole ball of yarn would unravel.

Tom walked through the halls of the main office building of Renegade Ranch and ended up in the armory. Tom always started with the ammo since it was the easiest. He began going through the spreadsheet that kept track of both incoming and outgoing ammunition and began to physically count the various pallets and stacks that were neatly organized by volume.

Oddly enough, it was off. Only by a few hundred, but it was never off. At least, not since he'd been on the team.

That's weird. Who would've signed out the ammo?

He checked the logs and found he had been the last person to sign anything out in the past week. He recalled clearly the range session and wondered if he'd made a mistake on the spreadsheet.

No, I remember double checking the amount, he thought to himself.

Baffled, he left the armory and went toward the front offices. There was one other person who knew this place like the back of her hand, and nothing got past her. He went down the hall and poked his head through the magnetically sealed secure doors leading into the lobby. In her usual spot, Lucy was there at her desk typing away.

"Hey, Tom. What's up?" she asked.

"Weird question for ya, Lucy. I was doing the inventory for Val, ya know, since he's got the semiannual meeting. Somethings off with the ammo count."

She peered up at him, pausing her work. "Not much of a question, but I'll bite. What do you mean 'off'?"

"We're missing a couple of cases. You know anything about it?"

She contemplated this for a moment. "Oh, you know what? I did run into Frank early this morning in the armory. I saw him loading up some ammo and grabbing some gear. He said he was helping Cody out with some training. Maybe you could try and give him a call? He might have grabbed some and forgot to sign it out."

Tom scratched his head and scrunched his face. That didn't add up. Frank didn't just make silly mistakes like that.

"Hmm, okay. I'll give him a shout. Did he say anything else or mention any other equipment he was going to use?" Tom asked.

"Yeah, actually. He asked me for $2,000 from the safe. Said he was going to buy a scope from Cody."

Tom frowned. "Okay. Thanks a lot, Lucy," he said with a wave.

Another red flag. Tom knew Cody wasn't much of a scope guy. He preferred the smaller, lighter red dots over the heavier-magnified optics. *This is getting weird.*

Tom headed back to the armory and began searching around for anything out of place. Sure enough, Frank's kit bags had been taken out of his cage. He moved to the electronics cage next, which—aside from the ammo—was the next most expensive stuff they had in the building. Two complete deployment sets of radios and a full rig of surveillance equipment was missing. Tom checked the sign out log. Nothing.

Why would Frank need all that for training? Was he in that big of a rush that he didn't sign it out?

Something wasn't adding up. He decided to call Frank. But when he tried, the phone went straight to voicemail. He couldn't help the weight that had settled in the pit of his stomach.

Try Cody. He'll know what's up, he thought.

Again, straight to voicemail.

Tom felt wedged between a rock and a hard place. He didn't necessarily want to run to Val at the first sign of trouble, but this had stench to it he didn't like. He walked back to the front lobby again, phone in hand. Lucy turned at the sound of the door opening behind her.

"Any luck? You get ahold of Frank?" she asked.

"No. Straight to voicemail, and the same for Cody. Did you know a bunch of surveillance equipment, radios, and the drone are gone?"

Her face paled a little. "What?!"

"Frank mention any of that?"

She shook her head.

Decision made. He ran a hand down the side of his face. "Okay, I need to call Val. Do me a favor please? Call the training facility where Cody works and see if anyone down there can get ahold of them. I just want to get to the bottom of it, but I've got a bad feeling about this."

"Will do," she replied and promptly searched her contacts, picking up the desk phone.

Tom stared at his phone for a few seconds. He knew involving Val would likely escalate things. A case of rifle ammo was one thing; that was only five hundred rounds. But several thousands of dollars' worth of custom electronics, some of which had military-grade encryption built into them was something entirely different. That was something that needed to be accounted for immediately.

Finally, he tapped Val's number in his digital contact card. The phone began to ring, which Val answered immediately. Tom took a deep breath and quickly caught him up to speed.

"Alright, I'm heading that way," the gruff voice replied.

It hadn't been more than twenty minutes and had just started to get dark outside when he strode in. Tom and Lucy stood in the front lobby waiting for him.

"Well, any news or word?" Val asked.

"Yes and no," Lucy answered.

Val raised an eyebrow.

"I called the facility where Cody works. Frank had told me he was going to help him out today training some cops. But Cody never showed up for work. He had a class scheduled and everything."

"That's not like him," Val replied, arms folded.

"Agreed. We tried calling Tessa," Tom said. "We figured maybe she would know what's up with him, but there was no answer there either."

Val suddenly remembered the invitation to her BBQ celebration.

"Oh yeah, she had some big news with her work. She was going on an archaeological dig to somewhere in South America I wanna say."

A soft tone alerting Lucy she had an incoming email diverted her attention. She looked down at the screen and skimmed through it quickly in disbelief.

"Uh, Val. I just got an invoice from Dirty Mike's secretary. It's for transportation services and fuel."

"Didn't we pay that already? Last time we flew with him was a few months ago," Val asked, frowning.

"Yeah, I did. This flight happened today. Notes says two passengers. Destination: Peru."

Val snapped his fingers. "Peru! That's where Tessa was going. Call Mike's secretary right now. I want either her or Mike in the next two minutes."

"You think they went to Peru with all that kit? For what?" Tom asked Val as Lucy walked briskly back to the desk phone.

"Who knows? Maybe Tessa was in some kind of trouble. The only thing we know right now is that we don't know anything."

The two Renegades remained quiet while Lucy was on the phone, which only lasted a couple minutes before she hung up.

"Okay, so here's the deal. She said Cody called Mike early this morning and told him you had tasked him with an S&R mission in Peru." She looked at Val. "Mike picked up both Cody and Frank, and they're on the way to Peru now, likely pretty close if not there already. She's going to try and get ahold of them. At the very least, she'll have Mike get in touch with you as soon as he can."

"What are you up to, Cody?" Val asked to no one directly, shaking his head as he brought one hand to his chin and rubbed it in thought.

"What do you wanna do, boss?" Tom asked.

After thinking a moment, he spoke up. "Pack your kit. We need to be ready to roll as soon as possible. Either Cody has gone completely rogue and somehow pulled Frank into it, or Tessa is in some seriously deep shit. Either way, we need to get down there ASAP."

20

After a solid six hours of sleep, Cody and Frank arose fresh and ready for the day's events. Both focused on their respective duties and responsibilities. Frank started on the coffee while Cody downloaded the mapping software to the iPad and wrist-mounted GPS devices. He had to estimate the area they'd need and chose to go slightly bigger just in case. While it took up more digital space on the devices, at least they didn't run the risk of walking off the map and getting lost.

After squaring away the navigation, Cody continued down his mental checklist, focusing on the radios. Luckily, he only had to worry about two of them this time around and quickly function-checked them both. He programmed primary, secondary, and tertiary channels into each and ensured they had a full battery before stuffing his into the radio pouch on his chest rig.

Cody laid the other next to Frank's kit and grabbed one spare battery for each. He stored the spare safely in his assault pack, in its usual place, laying Frank's spare within arm's reach.

Frank had managed to scrounge up some eggs and bacon Fernando had left in the outdated fridge in the other room. He set a plate on the counter with a cup of coffee, whistling to catch Cody's attention.

"Got it," Cody acknowledged with a shout back, continuing his last-minute checks and inspections.

Lastly, Renegade 02 slid his MCX from the Vertx backpack and turned on the red-dot optic. He inserted a fresh battery into the IR laser and switched the setting from "visible" to "check function." He worked the action a few times to make sure everything was properly lubricated, locking the bolt to the rear on the last cycle before attaching the SureFire SPS suppressor.

Cody looked around, searching for a loaded magazine he'd set aside. Sliding the magazine into its proper place, he released the bolt chambering a round in one fluid motion. After a quick press check, he ensured the weapon was on safely and then laid it down atop his chest rig and assault pack.

Content with his setup, Cody walked to the other room and started on the breakfast plate and coffee while Frank walked to the makeshift TOC, performing his own routine that was just as meticulous as Cody's in terms of setting up his fighting loadout.

They both knew it had to be an extension of their body in order for them to fight effectively. Frank didn't check the battery on his radio, trusting Cody wholeheartedly for having checked it already. He secured it on the left side of his chest rig and stored the battery carefully in his backpack. After checking his mags and loading his SPR, he laid it and the rest of his equipment next to the door and joined Cody in the adjacent room to finish off his food.

The morning was short on conversation, both Renegades focused on the trek to come. After stuffing down the last of their meal, they opened their duffle bags to change into appropriate jungle attire. Cody quickly pulled on a pair of dark green Kuhl pants and an earth-toned color, four-way stretch button-up shirt.

With any luck, they might pass for adventurers from the States fresh out the closest REI. He figured it would draw less attention than a full-blown combat uniform.

He slid his stiff nylon belt through the belt loops of his injection-molded holster and spare magazine pouch. Not wanting to draw too much attention, he pulled an oversized plaid cover shirt out to wear over his chest rig during the drive. It acted as a sort of camouflage to anyone driving past.

Finally, he pulled his old, worn, and perfectly broken-into Renegade baseball hat: a simple black hat with a small sewn-in American flag and hard-earned salt stains. For Cody, it was standard to wear on operations that didn't require a more clandestine approach.

As Frank was getting dressed, they heard a knock at the door. Instinctively suspicious, Cody's hand found the rough grip of his Glock. Frank zipped his pants and walked to the door, opening it just a crack while his pistol was concealed behind his leg.

Frank threw the door open when he saw their company. "'Sup, Fren. C'mon in. Ain't much breakfast left, but you're welcome to it," Frank said, allowing his guard down a bit.

"*No, gracias. Tengo tus llaves,*" Fren said, tossing Frank the keys.

"Sweet. What'd we get?" Frank asked, looking down at the key to see what make the vehicle was.

"Nissan Xterra. Tía Juanita call in favor for you. *¿Bueno?*" he asked, looking sheepishly at the pair of men, waiting for their response.

Frank looked at Cody, smiling wide, and found Cody doing the same. Fren could tell they were satisfied, causing him to break out in a large grin at their reactions.

"Oh yeah. *Muy bueno, mi amigo,*" Cody replied.

"Ugly. Run good," Fren stated in a thick accent with a shrug of his shoulder.

"Even better," Frank replied.

After Fren left, Cody stood in their gear room over organized piles of nylon packs, bags, and weapons' cases. He grabbed his things carefully, slid the MCX rifle back into the discreet, short rifle case, and pulled the zipper closed. Next, he slung his assault pack over his shoulder and was ready to go.

Frank had done the same. In less than sixty seconds, they were out the door. Fren even came back to escort them down the hallway and out the back, which he did carefully as to not draw them any attention.

Outside, the SUV was exactly as described. An early 2000-year model, it sported a heavy rust color mixed with what was once a nice silver. Cody opened the back liftgate to find a spare gas can already topped off, strapped down, and ready for use. He tossed his assault pack in and clambered in after it.

Frank walked to the driver's side, sliding his backpack to the last compartment. He closed the door and plopped down behind the wheel, praying it would still start. Much to his amazement, it fired to life relatively easily and sounded even better than expected.

Frank slammed the driver door shut and rolled down the manual window as Cody jumped in the passenger seat. They preferred traveling in this arrangement, Frank feeling most comfortable behind the wheel with Cody liking to keep an eye out for anything unusual. They found both their respective duties soothed any potential nerves.

With the vehicle idling, Cody felt it an appropriate time to say a quick silent prayer. Taking everything into consideration, he closed his eyes and addressed his Maker.

Lord, guide me on this journey. May You make my legs swift, my gun steady, and my mind clear. Please allow Frank and I to safely extract my sister from danger. May Your will be done. Amen.

The whole thing took less than ten seconds, and before he could open his eyes, he felt a calming sensation flow over his mind and soul like someone had pulled a cool blanket over him. Cody couldn't be sure whether it was from the prayer or the fact he was back in the saddle again. Either way, it was comforting.

He'd hoped Frank hadn't taken notice, but he wasn't that lucky. Opening his eyes, he turned to find Frank staring at him from the driver's seat.

"You good, bro?" Frank asked.

"Never better. Let's get to it," Cody shortly replied.

With a general wave of goodbye toward Fren and the hotel, Frank put the truck in gear while Cody rolled down the window to take in all the scenery and scents Peru had to offer. Truthfully, he wasn't impressed at first. Perhaps it was the nerves of being vulnerable in civilization getting the best of him. It wasn't exactly like Cody was in a people-friendly mood, nor was he there to sightsee. Luckily, the closer they got to their insertion point, the more nature took over the scenery, and the easier it became to take in Peru's beauty.

Cody was nearly glued to the map, making sure they stayed on course. He was slightly apprehensive about trekking through the jungle, trying to find an old Nazi's abandoned house with little-to-no real actionable intel. Something told him he was on the right path, but the analytical side of his mind desperately needed more.

The two Renegades talked little during the drive; the majority of the conversation was taken up by directions navigating their route. After thirty minutes of drive time, Cody checked the mapping software on Frank's iPad and realized they were at the infiltration point.

"Yo, looks like we're here. Find a decent spot to pull off the road and into some decent concealment. Fifty yards into the bush sound good?" Cody asked.

"Yeah, I'm good with that. Lemme find a good spot," Frank replied, looking around on both sides of the road, trying to find a suitable spot to stage the truck. Seeing a spot he liked, Frank waited a couple seconds to make sure no one else was on the road. Satisfied, he guided the steering wheel gently to the left, pulling off the road and into the thick triple-canopy rainforest.

As the rusty old vehicle came to a stop, neither Frank nor Cody wasted any time. They hopped out of the SUV as it came to a jolting halt. Cody opened the passenger door directly behind him and grabbed his backpack. With the practiced precision of a man who had done this more than once, he donned his equipment in his usual ritual.

Frank made his way to the back of the truck and dug through his pack to find the oversized camouflage netting he had prepacked to help conceal vehicles. He started covering his side of the vehicle while Cody finished setting himself up before switching roles. Frank made sure the side release buckles of his chest rig were securely clasped as Cody secured his side of the netting. To the well-trained eye, one could tell this wasn't their first rodeo. They moved with the efficiency only experience could offer.

Cody checked the handheld Garmin GPS device and ensured the satellite linked correctly before stuffing it inside a pouch on his chest rig. "My GPS is up. Yours good?" he asked.

Frank stared at the small LCD screen, waiting for it to acquire signal. After several seconds, the bars finally filled, giving him some relief.

"Yep, took a second, but I'm up. You on point?"

"Yeah. I set a waypoint for the Mengele house, or where it should be at least. We're not really expecting hostile contact, so let's not kill ourselves with the pace," Cody suggested.

"Good idea, bro," Frank said as he grabbed their weapons and slung his rifle over his shoulder.

Cody slung his suppressed rifle, adjusting the two-point sling to be snug against his body. Gaining his bearings, he looked up from the GPS and started walking through the thick foliage, Frank following close behind.

They maintained a watchful eye and kept both ears open as they fought their way through the humidity and intense undergrowth. Cody did his best to select the least taxing route as he and Frank crossed small streams, deadfall, and any potential natural dangers like steep elevation changes or loose rocks and debris.

Despite his best efforts, after more than an hour into the journey, Cody found himself a little more winded than he expected. His anxiety had been up so high over the last two days, he was burning the candle at both ends. Truth be told, his worry about Tessa's well-being was eating him up just as much as the environment.

Frank couldn't help but notice his friend's anxiety and thought there wasn't a better time to take advantage of bringing it up than right now. They had just stopped to take a quick water break, both Renegades sitting side by side on one of the many fallen trees. The encompassing jungle made sure its voice was heard, the noise of its wild birds and other critters living their simple life echoing around them. Cody listened to the sounds diligently, listening for any unordinary ones, as he sipped water from the water bladder. His unslung rifle laid across his lap.

He took a deep breath, trying to lower his heart rate a little at the prospect of what lay ahead. Frank gulped down a few ounces from his own hydration pouch and peered at Cody carefully. Realizing he was being watched at extremely close range, Cody snapped his head in Frank's direction with a puzzled look.

"Yes?" Cody asked with half a smile.

Frank maintained his serious gaze. "Dude, we need to talk."

"Now?" he said, surprised at the timing.

"Good a time as any," Frank said, his arms spread out to his sides, looking around as if mocking the fact that anyone would be nearby.

"Uh, okay. What's up?" Cody asked. He had a feeling he knew where this was headed.

"Listen, don't take this the wrong way, but we both know it's been a while since you've been in the field, and I'm worried about you. I know this is stressful, but I'm just used to seeing you in control and right now, you're not seeming it."

Frank paused a moment, collecting his thoughts and taking a deep breath. His exhale was louder than normal like someone who was about to break some bad news.

"I trust you and would do anything for you," Frank continued. "That's why I'm here. But you aren't acting like the Cody I know. You're the one who taught me to think first, then act. You're different this time around, and I'm worried it's because of—"

Cody cut him off before he could finish the sentence.

"Because of what, Frank? Because my wife and daughter are dead?"

Frank looked at him with a gentle gaze. "I was going to say because of the stress. I'm worried your emotional baggage is weighing you down. You can't see it, but you're so fuckin' worried about trying to save Tessa that I'm afraid you're going to make a mistake out here if, God forbid, she *is* in trouble. It's just the two of us, bro. Not to mention we're both probably off Renegade forever because of this stunt. I don't want to see you get hemmed up by some corrupt local PD or get yourself killed chasing ghosts."

Cody rolled his eyes. He looked up to the thick canopy above them and closed his eyes. How could he explain what he saw? How could he get Frank to feel what he felt? He'd already explained it to him before, but any reasonable person would've thought he was crazy the first time around. How could he blame Frank for thinking the same?

Am I a liability? Have I lost it?

He opened his eyes and turned back to Frank. "Listen dude, there's no way for me to thank you enough for backing me up on this. Having said that, there's also no way for me to get you to understand what I saw in that dream. I know what I saw, and I'm seeing this mission through one way or the other."

Cody held his friend's gaze, trying to read his thoughts. Frank did the same, hoping his best friend wasn't lost forever, unable to escape the past. Frank brought his hands to his face and wiped his brow.

"I'll follow you till the end, you know that. You're my brother. I just want to make sure you ain't letting all the extra stuff cloud your judgement. That's all," Frank said as sincerely as he could.

Cody nodded. "You're right though, Frank. I am out of practice. It's been . . . wow, a year and a half since I was actually in the field. So if at any point I put us in danger unnecessarily or pose a real risk to getting Tessa out of whatever mess she got herself into," he paused before looking right into Frank's eyes. "I personally authorize you to pop smoke and do what you have to, whether that means leaving me behind or taking charge of this whole operation."

The two men stared at one another, locked in a hardened understanding, before Frank nodded.

"I just want my sister back," Cody said softly. He stood and extended his hand to Frank. Frank took it and was pulled from the fallen log to his feet with their classic arm-wrestle handshake.

Releasing each other from their grips, Cody checked the GPS to see how much longer they had to walk to their destination. With at least another hour left on their trek, Cody and Frank adjusted their kit, tightened the straps to their packs, and set out again through the dense foliage. The humidity soaked their lightweight clothes, their nylon chest rigs and small assault packs heavy while battling the thick undergrowth. Neither knew what to expect as they made their way closer to their objective.

Cody hoped for the next pulled thread to lead him to his sister, although he was trying not to rely on high hopes. Deep down, he knew it wouldn't be that easy. Frank, on the other hand, was still acting like he suspected they'd find nothing and instead spent their journey sincerely hoping Tessa wasn't in trouble in the first place. After all, finding one specific woman in the depths of the Amazon would be near impossible without some serious help. Let alone doing so on a time crunch.

After checking the GPS again, the two-man Renegade team had to come within two hundred yards of Mengele's house before they spotted its low-sloped roof through the thick leafage. Cody used his hand to signal Frank, who made his way next to Cody. "We're two hundred yards out. Nonverbal from here, low and slow," Cody said in a near whisper.

Frank nodded in agreement as both men took a little more caution approaching their first objective. They carefully selected where each foot was placed, ensuring no excessive noise was made, while their hands held their rifles tightly, each ready to be used at a moment's notice.

Fifty yards from the house, Cody held his hand in a closed fist above his head, telling Frank to hold up. They both stood silently, taking in the environment to see if anything was out of place. Birds chirped in the distance, and all the familiar sounds of nature continued their usual melody.

Cody took a knee and remained motionless for the next ten minutes. Shortly thereafter, Frank quietly joined him, five feet away.

"You see or hear something?" Frank asked quietly.

"No, just being extra cautious. You ready?" Cody replied.

Frank nodded firmly. "Let's do it."

Both Renegades stood, clutched their weapons a little tighter, and continued their advance. Cody saw the rest of the dilapidated house first. One would almost miss it in the overgrowth without knowing its general location. It was clear the jungle had nearly reclaimed it in the decades since its abandonment. Thick bushes and vines grew up around the sides, showing there had been no clear signs of disturbance for a long time.

They approached the house from the rear, holding their customized rifles at the low, ready in the event an unseen threat showed itself. Cody pointed out potential danger areas with his nondominant hand so Frank knew where to direct the majority of his focus.

They circled around the back of the house counterclockwise until they got to the front. The door had been kicked in what seemed to be years earlier. As they approached, the two men could barely see five feet inside the structure.

Cody felt his heart rate stabilize, his subconscious taking over as he made his way to the entrance. Frank followed suit and took a position opposite Cody. They stood across one another on each side of the door.

Both pointed their rifles into the house, activating their attached weapon lights. Instantly the dark interior lit up as a thousand lumens illuminated the front room. Cody began slicing his piece of the pie, slowly, one step at a time, allowing him to see more of what was inside.

Frank did the same, waiting for the signal to enter. Cody waved the barrel of his MCX up, then down, giving Frank the indicator he was waiting for. Frank flowed into the open space like water, covering his sector of fire. The larger Renegade stopped at his point of domination, processing the information around him.

Frank stood a couple feet just off the wall, scanning the rest of the room. One thing was certain, nobody had been in here for a long time. The smell of rotting wood furniture filled his nostrils as he listened intently for any sound that might be out of place. Cody had done the same on the other side. Once the first room was clear, he and Cody stepped up to the next door to repeat the process.

Soon they had cleared the remainder of the house in the same methodical and practiced manner. Upon clearing the last room, they each lowered their weapons and relaxed their aggressive posture.

"Looks like a dry hole to me, bro," Frank said, stating the obvious.

Cody didn't reply and began searching the forgotten house for any clue that might lead him to the next step. Or, more importantly, Tessa. Mengele's house reminded him of all the abandoned homes in Austin he once had to check for homeless inhabitants.

Frank watched Cody turn over old tables and open drawers and cabinets like he was conducting a Sensitive Site Exploitation, or SSE. Frank eventually joined him. Neither were entirely sure of what they were looking for.

After a few minutes, Frank leaned against one of the doorways that led to a bedroom. Cody stopped his search and ran one hand absentmindedly through his hair.

"Whatcha looking for?" Frank asked, watching his friend closely.

"Not sure, but I'll know it when I see it," Cody replied matter-of-factly.

Cody remained standing in the living room and found himself staring at Mengele's bookshelf and reading collection. He found it surreal to be standing in the house of a Nazi war criminal decades after his escape and ultimate demise. It was an interesting thing to say the least, seeing how a hunted man lived once upon a time, looking at what he didn't deem important enough to take with him.

His eyes scanned the old books sitting on the shelves of the bookcase. Suddenly something struck him as odd. He began looking around the rest of the house like he'd dropped something important on the floor and was unable to find it.

"What's up? You lose something?" Frank questioned, watching Cody's curious behavior.

"No, but I might have found something," Cody replied with fervor.

Frank sprang from the doorway and looked around as Cody pointed all around him.

"Frank, what do you see?" Cody asked.

"Uh, I dunno. A fucked-up, rundown abandoned house that used to belong to a war criminal?" he replied.

"Exactly. Everything is torn apart by squatters, scavengers, or the environment, but take a look at the bookshelf." Cody made his way to the six-foot wooden structure against the wall.

Frank closed the distance to it, trying to connect the same dots as Cody. There were still several books on the floor, though one was left on the shelf undisturbed. Although covered in dust the bookshelf had remained relatively unscathed compared to the rest of the house.

Cody started wiping the dust from a few books to closer inspect them, several falling apart at the spine and their pages falling to the ground. After flipping through three or four, he grabbed for a fifth on the top edge of its spine, but to Cody's surprise, it refused to leave its place. Like on a hinge only, the top shifted a few degrees, followed by a solid click.

Frank's eyes went wide with amazement and instinctively lifted his rifle as the bookshelf rotated away from the wall on hidden hinges. Cody smiled ear to ear, knowing he'd found the next thread to pull.

"Dry hole, huh?" Cody said with no small amount of satisfaction.

"Why am I not surprised a Nazi had a safe room," Frank muttered as he used the muzzle of his gun to push open the door.

Both Renegades illuminated the downward-leading staircase with their weapon lights, senses on full alert. There was no telling who or what was down there.

Frank took point down the staircase, careful not to slip and covered the unknown with his muzzle. Truthfully, he was more concerned about the stairs holding his weight. At the bottom, the room opened up suddenly to reveal a twenty-by-twenty-foot room with an eight-foot ceiling. It was like a garage with a hidden door right under a house. Which, in this case, it pretty much was.

The air was damp and dank, though not quite as bad as the rest of the house upstairs. The lack of humidity did a decent job of preserving what lay inside.

Frank reached the bottom and lowered his rifle. It was empty, save for the work desk with scattered papers, journals, maps, pens, a filing cabinet in the corner, and a few boxes scattered on the ground.

Cody made his way down right behind Frank and kept his weapon light activated and pointed directly up, using it as an umbrella of light.

"What in the hell is all this?" Frank asked, sifting through the old papers and maps on the table.

He couldn't read the writing, as it was all in German. Among the writing were hand drawn pictures and sketches of human fetuses in the mother's womb.

"You weren't kidding, Cody. The Angel of Death was one sick bastard."

"Yeah, he was. He did all sorts of experiments on the Jews trying to perfect abortions and all sorts of other dark shit. There's a reason they wanted his ass so bad. Can you read any of this?"

Frank shook his head no, grabbing some other pages from the desk and flipping a couple of them over. Several revealed what looked to be maps. Cody recognized a few of the prominent land features from his topographical study that he conducted on the flight to Peru.

Mengele had circled three separate areas on the map within fifteen miles from his house. Cody lowered the map and studied it closely. *What were you looking for, dirtbag?* His mind raced as Frank continued to search the documents and sketches looking for anything useful. Suddenly, it connected.

The Nazi party, especially Hitler, was obsessed with the occult later on in the war. In perhaps what might have been desperation, they searched for ancient artifacts they believed might give them an edge over their enemies. Hollywood had even fictionalized similar stories like *Raiders of the Lost Ark,* which was one of Cody and Tessa's favorites growing up.

Did Mengele continue his search after the war? Was he looking for a secret weapon or some sort of lost knowledge to continue his experiment? Maybe that's what he was doing all this time in Peru.

Had he found something? Something like what Tessa's researching?

Cody took off his backpack and pulled the iPad from its protective case. He pulled up the high-res map and set it down on the table next to Mengele's paper map. Once he was sure the areas were correct, he retraced the same areas of interest onto his digital version and saved the overlay drawings.

"What do we got?" Frank asked, leaning over.

"I can't read what he wrote but it looks like Mengele was looking for something out here rather than just trying to hide. Frank, the Nazis were into the supernatural and thought they could find something to give them the upper hand later in the war." He jabbed the map with his finger. "What if Mengele didn't stop looking?"

Frank pondered the question before replying. "Yeah, but why? The war was over by then."

"Beats me. Why does any evil scientist do what they do? We're talking about a real-life Dr. Frankenstein, man. Maybe he was looking for supernatural stuff to help him with his experiments," Cody retorted.

"Yeah, I suppose that's possible, but how probable is that really?" Frank's skepticism was coming in loud and clear.

Cody raised his hands in mock surrender. "I don't know, man, but I'd like to at least check out these areas he was interested in." He couldn't help the hope that crept into his voice.

"What's there?" Frank asked, staring down at the map.

"From what I can see on the iPad, not much. Except for this one," he said, pointing out one area in particular. "It's out in the jungle a ways, but there's something weird on the topo. Like a waterfall or something. I think we should check it out," Cody said, zooming in on the digital image.

"I dunno, bro. I mean, yeah, we found some weird and cool shit about a historical figure, but I don't think that's got anything to do with Tessa. Kind of a stretch, don't you think?"

"What else do we have to go on?" Cody asked sternly.

"I think we should try something else. How is a dead occultic Nazi's map going to help us find Tessa?"

Cody sighed. Maybe it was a bit farfetched. "Look, we've been in the country less than twenty-four hours," Frank continued. "I told Juanita and Fernando to ask around and see if they can dig anything up. You know how it is—the locals know everything about what's going on in their area. No one can hide anything from them. I only let you drag me here to this dump first because, not gonna lie, I was hoping for some zombie Nazi action or something."

Cody peered at him. "You watched *Raiders* recently, didn't you?"

Frank shrugged, unabashed. "Don't hate. It's a flawless film, and you know it." Cody laughed. "But seriously, I think we should hear what the locals say first," Frank finished.

"You're right, good call. And here I was worried you'd slow me down," Cody shot back.

Frank rolled his eyes while pulling his phone from his chest rig. He'd missed a couple messages from Fernando while they had been searching the house.

"Well well well."

"What's up?" Cody asked, looking up from the map.

"Fernando might have found something. Said he started asking around town like I asked him to, and he said a friend of his overheard his uncle talking a couple days ago about working in some cave out in the jungle. Several Americans are out there as well. They're all staying at an upscale hotel on the other side of town."

"Well now, that does sound promising. Let's wrap up here and get moving. Maybe we can collect some intel and see where this leads."

"Agreed," Frank replied.

Cody left Mengele's map on the table. He took one last look at the writings and saw a leather book underneath a few shuffled papers. Curious, he grabbed it and wiped it clean. As he flipped through the handwritten pages, he realized it was Mengele's personal journal. The writing was German of course, with only a few sketches found throughout.

Who knows what dark secrets are in here? he thought. Then he paused. He shoved it in his backpack to take with him. Perhaps it would be worth something to the right guy.

21

Joshua Michaels landed in Peru and checked into his hotel room without any issue whatsoever. He'd only been with North Spear a few years, but he knew they really had their stuff together when it came to pulling strings and getting things done. Their seriously deep pockets certainly helped. Which is why when he'd been contacted by Mr. Adams directly and instructed to fly to Peru and relieve Bart Cox, he hadn't questioned it.

Joshua had not worked with Bart directly, but he knew his reputation. He was known in North Spear management as a man who could get things done, so he was quite surprised to find that Bart was being relieved in this manner. Hopefully Bart saw this for what it was and wouldn't hold any grudges. This was business after all, and they were peers.

Michaels walked down the stairs into the lobby where he saw a pair of men. They wore cargo pants and polos with the North Spear logo. They must have been his security escort. He walked to them and greeted them in the typical fashion you'd expect from an executive.

"Where is Bart? I thought he was going to meet me?"

"Sir, Mr. Cox sends his apologies. There's been a recent discovery at the site that required his attention. He asked that we escort you to him so he can show you around Azazel more thoroughly."

"Very well. Let's get on with it."

Joshua found the drive quite scenic, though he much preferred his concrete jungle to the real one. At least in his usual jungle there weren't as many bugs, and the roads weren't as rough nor the air so humid. He was certainly grateful for the air conditioning inside the Land Rover. Hopefully he would be able to clear up whatever mess had transpired and be out of here in a couple of weeks.

At long last, the winding drive through the jungle came to a close. The security men drove as close as they could to the entrance and then led him inside. Though he was not comfortable outdoors as he was in somewhere like his corporate suite, he couldn't help but be impressed with the magnitude and scale of both the waterfall and entrance of the cave.

The escort showed him the way through the twisting tunnels to the main chamber just outside the temple. As he walked, they passed the tents and various teams working and moving about. Things seemed to be in order, which was a good sign. Directly ahead there was a tent larger than the rest of them. Just as he identified it, the flap flew open and Bart Cox exited.

Bart was not happy—as to be expected. However, like the professional he was, he concealed it behind a fake smile. If Joshua noticed the façade, he didn't say anything. Bart closed the distance to the newcomer, arm extended for a handshake.

"Mr. Michaels, I presume?"

"Indeed, and you must be Cox," he said, grasping and shaking his hand firmly.

"I am. Please, come inside," he said, arm extended toward the tent flap. "Let's talk a bit before I show you around."

Inside, the pair sat across from one another, legs crossed in their respective chairs. Both knew the game and were trying to feel each other out. Michaels wondered just how tight Bart was going to hold onto this project.

"Would like something to drink?" Bart asked. "Coffee? Tea? Anything?"

"Tea would be nice. One sugar and cream," Michaels replied.

Bart yelled for a security member, who promptly took the order and left the tent.

"So let's get to it, shall we? What seems to be the holdup out here?" Michaels asked.

Bart pretended to think hard and shamedly about it. "Difficult to say, really. Some weeks ago, I brought on a young archaeologist, Tessa Willis. She has been on our radar for some time given her areas of study and expertise. Her skills proved useful in helping us learn the secret to the Nephilim tomb; however, she abruptly decided to abandon her work and ultimately this project, which, as you know, Mr. Adams will not accept."

"I see. Has she specified why?"

"She has not."

"Where is she now?"

"She is still at her hotel, refuses to leave her room," he lied easily.

"How close are we to opening the tomb?"

"I honestly feel we're on the brink of a discovery, which I believe is why she wants to quit."

Joshua frowned. "How do you mean?"

"I suspect some form of . . . espionage. Either someone else has gotten to her or she realizes the worth of what's at stake. Either way, she's the linchpin. She holds the cards and, quite frankly, she has us by the balls," Bart lied again.

"I'll see what I can do about a replacement for her. In the meantime, I'll have the lawyers draft up some paperwork in regard to suing her into oblivion. Perhaps that will motivate her to continue."

Bart cracked a smile. "Be aware, she's quite stubborn."

Just then, the security man entered and set down the cup of tea. "I have ways of dealing with that," Michaels replied before taking a sip.

The North Spear executive made a face of disgust at his drink while Bart did his best for his face to not flush in anger. The mere presence of Michaels had been nearly enough to send him into a blind rage, but he had held it together thus far. *Just a little longer now.*

After all, Bart wasn't going to allow him to just waltz in here and simply take control. Not after everything Bart had done to get here. Bart was not going to let go. Not now, not ever.

"Ugh, you call this tea, Cox?"

Bart did not respond.

"I want to see the tomb in question. I understand a new discovery was made recently. Is that so?" Michaels asked.

"As a matter of fact, it is. Please, allow me to show you around the temple," Bart replied, faking the enthusiasm.

Both men stood, Michaels eagerly exited, brushing off his shoulders in fear of ruining his new suit. Bart remained in the tent for a moment. He opened one of his trunks and found the item he wanted, stuffing it quietly into his pocket.

They entered the underground cave temple. Light, meaningless conversation filled the silence as Bart showed him the way to the most recent excavation discovery. The small opening the crew had uncovered had been enlarged and the debris moved out of the way, allowing both men to simply walk in.

The crew had erected light panels on tripods, which eliminated the use of flashlights and flooded the room with gleams. Bart waved the team out and told them to give them a few minutes. Once they had left, Joshua Michaels walked over and stood in front of one of the stone statues, marveling at the detailed carvings. It was clear this one in particular fascinated him.

"What is this room exactly?" Joshua asked.

"My team tells me this was likely a ceremonial burial chamber for the tribal chiefs who gave their daughters to be either sacrificed or married to a Nephilim. The statues depict them as warriors to honor them."

"I see," Joshua snorted. "The ones that give away their daughters are the ones to be presented as warriors while the ones sacrificed, well . . . Just a case of bad luck and that's about it. Ironic, wouldn't you say?" he said, laughing like it was the funniest joke he had heard.

Bart just smiled. "Quite," he replied, and Joshua shook his head as if Bart didn't get the punch line.

"Anyway, have you had any luck with uncovering these tombs?" the man asked, but Bart shook his head.

"No, they're constructed the exact same as the giant's tomb, just scaled down."

"I like this one," Joshua said, staring into the eyes of the statue. "Perhaps I'll have this one removed from the wall and take it with me when I'm done. I believe it would look quite fitting in my flat. Once it's cleaned up, of course."

Bart stood on the other side of the tomb at Michaels's three o'clock. Bart reached into his pocket and felt his hands wrap around the grip of the small pistol. He slid the firearm out with ease and pointed it directly at Michaels's head only a few feet away.

"What do you think, Cox?" he asked as his head turned toward Bart.

"I think you're not taking anything from me," he said before pulling the trigger.

The report was deafening. Bart watched as blood and brain matter sprayed out the back of Joshua Michaels's skull as it followed the path of the bullet. The North Spear executive was dead before he even had time to react. It hadn't helped him any when he had tried to take a step back right before the high-speed projectile entered the bridge of his nose. That momentum continued as his body slumped unnaturally backward toward the tomb of the tribal chief.

Bart's heart beat like never before. He felt truly alive, powerful, aroused even. He looked down at his would-be replacement in elation as the massive headwound bled profusely. Suddenly, Bart heard stone grinding against itself as the grooves channeled the blood into the ancient mechanism. It slid head to foot with ease as Bart's eyes wide in amazement.

That was it. This was the key. Blood. Human *blood.*

Bart could hear the footsteps approaching quickly, no doubt to investigate the gunshot. He was so blinded by rage he hadn't considered the consequences of murdering his replacement. Quickly he reached down and rubbed his hands in Joshua Michaels's blood and wiped it across his face, just before a few security men ran inside weapons drawn.

"Mr. Cox, are you okay?" they asked, unable to take their eyes off the dead body.

"Yes, yes, please help me," he feigned, leaning tiredly against the stone.

"What happened?" they asked.

Bart pointed at Michaels's body. "He, he tried to kill me. I fought back and defended myself."

In the midst of the chaotic scene, it seemed a logical explanation to the inexperienced young men. They helped Bart to his feet and out of the room.

"Tell Al that I need to talk with him right away," Bart said as he took one last look at Michaels's dead body. He couldn't help his smile.

22

Tessa thought torture would be coming at any minute. Both her and Jake had been held hostage in her hotel room going on two days and knew they'd be foolish to think they would be released anytime soon. Al had posted a guard in the room on an eight hour rotation, twenty-four hours a day.

Both she and Jake knew they had no bargaining chips. The guard had not prevented them from talking so they continued doing what they could to unlock the mystery at hand. If they discovered the secret to the tomb, then at least Tessa figured they'd have something to use; otherwise, they were useless. And Tessa had a feeling she knew what North Spear did with useless people.

"You know, Tessa, I've had a theory for some time now about the descendants of the Nephilim," Jake said. He still had a nasty bruise from the hefty right cross that had grounded him when he had bravely tried to help her. The guard hadn't even bothered to get him ice.

"What kind of theory?" she asked quietly out of the corner of her mouth, flipping through the pages of a book. She didn't trust the guard any farther than she could throw him. She and Jake sat on one of the couches, their notes and research spread out on the coffee table before them. The guard didn't seem to be paying them much attention, but she wanted to make sure he didn't know anything more than he had to.

"The bible is very clear the Nephilim were on the Earth before *and* after the flood," Jake said, facing her. "The pages of the Old Testament and the Tanakh are filled with stories of God's people overcoming them to take control of the promised land. What if David and his mighty men didn't get them all? What if they survived and their bloodline was so diluted, so watered down, that most of their genetic expressions were muted or hidden?"

"Interesting thought, but I don't see how that helps us out in our current situation, Jake."

Jake frowned. "No, it doesn't. I was just thinking about who Bart keeps calling. Who does he answer to?"

"And what, you're suggesting he answers to someone with Nephilim lineage? Like a Canaanite?" she sighed. The Canaanites were the alleged descendants of the Nephilim. Constantly at war with the Jews, they were driven out of the so-called promised land and thought to be extinct. Only a few artifacts from them remained.

"Perhaps," Jake said with a shrug of his shoulders. As far as Tessa was concerned, they had problems more prominent at hand than Bart's faraway boss's potential lineage.

Suddenly, something hidden in the pages of the book she was holding caught her eye. She'd read it at least a hundred times, but this time a picture she almost blew past stood out. She flipped back for a closer look. Detailed in the grainy image was an ancient altar of sorts. It was the shape and arrangement in particular that stuck out to her. The structure was made of basketball-sized stones in a circular pattern about twenty-five feet in diameter and stood five feet high with a set of stone steps leading to the top.

Nothing else lay atop the butte-shaped altar. The text beneath the picture read CANAANITE ALTAR, the same Canaanites Jake had been talking about. The more she studied the sacrificial altar, the more she realized it looked eerily similar to the one in her dream at

Azazel. As a matter of fact, this could easily have been a recreation of the very same one.

She skimmed through the author's explanation, which stated the altar was presumably constructed for human sacrifice to appease pagan gods. In one of the paragraphs, she'd read that grooves had been cut into the surface of the structure. A close-up picture was used as reference next to it, looking nearly identical to the Nephilim tomb in Azazel. The paragraph went on to describe how cups were placed to collect the sacrificed humans' blood for ceremonial purposes.

In a moment, everything clicked. These enemies of the Israelites performed all manner of human sacrifices to their so-called gods, presumably the same fallen angels from whom they descended. The secret was blood.

The angel in her dream had shown her what was going on right in front of her and still she'd missed it. The intricately carved lines on the top of the tomb were designed as a serpentine to direct the blood flow in a specific manner. That explained the small pen-sized holes leading down into the tomb. Blood was the key.

The sarcophagus is an altar! How could I be so stupid? It was right there in front of me the whole time.

A human sacrifice unlocks the tomb.

In her excitement, she looked up to see if the North Spear guard had noticed her elation and caught on to her discovery. Luckily, he was busy raiding her mini-fridge, searching for something to drink.

"Jake, I just figured it out," she said quietly.

"What?! How?" he asked.

"Look here at this picture. Look familiar?"

He stared at it for a moment, and she knew he was catching on. "Sure does," he replied softly. "You don't think—"

"Those serpentine grooves are almost just like the ones on top of the Azazel tomb. They must direct the flow. Says here they used to collect the blood for ceremonial purposes."

He looked up at her as their eyes met. "Are you saying that to open the Nephilim sarcophagus, we need human blood?" he whispered.

She nodded. Though Tessa was young for her field, she certainly wasn't stupid. She knew if Bart found out the secret, there was nothing stopping him from sacrificing her on top of that altar. She thought about Cody, wishing that if she just hoped hard enough, he'd come bursting through the door and take them far, far away from here.

When Bart had questioned her about who she called, she had eventually told him that she called her brother only to stop the vein in his neck from popping, leaving it intentionally as vague as she could. With North Spear's resources, she figured they'd identify him sooner or later but took the chance that they wouldn't know enough about him to think he'd be able to do anything about it. She could only hope that her call had gone through, although she feared the worst.

Suddenly, the door sprang open, startling the North Spear guard who instinctively thrust his hand to the pistol on his hip. Realizing it was Bart, he released his grip on the gun.

With a start, Tessa noticed dried blood on the collar of his shirt. He was clearly amped up. Her body tensed as she discreetly closed the book in front of her, trying to conceal the piece of the puzzle that led to her discovery. Bart didn't notice, and instead continued to stare at Tessa and Jake for what seemed like eternity.

He looked at their makeshift workstation with her small library of books spread across the table with loose sheets of paper strewn about. Helping himself, he grabbed a few to see what they said as if he were actually interested. Tessa knew it was all for show. She'd grown accustomed to his flair for dramatics and love for power plays.

"No progress, I take it?" he asked with a smile.

"Bart, I've told you time and again, I have no idea," she lied through gritted teeth.

"Hmm, that's very unfortunate. For both of you, honestly. You see, the people I work for, the ones who own North Spear . . . " Bart paused for dramatic effect. "They don't accept failure, and by proxy, that means *I* don't accept failure."

"Please just let us go. We don't have what you want, Bart," Jake said pleadingly, looking up at him.

Bart turned toward him. "Actually you do, but we'll get to that later." He turned away from him and instead faced Tessa. "Tell me about your brother, Tessa," he stated.

Tessa's eyebrows knitted together in confusion. "There's nothing to tell really. He was a cop, and he lives in Texas." She had realized it was better to give Bart what he wanted in small doses rather than not giving him at all. As long as she stayed vague, she might just stay ahead of him. But while Tessa might not have realized her choice of words, Bart certainly did.

"What do you mean *was*?" he asked, watching her reaction closely. Her shift in posture and body language was undeniable as she tried to backpedal unsuccessfully.

She tried to appear nonchalant as she spoke. "He used to be a cop, but now he just trains people. He works for some company that sets it up. But I'm not even sure if he does that anymore. We're not that close," Tessa lied as she shifted uncomfortably to an upright seated position.

Bart paused, considering. "That sounds like a man with skills. Skills that could be useful to you right now. So, tell me, Tessa, when you made this phone call to this brother of yours . . . did you tell him about what we're doing down here?"

Tessa's heart sunk into her stomach. She knew Bart would see right through her if she wasn't careful. And he was right about one thing: she was in a world she didn't understand and one she didn't know how to navigate. Her hands began to tremble. She needed to lie, and she needed to lie well.

"I just tried to call him to let him know I was coming home early and to tell him I would need a ride from the airport. He was worried about me working outside of the US," she said.

"Rightly so. It's a dangerous world out there, you know. Accidents happen all the time." Bart studied her carefully, hoping to induce as much fear as possible. "Especially in the jungles of South America."

He felt the familiar feeling of power course through his veins at the glimmer of terror in her eyes. Bart Cox had not reached his position within North Spear by taking excessive risks. He fancied himself careful, calculating, ambitious— some might even say manipulative. Nevertheless, he knew he needed to shorten up some loose ends.

Turning to the guard standing behind him, he ordered. "Call Al and tell him I'm going to need my car ready to go in fifteen minutes.

We'll need an armed escort. The three of us have some unfinished business at Azazel to sort out."

"Why? We already told you we don't know how to open the tomb, Bart," Tessa said quickly.

"Yes, I'm aware, you both have said as much several times. But as it turns out, I do," he gloated, his arms spread wide.

Jake and Tessa looked at each other in fear.

The guard immediately started fulfilling his boss's order. Bart snapped his fingers at them to get moving. When Tessa went to go grab a few articles of clothing to stuff inside her backpack, he held out a hand to stop her.

"Don't bother. You won't need it," he said.

The young archaeologist shuddered at the thought and said a silent prayer.

23

After yesterday's trek through the dense, humid Amazonian rainforest, Cody was somewhat relieved to find that he still had what it takes to do the job, though he didn't remember having to work so hard just to cover a few hundred yards—although he'd never admit it to Frank. After all, he couldn't have Frank thinking he was actually getting old and out of shape.

Cody knew he wasn't exactly the man he used to be after being out of the field for as long as he had been. Frankly, he was silently thankful for the rest their surveillance position offered. The air conditioning in the busted-up Nissan didn't work really well, but it was something, and with the windows down, it felt pretty nice. But despite the slight change in his capabilities, deep down he knew he still had more-than-enough nerve to make up for them and get the job done.

Frank had taken the lead on today's objective. As usual, he drove while Cody rode shotgun. As they rode, Cody mulled on something Frank had said: that he wasn't one to let a good idea go to waste simply because his own ego was an obstacle. He had made a good point, and Cody knew it. So they'd packed the car the same as the day before, unsure of what they might get themselves into. The old adage "It's better to have and not need it, than need it and not have it" ran in the back of their minds. Cody had thrown some old blankets over their equipment to help conceal them from onlookers in the case of dismounting in an urban area and leaving the car behind.

Out of habit, he couldn't help but keep his MCX rifle shoved between the torn-up seats and center console for easy access, concealed by with an oily rag he found in the floorboard. Cody checked his Garmin Instinct 2 smartwatch and realized he and Frank had been outside of the five-star hotel for over an hour without seeing anything that caught their interest.

"Dude, how long you wanna stay out here watching tourists enjoy their vacation?" Cody asked with an abrupt tone.

"Aren't you the one who taught me patience is king when it comes to hunting?" Frank shot back.

Damn, he's got me on that one. Though he kept that to himself.

"Just remember, Frank, I taught you everything *you* know, not everything *I* know!" Cody said as he looked through a set of ten-power binoculars.

"Mm-hmm," Frank replied in dismissal.

They sat quietly for the next fifteen minutes, hoping to see something, anything, that was out of place. Suddenly, Cody focused on an expensive vehicle driving up to the front entrance.

"I might have something. Brand new black Land Rover, front entrance," Cody said succinctly as Frank turned his attention.

"Fernando's contact said the people up top have been driving black SUVs in and out of the jungle."

Renegade 02 could see that the fancy SUV had every bell and whistle, but then he saw something that definitely caught his trained eye: dirt and mud, caked on the running boards and wheels—signs of off-road travel.

"Got mud and dirt on the wheels. Could be transport to an excavation site," he announced to Frank.

"Or some rich guy who wants to take his sweet ride for an outdoor adventure. Let's not make any assumptions just yet, bro. Though that is a flashy ride to take into the jungle," Frank said, wishing he'd brought another pair of BINOS or even a small monocular.

Through the binoculars, Cody saw the driver exit. He was a man of average size who had definitely spent some time working on his "don't mess with me" look. Cody immediately pegged him as low-level security itching to get into a fight. Immediately he dubbed the man Bro Vet, simply based on his demeanor. It was derogatory term used for veterans who liked to visually announce they were a veteran of the military but were all too often far more bark than bite.

He was dressed in the classic security tough-guy outfit: cargo pants and a size-too-small polo with an ID badge hanging from a lanyard. He couldn't be sure, but he thought there was a slight bulge on his hip underneath his shirt, possibly from a firearm. The distance was just a bit too far to positively identify it.

Cody watched their every move as the driver opened the back door for his passenger: a well-dressed businessman. Instinctively he named him the Suit. He couldn't help but assign his own nicknames to his surveillance targets. It helped him remember who was whom.

"Bro Vet is opening the door for the Suit," Cody relayed.

"Okay, I see 'em. They're heading toward the main entrance," Frank replied.

Both Renegades watched as the pair made their way inside, acknowledging the door man on the way in. Cody's mind raced and wished there was more he could do. He was a man of action; he hated waiting around.

Looks like ol' Frank might have made a damn good call, but how do we get in there to get some more intel? Bribe the desk clerk? Use the "I'm looking for my friend" routine? Nah, too obvious, he thought to himself.

Cody turned to look at Frank, hoping for some ideas he hadn't considered yet. Thus far, Frank had remained quiet, but Cody could see Frank's wheels turning same as his.

"Whatcha thinking?" Cody asked. "Talk to me, bro."

"I'm thinking what you're probably thinking. They smell fishy, and it would be nice to get inside."

"Any ideas on how to do that?"

"Not just yet," Frank replied.

As they discussed ideas, a pair of identical Land Rovers drove up and parked directly behind the first. Cody pulled the binoculars up to his face to get a better look. He saw a large, muscular man step out of the lead vehicle followed by another, similar in size. Two more followed from the last vehicle. All were wearing the same outfit, uniforms really. They were some type of private security for sure.

"Alright, I got Muscles and three more heading in. Looks like some sort of uniform. I count five dudes plus the Suit. Private security, you think?" Cody asked his little brother.

"No doubt. But we still don't have any idea if that leads to Tessa. I mean, do archaeologists usually need security?" Frank asked.

Cody discreetly pulled his MCX from its stowed position between the seat and center console.

"What the hell are you doing?" Frank questioned in a serious tone.

"Relax, I'm putting it away . . . in the backpack," Cody replied.

Cody detached the suppressor from the muzzle and slid the compact rifle into the discreet non-militarized backpack. With the stock folded, it was a perfect fit and easy way to carry around some extra firepower that wasn't going to draw any extra attention. He zipped up the backpack and made sure his plaid Kuhl shirt was sufficiently buttoned to conceal his appendix-carried Glock as he stepped out of the vehicle. Frank quickly did the same.

"This is exactly what I was worried about, Cody. You gonna let me in on what you're doing?" Frank asked from across the hood of the truck.

"Well, I was thinking that maybe we could partake in some social conversation with those dudes that just walked in there. Care to join me?"

Frank's head dropped down out of frustration. "Of course, I'm coming with you. We can't risk you shooting up some five-star hotel over a damn hunch."

"I'll be on my best behavior, I promise. Besides, this is such a nice hotel, they have to have a good bar. You think they'll have jalapeño margaritas?" Cody said over his shoulder where he had slung the backpack.

Both men strolled into the front entrance casually, like guests. They entered the foyer and scanned their surroundings, taking note where the elevators, lobby desk and so on were to gain situational awareness. To his left, Cody observed Bro Vet at the bar sitting by himself.

Must be my lucky day. Time to work that Renegade magic, Cody smiled to himself.

He nudged Frank and nodded in Bro Vet's direction. Frank winked at him, and both continued in that direction. Not entirely out of place, both Cody and Frank were dressed in casual outdoor attire and looked like they'd just come from an outdoor adventure or hike, which they had done the day before.

Cody casually walked up to the bar and stood next to Bro Vet who was babysitting what looked like sparkling water. He paid no attention to Cody who ordered his signature spicy beverage complete with the bowl-style glass rimmed with Tajin—just the way he liked it. Bro Vet was too preoccupied with Instagram to be concerned with things like his surroundings. Frank took the seat on Cody's left side, leaving Cody between his large friend and their target.

The senior Renegade waited until his subject brought the glass up to his lips to take a sip and let his Vertx backpack slip off his shoulder, bumping into Bro Vet. His drink spilled onto his tight polo shirt and smartphone. Immediately he jumped from his seated position, obviously angry and glaring daggers at Cody.

"What the hell!" he protested in anger, fists clenched.

"Oh shit, I'm so sorry, man! My bad," Cody feigned as he grabbed some nearby napkins and started patting him down, pretending to dry him off. He grabbed his ID card lanyard and started wiping it off in hopes he'd catch the company name. Cody's heart started racing when he saw North Spear printed at the top. Bro Vet pulled the ID from Cody's grasp.

"Dude, chill out. I got it," he said aggravated at Cody's reaction, reaching for more napkins to wipe his phone.

"I'm so embarrassed. Lemme make it up to you. Can I buy you another round?" Cody inquired.

"Nah man, you're good," Bro Vet said, but it was laced with a hint of arrogance.

"Please, it's the least I can do," Cody tried again.

Bro Vet relented and sat down, displeased. "Alright."

"I'm Cody," he said, holding out his hand for a handshake. Bro Vet took it reluctantly. The first thing Cody noticed was the overly firm grip he applied, befitting his nickname.

"Deon," he replied gruffly.

"Wow! You got a strong grip there, Deon," Cody complimented, trying to break the ice with his target.

"If you say so," Deon shrugged, dismissive and more intent on continuing to wipe down his shirt.

"I couldn't help but notice your tattoos. They're pretty cool. Were you in the army or something?" Cody asked, nodding his head in thanks to the bartender who had brought his drink.

After years of experience as a street cop, Cody had learned to gain valuable details from people after just a few minutes and perhaps some brief speech. He was a keen observer, which made him so successful both in his previous career field and with Renegade. The same held true for his sister with her own career.

Cody saw Deon's overly obvious torn-American-flag tattoo on his right forearm when he lifted his drink. The design gave the appearance the flag was underneath the skin. On Deon's hands were the words HOLD FAST tattooed with each letter on a separate finger. It was indicative of time spent at sea or service in the navy, handling the large lines of boats and ships—and an immediate peg of military service.

"Nah, I was in the navy. Did my four and got out," Deon said, obviously annoyed.

"Wow, I bet you've seen some awesome stuff, huh? I had a buddy from high school who joined the army, but I just couldn't do it. I went to college instead. I don't like violence and guns and all that. I appreciate guys like you. Are you still with the navy?" Cody asked.

"No, I got out last year. I contract for a private company now. Security stuff. Can't really talk about it."

Bingo. Just keep reeling him in, don't overreach, Cody.

"Oh wow, I don't know what that means, but it sure sounds cool," Cody said casually, sipping on his drink. "Thank you for your service. How'd you get into that? My little brother over here has been talking about doing something with his life. He works in an office and wants a little action. You got a card or anything?" Cody asked, hoping he'd score a website, phone number, or something to dig a little deeper. Frank toasted his beer with a friendly smile, but Deon just glared at the pair of them.

"Listen man, can you just leave me alone?"

Deon's phone buzzed on the hard surface of the bar. With no hesitation, the North Spear man reached for it to see who was calling. He swiped the screen, taking the call. Cody figured it was his boss, the Suit, dishing out orders.

"Go for Deon," he said into the handheld device.

Cody nursed the spicy margarita while his ears strained to hear what orders were being issued. Deon hung up the phone without another word to the caller. Cody would've given his left arm to know who was on the other end and what was said.

Deon stood from his chair and slipped the phone into his cargo pocket. Instinctively he reached down to adjust his belt, the weight of his pistol tugging at this belt line. Cody noticed the movement and mentally checked the box, knowing for sure he was armed. He looked to Cody and gave him a nod, letting him know he was taking off.

"Duty calls, huh? Be safe out there," Cody said, watching him as he walked to the lobby.

Renegade 02 kept an eye on Deon as the man stood in the lobby, carefully watching the elevator. Maintaining his view on his subject, he leaned his head over his shoulder to make sure Frank could hear him, his tone barely above a whisper.

"Confirmed North Spear. That's the company Tessa said over the phone. I saw the badge. Let's be eyes up, dude. See him checking out the elevators? Probably waiting on someone. Get pictures if possible."

Frank didn't respond and didn't need to. He reached for his phone while Cody shifted the backpack to the seat Deon had occupied moments earlier.

Enjoying his adult libation, Cody saw Deon perk up and assumed it was go time. He watched as several other members of North Spear dressed in the same cargo pants and polo came out of the elevator and crossed into his line of sight. They were followed by the Suit, an older white guy, and finally his sister.

Cody's heartrate spiked, and his vision narrowed. In it he could only see Tessa. The entire world around him faded away as he watched his sister being escorted by five security guards and a few others, the Suit among them.

Without thinking through the second- and third-order effects, he unzipped the backpack and began to slide out his folded rifle. He was going to end this here and now.

His left hand flung the folding stock to the locked position and he crossed the room quickly, closing the distance between him and Deon, who was the closest to him.

Frank saw Cody moving, realizing he was committed and wouldn't be able to stop him if he tried. He looked past Cody, seeing Tessa in the custody of a group of men more than twice their number. He pulled his own pistol from concealment and moved to help cover Cody, knowing what was likely to come next.

Deon saw the movement coming at him quickly and turned to identify what it was. His eyes went wide when he saw Cody steadily closing the distance like a freight train. He didn't, however, see the stock of Cody's rifle until it smashed his nose, exploding the cartilage inside. The butt stroke had a simultaneous effect of knocking him unconscious, his body dropping lifeless to the hard tile floor. Around them, several of the other guests and staff had noticed the commotion. Several of them screamed and began to run.

The remaining four North Spear guards watched in momentary bewilderment before drawing their own weapons and taking a defensive posture around the group. They started shouting commands to Cody to put the gun down, but he couldn't hear them.

"Cody!" Tessa screamed, reaching for him through the mass of men in front of her.

Tessa's eyes were filled with tears and fear. She was clearly shaken by the focused violence taking place up close. Surrounded by the security detail in a semicircle, she couldn't do anything as Muscles grabbed her by the arm and leveled the barrel of his pistol to her temple. Cody stopped his forward movement, knowing it would an easier shot if he remained still. His mind raced through various shooting solutions, trying to calculate the best angle to free his sister. None of them were great. *Too many people.*

The Suit dove behind Muscles, cowering. Muscles began shouting orders to his men as the other guests ran in fear.

"Back up or I'll kill her. Back! Up!" Al shouted, staring into Cody's expressionless face.

"Let. My. Sister. Go. Or I'll put a bullet between your eyes."

"Tough talk for a man who's in no position to negotiate," Al replied.

Cody felt like an hour had passed since he'd broken Deon's nose. In truth, no more than five seconds had gone by. His senses were firing on all cylinders, and his vision began to widen as he processed his environment.

He knew he was out gunned. The likelihood of surviving a gunfight at this range was impossible. He cursed himself and redirected his focus from Al to Tessa, locking eyes with her. She was clearly trying not to show she was freaking out, but he noticed her eyes welling up with tears and watched as she cowered away from the gun pressed against her temple. Despite having wanted recently nothing more than for her brother to save her, she now feared for not only her own life but his. And her brother knew now wasn't the right time to do so. He needed to regain control. The pressure he'd maintained on the safety released only slightly, though he maintained his red-dot sight just above Al's forehead, accounting for close range holdover in the chance an acceptable firing solution presented itself.

"What's the plan, bro?" Frank asked, standing shoulder to shoulder with Cody, his pistol at the ready.

"Get us out of here, Al," Bart growled, from behind the men with guns.

"Cody . . ." Tessa said, the fear apparent in her voice.

"It's okay, Tessa. Everything's going to be okay."

Everyone's weapons were still trained on one another. Al and his security team began walking backward toward the doors leading outside. He continued to shuffle step, barking an order for someone to retrieve Deon. Tessa, still locked in his grip, didn't dare try to escape, her eyes never leaving her brother as she was led away.

Cody came to the realization that he would have to let his sister go. All the worry, anxiety, and fear came in a wild rush at this moment. He'd found her, accomplished his main objective, and now he had to watch her slip away back into danger and do so all by herself.

"We seriously gonna let her go?" Frank asked incredulously.

"Have to, or we risk killing all of us," Cody replied in a quiet, controlled tone.

Cody and Frank followed Al and his team to the doors where his men stopped, offering their team leader some cover as Bart ran to the doors and dove into the safety of the Land Rovers waiting outside. One of the men had grabbed Deon by the wrist and was dragging his limp body while Al pulled Tessa and Jake at a sprint with him to the car, forcing them in the back seat like a bag of groceries. The remaining members of the North Spear security detail conducted a bounding overwatch maneuver, leaping past one another to their getaway vehicles.

Both Renegades stood helplessly watching them speed away from the hotel, with Tessa held against her will in their custody.

We'll be seeing you again, Cody thought, staring at the back of the cars as they sped away.

Suddenly, Frank made for their old truck at a sprint, pistol still in hand. Cody took off right behind him.

"Pursue?" Cody asked his little brother, trying to close the gap.

"Yeah, you drive. Keep your distance though. Don't wanna spook them," he yelled over his shoulder, reaching the truck first.

Instead of jumping in the driver's seat and firing up the engine, Frank ran to the back and pulled out his surveillance gear. Hopping in the passenger side door, he quickly tore open the hard case and pulled out Bubo, his modified drone.

"Grab the iPad. Hurry!" Frank snapped at him as Cody reached the car.

"On it!" Cody said after he pulled the door so hard he thought it might come off the hinges. He retrieved the iPad, jumped in, and started up the Xterra while Frank prepped the drone for launch.

Frank leaned over and snatched the iPad from Cody's lap, quickly tapping the screen as if that would will it to connect faster. He rolled down the passenger window and launched the drone, eyes still locked on the screen.

Soaring above the ground, Frank acquired the Land Rovers driving away as fast as they drivers could navigate the turns. He tapped the screen, telling the drone to lock onto the cars.

"Go go go! I got a lock. To the right. To the *right*!" Frank said, watching the Land Rovers' every turn.

24

It had been a while since Cody had driven in pursuit of a target vehicle. Though it was less of a pursuit than it was making sure the drone stayed within range. He took his turn-by-turn directions from Frank who only glanced up to verify they were on the correct trail. The difficult part was the lag, although they were managing so far. Had the circumstances not been so dire, he might have even called this fun.

The North Spear Land Rovers had a decent head start, which was perhaps a good thing; Cody wanted them to feel at ease. As the vehicles began to distance themselves from town and made their way into the jungle, it became easier to keep track of them. Brand-new, state-of-the-art, luxury SUVs tended to stick out like a sore thumb in Peru.

While Frank's quick thinking had prevented them from losing Tessa altogether, the jungle played havoc on Bubo's locking signal. The thick canopy of the rainforest threatened to lose the vehicles, only to be reacquired a few seconds later. Frank recalled the drone for a quick battery swap. He especially didn't want to lose Bubo altogether if it crashed somewhere way out in the jungle and the battery died. Luckily for them, as they headed deeper and deeper into the Amazon, they were on a single-lane road, so there wasn't much to get lost to.

"Where the hell do you think they're going? We're heading out to the middle of nowhere. If they dismount and set up a hasty ambush while the drone is down…" Cody trailed off, speaking more so to himself than Frank.

Frank caught on to what he was trying to say. "Good point. Let's stop for a second and see if there's anything up ahead on the map. That'll give me a chance to check the battery too. Damn, I was so focused on not losing them, I didn't think to see where they might be headed," Frank replied.

Some parts of the off-road travel got easier as the sun dried out the thick clay-like mud. Other spots were still wet and required him to slow down to navigate or else get stuck. The one nice thing about that was it made tracking the Land Rovers easier. The ruts in the mud were a clear indicator.

"Uh, Cody," Frank said, hesitation thick in his voice.

Cody glanced at Frank, unsure if he was worried about something on the screen or the road. "What? Tell me." His stomach plummeted as he became afraid for the worst. He couldn't help but think something horrible had happened, imagining Frank was about to point out his sister had just been executed on the side of the road or something.

"You ain't gonna believe this. I followed the dirt trails as far as the satellite imagery would allow. Honestly, it's just my best guess, but take a stab at where it leads?" Frank said with a grin.

"I dunno, man. Just friggin' tell me," Cody snapped. He was in no mood for suspense.

"Deep in the jungle. To a waterfall. The same area Mengele had circled."

Without a word, Cody threw the vehicle in park and snatched the tablet from Frank to take a look for himself. *What are the chances of that?* he thought.

Staring at the screen, he pored over the satellite image, gaining his bearings to see if he could make sure it was, in fact, the very same waterfall. It was South America after all, and waterfalls in the jungle were plentiful. But either way, it was a start.

If North Spear is on the hunt for the same thing as a Nazi war criminal, that can't be good.

And if that were true, one thing was certain: he had to get his sister away from them as fast as he could. He set the tablet down in his lap, closed his eyes, and silently asked for help.

Lord, help me be fast and accurate. Let me be your weapon against evil today. If the somebody in the Willis family needs to die today, I pray that it be me. I can't bear another loss. Here I am, offering myself in exchange. Take me.

"You good?" Frank asked, looking at Cody intently.

"Yeah, I'm good. Just needed to clear something up really quick."

"Just want to make sure you're up to this. Tessa needs us *both* in top shape right now."

"Trust me, Frank, I'm aware. I said I'm good. Let's get there and save my sister."

For the first time in several days, Tessa had felt hope, only to have it stripped away from her. After the intense scene in the hotel lobby, she seemed to have lost her sense of time. Completely caught up in the events, she had no idea how long they'd been on the road or where they were going. Had she not been so stressed, she would've recognized the trip to Azazel.

The Land Rover slowed in the area leading up to the waterfall. As the vehicles stopped, she suddenly realized where they were and felt her body shiver. Her palms felt cold and clammy looking upon the ancient site. She now saw it for what it was, and felt remorseful for her own stupidity.

Al threw the gear shift into park, simultaneously shutting off the engine. Stepping out of the driver's side, he opened the back door and offered his hand to help her out. She refused and stepped out on her own. From another vehicle, Bart exploded out of the backseat toward her.

"Who the hell was that at the hotel? If you lie to me, I will kill you where you stand!" Bart shouted with a raised fist, a mix of fury and fear in his eyes.

"That . . . that was my brother," she replied numbly. If she hadn't been so shellshocked, her senses might have told her to lie. But a part of her still didn't believe it. *Cody? Here?*

"How did he know where you were? What does he know? Who was the other guy with him?" Bart interrogated through gritted teeth.

"I don't know, I just told him I was coming home early. I've never seen the other guy before. That's all, I swear!" Tessa lied again, trying to stop herself from shaking. She was suddenly very aware of the number of people who had guns around her.

Bart must have remembered his own because he suddenly pulled the small pistol from his pocket and pointed it directly at her. Tessa couldn't hold it together any longer. She was going to die. Just before she felt herself about to burst into sobs, she heard a voice yelling from outside one of the other cars. The shout was getting closer and louder.

"Bart, put the gun down right now!" Jake yelled, charging in his direction.

He wasn't even within arm's reach before Al knocked the mid-fifty-year-old to the ground with a solid punch to the face. Bart didn't even flinch. His attention remained on Tessa.

"You think you're so smart, don't you? Well guess what kid, you're not as smart as you think. I figured out the secret. I have everything I need to open the tomb, and now you're useless to me." Tessa felt her skin go cold. "Well, not entirely," he then said, a sinister smile forming across his face.

"No, you can't!" Jake said from the ground, holding his bleeding nose.

"Can't what?" Bart asked, looking down at the grounded man with a puzzled expression. He suddenly realized Jake knew more than he had led on. He turned back toward Tessa, waving the gun threateningly at her.

"Let me be very clear with both of you. *I'm* the one in charge out here, and *I* can do whatever the hell I want. Look around," Bart waved his arms, beckoning toward the jungle around them. "Do you see anyone that's going to stop me? Huh?"

"Bart, please, let's talk about this," Tessa said, raising a hand in a reassuring manner, but Bart shook his head.

"You don't get it, do you? The time for that is *over*, Tessa. I gave you the opportunity to open the tomb and prove yourself. You squandered it away and then betrayed me by quitting. I gave you the means to have the very world at your fingertips, and all you had to do was make it happen. You *are* going to open the Nephilim tomb. Though now, it's going to take a little more out of you than you realize." He turned toward the armed guards. "Grab them and bring them inside."

Al did as he was told, though Tessa could see the look of his own reservations. Tessa tried to appeal to him as he grabbed her arm and dragged her along.

"Please, Al, don't do this," she said. But he remained silent.

As they made their way to the waterfall entrance, Tessa found herself looking around the jungle in every direction, hoping for a miraculous rescue from her brother and Frank. She prayed they were nearby, just waiting for the right moment to strike. But as they came up to the large cave entrance, her heart sank as she realized they weren't there. She was alone. Ahead, she saw the inscription she'd translated weeks prior: Death is only the beginning.

They made their way through the cave to the tent city just outside the temple. The usual teams were doing their normal routines, and Tessa—in a brief moment of desperation—thought to call out to them for help. But Al seemingly read her mind as she felt the barrel of his pistol press into her back. "Don't even think about it," he growled behind her.

Jake and Tessa were thrown roughly into seats inside Bart's tent. The security guards remained outside as Bart sat across from them after pouring himself a drink. He took a large gulp and let out a sigh of both pleasure and relief.

"So, let's all be honest, shall we? Can we quit beating around the bush?" Bart said. Neither of them said anything. "You know how it opens, don't you?" he eventually asked, looking to both in turn, eyebrows raised.

Tessa realized playing the idiot wasn't going to work anymore. She had no hand to play if Bart really knew the answer was human sacrifice. She saw the blood on the collar of his shirt and figured it was a safe bet he did.

She nodded, hands fidgeting with the fabric of her pants. "Yes, we figured it out in the hotel," she said quietly.

"Why keep it to yourself?" he asked. His tone almost replicated that of a teacher scolding two students.

"Because we knew that even that wouldn't stop you. You'd stop at nothing to open it up," Tessa said, her voice a little stronger. "And you know, Bart, you keep telling me I'm messing around with people and things I don't understand, well guess what? So are you. You have no *idea*. And I think that scares you."

"Oh really?" he said. An overly confident, smug look formed as he brought the glass to his lips.

"You don't know what you're messing with, Bart," she repeated, straightening up. "The Nephilim are pure-concentrated evil, and if you start playing around with their DNA, I promise God will pay you a visit."

Bart just smiled. "I certainly hope He does. I have a few things to say to Him in person," he said in a pompous tone.

If my brother gets ahold of you, you'll get the chance, she thought.

"I warned you about this, Bart. You're going to end up unleashing an evil that will dominate the human race if given the opportunity," Jake said from next to Tessa.

Tessa thought about the ancient Enochian on the Nephilim tomb: "Death is but the doorway to life. We live today. We shall live again. In many forms, we shall return." This was part of the Nephilim agenda. Bart's ego and desire for power was exactly what they wanted. In fact, they were counting on it.

"From the way I look at it, I don't care who is on the bottom so long as I am on top," he said before draining the last of his glass. "Now, let's get on with it. My prize awaits," he said, standing up with a flourish and calling for Al, who entered and grabbed Tessa by the arm. She knew one thing: death was certainly waiting for her inside Azazel. Luckily, despite the bleak concept of the matter, her dad had taught her a vital thing before he had died: to not ever give up. If she didn't act quickly, she would be dead in the next several hours.

She did the first thing she could think of: she drove her knee as hard as she could directly into Al's balls. As soon as he began to double over, she made a run for it.

25

Frank and Cody had tailed the small North Spear convoy as far as they could while still feeling safe enough to avoid detection. They gave a generous tether to the getaway vehicles now that they had a decent general destination. Nevertheless, while they did, they kept a sharp eye out since they feared driving straight into an ambush or encountering a QRF or quick reaction force.

Bubo had once again proved his worth, keeping eyes on the vehicles until it was confirmed that the Land Rovers were at the waterfall. The two-man team pulled off the side of the road and camouflaged their beater ride. Both quickly donned their chest rigs with spare ammo and radios. Cody opted to don his Volund assault belt, giving him access to faster reloads and a more overt holster for his pistol, should he need to transition. Neither had packed their plate carriers, so they would have to infiltrate without the added protection. At least the chest rigs would allow them to remain light and fast, so the trade-off was fair enough. The sun was getting low on the horizon and night started to approach, which was unfortunate since neither thought to bring their helmets or night vision.

Given the circumstances, Cody's nerves had remained relatively steady. Jumping headfirst back into this lifestyle was becoming second nature once again. It had only taken a couple days, but the stakes had never been higher for him personally. This was a no-fail mission.

Cody attached the SureFire suppressor to his rifle and checked his pistol one last time before he looked to Frank and spoke in a low tone. "According to the map, we're about a few hundred yards out. I say we find a break in the canopy and launch Bubo. Let him hover just over the trees to confirm the vehicles are there. Whaddya think?" he asked.

"Yeah man, I totally agree. We have no idea what we're up against. Could be ten dudes out there. Could be fifty."

Cody nodded. Frank launched the drone, sending it up near the roadway with a clear view to the sky. He worried about flying too low to the treetops, lest Bubo get caught on a stray branch or a random bird was spooked and crashed into it.

He saw the mist of the waterfall in sight, slowing the aerial vehicle down to prevent it from being seen. The sun was due to set soon, but luckily it still provided just enough light for him to get a good view of the site below. Frank started calling out anything that could be useful to them so he and Cody were on the same page.

"I got vehicles. Confirmed, black Land Rovers. Panning now . . . No sign of people—whoa!" he said incredulously, laying eyes on the massive twin angel statues.

"What?! What is it?" Cody said, anticipation pulling at his core.

"You gotta come look at this, that's one of the coolest things I've ever seen." Frank handed the tablet to Cody.

"Whoa, look at how big those bastards are compared to the trucks," Cody marveled.

"Dude, I know. They gotta be like a hundred feet tall. Looks like some sorta entrance or checkpoint," Frank guessed.

Both Renegades hovered over the tablet, staring at the digital screen in amazement. Cody zoomed the lens to see how deep the entrance went, surprised to see it came to an abrupt stop at a stone wall. He continued to pan around, looking for any sign of a dig site and finding none.

"Bro, I ain't seeing anything other than the waterfall, some big angel statues, and the cars. Did I miss something?" Cody asked.

"Nah, I got the same. You think they swapped vehicles trying to shake us? Snagged a helicopter ride outta Dodge or what?" Frank supposed.

"Doubt it. The canopy is a little too thick, but I'd say it's worth a look in person. Only way to be sure. We should take all the kit with us just in case we can't make it back to the car," Cody said.

"Clear," Frank replied, stuffing the remaining gear inside his backpack.

The next words they spoke were only to conduct quick and simple radio checks. Their gear adjusted and the vehicle stowed, both Renegades made their way into the jungle once again just off the beaten path. They moved swiftly through the dense foliage, being careful not to make too much noise but compromising to some degree to move faster and cover greater distance.

Cody stopped to take a break, the thick, humid air filling his nostrils. He subconsciously started combat breathing, an effective tactic to reduce heart rate and control stress. He inhaled four seconds, held for four, exhaled for four, then repeated the process. First learning the technique from Val, it had proven useful for just about everything.

Bringing his wrist into view, he checked his GPS. It showed them less than three hundred yards from his set destination: the waterfall. He mimed the numbers with his hands to Frank off to his right. They didn't want to stay too close to one another in the event shooting erupted. Their distance was just close enough to see each other, but the light was quickly fading. Cody could barely make out a nod from Frank's shadowy outline.

With each step, they grew closer to their objective, intentionally slowing their pace and carefully moving branches out of the way so as not to make any excessive movement or noise.

Cody could hear the roaring of the water for the last few minutes, drawing him in like a Greek siren. It was almost deafening. He was sure Frank and him could shout at each other and no one in the vicinity would hear. Just ahead, roughly twenty yards or so, he could see the trees clear out and the last remaining rays of sunlight shining through an opening.

We have to be close.

He knelt on one knee, watching, waiting, listening. The only thing he could hear was the crashing of the water. He looked to Frank, who had drifted over in his direction. With his hand flat he pushed it low to the ground, like he was giving a dog the command to sit. In truth, it was a signal to go prone or lie on your belly. Frank understood immediately and got as low as he could.

The two-man assault team low-crawled the last remaining distance, taking cover behind some large rocks surrounding the perimeter of the pool. One at a time, they peeked their heads up to get a better view of their surroundings. After a quick scan, neither could help but stare at the massive stone angels just to the side of the now-visible waterfall. The satellite imagery hadn't shown the ancient stonework at all, likely hidden from the dense overgrowth of the jungle, which had clearly reclaimed its land from inhabitants long ago.

Cody crawled closer to Frank, who was still staring at the statues.

"You see anybody?" Cody asked.

"Nobody. Nothing," Frank answered, peering around at it all. "What *is* this place?"

"No idea, but it looks old as hell. Just the kind of place Tessa would love," Cody replied softly. If there was any place she would be, it was here. He was sure of it.

"Let's hang out here for a minute and—" Cody started when suddenly a sound caught their attention. Both stopped talking immediately and were on full alert. It was the sound of a car engine heading in their direction. Instinctively they gripped their rifles and brought them to a low ready position should they need them in a hurry.

"Vic coming in," Frank said hastily.

"Yeah, I heard it too. North Spear?" Cody asked.

"Unknown. Standby," he replied.

The vehicle drove in, careful of the dirt road. As it closed the distance, it was indeed another Land Rover, exactly like the others already parked across the water. From their position of observation, the distance was about thirty-five to forty yards. The vehicle came to a stop, and all the doors popped open. Cody slowly popped his head above the large rock to have a look for himself and get a grasp on their new company.

Cody and Frank could barely hear the muffled voices over the roaring of the water. Four men exited the expensive four-wheel drive SUV, grabbing bags and backpacks from the back storage compartment. Two were wearing the same uniform as the guys before; the other two were in civilian attire.

Neither Cody nor Frank said a word as they discreetly watched the men seemingly go about their business, but where were they going? Were they prepping themselves for a hike into the jungle?

The North Spear quartet closed the car doors and began to walk toward the pool and the statues. The group walked along the bank closest to the angel carvings before jumping into the water. Suddenly, one stood motionless for a few seconds, and Cody heard him shouting something as he beckoned toward the car at his three colleagues who waved him away. He could see the guy again feeling around the outside of his pockets looking for something. Cell phone or cigarettes perhaps.

Cody's best guess was he forgot something in the vehicle and had to return to get it and the other men didn't want to wait up. A second later this seemed to be the case. The lone guard retraced his steps heading back toward the Land Rover. Suddenly Cody had an idea and knew Frank had to be thinking the same. He watched the rest of the trio slosh their way through the water before making their way between the massive, winged warriors.

His curiosity was enough to kill him, and he started nudging Frank with his elbow to watch them closely. Frank turned his head to see the three men walk into the opening as one put his hands on the massive stone wall and pushed it open. Both Cody's and Frank's jaws nearly hit the ground, amazed at what they saw as the trio disappeared through the entrance.

"Did you see that?" Frank said incredulously.

"I'm seeing it, but I don't know if I believe it," Cody replied.

They each had to force themselves to pull their focus back to the solo security man, who was already halfway back to his vehicle. Cody remained hunched over, using the rocks for some type of concealment as he closed the distance to the parked cars. Without reservation, Frank followed closely behind.

The pool of water bottlenecked into a crossable stream roughly about six feet wide. By the time Cody and Frank slipped into the water, the lone man had the car door open and was digging around the floorboard for his missing item.

Luckily, thanks to the downpour of the waterfall, their footsteps had been dampened as they had broken concealment. Not that it mattered much. The man seemed to be preoccupied with other things at the moment. Both rifles were trained on the vehicle, Frank crossing the water first, then stopping to stand watch as Cody followed suit.

The North Spear man's head was looking under the passenger seat when he was unknowingly approached. The man's arm stretched out, and his fingers closed around the object of his desire: a pack of cigarettes.

Frank stood on the opposite side of the vehicle as their target did, his Geissele SPR at the ready. Cody moved around to the back of the vehicle, stopping once he had the man clear in his sights. He stayed at the rear of the vehicle and waited until Frank moved around behind him, trapping the North Spear guard in a perfectly positioned short-range ambush. They counted themselves lucky he had no situational awareness. Cody gave Frank a nod without taking his eyes or muzzle off the target.

"Excuse me, sir, I was wondering if you could tell me how to get inside the big *Uncharted* cave-looking thing?" Frank asked, weapon bearing down directly at the man's head.

The man had jumped up and spun around at the unfamiliar voice, and his eyes went wide at the sight of the tall commando-dressed man. His heart rate spiked, hands shaking uncontrollably. Cody stepped from the rear of the vehicle, causing him to take a step back.

"Who . . . who are you?" he asked.

"Doesn't matter. I'm asking the questions, and you're going to tell us exactly what we want to know," Frank said with no emotion, his eyes piercing the man's soul.

Cody slung his rifle and pulled a set of flex cuffs from his pack. Frank held the man at gunpoint until he was checked for weapons and his hands were secured. After finding he had only been armed with a Glock pistol and pocketknife and stripping him of both, they sat him down away from any potential prying eyes and Cody took the lead.

"Listen, we came here for a very specific purpose, and we're not leaving until we get what we came for. I'll make this brief so there's no confusion. Help us get inside, or we'll put a bullet in your head and leave your body here to rot. Make sense?" he said in a tone that sounded more like he was explaining basic math than threatening a man's life.

"I can help you, just please don't kill me. I'm an American!" the man sobbed.

"Good for you. What's your name?" Cody questioned.

"Brandon," he answered.

"Can you get us into the . . . whatever that is over there?" Cody pointed to the temple.

"Are . . . are you going to k . . . kill me?" Brandon asked, eyes widening even further.

"Focus, Brandon. We're short on time. Yes or no?"

"Yes, I . . . I can. Look, I'm not even supposed to be here technically. My boss issued a recall to come back. Some sort of security threat to the worksite," Brandon confessed.

Cody looked at Frank, his eyebrows raised. Both were fully aware that the enhanced security posture was likely a result of their interaction back at the hotel.

"Okay, Brandon, here's what we're going to do. We're going to follow you into this worksite, and you're going to tell us everything you know on the way. If you screw us in any way, we will kill you. Understand?" Cody said in a light tone, not at all consistent with his verbiage.

"Yeah," Brandon answered, voice shaky and lips quivering.

Frank hefted the man to his feet, Brandon's knees wobbling like a baby deer. It was clear he'd never experienced any kind of stress like this before. Frank hoped the rest of his colleagues were as inexperienced as Brandon.

"How many other security guys are there like you?" Frank asked.

"About twenty total," Brandon replied quickly.

"All inside?"

"Most of them. Some of them are still probably out in town on their day off, like I was before I got recalled."

"Got it. Who's in charge of security for North Spear? What's his name?" Cody asked firmly.

"Alberto. Goes by Al. Big guy, combat vet. Marine, I think," he said, wiping his eyes with his shirt sleeve as best as he could in the position of his hands being tied up.

"Muscles," Cody chimed in, shooting a look over at Frank.

He turned back to the man. "Any shooters or real experienced guys with y'all? You know what I mean. Former SEALs, Special Forces—anybody like that?"

"No, no. This is my first security contract. Same for most of the guys. A few of them have been on one or two before, but that's it," he replied with a shaking voice.

The questions continued, and they found Brandon didn't know much about the Suit but did know that Al reported to him. The young North Spear man didn't know much about the temple either, just that he was supposed to protect both what was inside and the scientists. He explained the temple in vague detail, hoping it was enough to prevent a bullet from going through his head.

All three men stepped down into the shallow waters of the pool, Brandon needing help due to his hands being bound behind his back. They reached the stone wall with the inscription. "So what's the secret? This some kind of James Bond lair?" Cody asked, peering around.

"No, just push it open. It's a door," Brandon replied sniffingly as he beckoned toward the wall with his head.

Cody and Frank pushed Brandon against the wall as they approached, rifles at the ready. With a threatening look toward Brandon silently ordering him not to move, Cody readied himself to push the seemingly solid surface while Frank stood at where the crack would be, ready to engage anyone or anything on the other side. Nodding in approval, Cody pushed against the wall with his free hand. To his surprise, it swung open freely, the gargantuan stone door revealing itself just as they had seen from afar. Seeing it up close was even more impressive. Frank immediately activated his weapon-mounted light, illuminating the dark cave. His eyes scanned side to side, searching for threats. Finding none, he waved his barrel up, then down, quickly in a single motion, signaling to Cody he was clear to enter.

Cody grabbed Brandon, still shoved against the wall, by the shoulder and had him take the lead into the cave. He didn't want his prisoner leading them directly into a trap and wanted to be sure Brandon would take the brunt of it if he did.

Inside the cave, they followed their unwilling guide. Through the various tunnels they carefully trailed him, not knowing if someone was going to pop out just around the corner, armed or otherwise.

Frank heard voices and grabbed Brandon by the arm, pushing him to the side of the cave wall, forcing him to sit down. Cody heard the same and closed the distance, squeezing Frank's shoulder, letting him know he was ready to advance with him.

Silently they stood still, listening to the sound of various voices. The words were indistinguishable. With short, light steps, they eased through the tunnel cave, inching into view of the massive chamber room. Frank leaned his head to the side, surveying the large underground opening. All he could see were various figures moving around a congregation of tents. He couldn't make out any details or faces; the distance was too great and the lighting too dim.

"I got people. All unknowns. No eyes on Tessa," he said in a low tone.

"Copy. Let's stay put, let our eyes adapt and see if she pops up," Cody offered.

"Check," he replied succinctly.

Frank continued to scan, bringing his scoped rifle to his eye. The magnified optic allowed him to see better as he scanned the various tents, looking for threats. In the distance, he saw one tent that was larger than the others. He adjusted the zoom on his scope to get a better look just as the flap door flung open. Tessa barged out with armed men right behind her.

"I got her, dude. I got eyes on Tessa!" Frank said a little louder than he expected, and Cody's heart leapt.

Just as he got the words out, a North Spear guard grabbed her by the collar and pulled her back into his grasp.

Purely out of instinct and training, Frank naturally lined up the crosshairs on the man's head just as Cody came up next to him to take a look. Frank exhaled softly, emptying his lungs of air, which helped steady the rifle against the cave wall. He effortlessly flipped the selector to fire and took up the first stage on the match trigger. Satisfied with his sight picture he continued through the second stage of the trigger until it broke clean. Time slowed as Frank saw the man's head explode into a pink mist, his body falling lifeless like a puppet whose strings were cut. He heard the single piece of brass clinking on the hard, rocky surface.

All of Cody's blood rushed to his legs, knowing this was his chance. He took off at a sprint, MCX in hand, Frank right behind him as they left Brandon far behind. Luckily, it seemed the element of surprise was in their favor. Everyone they ran past seemed to jump out of their way in fright. After Cody and Frank weaved through the scattering of people and tents, both Renegades finally reached Tessa, who stood frozen in fear, blood spattered across her face. Unsure of what happened, she looked down at the mangled head on the body behind her. Her ears rang, high-pitched and shrill. Suddenly she heard a voice, distant at first and almost muted, but it began to grow louder as the auditory exclusion wore off.

"Tessa! Shake it off. We gotta go now! *Now*!" Cody yelled, now within arm's reach.

Gunfire erupted from the direction of tent city. The initial element of surprise was over. North Spear was now aware they had been infiltrated. Cody brought his rifle up as two guards came into view around the side of the closest tent. They looked stunned to see him so close. Cody let out a controlled pair for each man, left to right, no discernible break in cadence as the sound of four consecutive shots rang out. They both dropped before they could bring their weapons to bear.

More gunfire began to break out, this time with screams as the scientists and workers scurried around, fearing for their lives. Frank shouldered his rifle, acquiring armed targets of his own and breaking shots in their direction. Cody grabbed his sister by the shoulder, shaking her abruptly.

He pulled her over the boxes, letting her run past him as he and Frank provided cover for her escape. Simultaneously they walked backward a few steps, firing their suppressed weapons as North Spear contractors fired at them, exposing their positions. Cody saw Al round the corner in the distance. They locked eyes as Cody paused just long enough to give him the finger.

Frank saw him too and fired three quick succession rounds in greeting toward Al's general direction, though none hit their mark. It did have the desired effect, causing Al to duck and cover. Frank felt his bolt lock back to the rear, subconsciously dropping his magazine, pulling another from his chest rig. He reloaded his rifle, Cody firing intermittently.

The two-man assault team bounded backward into the tunnel that led them to their mission. Frank passed Brandon and saw he hadn't moved, sitting in a puddle of his own urine and tears. He rounded the next corner and stopped, bracing against the side of the wall, ready to engage anyone brave enough to pursue them, although it seemed no one was.

Cody passed by Frank as he tapped him on the shoulder and called, "Last man." He ran to catch up with Tessa. He saw his sister up ahead, rounding another corner. Cody stopped himself once more to provide cover for Frank to move.

"Set!" Cody yelled out as loud as he could, his voice echoing through the cave.

"Moving!" Frank replied, firing suppressed shots directly after.

"Move," Cody said in the final reply.

He heard Frank's heavy footsteps barreling down the tunnel toward his direction, making a conscious effort to keep his finger off the trigger until Frank was past him. Frank stopped directly behind Cody, pulling his backpack off and tearing it open. Cody heard the zippers and wondered what Frank was doing.

"Are you up?" Cody asked, fearing he'd taken a stray round.

"Grabbin' some smoke. Got it. Smoke out," Frank replied, pulling the pin from the smoke grenade and tossing it down the cave, the spoon flying free from the can and releasing a thick plume of purple smoke.

"Should give us a little extra time. C'mon, let's boogey," Frank said with a slap to Cody's shoulder.

Both Renegades took off at a sprint, catching up with Tessa at the waterfall entrance. Cody grabbed the door and pulled it closed for added measure. Night had fully taken over the rainforest, and visibility was impossible without some source of illumination.

Sure wish I had my NODs with me right about now.

"Where's Jake?" Tessa asked, whipping around to see who was in their party.

"Who?" Cody yelled over the sound of the waterfall.

"The guy who was with me in the tent. My friend Jake. Fifty-something-year-old white guy."

"Didn't see him. C'mon," he implored, going to grab her arm.

"Cody, I can't just leave him in there," she pleaded, yanking out of his grip.

"If you want to survive this, you're gonna have to, sis."

All three jumped down into the shallow water, not taking any time to celebrate or reunite officially just yet. Frank saw the Land Rovers and didn't think twice. He took off through the water to the bank as quickly as he could. The Willis siblings followed close behind.

The sound of commotion made them turn. They could see that Al had just led the charge out of the cave through the smoke. Himself and ten North Spear gunmen poured out it, coughing furiously as their eyes searched for movement.

"C'mon!" Cody shouted, shoving his sister forward. Al's eyes met Cody, Frank, and Tessa who were clearly making a run for the cars. Flipping the safety selector on his M4 rifle to full auto, he let an uncontrollable burst fly in their direction.

Bullets sprayed wildly into the trees. Luckily most of them flew over their heads. Frank, Cody, and Tessa took cover on the opposite side of the beefy SUV while Cody pulled Tessa down next to him and put her directly behind the wheel well, giving her the added protection. He himself took a prone position underneath in order to acquire a target while Frank opted to use the back wheel for cover, kneeling to return fire.

"We can't keep this up! They're bounding toward us!" Frank yelled.

"I know!" Cody replied in between shots.

More North Spear bullets struck the vehicles, deflating the tires. Tessa's eyes closed shut, her hands clasped tightly over her ears. Stray bullets zinged over the car into the trees behind them while the ones that struck closer mashed into the car doors, some piercing the metal through and through. Cody changed positions, shooting around the front bumper, using the engine block as cover. He looked to his left, at the other vehicles, wondering if he should chance it. If they didn't move soon, they'd be quickly overrun and killed.

Outnumbered five to one, Cody knew this was eventually a losing battle. They could only keep this up so long before both he and Frank ran out of ammo. Suddenly the chaotic scene became eerily tranquil, and Cody heard a ringing voice clearly in his head. It was masculine and strong, though calm and confident.

Use the jungle, Cody.

He whipped his head around to find the source even though he knew the voice hadn't spoken out loud. It was like the voice had spoken directly inside his head. Turning to the thick rainforest, he knew it wouldn't be safe when the sun went down. It would be hard enough to see just to walk at an easy pace, let alone running away from the weaponized men that would pursue.

Trust in me, and I will provide refuge, the voice said.

He called out to Frank, "Too risky for the vehicles. They're bullet magnets. We can lose them in the jungle."

"Are you crazy?" Frank exclaimed.

"Probably," he said with a grin, and Frank shook his head exasperatedly. "I suppose it's better than dying here and now. Y'all first. I'll cover."

"Check. You ready, Tessa?" Cody asked, nudging his sister.

"I . . . I think so."

"Nothing to it. Just run when I run and stop when I stop," Cody said.

"Okay, I can do that," Tessa replied. Cody was reassured by the determined look on her face.

"Moving," Cody said, jumping to his feet, hunching over, and sprinting toward the jungle. Under the thick triple canopy, the light was already gone. If they were lucky, they could avoid contact long enough either for his pursuers to lose interest or not want to take the risks of low visibility for themselves. Using the thick foliage as concealment, he hopped over a fallen log, calling out to Frank to move.

Using the same leapfrog tactic as before, Cody oriented his muzzle downrange as Frank ran past him. One of the oldest tactics in the book, it was typically very effective as long as your teammate didn't cross your line of fire or, of course, have a weapon malfunction.

Cody saw the North Spear goons running up to the vehicles. One in particular had exposed himself too long before seeking cover. Cody centered the red dot on the man's chest and squeezed the trigger. A subsonic match grade bullet slammed into the man's upper chest. His body dropped behind the truck and out of sight.

Well, that's one less dude for sure, Cody thought to himself.

He saw Muscles poke his head up over his cover. Cody took aim and squeezed the trigger just as his head moved. The subsonic bullet whizzed past him with a hiss, only missing its target by inches. Cody cursed under his breath before he caught movement to his right—North Spear was trying to flank them.

He keyed his radio, hoping Frank would catch the radio traffic.

"They're moving to box us in. We need to pick up the speed or we're gonna run outta ammo."

Cody heard his radio crackle in his ear before Frank's voice filled his earpiece. "Yeah, I hear movement. Let's follow the creek. Maybe it feeds into a bigger river link up there."

"Yeah, ten-four," he said into his mike.

Cody checked to make sure no one had a direct line of sight on him and stood to cover some distance. He took off at a run, making sure his sister was right behind him. He could barely see his surroundings in front of him, but he could hear the flowing water coming from the Azazel pool that ran to his right.

"I hear movement coming my direction. That you?" Frank asked via radio.

Cody stopped and took cover behind a tree, checking behind him and Tessa for any pursuers. "Seven," he called out loud over his shoulder, using a challenge and reply. He could pick any number and so long as the other person called another number that when added together would equal ten, he would know they were in safe company. Simple and effective.

"Three," Frank replied, and he could hear his from twenty yards behind them.

Cody and Tessa made their way to the voice quietly, their eyes not yet adapted to the near black conditions of the thick canopy of the rainforest. The trio stopped together, everyone out of breath.

"These dudes are relentless. They don't wanna give you up, girly. What the hell did you get yourself into?" Frank asked quietly, breathing heavily.

"You know, I've been asking myself that same question," Tessa said, huffing and pushing up her sleeves. "It's a long story, one I hope to tell if we make it outta here alive. It's good to see y'all. Thank you both for coming to save me."

"Don't thank us yet. We're still a long way from home. We need to keep quiet until we know we're clear," her brother replied.

The small talk over, they remained hidden behind some deadfall and shrubs, the running water the only audible sound. Just as their heart rates slowed enough to keep moving, the bushes rustled. Low voices were heard. Tessa held her breath, her eyes starting to adapt. She saw her brother and Frank ready to engage, scanning for potential targets. They remained perfectly still, hoping they'd go undetected, but the voices got closer.

"I swear I heard them head this way," one of the North Spear man said.

Cody tapped Frank's shoulder, pointed to Tessa then downstream, telling him to take her and go. Both knew his 300 BLK MCX was much quieter and more difficult to detect if he had to shoot. He reluctantly agreed, not wanting to leave Cody alone against an unknown number of assailants. But their objective was getting Tessa out safely, and they both knew that.

So Frank and Tessa slid out as quietly as they could, careful not to make any unnecessary noise. With limited visibility, all the other senses had become much more acute, especially their hearing. Cody remained stock still, ready to vanquish anyone hellbent on harming his family.

"Shh, you hear that?" an unseen voice said. An intensely bright light turned on in Cody's direction. He couldn't risk them seeing Frank or Tessa. He brought his rifle to his shoulder and aimed toward the light. Cody sent three shots as fast as he could, though the light made it difficult to see his targets and red dot clearly.

He heard a male voice cry out in agonizing pain. The light flipped over, consequently illuminating his partner. Cody looked through his red-dot optic, put the circular fireball on the man's chest, and sent another volley. Rushing the shot a little too quick, the heavy bullet struck the man in the shoulder. He, too, cried out as more voices and rustling started coming their way.

After incapacitating the two gunmen, Cody wanted to give Frank and Tessa their best chance to get away. As the voices grew louder and closer, he slipped his assault pack from his shoulders and dug through its contents until he found more smoke grenades. He popped one immediately to cover his own movement in case North Spear used their flashlights to identify him.

Cody heard Frank in his earpiece. "Gonna try and head downstream a little ways and find a place to cross. If we get split up, primary RV is the hotel. Secondary RV is Mengele's house. Copy?"

"Zero Two copies all. Enroute," Cody replied, panting heavily.

Cody heard the river and knew he was close. Turning to run, he stumbled on a rock, quickly catching himself before he could fully fall. He slowed his pace enough to reduce the risk of falling down again or, worse, breaking a leg. He activated his weapon light and saw water moving swiftly, large rocks jutting upward to the sky, but he couldn't tell how deep. Neither Frank nor Tessa was anywhere in sight.

He tried the radio. "This is two. Status?" Cody inquired.

There was static in his earpiece, and he could tell a transmission was trying to come in, but it was far too garbled to understand. It sounded like a hair dryer was being blown directly into the mike and assumed they were already down river, hopefully crossing.

The water was clearly moving rapidly and for a moment he feared being swept away. Cody had hoped the bank would slope down easily into the water, but he was wrong. Right underneath him was a sheer drop of about six feet. He could see the large rocks sticking out amongst the rapids and knew he didn't quite feel like being smashed between that and the powerfully massive amounts of water. But what choice did he have? Behind him in the distance, he heard the remaining North Spear guys closing in. Their lights bounced back and forth through trees. If he jumped, he might be able to lose his pursuers, but in the river, he knew he'd have little control.

I hope this works, he thought as he unslung his MCX and took a leap of faith into the murky waters below.

26

Frank and Tessa had taken off at a dead run toward the stream. Frank activated his own weapon-mounted light to help him see, if only a little, to prevent him from running off a cliff or faceplanting straight into a tree. As they had entered the water, they quickly realized the creek was far deeper than he thought. He tried to remain close to the bank, but the jungle vines and branches tore at his arms and gear, refusing to release him. Luckily, Tessa had a much easier time, not weighed down with ammunition, weapons, and surveillance equipment, and she did her best to help him where she could as they made their way.

The creek began to widen more and more, clearly leading to a larger water source. Frank and Tessa heard suppressed gunfire from Cody followed by shouts in the distance. No radio traffic had come out; in this case, that was a good thing. No news was good news. Up ahead, Frank realized he could see better than usual, sparse moonlight shining through a break in the canopy. He stopped momentarily to ease the stitch in his side and figured Tessa's lungs were probably on fire as well.

But the powerful water surging around them seemed to have only gotten stronger as they navigated the current. It swept around Frank and

Tessa's hips, tugging on their clothing and continuously trying to pull them under, threatening to drag them into the darkness.

"I'm not sure how much farther we can go with this current!" Frank yelled to Tessa over the water.

He could hardly see her even though she was only a few feet in front of him. The duo stuck close to the banks, trying to maintain their footing on the rocks below. Just in front of Frank, Tessa lost her ground and disappeared underneath the water.

"Tessa!" Frank called and reached a hand out in front of him. Nothing. No one was there.

"Tessa!" he called again.

"Yeah! I'm here," he heard her call back, sputtering after she had found her footing and surfaced. "Careful. It drops a bit right here," she shouted.

"The current is too strong! C'mon, we need to get out of the water before it—"

Suddenly, one of the branches Frank had been using for support snapped, and he plunged down into the water. Without the grapple of the branches, the current threatened to take him away. In the darkness, his hand reached out and found grip on another root that, thankfully, held firm. He regained his footing, the soles of his boots finding the bottom of the river again.

Tessa had heard the splash and could only shout helplessly for Frank until he watched him surface once more. "Stay there!" he shouted, and she held her place until she felt Frank's hand find her. She was holding on for dear life to some bramble from the bank as the water threatened to push them along, trying to force them downstream.

"You okay?" she called back, fighting to keep her own footing.

"Yeah. C'mon!" he yelled again.

But as they tried to take another step to escape the tug of water, their feet met another unsteady part of the muddy river floor, and their footing was whipped out from under them. With no grip, the surge from the current smashed into Frank's behind with the force of an NFL linebacker. All control was lost as the roots they had been clutching were ripped from the banks. Neither of them could do anything but fight to keep a hold of one another. Both he and Tessa were hurled down the river as quick as the water could carry them. Tessa choked as she thrashed to find the surface, unwillingly taking in mouthful of the murky water as she thrashed blindly toward Frank. But it was no use. Just a few feet away, Frank was fighting just as hard to reach Tessa, but it was impossible to see, feel, or hear her.

Though Tessa had always been a strong swimmer, there was nothing she could do against this sheer force of nature. She fought to stay above the surface and barely had time to register the dark silhouette of an object approaching rapidly. By the time she realized the rock, it was too late. The river spun her body around, her head and shoulder striking it hard. She felt the impact harshly, but oddly enough, it didn't hurt. There was a few moments of just pure darkness. Where had the water gone? Where was the roar of the current?

Suddenly Tessa felt warm and at home. Like a switch had been flipped, she was now comfortable; the reality of running for her life felt like a distant memory. She realized she was floating. Opening her eyes, she blinked dazedly at the stars that shone blurrily through the water and rainforest canopy.

Slowly Tessa's senses came back to her when she heard something in the distance—a voice, perhaps—getting louder. *Frank!* she thought.

Suddenly aware of her surroundings, she reached out and felt her hand break the surface. A dip in the river threatened to pull her under, but Tessa strove to keep fighting with everything she had. Eventually, after several long moments of clawing her way up to the surface to find air, she felt it hit her face. Her muscles and lungs burned from the lack of oxygen as she spluttered the water from her lungs. She looked around quickly for any landmarks, but she didn't even know where she was.

She called out to Frank, her voice croaky at first and then louder, hoping he could hear her.

"Frank!" she yelled, coughing. Several petrifying seconds of silence passed. And then several others before she heard him.

"I'm here," he called from behind her.

He could just barely make out her outline only fifteen yards ahead, ensuring he kept an eye on her before she was swept too far from him to see. Frank tried to maintain as much control of his movement as possible, hoping to steer closer to her, but the water kept whipping him in the face and making it hard to breathe or maintain any directional bearing. Before he saw it, a car-sized boulder flew past his head by mere inches.

The next one, however, was unavoidable. Frank's right torso slammed into it, knocking what little air he had out of him. Under the surface, he grunted with pain after he felt two distinct, sharp, painful snaps. There was no doubt; several of his ribs had broken.

Tessa tried to orient herself toward his voice when she suddenly felt herself go weightless. For a moment in her dazed confusion, she thought she had escaped the river somehow. Instead, she felt herself plunged into freefall as her body was cast over the edge of the previously unseen waterfall. Moments later, the same fate befell Frank as the earth dropped out from beneath him and he, too, was sent tumbling to the aquatic darkness below.

Tessa hit the pool below with a splash. Thankfully, the drop was only ten feet, but for all either of them knew during the plunge, it was going to be thirty. Miraculously when she came up for air once more after hitting the surface of the water, she realized she had been lucky to avoid any rocks below that would have done any permanent damage. She pulled herself to the bank as the current from the pool pushed her into a shallower part of the water, layered with a patch of tall grass. Working herself out of it, she began to crawl up the small riverbank and through the thicket of foliage. Scratches, cuts, and what would soon be bruises covered her from head to toe. Dizziness filled her head, and she thought for a moment that she would vomit. Just seconds later, she was right. Tessa heaved over in convulsion, her body trying to rid itself of the ingested water.

Any sense of direction she had prior to getting in the water was now gone.

As soon as she finished, her head whipped around, looking for Frank, desperate to find him. The only sound she could hear was the rushing waterfall hitting the pool below. Fearing the worst, she began to yell out to him.

"Frank! *Frank*!" Her eyes scanned the dimly lit banks, hoping to catch a glimpse of him.

She began walking down the bank away from the waterfall, pushing the tall grass aside as she continued her search. The sound of the jungle creatures began to overshadow the rushing water.

With no sign of him and suddenly overcome with the fear that the river had overpowered him, she felt tears begin to stream down her face.

"Please, I'm so scared," she confessed in a whisper, her hands over her face in an attempt to shut out the world around her. A world where Frank didn't exist.

"Yeah, that'll happen when you get shit out of a waterfall," a voice said nearby, faint but unmistakable.

"Frank!" she yelled aloud, tearing her hands from her face and searching the ground for the voice's source.

Sure enough, Tessa could just make out the faint outline of a silhouette in the grass ahead. She rushed over to help him. The tall grass near the bank had camouflaged him so well, he was nearly invisible. Filled with joy, she dropped to his side and kneeled beside him. Immediately she knew he was badly injured. He sported a large gash above his left eye and was tightly clutching his right abdomen.

"I took a pretty bad hit before I went over," he explained when he saw her look of concern.

He tried to get up before Tessa could stop him, but the pain was too excruciating. He managed to get to a knee while Tessa threw his arm over her for support. She helped him away from the water and sat him next to a large rock.

"What's the worst part?" she asked, trying to decipher their list of medical priorities.

"I'll live," he said, shrugging. At her pointed look, he sighed. "It's just my ribs. I don't think they punctured anything, just hurts like hell." And she nodded, straightening up.

"First things first, we need to find a better place to go. Do you have any idea which direction we can head?" she asked, trying to take his mind off whatever pain he was feeling. "I can make a crutch for you out of some branches, and we'll take it slow," she reassured him.

"Well." He paused for a breath. "Mind if I take a nap first?" he suggested, looking over to her with a half grin, which was cut short by sharp pain from the movement.

"Ha ha, very funny. Do you have any idea where we are?" Tessa asked as she looked up the bank in the direction of downstream. "I can navigate if you just give me a heads up on the area."

"Not a clue, but in my backpack, I have a GPS. Let's take some cover so we're not too exposed. Help me get over there under those trees. I need to rest a minute and try to get in touch with Cody." Frank motioned with a faint wave of his hand. Tessa was growing more worried about him as she watched the color drain from his face, hoping the broken ribs were the extent of the injuries.

She helped him over to the trunk of a smaller tree and leaned him against it, but it seemed no matter how she adjusted him, he was in pain. His earpiece had been ripped out of his ear from the chaos of the water. He reached down to where his radio was supposed to be to find it cracked in two. That explained the broken ribs.

"Well, so much for getting in touch with Cody," he said, holding up what was left of his radio.

She pushed aside the intense worry for her brother and focused on the problem at hand. "You said you have a GPS? Let me get it, and we'll go from there."

She dug through his backpack before finding what she was looking for. Powering it on, she handed it over to Frank, who punched a few buttons as he stared into the dimly lit screen.

"Well shit," he said finally.

"What?"

"Looks like we're real far from our primary RV point back in town, but our secondary RV is about half the distance. I don't think I could make the primary in my condition, but the secondary is a realistic option. I just need to rest for a while, then we can start that way. The problem is I don't have a way to let Cody know."

"Forget it. Let's take this one step at a time. Why don't I do a supply check and see what we still have on us that works?"

He was looking at her with what almost looked to be a soft expression on his face. "Come here first," he said, reaching up to take her hand.

Frank pulled her ever so gently to the ground beside him. She moved closer and put her back against the same tree. Frank slowly turned toward her and nudged her shoulder with his.

"You know last time I saw you, I got a kiss on the cheek," he said, a twinkle in his eye.

"Last time you saw me, I wasn't running for my life," she quipped. "But I suppose since you helped saved my life, I owe you one."

Her muddy hands reached up and cupped his cheeks as she gently kissed his lips. The moment was short-lived, however, as Frank recoiled and winced in pain from his ribs. After a small readjustment to his position, he leaned in again for another, but she had pulled away.

"Excuse me, sir, those aren't for free, ya know? You have to earn them."

He frowned for a moment. "Can I get a line of credit?" he asked with a hopeful expression. They couldn't help it. They both erupted in laughter.

"I suppose one more on the house wouldn't hurt," she replied and kissed him softly again.

"There's something I need to tell you," he said, resting his forehead against hers, obviously exhausted. "I missed you."

Tessa held his hand with one of her own and caressed his cheek with her other. Despite his austere appearance, all she saw was a man who was willing to risk life and limb to help save her. Along with her brother, he'd pulled her from the clutches of certain death. Tessa brushed strands of Frank's long, dirty hair out of his face and behind his ears with the tips of her fingers.

"I've missed you too," she said softly. "Now get some rest and let me take care of you for a little bit," she said as she kissed his forehead and let him fall asleep to the sound of the waterfall.

27

Cody struggled to keep his head above water. The choppy waves enveloped him every time he tried to catch a breath of air. He wanted to stiffen his legs in hopes of bracing against a rock but feared he'd break them or worse, get caught by something and dragged under.

In an effort to keep his head up, Cody slipped off his backpack to lighten his load. As the straps slid off his shoulders, he reluctantly loosened his grip on the rifle. Just as his firing hand let go of the pistol grip, an unseen rock appeared right in front of him, sticking out of the water like an obelisk. The force of the current slammed him into it, causing the weapon to fly in one direction, and his body in another.

Clawing at the stony surface, he knew it was too smooth and wet to get a decent finger hold. Another splash of water to the face forced its way down this throat while he tried to catch another breath. Turning to navigate on his side, he began to pull and claw at the water with everything he had in the best combat sidestroke he could manage in order to escape the current. Cody's arms felt like dumbbells as he fought against the rushing water. The entirety of the day's events were catching up to him and he most certainly felt it now. He was drained.

As the water thrashed around Cody, he caught a glimpse of a low-hanging tree. Some of its branches dipped into the river. It was his only option at this point. He feared the river would overcome him soon. He began to claw his way toward the tree, hoping the momentum of the water wouldn't carry him past. The first branch touched his fingers but slipped through his grasp. He reached for the next and managed to secure a good hold.

The force of the river pulled his body, threatening to break his grip. His arms and hands burned from the exertion. Cody pulled himself out of the water enough to catch a good breath but didn't know how much longer he could hold on. For a brief moment, a tiny voice in his head, different from the calm and reassuring one from before, told him to let go. It would be so much easier to give up. Maybe it would be this river that would kill him, or perhaps the placement of a good rock, and he'd finally be able to see his wife and daughter again.

He looked to the riverbank, his grip failing and saw that underneath the tree sat a lion. Though it wasn't just any lion. It was the same lion from his dream.

Am I going crazy? There aren't any lions in South America.

Cody held his grip of the branch as the lion stared directly at him. For a moment, they held one another's gaze. Not a moment later, he heard a voice in his head say one word. This voice was the stronger, calming one from before when they were taking cover from North Spear's gunfire. This one overpowered all other ones.

Fight.

Cody kicked his legs and pulled with everything he had, hoping the branch wouldn't break. Inch by inch, he pulled himself closer to the bank until finally he was able to pull himself up onto a nearby rock. Coughing, he scrambled to look at the maned cat, only to find he'd disappeared.

Maybe I am going crazy. No, I know I didn't imagine that. He was right there, I saw him. Was it His voice that I heard?

He rolled to his back on the rock, exhausted. The bank was still steep but more manageable where he was at now. Luckily another hanging tree branch gave him the structure he needed to pull himself completely out. As soon as his boots felt the earth beneath him once again, relief filled his soul. Soaked from the inside out, he laid down behind a Volkswagen-sized boulder that had found its home on the bank. Coughing the last remaining ounces of water out, he paused, hoping to hear some sign of Frank or Tessa.

Instead all that greeted him were the sounds of the jungle river and various nightlife. The sound of birds, rushing water, and wind in the trees echoed all around. He looked to the sky, seeing a few stars above, thankful he was alive to see them. Now he had to survive. Instinctively he reached down to his hip, feeling for the only remaining firearm he had left, his faithful Glock. To his amazement it was still there, held securely by the Safariland holster. His spare mags managed to remain with him as well. His radio, however, had not been so lucky. The screen was cracked, and he cursed as nothing happened when he turned the power knob.

Crawling around the rock, Cody laid prone looking upriver. Without any artificial light, he couldn't judge how far he'd travelled. He was thankful he didn't see any North Spear lights searching for him. Hopefully the smoke grenades had worked, giving him the distance he needed. Perhaps they didn't think he was crazy enough to actually jump.

He'd considered walking up and down the riverbank yelling for Tessa and Frank but knew it was too risky. He didn't want to increase his chances of North Spear finding him again after he nearly drowned trying to get away.

Checking his wrist-mounted GPS, he tapped one of the side buttons, hoping it hadn't suffered the same fate as his radio during the aquatic onslaught. The LCD screen lit up and looked no worse for wear. He checked his waypoints and quickly realized he only had access to one: the hotel safehouse. Although he'd saved the coordinates to Mengele's house on his handheld Garmin, he had forgotten to do the same for the smaller and simpler wrist-mounted device.

Rookie move, Cody. Dammit! He knew it would be closer than trying to trek through the jungle back to the hotel. For a moment he thought about trying to find Mengele's house without the aid of satellite navigation. But ultimately he knew the risk of getting lost was too high.

He knew he only had one option at this point: he needed to make it to the safehouse. From there he could refit, rearm, and reorganize enough to figure things out. It was the only choice he had. Cody also knew that he wasn't going to wish himself there either. It had to start by putting one foot in front of the other. This was no time to start feeling sorry for himself. He just hoped Tessa and Frank were better off than him right now. He checked the wrist-mounted GPS one more time and began his trek through the jungle.

Hours had passed as Cody navigated through some of the thickest foliage he'd ever encountered. Fortunately it had the added benefit of distracting him from worrying about Tessa. Being anxious about her and Frank wasn't going to help them. He needed to stay focused on the objective: getting to the safehouse.

Being alone in the jungle didn't bother him, so long as the GPS battery held up. He checked his watch and saw it was closing in on 04:00 a.m. If he was lucky, he'd find a dirt road or something that could lead him toward town. Cody found himself realizing how much easier operations like this had been with a full team. If Val and Tom had been with them, they'd have made short work of those assholes back at the cave and likely had been able to exfil in a vehicle.

Sure would have been nice to avoid that whole river from the get-go. The thought of his team by his side made him smile as he walked. Daylight was still a ways off, but his eyes had adapted significantly better since everything had kicked off. The adrenaline dump had certainly taken its effect on his movement, but he pushed forward, one step at a time like he told himself he would.

Cody heard familiar mechanical sounds coming from just up ahead. The sound jerked him out of his exhausted state, his senses on full alert. He drew his Glock and approached carefully. Light illuminated the jungle, but it was static. Cody peeked around a tree and saw it was two vehicles, one parked behind the other. After carefully watching the occupants, it appeared the lead car had been having some kind of engine trouble. As Cody observed, they tested the vehicle once more, shouting in hurrah as the vehicle suddenly roared to life with a sputter. He could hear a slightly unfamiliar language at a distance as the two men spoke, but from what Cody could translate, they didn't sound like North Spear.

After consideration, Cody holstered his pistol and moved in to take a closer look. He saw two older men in their fifties. Both were conservatively dressed and definitely local. Not wanting to spook them and cause an untimely heart attack, he stood in the open and called out loud, "*Hola, caballeros.*"

The men were bent over the lead car's engine, and despite Cody trying not to spook them, both nearly jumped out of their skin at the greeting. Their eyes went wide looking at the young American, caked in mud and soaking wet. They glanced at his chest rig and finally on his pistol. Cody resisted the urge to put his hand on the gun, fearing it would provoke them.

He lifted his hands up to show them he meant no harm. Their body language shifted slightly, relaxing at the realization they weren't being robbed. Wishing he'd worked on Spanish more often, Cody tried to communicate.

"*¿Tu hablas inglés*?" he asked.

"*Hablo español*," they replied simultaneously.

Well shit. What was the word for city or town? Ciudad *or* cuidado*? Screw it, Cody, just pick one.*

"*Cuidado*?" Cody asked, unsure of his pronunciation.

Both men looked at him curiously, then at each other before one responded. "*¿Para que*?" he replied.

Okay, let's try the other one.

"*¿Ciudad*? *¿Iquitos*?" Cody tried again, hoping he got his point across.

The men's eyes lit up, now understanding the gringo's mistake. They chuckled at each other and said something way too fast for Cody to catch. The language barrier had been crossed if only for a moment. The two men spoke, agreed on something, and shook hands.

One of them pointed toward the rear car and then waved at Cody to follow. He appeared to be offering him a ride. The American knew the dangers of hitching in third world countries, but chances were his newfound friend was more scared of him than the alternative.

The man pointed to himself. "Alonzo," he said. Cody shook his head and introduced himself as well. The man said something else in Spanish but either spoke too fast for Cody to interpret or Cody was too exhausted to interpret it in the first place. Either way, Cody pretended to understand and jumped into the passenger seat with a general wave of goodbye toward the man's companion, who returned the same. Now, Cody's biggest fear was nodding off into dreamland, wanting to make sure he stayed aware of his surroundings as they drove and that he and his driver were on the same page for their destination. Besides, he didn't want his escort to drive right up to the dilapidated hotel while he was passed out like a kid riding the school bus.

After hopping into the car himself, the man seemed to think of himself as a tour guide, pointing out different features of the land, talking so fast he never understood a word the man said, but Cody nodded in agreement nevertheless. Soon enough, Cody saw the lights of the city up ahead.

He asked the man to stop, putting his hand out to convey this, which the man did with a curious face. Cody jumped out of the passenger seat after which he caught sight of an old wool blanket in the backseat. Not wanting to steal it, Cody dug through his chest pocket and found a hundred-dollar bill he always tucked away in case of emergency, happy to finally put it to good use. The driver happily parted with the old piece of fabric for such a price. They exchanged basic pleasantries of thanks before the man drove away. The sun was going to break soon, and Cody wanted to maintain some concealment as he made his way into town. He draped the old blanket over his head and shoulders, trying to play the part of a vagabond.

On the outskirts of the town, he recognized the basic layout. He saw familiar buildings from the last couple days and followed the route he knew that led to the hotel safehouse. Cody estimated he was only a half mile away.

He navigated through the streets, careful not to draw any attention. Within fifteen minutes, he was standing two buildings down from the hotel. He leaned against the corner of an opposing structure, watching the hotel for any signs of North Spear. After watching the area for a bit, he proceeded around the corner to the back entrance Fernando had shown him.

He walked through the building and up the stairs until he got to one of their rooms. The door was slightly ajar, which immediately put Cody on edge. Walking on the balls of his feet to reduce noise on the creaky floor, he closed the distance to the entrance. He listened for anyone inside and heard nothing but silence.

Pulling his pistol from the holster, he held it at a low ready and shrugged the blanket off his shoulders. Cody hoped Tessa and Frank were inside waiting for him, but he couldn't be too careful. He especially didn't want to run in blindly, not by himself. He pushed the door open ready to engage any threats as he cleared the room from the hallway.

Inside, the early morning light shone through a window, illuminating the one face Cody never expected: Val, who looked none too happy. Cody saw Val's HK 416 sitting across his lap, and Cody had a brief moment of uncertainty, wondering if it was meant for him or not.

Cody held eye contact with him for a few seconds before Val casually glanced at this signature Tudor timepiece.

"Good time to talk?" Renegade Actual asked as he spat tobacco juice into a cup.

28

Al and what was left of his men that chased Cody and Frank into the jungle returned to Azazel wearing defeat on their faces. Three men had been killed, and two more seriously wounded. Two men had effectively crippled his fighting force, cutting their numbers in half. Luckily it was only a quarter of the men he had available to him.

They entered the main cave chamber that housed tent city and saw a large group gathered at the front steps of the temple. At the top of the steps, Bart stood, talking with the crowd. Al and his men remained in the rear, listening.

"Who were those guys, Bart? You assured us this place was safe!" a voice said. Several others resounded in affirmation.

"I've talked with my lead security officer, and we have concluded that we were attacked by competitors in the field. I know, this is all quite traumatic for you, just as it is me," he said, peering into as many faces as he could. "I wished to keep this information confidential, but since it has affected all of us, there's no sense in trying to hide it any longer. I, too, was attacked in an assassination attempt earlier today. Our work here is important, and the impact this project will have on the world will last generations. But there are people out there who want to take that away from us . . . to steal it for themselves."

He had their full attention while he paced back and forth. His arms waved as the lies and deceit poured out from his politician-like speech.

"After the failed attempt on my own life, they sent more attackers and kidnapped our very own Tessa Willis. They knew her value to this team and clearly understood her importance to our work. I will be working with Al and his men to retrieve her with the help of local authorities. The best thing we can do right now is remain here inside the cave for the night. I will have guards posted to ensure no one can harm any of us again. Now if you'll excuse me, I have a few things to attend to so that we are all safe."

"What about Dr. Reynolds?" one of the scientists asked.

Bart thought quickly. "Unfortunately, our dear friend Dr. Reynolds was struck by a bullet and killed. We have secluded his remains until we can properly take care of him. I will be notifying his family at my earliest convenience. Are there any further questions?"

"Yeah," someone called from the crowd. "When are we getting out of here?"

"I assure you, as soon as it is safe, we will all be relocating to the hotel, but right now, it is imperative that we remain right here until Al gets things under control." He grit his teeth. "Anything else?"

If anyone had anything left to say, they didn't voice it to him. They began to depart to their tents and workstations.

Bart descended the steps and waved Al away from the crowd.

"Well?" Bart asked impatiently.

"We were not able to stop them, sir. I chased them into the jungle where we lost sight of them and took heavy casualties. I lost five men—"

Bart cut him off. "I don't give a shit about five men, Al," he growled. "I want her found. She knows too much at this point and could ruin everything. I had it all figured out and everything was going so perfectly beforehand. I want it back that way now, dammit!"

Al's anger flared momentarily at Bart's dismissal of his troops. He knew those men—good men, just like the guys he'd served with years before. He thought about them and how badly he wanted to exact revenge on those who killed them. He was just assessing how he would even go about tracking them down when an idea began to form.

"Sir, didn't Tessa make a call on a satellite phone a couple of days ago?"

Not seeing where this was going, Bart answered, "Yes. Why?"

"If we had access to her phone, we could possibly identify the number she called and track the device that was used. If they're still here in Peru, maybe we could intercept them and recover her and tie up any loose ends."

Bart looked Al in the eyes. "I knew pulling you out of that gutter in Thailand years ago would pay off eventually. The phone is in my tent. I'll make a call up the ladder and get it authorized," and Al nodded.

Bart knew once he called, he'd have to explain Michaels's death anyhow, or at least have *an* answer. He was already formulating what he would say, but that would not be something for Bart to face until a later moment. For now, he needed Al.

"Pick someone to lead them and get it organized," Bart ordered. "I don't care who you send or how many, but I want it done as clean and as quiet as possible. Make sure they don't make a scene. Think they can handle that?"

Al nodded resolutely. "Yes, sir."

"The last thing we need is Peruvian government down our necks," Bart continued. "It was already expensive enough to get the licenses and permits just to excavate here, let alone pay off the officials. We cannot afford that kind of heat. As for you, I want you here with me."

"Yes, sir. What do we do with Dr. Reynolds?" Al asked.

"Ah yes, Jake. He's subdued in my tent under guard. He won't be a problem. Though it would be poetic, and I would greatly prefer her blood to open the tomb, I suppose he could stand in for Tessa in the event your team is unable to recover her."

"Understood, sir. I'll assemble them immediately," Al said before departing.

Bart began to think through the second—and third—order effects. If he could spin this the right way, there was a chance he could eat his cake and have it too. His entire life had led him to this point, and he'd be damned if anyone was going to stop him.

First thing was first: he needed to update Mr. Adams. Bart exited the cave and stood outside staring at the night sky as he waited for the phone to connect and went over his carefully planned lines.

"If you're calling to grovel, Cox, don't bother," the voice said as soon as the phone connected,

"On the contrary, sir, there's been a development that you need to be made aware of. Joshua Michaels has been killed."

There was a pause before he replied. "What have you done, Bart?"

Bart thought of a few words Hillary Clinton once spoke: "Never waste a good crisis."

"We've been attacked, sir. *Here*, at the site," Bart quickly said. "I am certain it was Ms. Willis's brother, a former police officer, and his accomplice. Michaels and I were conducting our turnover when they launched their attack, seemingly to take custody of her, which they did. Our security tried to repel them, but unfortunately, Michaels was killed in the process."

"How fortunate for you," Mr. Adams said, his voice laced with suspicion.

Anxious to throw Adams off his trail, Bart offered up a solution as well as the juiciest update yet.

"I do have two bits of good information however, sir. One, and most importantly, I have discovered the secret to opening the tomb. Secondly, we possibly have a way to track down Ms. Willis and her friends. Sir, I believe she knows far too much to be left hanging in the wind. I am requesting you track a phone and allow me to clean this up properly."

"So, she is no longer necessary?" the cold voice pried.

Bart thought about the question for a moment, and though technically that was true, he couldn't let it go. No, he couldn't let *her* go. Mr. Adams wouldn't care as to how or who opened the tomb so long as it was opened. Bart, however, was emotionally involved now, and he knew he'd need the authorization to track them down regardless. Tessa therefore had to remain in play.

"Not entirely, sir. She presents a loose thread that needs to be clipped. If we want this to remain discreet, her silence is necessary."

Another pause.

"Very well, I'll get it to you. Do I need to send my specialist and his team down there to handle it?"

Bart had heard rumors about Adams's specialist. He was a man of no remorse; someone Bart did not want involved.

"No, sir. It's only two men and a girl. My men can handle it."

"Call me back when you have this cleaned up."

And with a click, the line went dead.

29

Cody didn't waste any time. "No, Val, actually now is not a good time." Cody spoke matter-of-factly. When Cody didn't clarify, Val raised an eyebrow.

"Well, you gonna tell me what's going on or keep me waiting?" he asked.

Cody shut the door behind him. "Listen, Val, I'm sure you're pissed, but seriously now is not the time to do this. Frank and Tessa need my help."

"No. Pissed is putting it lightly. You need to tell me what you've gotten yourself into *now*." The frustration in his voice was apparent. His fingers drummed impatiently against the weapon in his lap.

"I'm not entirely sure you'd believe me if I told you," Cody replied shortly.

"Humor me," he said, standing from the chair and placing the rifle on the table in front of him. He crossed his arms, waiting for Cody to speak.

Cody paid no attention to the anger laced on his face and instead moved to his gear on the other side of the room, kneeling down and beginning to prep his equipment while he talked. He did so quickly.

"Tessa called me two days ago on my SAT phone," he said, picking it up from his pile of gear for emphasis. "The connection was spotty, but she was in danger and I knew it. She used the family code phrase from when we were kids. She needed me, Val, and I wasn't going to let her down, not like I let the girls down," Cody said, his mind flashing with Jen and Elena's faces.

"Where is she now? Is Frank with her?" Val asked. It was hard to read the expression on his face. It wasn't as red now, which Cody took for a good sign.

"I don't know. I was hoping I'd find them here," Cody said, not making eye contact with Val and trying to push down the fear he had felt at the sight of their absence. Why weren't they? Did they go to the other RV point? Had they made it?

"I've been here all night and haven't seen them," Val said, which made Cody's heart lurched. "Fill me in on some more details."

He watched as Cody busied himself with his equipment. "Frank and I made our way down here and found her being held hostage by the company who hired her. They fled to the excavation site in the jungle where Frank and I were able to do an in-extremis rescue. We tried to E&E through the jungle but got split up at the river. I was coming back to reorganize and go back out there."

"Did you have a secondary RV?"

"We did, that's where I'm headed."

"No, you're not," Val said firmly.

"You going to stop me?" Cody asked, looking up at him before standing up to face him. "I don't work for you anymore, *remember*?"

"Didn't I teach you anything?" Val groaned. His frustration was back. "What happens if you go to the secondary and they try to meet you here? You guys could be chasing each other all over Peru."

Cody hated that Val was right. He realized just how tired he was if he was making those kinds of mistakes.

"Alright then, what do you suggest? Making a pizza run and just hoping they'll eventually show?" Cody asked sarcastically.

Val must have seen Cody's stress levels because he didn't make a comment on Cody's mockery. Val wouldn't have let it slide otherwise.

"I've got Tom down here with me. He's out driving around town scanning the radios for any signals from you guys. We'd hoped to pick up something that would help point us in the right direction. Let me give him a call and let him know I've found you, at least. He'll come by, then the three of us can start trying to figure out how we're going to find Frank and your sister if they aren't at that second RV. We can keep one of us stationed here in case they show," Val said and rubbed his head, nursing an already-forming headache.

"Wait a minute, if he's out there scanning for our cell signals or radio transmissions, how'd you know to come here to this hotel room? How'd you know you'd find me here?"

"I made a call to an old friend in the Activity who helped me track your SAT phone. I was counting on you bringing it along," Val replied, bringing the phone to his ear to talk with Tom.

Cody looked at the SAT phone still in his hand as the door was shoved open. There was a familiar metallic clink as the small object rolled across the floor. A flashbang. Before either of them could say anything, their world erupted in a blinding flash of white light.

Cody took the brunt of the blast while Val's body had been turned partially away. Val had been exposed to more flashbangs in his lifetime than any one man could count, but that didn't make him immune. Directly after the blast of the distractionary device, his body dropped to the floor, releasing the phone. He rolled to his back and grabbed for his weapon on the table, leveling his suppressed HK416 at where he knew the door to be just as a young man poured in the room. Val flipped his selector to fire and started pulling the trigger as fast as he could. The 75 grain Gold Dot did its job, blossoming beautifully into a jagged, hot flower petal of destruction right in the center of the man's chest. Instantly, the intruder folded and crumpled to the floor. There was a momentary pause before the next man entered the room, giving Val a chance to seek cover behind the couch. As he did, Renegade Actual took a step back, his foot stepping on the phone he'd dropped no more than seconds earlier. It connected.

Cody drew his pistol but couldn't see anything well enough to fire any well-aimed shots. He was too experienced to fire blindly for fear of hitting Val. He suddenly felt the impact of someone grabbing at him, landing on Cody's back before Cody was able to wrestle him off. The fight was on. Cody held the man's head tight to himself and threw his elbows as hard as possible while simultaneously bucking his hips up to throw his assailant off balance. It worked. As he thrust up and out, he flipped the man harshly onto his back just as Cody's eyesight began to return.

Val brought his weapon to bear around the side of the couch, searching for targets. He had not been able to engage the guy who tackled Cody out of fear of striking Cody instead but figured Cody could hold him off a bit longer. They had to take this problem one bite at a time.

Two more men entered the room, clearly unsure of what to do or where to go, giving Val an opening. Like he'd done a thousand times before, Val took a sight picture through his optic and fired three rounds into one man before immediately transitioning and firing another three into his partner. All six shots were seamless. As soon as he ensured he did not see any further threats in the room, he moved to help Cody, who was still fighting his man on the ground.

With Cody on top, Cody held one of his hands on the man's throat while his other reached for the pistol he'd dropped on the floor earlier. He had barely grabbed it before he realized the man below him was none other than Bro Vet Deon. The sudden pause gave Deon the break he needed. He fished his index finger into Cody's mouth to pull him down and to the side. Cody released his grip on Deon's throat and abandoned the reach for the gun, instead choosing to trap Deon's hand so he could maintain control on top.

Cody bit down on the finger in his mouth just as Deon's other hand cold clocked him from the side. Unintentionally he clenched his jaw to take the impact and bit Deon's finger clean off.

Cody spit it out just as Deon began to scream in pain. When Val reached them, he fired one round into the man's forehead, ending the fight for good. Cody doubled over gagging.

"Can't say I've ever seen that before," Val said with a cocked head, looking at the severed digit. "We need to get the hell outta here. Grab your kit."

Cody nodded in agreement, wiped his mouth, and shuffled over to his gear pile. He collected his pistol from the floor and shoved it in his holster while pulling his trusty Hodge rifle from his deployment bag. He began stuffing magazines in the empty slots on his chest rig while Val went to the window to peek outside. The frame exploded in a burst of wood splinters and hot lead as incoming fire rained up from outside.

"I'm good. Landslide, landslide, landslide!" Val yelled their team's hot word that meant, "Get the hell out of dodge right now."

Cody acknowledged it by running to the door. Just as he began to peek outside it to get his bearings, the same thing occurred. Gunfire rang out from down the corridor as bullets skipped down the walls and slammed into the end of the hallway, blocking their exit.

"Any bright ideas?" Cody asked, ducking back inside the room.

Val shook his head. "No, we're boxed in. Looks like this might be our last stand, Cody."

30

Tom Lorry had answered the phone as he drove, looking at the shanty buildings on both his left and right. He was always amazed at the living conditions outside the United States. No amount of time spent overseas would ever make up for it.

"What's up, boss? You got something?" he asked immediately.

In response, Tom heard several loud bits of commotion on the other end of the line that, in a momentary second of confusion, he couldn't place at first. But after a few seconds, he quickly recognized the all-too-familiar sounds of suppressed gunfire. His boys were in trouble, and he needed to get moving fast.

His foot smashed the gas pedal, pushing the vehicle to five thousand RPM in an instant.

"Val?! Talk to me, boss," Tom yelled to the Bluetooth-connected phone.

He turned left and right, working the steering wheel and emergency brake like a professional driver, silently thankful for the offensive driving course he'd taken last year. He raced toward the hotel where he'd dropped Val off and slowed a bit. It wouldn't do him any good if he drove right up to a group of people who wouldn't hesitate to shoot him through the windshield. He saw parked cars on either side and locals run every direction.

Looks like I'm heading in the right direction.

Two hundred yards ahead, he processed the scene in front of him. Two brand-new, muddy Land Rovers were parked in the middle of the street. Two men stood behind it.

One man was dumping bullets into the second story with an automatic rifle. Tom stopped the car in the middle of the street, angling the car's passenger side toward the threat to give him more cover and concealment. He darted out of the driver's seat and opened the backseat to arm himself. Tom was a man of unique talents. He could, simultaneously, be both a blunt force object that inflicted heavy damage *and* a precision instrument of death—something his choice of weaponry definitely reflected.

In the backseat he'd stored a short-barreled belt fed MK46 suppressed machine gun and a SR-25 sniper rifle. The lives of his teammates were at stake, so he knew he had to choose quickly. He popped his head up to look through the passenger's side windows to gauge the engagement distance.

In the moment, Tom opted for precision and grabbed the SR-25. He didn't want any dead civilians on his conscience today. He opened the stock to full extension and deployed the bipod. He took a prone position using the rear wheels as cover.

With the scope covers flipped up, he settled the Horus reticle on his target. Tom had a clear, full-body side shot, but he was concerned about over-penetration. He calmed his breath as the shooter stopped to reload. The man turned to take cover behind the Land Rover, giving Tom a full-frontal view of his target. Just as the North Spear man had identified something underneath the vehicle down the road, he felt the impact of the match-grade .308 round slam into his chest. His armor had taken most of the impact, knocking him flat on his back. He rolled to his stomach and tried to crawl to the other side of the Land Rover. He never made it as Tom sent another that entered the man's hip at an angle and traveled through his torso, finally exiting out the opposite shoulder. The bullet decimated his heart almost instantly. When Tom didn't see anyone else, he lifted his head from the scope to inspect the surroundings. He had just heard the report of a rifle when a high-velocity round impacted the ground just in front of him spraying dirty and debris in all directions.

He tucked himself behind the Toyota and came to a kneeling position. Tom moved to the other side of the car in the event his opponent was waiting for him to pop out. Tom could now see the second gunman who was firing directly at him take cover behind a car parked next to the sidewalk. Two rounds hissed directly over his head, forcing Tom back.

"Alright dude, you wanna play hardball? Let's play," Tom said, catching a glimpse of the shooter trying to move up to get a better shot.

Tom went prone again and saw the North Spear gunman's feet and lower leg under the vehicle. With the bipod attached he couldn't get the rifle low enough and turned it onto its side to lower the profile. With the gun turned ninety degrees, Tom adjusted his point of aim higher and to the magazine's side to ensure a hit. He squeezed the trigger; the match-grade bullet connected with his target's shin. His body fell to the ground as he clearly screamed in pain, which was visible through Tom's scope. Tom adjusted his point of aim, pulled the gun tight into his shoulder, and fired two shots in rapid succession to put the man out of his misery. The second bullet unintentionally struck his head, which exploded like a watermelon, chunks of skull and blood spraying the wall behind him.

Just as Tom had finished that guy off, three more poured out of the hotel from the front entrance and fired at him. They knew exactly where he was and were delivering accurate fire. Rounds impacted both the vehicle and the area around Tom, spitting dirt up all around.

It was time to change tactics. Tom knew just what to do. He left the precision rifle laying on the ground and pulled the belt-fed machine gun from the back seat. Tom opened the tray to ensure the belt was seated properly. Satisfied, he slammed it closed, pulling the bolt rearward, then forward, ready to unleash his fury.

This ends now!

Tom peeked around the rear bumper of the Toyota and sent a burst toward the men. All three ducked in cover. Tom ran as fast as he could to the side of the street to take cover behind another parked car. He moved as efficiently and quickly as he could, hoping to flank them, knowing speed was his security now. Tom stopped when he saw one of them looking to do the same, so he lifted the heavy machine gun and settled the red-dot sight on his target before letting loose a burst. The man tried to turn and run, but Tom kept the trigger pinned to the rear as he continued to move laterally. The man couldn't react in time, and his body was quickly riddled with bullets. He was dead before he hit the ground.

The two remaining North Spear gunman hadn't seen Tom yet. They didn't think anyone could have moved up on them that fast. They looked around in panic, trying to pinpoint his location as Tom continued in duck walk, concealed by the parked vehicles. He made his way directly in front of the Land Rover and could see the men moving from front to back, afraid of what was to come.

Tom had full view of both, and he was ready to pounce. He pinned the trigger down and let the machine gun do the rest. He didn't let go until he was satisfied both men had either changed shape or caught fire. The smoke from the suppressor and barrel was so thick he couldn't see them, but he let his imagination fill in the blanks. Tom heard a familiar voice call out from behind him.

"Two coming out!"

Tom turned to see Val and Cody standing at the door to the hotel waiting for his response.

"Come out. Y'all good?" Tom shouted at them, and although they looked a little worse for wear, they nodded.

As the pair walked out, they couldn't help but stare at Tom's handiwork. Cody whistled.

"Well, if we weren't before, we certainly are now. Damn bro, you smoked those fools," Cody said, looking down at one of the mangled bodies.

"Nicely done," Val added, looking at the carnage and the five dead bodies strew about. "No doubt that would've made your old CSM proud," he said with a slap to Tom's shoulder.

Tom smiled. "You know me, just glad to lend a helping hand."

"Well, I'd say we've drawn enough attention for one day. Grab everything we can, and let's get the hell outta here before anyone else shows," Val said, beckoning them away.

Cody and Tom agreed with a nod. They collected all their sensitive gear and weapons and piled them into one of the serviceable Land Rovers and Tom's Toyota before the three of them departed the town and made their way toward RV point two, Mengele's house.

31

The sun was just cresting the horizon, providing some much-needed light for Tessa and Frank. They had been able to move steadily toward the rendezvous point, but it had been slow going due to Frank's broken ribs. The once-agile six-foot-three athlete was restricted to a snail's pace, even using the makeshift crutch Tessa had fastened for him out of some branches and vines.

Tessa had also tried to help by carrying some of Frank's equipment to lighten the overall strain, but it was only mildly effective. They had pushed on through the night one step at a time until they came within a couple hundred yards of their destination at daybreak. It was impossible to see the house through the thick jungle even at that range.

Frank had to use his GPS to confirm their proximity before he looked at Tessa.

"Listen, we don't know what's out there, okay? We don't know where Cody is or if they captured him or what. I want you to stay behind me, and I'll wave you up when it's clear. Got it?" he instructed.

"Got it," she replied.

He nodded and set down the makeshift crutch at the bottom of a tree trunk. He would prefer the use of both arms if he had to. "Alright, let's go," he said.

Together, they carefully and quietly moved through the jungle toward the old Nazi's house. Through the trees, Frank could make out two vehicles close to the house, one of which was a black Land Rover.

Not a good sign, he thought.

Palm down, he waved his hand up and down to signal Tessa to get low. When he turned back, he saw someone emerge from the house, and his heart skipped a beat. Instinctively he drew a deep breath as he recognized the figure and was rewarded with sharp searing pain for it. It was Val.

"Think you could lend a hand?" he yelled toward Val, pushing the pain aside.

Startled, Val turned, gripping his pistol. But even from a distance, he recognized the tall frame. Lowering his defenses just slightly, he yelled toward the house for additional help. Cody and Tom both ran out, weapons drawn and ready to fight, but Val waved them down and pointed towards the newcomers. Cody let out a shout of greeting and ran to Tessa, who wrapped him in a tight hug, while Tom and Val helped Frank toward the vehicles. Within a few minutes, all four Renegades and Tessa were gathered around the two cars.

"What the hell happened? You take a round?" Val asked as Frank leaned heavily against the vehicle.

"No, I took a boulder to the side right before I went over a waterfall, *Predator* style."

"Not gonna lie, that sounds kinda cool," Tom blurted.

"Well I can assure you, it sounds a lot cooler than it is," Frank replied, nursing his side.

"How about you, sis? You okay?" Cody asked, turning to his sister, his face filled with concern.

"Better off than Frank at the moment. You?"

"Other than the taste of finger in my mouth, I'm no worse for wear," Cody replied, wiping the back of his neck.

Tessa shot him an odd look. "If that's a joke, I don't get it," she said.

"Unfortunately, it's not, but I'll tell ya later," Cody replied.

Val cut in, taking charge of the conversation. "Alright, first off, I'm glad nobody is seriously hurt. A lot has happened in the last couple of days that I need to get caught up to speed on so I can figure out how to deal with this mess. Tessa, you're up first."

Without any hesitation she jumped right in, starting with how she was approached by Bart and offered the position. She told them all about the ancient Nephilim temple and her work trying to decode the Enochian, believing it would provide the secret to opening the giant tomb. She paused for a moment trying to find the right words when she got to the dream. Tessa knew it sounded crazy, and perhaps she was a little vague as she herself was still trying to wrap her head around it even as she spoke, but she continued anyway. She told them about learning the secret with Jake and finally ended with Bart, hellbent on sacrificing her atop the Nephilim tomb to access the remains inside.

Processing what they heard, all four men stood silently for several moments after her story. Tom broke the silence with a low whistle. Val was the first to speak.

"Do you know for certain that he can open it?" he asked quietly.

"I mean, I didn't see one open, but given what I could tell from Bart, he was certain. So yes, it's a pretty safe bet. And trust me, he doesn't seem the bluffing type," Tessa said. There was a pause as they all took what she was saying in.

"And you . . ." Tom looked around a bit sheepishly before turning to Tessa. "You believe that opening it will . . . you know, do something?" Tessa sighed, knowing Tom likely wasn't the only one in the group with this opinion of disbelief. She could hardly blame them.

She took a deep breath. "I do. But you don't have to believe me. Either way, we have to go back to do something about Jake," she said resolutely.

That caught Frank's attention. "Whoa, Tessa, I'm not trying to be an inconsiderate asshole here, but we came for *you*. Who cares if some giant-worshipping dirtbag uses some old guy to open an old casket?" Frank said.

"*I* care, Frank, because he's my friend. And I'm not going to let Bart slit his throat to do it. Besides, none of you are getting it. Whether he uses Jake or someone else to open that tomb, if he gets access to the remains of that Nephilim body, the bad guys win. End of story. Whether you believe me or not about what will happen if that tomb is opened, we can't let this happen," she said, slamming her palm against the hood of the car, but the rest of the guys looked uncertain.

"Look, Frank's got a point, Tessa," Cody said, "I know what you mean about wanting to stop evil, trust me, I really do. I've had experiences during this that I can't really explain either, but this isn't what we're here for. Hell, Val and Tom are only here in the first place because they got mixed up in this mess thanks to me. And Frank and I? We chose to come down here to get you out. *You*. The four of us," he glanced at Frank, "well, three and a half of us, aren't equipped or prepared to do something like this."

Frank gave him the middle finger.

Something Tessa said had caught Val's ear.

"Back up a bit here. What do you mean by, 'whether we believe you or not about what will happen if that tomb is opened,' Tessa?" he asked, and she looked a little hesitant to explain in further detail, knowing it was the craziest part about what she had told them. "Details, Tess," he said firmly, and she sighed.

"When I was visited by the angel in my dream, he showed me who and what the Nephilim really are and what they're capable of. They're a plague that would destroy the human race—the world. The ancient Jews believed that demons were the disembodied spirits for the dead Nephilim. If they're allowed to return to physical form, I don't even know what would happen, but I do know it would be catastrophic."

"I don't get it. How would they come back if they're already dead?" Tom asked, itching a spot on his cheek.

"North Spear is planning to harvest the DNA from the skeleton with the hope of studying it as an 'enhancement' to the human genome. Their hubris is playing straight into the same Nephilim agenda from thousands of years ago. Anyone with this so called 'upgrade' becomes bonded with them forever. You become a suitable host for demonic possession—and not just you either. Your children, and your children's children and so on. This is why God chose to step in and flood the world. He did it to save what little was left of it."

The four-man team stared at her at the influx of information. She glared at them. "Anyone here remember what Edmund Burke said?

'The only thing necessary for the triumph of evil, is for good men to do nothing.' You're good men, aren't you? Rebels with a cause?"

Cody thought about his own unexplainable events the last couple of days. Was this why they were here? Was this the purpose all along? Surely it all had to be a coincidence. It was suicide, to say the least, but maybe this is exactly why they were brought here together.

He looked to everyone in turn as he spoke. "I know you came down here to bring me home, but . . . I can't leave. If Tessa believes in this, then so do I," he said, looking at his sister. She nodded solemnly in appreciation before he continued. "Ever since my girls were killed in that car crash, I've been blaming myself. Jen told me that night on the phone she wanted me to stop working for ProCorp and come home after that mission. At the end of the night, I chose the job over them. Suddenly now, I realize this is my opportunity to make it right."

He straightened up. "I'll stay behind and stop them from opening that tomb. You guys leave, get my sister out of here, and blame the whole mess on me. That way you keep your noses clean with ProCorp."

Val looked at Cody, surprise flickering on his face. He was looking at a different man than the one he kicked off Renegade a little over a year ago. Before him was a man who understood what sacrifice was and was willing to pay the price. He'd taken responsibility for his actions and was doing what he could to make things right. Val realized it *was* time to bring Cody home, back to Renegade.

"Oh no, you don't. You're not getting off that easy. You think you can just stir up a hornet's nest down here in Peru and then go off by yourself to stop a bunch of giant-worshipping contractors from opening an ancient, sacred tomb? No way you make it inside that temple by yourself without getting yourself killed. We better tag along and make sure you don't screw anything up. Isn't that right, boys?"

Frank and Tom both grinned at each other before replying with a resounding yes.

"Question is, what do we do with girly here?" Frank asked, beckoning toward Tessa.

"What do you mean 'what do you with me?' I'm going in with y'all," she said, frowning.

"The hell you are," Cody said before Val could reply with his "Absolutely not."

She looked them both dead in the eye one at a time. "Do either of y'all know your way around said Nephilim cave temple?" Neither responded. "I thought not. When do we leave?"

32

Hours had passed since Al had deployed their "recovery teams," and still no word. Bart sat in his tent, swirling a glass of liquor while Jake remained bound and gagged on the floor. Bart could only wonder if this was how a cat felt when it played with a mouse before ultimately devouring it.

Al ran into Bart's tent, clearly worried, with his phone in hand.

"Sir, we have a problem," Al said, panting from his run outside.

Bart sat up in his chair, ready to receive the news. "Well?" he barked.

"I just heard back from one of the teams. One team got a flat tire just outside of town and stopped to fix it. The other team continued tracking the phone to a hotel room. They ran in without waiting for the second team to back them up. One of the guys said Deon was in charge of that group and didn't want to wait. They said he wanted payback for what happened in the hotel and was going in."

"And?" Bart pressed.

"By the time the other team fixed the tire and got there, the local Peruvian authorities were all over the area. They could see some our guys lying dead in the street."

"You assured me they could handle it, Al," Bart growled.

"I should have been with them, but you insisted I stay here, *sir*," he snapped back, hissing the last word.

Bart considered a response but let it slide. There was no use in arguing; the damage was done. The only objective to do next was move along with plan B. He looked to Jake, still gagged and bound to the floor.

"When the remainder of your men get back, I want you to get Dr. Reynolds here ready."

"They're on their way back now, they'll be here by nightfall. I've recalled everyone else that's left. They're coming in sporadically."

"Excellent. We'll wait till they arrive. I want to make sure I'm not bothered once I start," Bart said.

"Are we really going to kill him, just to see what's inside?" Al asked, looking down at Jake.

"Yes, if that's what it takes." Jake whimpered from the floor. Bart ignored him. "I've worked too damn hard for far too long to stop now. And so have you, Al, haven't you? Once we access the Nephilim genome, the sky is the limit. Their DNA can unlock the secrets to hybridization across species. How would you like to have the strength of a bear, or better yet, the natural night vision of an owl? Why not both? Surely that would come in handy for a man of your skills. We can be at the forefront of this evolution, Al. We can start fixing problems that have plagued mankind since the beginning. Problems like death. Once we discover the angel strand, my friend, we can live forever."

Al thought about the possibilities. He didn't want the strength of a bear; he wanted the strength of ten. Mr. Cox had always been a sick, twisted man—Al knew that. Al also knew that Bart was a man of his word, and he planned to hold him to it. Yes, Al was going to help him, but he was also going to get what he wanted out of it. At the end of this deal, he was going to be immortal.

33

"Alright, let's split it this way: Tom and Cody on point with me in the lead car. We'll take the Land Rover in like a Trojan horse in case North Spear has a checkpoint set up. Frank and Tessa, you guys trail behind us in the other car. Once we get close to the objective, we dismount and foot-mobile it from there. Tessa, are there any other entrances or exits that you've found?" Val asked. The team had gathered just inside the house so that they wouldn't be as vulnerable as they would be standing outside. The humid air still clung to their skin, and they all had to keep wiping their foreheads to stop the sweat from dripping down.

"Yeah, that's gonna be the problem. I've only ever seen one way in and one way out, and that's through the main door next to the waterfall," Tessa said.

Val rubbed his chin thoughtfully. "Hmm, usually caves that large lead back to the surface somewhere."

"I'm not saying it doesn't, just that I haven't seen it. The temple is massive, and we were uncovering and mapping new areas every day. By a rough estimation, it's roughly the size of the Great Pyramid of Cholula in Mexico."

"That means nothing to me," Tom said just as Cody asked, "Wait, there's a pyramid in Mexico?"

Tessa ignored Tom but rolled her eyes at her brother. "Yes, dummy. Didn't you pay attention in school?" Cody opened his mouth to answer her, but she cut him off. "You don't have to answer that. I know you didn't. But yes, largest in the world, actually—by volume anyhow. Not as tall as the Pyramid of Giza, but much, much wider. Something like five miles worth of tunnels inside. I wouldn't be surprised if Azazel was actually a pyramid if we 3D mapped it."

"And you expect us to find one person inside all that? Assuming he's still alive?" Tom asked.

"Really, dude? Right in front of her?" Frank asked.

Tom shrugged his shoulder and held up his hands. "What? I'm just being honest here."

"Tom's right about the tunnels, though. That's an awful lot of ground to cover for just the three of us," Val said.

"Four," Frank objected.

"You're busted up, bro. You're better off staying with Tessa," Cody said.

"I told you, I'm coming with you guys," Tessa replied.

"No you're not, Tessa. It's too much of a liability. We're going to have enough to worry in there without having to watch out for you. The best thing for you to do is stay out here with Frank to provide overwatch and protect the vehicles," Cody replied.

"Hang on a minute, Cody. She might be right. She *is* the only one who has seen this place in person. We shouldn't discount what she can offer," Val asked.

"C'mon, Val, you can't be serious?" Frank asked.

"Do either of y'all have a better idea?" Val retorted, arms crossed. Neither answered. "I didn't think so. Listen, we can do this. Frank, you take Tessa with you and trail us once we get inside. The three of us can handle some low-level contractors. Speaking of which, how many we looking at here?" he asked Tessa directly.

She thought about it for a minute, trying to remember. "Uh, I'm not entirely sure. Maybe twenty-five to thirty, minus the ones you guys have already dealt with or put down or neutralized or whatever you guys say."

Cody nodded. "I'd say that puts us at roughly half that after what Frank and I dealt with last night."

"About thirteen to fifteen ain't bad against the four of us. Well . . ." Tom trailed off with an apologetic look toward Frank. "Three. Sorry, Frank, but we've dealt with worse odds before."

Frank ignored the jab. "Tom's got a point. The guys Cody and I engaged aren't real good and don't seem experienced. I'd say we have a better-than-average chance, especially if we wait for nightfall and approach the cave with NODs under cover of darkness. The waterfall is so loud they wouldn't hear us coming."

"The entire cave is artificially lit, but you could disable whatever generators you wanted to give you the edge," Tessa added.

Val smiled. "Well, it looks like we own the night, gentlemen. Get your kit sorted. We only have two more hours of daylight left."

They collected their gear and began setting up for their assault. They all knew it was risky, but they were used to taking risks. That's what made them who they were.

Renegade changed into their MultiCam Tropic Crye combat uniforms and donned their assault. Each man grabbed their rifle and checked to ensure it was loaded. Cody grabbed his beloved Hodge, inserted a magazine, and chambered a round. He hoisted his plate carrier over his head and adjusted it accordingly. He looked over to see his sister, who was helping Frank do the same. He couldn't believe he was agreeing to her tagging along, but like Val said, he didn't see any other option. For a second, he saw Tessa look at Frank with something that almost looked like tenderness before she stepped away to help anywhere else that she could.

He decided he wanted to get a few things off his chest before they departed.

"Frank, I'm sure we could head back to town really quick and get you a wheelchair or something," he poked.

"Ha ha, very funny," Frank replied.

"Look, I know you care about Tessa too, so this is your chance to prove it. Don't let anything happen to her, or I'm coming after you as soon as I handle these North Spear assholes."

Frank met his gaze, his face serious. "I promise, I will. Besides, I've seen you shoot and fight. Even with a couple broken ribs, I'd kick your ass any day."

They clasped hands in the classic bro handshake when Tessa's voice chimed in from across the room. Perception really was a Willis sibling trait. "Maybe you two should just kiss already and get it over with."

"Shut up," Cody said with an annoyed look at his sister. He then turned to her and said, "Listen to what he tells you, and everything will be fine."

Tessa just gave him a wink.

The ProCorp Applied Sciences team packed what was left of their equipment and settled in their vehicles. Cody shoved his 12.5 Hodge between the console and driver seat of the Land Rover and looked around. He felt at home.

"Alright, let's go do the Lord's work," he muttered under his breath and put the SUV in drive.

34

One by one, they kept insisting on speaking with him, which really posed a problem, of course. Bart knew they wanted answers, particularly when they'd be able to leave. Unfortunately, he didn't have an answer. He was waiting for the remainder of Al's teams to return. The rest of the archaeological team couldn't know he was holding Jake for his own special purpose. After all, they all thought he'd been killed when Tessa was taken. All he had to do was keep them at ease a little while longer.

Bart wiggled uncomfortably in his chair. He'd been stuck in this cave longer than he liked. Bart looked at his watch, anxious to get this over with; the time read 09:00 p.m. Suddenly he heard the tent flap open and saw Al approaching him.

"Sir, my guys are back. I've got two posted guard at the front leading to the cave. I'll leave about five or so guys here to watch the scientists to make sure they stay put. Maybe put another three on the outskirts here for cover. That leaves another six with us, which we're gonna need if we plan to get the good doctor up on that tomb."

"Excellent. Inform your men, and I'll get Dr. Reynolds ready to move."

"Right away."

Al departed to update his guys. Most were walking aimlessly amongst the tents, mingling and chatting with the excavation and archaeological teams. He saw one of them flirting and whistled to get his attention. Immediately the man snapped to and moved quickly to see what his boss needed.

"Yes, sir?" he asked sheepishly.

"I need you to pick about five or so guys and watch the scientists for a bit. Maybe take another few men and keep them posted around the edges. Mr. Cox and I need to take care of a few things in the temple. They're some artifacts he wants secured before we leave. It looks like we'll be able to get out of here by morning at the latest. I need you to make sure none of them leave. They have to stay here. Is that clear?"

"Yes, sir."

"All you have to do is make sure they don't try to follow us into the temple. You can go back to flirting with whomever you want if that keeps them here."

The young man smiled. "Understood, sir."

Al nodded and began to walk away. He knew it was close to being over now.

No, it was close to the *beginning.*

35

Renegade arrived at the waterfall not long after dark. They got to their destination as close as they dared so as not to alert any potential sentries and then concealed their vehicles. Each man donned his helmet and activated his night vision goggles.

As agreed earlier, Cody, Val, and Tom began their movement toward their objective, Tessa and Frank trailing behind them. They slowly pushed aside large vegetation leaves and branches from their intended path. The team followed the stream that wound its way to the massive pool beneath the thundering waterfall. Tom had taken point, leading the patrol. Raising his hand straight up, arm bent at ninety degrees, he signaled his teammates to stop. Val stepped past Cody and whispered in Tom's ear.

"Whatcha got?"

"Sentries. Two of them," Tom replied, not taking his eyes off the identified threat.

Val came shoulder to shoulder with Tom to get a better look. He could see the pair of men in the soft glow of his panoramic goggles. They were definitely sentries and were armed with rifles—M4 carbines from the look of it.

Val squeezed Tom's shoulder, giving Tom the only signal he needed to continue. They all continued their tedious approach through the thick foliage. Each step was carefully placed so as not to give away too much sound or take a tumble.

Tom continued toward the guards, refusing to take his attention away from them. He hoped they didn't have a handheld thermal imager, or the jig was up. Cody followed right behind, with Val directly on his heels. Frank paused, maintaining a safe distance behind with his precious cargo.

The trio crept forward to the unsuspecting guards, the sound of the waterfall covering their footsteps. Once they were within a close enough distance to guarantee an easy hit, Tom stopped and activated his IR laser. Cody stepped shoulder-to-shoulder and did the same, centering his beam on the other sentry.

"Ready?" Cody whispered to his partner.

Tom let out a burst of three to five suppressed rounds into the first man. Cody placed two well-aimed hits to his target's upper-thoracic cavity. Both went down without a fight. Val looked over his shoulder and waved his arm. Frank recognized the signal and urged Tessa to move with him.

Together, they all moved to the ancient, megalithic entrance. Tom and Val peered up to the angelic statues on either side.

"This is some serious *Tomb Raider* shit right here," Tom couldn't help but say aloud.

"You could say that again," Val concurred.

Cody took the lead, pushed the massive door open, and used his IR illuminator to see into the tunnels. It was clear. He led the team forward through the elaborate tunnel system from memory until they arrived at the tent city. The overwhelming brightness caused him to flip up his night vision goggles and saw his team members doing the same. He could see all sorts of people milling around aimlessly. He signaled for the team to stop.

"What we got?" Val asked.

"This is the tent city where we rescued Tessa. I don't know what's what after this."

"Standby," he replied and moved back to speak with Tessa directly, who was standing a safer distance back.

"Alright, we're at the tent city. Now what?"

"Just past the tents to the right is the entrance to the temple. It's carved directly out of the cave. We can either enter the main chamber and follow the wall all the way around or try to weave through the tents. Are there people there?" she asked.

"Yeah, we saw a bunch of 'em standing around. Who are they?" Val inquired.

"Probably my team. I'm not surprised Bart would've kept them here all this time."

Tom backed up a bit toward Val, Tessa, and Frank to give his two cents. "Sounds like good concealment moving through tents, but we might run into some of the security dudes."

"Yeah, and from what I remember, we'd be too exposed if we just tried to book it to the temple, but going the long way around the cave wall would put us in same position," Frank chimed in.

"I have an idea. What if I can fill my team in on what's really going down. If I can convince them to leave, that would remove them from the equation," Tessa said.

"I don't know . . . that sounds awful risky," Frank replied, looking a long time at her.

"Yeah, but I can blend in with the group. They're my people," she said back. "No offense, but you guys look like you just stepped off the set of *Predator*."

"It would simplify things. If she could get them out, then anybody else we come across would likely be security," Val admitted.

"Worth a shot," Tom said.

"Alright, I'll tell Cody. He'll take it better coming from me," Val said.

Val moved forward and caught Cody up to speed, but Cody shook his head resolutely in a resounding no.

"What? We just gonna let a noncombatant run around doing whatever the hell she wants?"

"It's probably our best shot. Besides, she's practically a Renegade now. Remember, it's not just a callsign; it's an ethos," Val said.

"For the record, I hate you right now."

36

Tessa Willis walked as casually as she could manage to the first tent in front of her. She could feel her pulse racing all the way up to her neck, certain that if it increased another ten beats a minute, her head might explode. She made sure to keep her head down as she walked just in case. Although she trusted her team, it wouldn't help if they, unknowing of the consequences, revealed to Bart she was now back in his clutches.

No wonder the boys love this sneaking around, she thought. The adrenaline pump was like nothing she'd ever experienced. She stopped and looked back toward the cave's entrance tunnel, barely able to see Cody or the others. Tessa gave them a subtle thumbs up while she took a deep breath. *You can do this.*

Her hands began to tremble by her side as she walked between the tents and headed toward her friends, or at least where she thought they would be. Tessa turned the corner and almost ran directly into a North Spear guard from behind. Her heart rate spiked, and her stomach dropped. Without so much as a breath, she turned around and went another direction.

She wasn't sure if he would have recognized her or not but didn't want to take the chance. Tessa bobbed and weaved until she finally came to Amanda's tent. She went in quickly and peeked back out once inside, checking to see if anyone had noticed her.

"Excuse me, I think you're in the wrong tent," Amanda said without looking at her.

Tessa approached and held her index finger to her lips. Amanda looked around suspiciously, unsure at first what was occurring. When she finally glanced toward her, recognition spread across her face. She shot up from her cot to greet her friend.

"What the hell happened to you? Bart said you'd been kidnapped!"

"I was wondering what lie he'd come up with. Listen, Amanda, Bart is crazy—"

Amanda rolled her eyes. "Yeah, I've been getting the feeling," she scoffed.

"No, you don't understand. He's so hellbent on getting that tomb open, he was going to sacrifice me on top of it," Tessa said breathlessly.

Amanda gave a shaky laugh. "Why would he do that?" she asked before looking at her friend with concern. "You okay, Tessa? Maybe you should see a medic—"

"No, no, I'm *fine.* Look, I need you to listen to me, and I need you to believe me. He was going to sacrifice me on top of it because that's the secret—the Nephilim constructed it to only open with human blood. It runs down into the grooves. I think and unlocks some form of mechanism. Look, believe me or don't, but we're all in serious trouble here. Where's Jake? Have you seen him? He can help me explain better."

Amanda's face was suddenly sullen. "Tessa, there's something you should know. Dr. Reynolds is dead. Bart said he'd been shot when those men took you."

Tessa's heart, moments ago pounding furiously, seemed to stop. "That's a lie. There's no way. Cody and Frank wouldn't have missed like that."

"Who?"

"Sorry, my brother and his friend. Either way, they're the ones who rescued me. Listen, I'll happily explain all of this to you later, but I'm here to get you and everyone else out. I need you to trust me."

"You came back by yourself?" Amanda asked with a puzzled expression.

"No, my brother and his friends are here with me. They can protect us. They're in the tunnel waiting, but I need you to go get the rest of the team and anyone else who will come along so we can get you out of here. We're going to stop Bart from opening that Nephilim tomb."

Amanda took a deep breath. "I feel like I'm in a movie," she said, pressing her hands against her face at the influx of information.

"Welcome to the club," Tessa replied.

But then Amanda straightened up. "Okay, okay. This place has gotten shady anyway. Lemme get my things," she said, and Tessa nodded, relieved.

Amanda scurried about her tent, stuffing clothes in a backpack. Satisfied she had what she needed, she looked at Tessa for what to do next.

"Alright, get everyone else together and meet me right back here in your tent. That way we don't risk Bart or anyone else seeing me." Amanda nodded. "Then I'll lead you guys to my brother and his team. They're over that way," she said, pointing in their general location.

"Alright, I'll be back in a jiff," she said in her usual peppy way as if she was going to run a quick errand.

After about thirty seconds after Amanda had taken off, the tent flap opened again. Tessa, expecting to see her friend, turned toward it. Instead, Al stepped inside.

"Well, well, well. Look who stopped in to visit."

It was at that moment Tessa realized she had just stepped out of the frying pan and landed knee deep into the fire. She thought about yelling in hopes that it would attract Amanda's or anyone else from her team's attention. After all, if she was going to get her team to believe her about the danger they were in, being killed in front of them seemed like a good point to make. But Tessa was too stunned to react. Her body wasn't used to this type of stress until recently, and unfortunately for her, it chose to freeze.

"Where's your brother and his friend? I can't imagine they're too far away," Al asked as he pulled his P320 from its holster and aimed it at her from the waist.

Her mind ran fast with possible answers. She did her best to make her voice crack. "Dead, both of them," she croaked. "My brother was shot by one of you assholes and bled out in the jungle. His friend broke his neck at the bottom of a waterfall." She pinched herself to make her eyes well up with tears.

Al momentarily closed his eyes and tilted his head back with a sigh of relief.

"You know that's the best news I've heard in two days. Thank you for that. I was getting real tired of looking over my shoulder. It would appear that these Nephilim demigods have seen to it to bring you back to us. We better not keep Mr. Cox waiting. Let's go," Al said, waving the weapon toward the tent's exit.

A few mere moments later, Amanda returned with a few members of the archaeological team. She tore open the tent flap only to find her tent empty, her friend gone. Perplexed, she closed the tent and looked around, searching for an answer. On the other side of the tent and heading away, she saw Tessa with Al, who followed directly behind. Amanda couldn't be sure, but it looked like Al was holding a gun to her back.

"Oh shit."

37

"Something's not right. It shouldn't have taken this long," Cody said. He had lost sight of his sister just a bit after she had given them a thumbs-up and disappeared amongst the influx of tents.

"Relax, have a little faith. She can get this done. After all, she's a Willis. There ain't a whole lot that can keep you people down," Val replied.

"Thanks . . . I think."

"Heads up, we got movement," Val announced just loud enough for the team to hear.

"I got eyes on a small group of people. Might be heading our way," Cody said, clutching his rifle a little tighter.

The small gaggle of five or six stopped at their last point of concealment by the tents. It was clear by their body language they were attempting to sneak out.

This must be them, but where's Tessa? Cody asked himself, his eyes scanning back and forth wildly, hoping to see her. He wasn't sure if they could see him since they'd tried to remain in the shadows. Suddenly alarmed, the group turned away toward something or someone they could not yet see. Cody could only hear voices.

"Heads up, boys, I think we have a problem," Cody said, seating the stock of his rifle in the pocket of his shoulder, his thumb riding the safety selector, ready to fire at a moment's notice.

Two men wearing the stereotypical contractor outfit came into view, holding their M4 rifles. They were saying something to the group, obviously questioning them about what they were doing. The blonde one in front glanced in Cody's direction, and he knew that she knew they were here, whether she could see him or not. The two North Spear men also caught on, one of them turning to see what she had looked at.

Cody didn't want to risk being compromised and brought the Hodge to bear, thumb swiping the safety without conscious thought. He put the two MOA red dots from his Aimpoint on the left man's chest and pulled through both stages of his trigger. The SureFire MINI 2 suppressor helped reduce the signature of the gunshot, but overall in a confined space like a cave, it still rang out quite loudly.

Val moved around to get in line with Cody and engaged the second the other target tried to bring his gun up to fire. Unfortunately for him, he processed what was going on too slowly and got stitched from his abdomen to his neck with three rounds. The third and final round severed the man's spinal cord at the base of the skull, effectively turning the lights off upstairs. It was Val's cleanest kill ever, and he had even managed not to hit any of the scientists with it.

"Fight's on!" Val yelled to the team, who stood and rushed to the would-be escapees. They cowered in fear, unable to process what had just happened. Several were overcome emotionally and stood frozen. Cody ran to the blonde who'd been leading them.

"Where's Tessa?" he said, grabbing Amanda's shoulder.

"She . . . she," Amanda stuttered.

Cody grabbed her by both shoulders. "*Where is she*?!"

"Al had her. I think he was taking her to the temple. That way," she managed to get out, her brain already foggy from the traumatic stress.

Muscles. Cody felt rage, the same rage he felt when saw the child trafficker, and he allowed himself about one moment to fight to control it. He knew he couldn't afford to go berserk, not when both his sister and Renegade were depending on him. He had to stay focused.

Val did what he did best and took command. He had heard Amanda and knew they needed to act quickly before the rest of North Spear caught on to what was happening.

"Frank, you're with me. Tom, with Cody. We use the tents for concealment and bound in two teams. We got right. Cody, you guys have left. Weapons free on anyone with a gun. Move."

There was no talking, no affirmations or acknowledgements—just action. Each man fell into place, knowing each other's movements like their own. They moved quickly and found two more armed men who began firing at them.

Cody and Tom continued to move while Val and Frank covered their teammates. Frank brought his rifle up, his ribs searing in pain. He pushed it aside and began firing at one of the men in a rapid cadence. His intent was not as much to hit him as it was to force him to stop shooting and take cover. Val did the same. Both of the North Spear men were hit in the lower extremities, rendering them incapacitated.

Once Tom and Cody arrived at their next point of concealment behind a large equipment box, Tom sprayed them both with a burst from the suppressed MK46. Satisfied they were on their way to judgment, Cody looked up to see Al in the far distance ahead, dragging his sister with him.

Al maintained at least an arm's reach away from Tessa. She figured he'd learned from his last mistake and wouldn't chance another knee to the balls. Tessa thought about simply taking off at a sprint, but knew Al was too close. All he really had to do was reach out and grab her. Plus, despite her speed, even she couldn't outrun a bullet.

They approached Bart's tent and could see a group of North Spear security men standing by, waiting. Tessa caught a couple of odd looks exchanged between the pair of them, knowing they were asking themselves how or why she'd returned. She wondered how they could be so complicit in all this and realized that, often, the bad guy never sees himself as such. Al grabbed her arm so tightly it hurt as he pressed the pistol hard into her back.

"Mr. Cox, you have a visitor," Al called out with a smile.

Tessa wondered what had gone wrong in Al's life that he required Bart's approval so badly. Did his parents not hug him enough? Unnecessarily high expectations from his dad? Who knew.

"What now? I told you I didn't want to be bothered until—" Bart stepped out of the tent, and his face registered complete shock. His eyes went back and forth from Tessa to Al, trying to piece together how she was standing right in front of him. A sinister smile slowly formed across his face as he folded his arms across his chest in pride.

Before the tent flap had shut closed, Tessa had caught a glimpse of Jake, tied and gagged on the floor but alive. The relief at seeing her friend seeped through her. She also realized that meant the tomb was still closed. Bart's voice broke her thought process.

"It seems that the Dr. Reynolds' faith in Yahweh has paid off for him, and that my faith in the Nephilim has done the same for me."

"It didn't work out so well for them in the end, Bart, don't forget," she said with gritted teeth.

"It's working out a lot better for me than it is for you," he quipped.

Tessa had not considered herself religious, but found herself silently praying that the ace up her sleeve, or more accurately in the tunnel, made an appearance sooner rather than later.

Bart lifted the flap to his tent. "Dr. Reynolds, you are relieved of your responsibilities. Looks like you'll have to meet your divine creator another time. Pardon us, while we—"

The suppressed gunshots, now closer and in hearing distance, began to echo off the cave walls. Al grabbed Tessa by the arm and looked to Bart.

"Al, get her to the tomb," Bart yelled. "You men stay with us, and do not let *anyone* else inside the ruins."

Altogether they took off, sprinting toward Azazel.

38

Cody pressed the push-to-talk attached to his plate carrier. "I have eyes on Tessa. North Spear has her. All callsigns converge to the temple entrance. I say again, temple entrance," he said into the boom mike of his Ops-Core AMPS, thankful Val and Tom had brought spare radios.

Closely following Muscles and Tessa, Cody observed the Suit and five or six men who had run in behind them. They couldn't let them get too far ahead, or they'd run the risk of losing them in the continuing maze Tessa had described. He looked to his right and saw a generator with large power cables leading up the steps and into the ancient passageway.

Cody dumped eight to ten rounds into it, hoping the darkness would slow them down a bit. In an instant, the main chamber outside the cave went dark with the exception of a few torches in front of the temple. Renegade flipped down their night vision goggles, giving them the advantage. Cody scanned his surroundings before leaving his last point of cover. There seemed to be three remaining North Spear contractors who were attempting to bolt for the temple, the light from the torches their only visible guide.

Cody caught the movement in the bluish-white glow of his NVG's and activated his IR laser before actively targeting one of the running men. He saw three additional lasers appear as the other members of Renegade acquired the other two. Muffled gunfire rang out from the dark as the men took rounds. One died instantly as a high-velocity rifle round entered just under his armpit, hitting his heart on its way through. The other two screamed in pain and fell to the ground face first.

Their bodies slid another five feet as the lasers stopped again on their bodies and danced up and down with each follow up shot, finishing them off. Renegade jumped to their feet and ran the fifty yards to the temple entrance, hurrying to catch up.

Bart ran through the tunnels of Azazel with a speed he thought was long forgotten due to his age. When the lights went out, he stopped, frozen in fear until Al turned on a light attached to his pistol. He found himself relieved and thankful for Al's readiness.

They pushed ahead at a slower pace to catch their breath, the route to the tomb committed to memory. Finally they rounded a corner and saw the entrance. They had made it. He looked to the massive sarcophagus in the middle of the room and began to walk around it, his fingertips lightly touching the hieroglyphs and Enochian carvings. Bart knew that, in a mere few minutes, the contents inside would be his at long last.

All his years of hard work had boiled down to this one event. Bart knew he needed to focus on one problem at a time. The last thing he wanted was his moment to be ruined. And how could he enjoy his moment while these men wouldn't stop breathing down his neck?

He looked to Al and his men who had begun turning on the battery-powered light stands to illuminate the massive ancient tomb.

"I want you and your men to go back out there and kill those assholes following us," Bart said.

Al smiled. "I thought you'd never ask." Then he turned to address the last of his North Spear contractors. "Listen guys, maximize your cover, and if you have a light, use it. If they're using night vision, just shine your light in their direction. It will blind them. Set up with a good piece of cover and let them get close. Don't start shooting until I do, and wait for my signal, is that clear?" he asked, locking eyes with each of them. They all nodded in agreement before they turned and left the tomb.

Bart turned toward Tessa, still caressing the tomb. She watched as he walked back and forth, touching the Nephilim tomb as he did.

"Looks like it's just you and me. Who would have thought this is where we'd end up, huh? I mean, I always knew we were going to open this tomb together, but not like this. I said to myself when I first saw you giving that presentation asking for funding, 'That's a girl that can get things done.' I've always liked that you have spirit, Tessa, although I have to admit, here at the end of the road, it has really been a pain in my ass. I was hurt, Tessa, when you left. I really was. I thought better of you . . . that you knew what this would mean. Why? Why did you abandon us in the first place?"

Tessa looked around, her eye catching a set of tools on a makeshift table nearby. She stepped toward them, engaging Bart in conversation and making sure his attention stayed on her words rather than her hands.

"Would it make any difference to you?"

"Probably not, but you owe me that at least. After all I've done for you?"

"I was visited by an angel," she said simply. "He showed me the true purpose of the Nephilim. They're the antithesis of all that is good, pure, and true. God lowered himself and took human form, offering *Himself* as a sacrifice for all mankind. The Nephilim were the exact opposite. They opposed Him, elevating themselves as kings above all, not afraid to sacrifice men for their own selfish lusts and desires. They pollute the very makeup of what it means to be made in the image of God and imagine themselves as God Himself instead," she finished, her feet stopping in front of the table as her hands searched blindly behind her for anything she could use as a weapon.

"Insightful," Bart breathed. "And why do you suppose he showed this to *you* of all people?"

"God only knows, but there was something my mom used to say before she passed. 'It takes all kinds, Tessa.' I never really knew what that meant until recently," she replied, her fingers recognizing the feel of a chisel.

"Wise woman," Bart replied with a smile. "Soon enough, you'll be reunited with her, and all of this will be behind you."

"Don't be so certain, Bart. God has a way of pulling his people out of situations just like this, ya know." She clutched the hardened-steel tool tightly in her hand, making sure she had a firm grip.

"Oh really? Then why doesn't He show Himself now?" Bart asked lightly, spreading his arms out in mockery.

No sooner had he uttered the words when gunfire broke out in the tunnels. Startled, Bart closed the distance and grabbed Tessa. He used her body to shield his own, turning her to face the massive doorway, pistol pressed against her head.

39

Val took the lead, his quad-tube GPNVG struggling to illuminate the dark hallway leading into the temple. He activated his IR task light on his helmet, giving his night vision the necessary light to amplify. It allowed him to see wherever his head was oriented but gave off a faint red glow to anyone looking his direction. He scanned up and down, taking note of the intricate stonework carved into the sides and roof through the green hue of his alien-like goggles. Cody kept up right behind him.

Frank and Tom arrived last due to Tom's extra weight with the bigger gun and Frank's injured ribs. Tom cracked IR chemical lights, or glowsticks, every hundred yards to give them a trail of breadcrumbs to follow out.

Neither Cody nor Val detected any sign of their quarry as they moved down the wide tunnel shoulder to shoulder. They came to a large intersection that split both left and right. Covering the opening opposite their side of the tunnel, they prepared for a movement called "cross cover." Tom and Frank stood behind them, who looked at each to ensure their readiness and then gave a nod to signal the man in front of them to snap into the hallway, covering both directions simultaneously.

As they did, the cave temple erupted in gunfire from the left—Cody's direction. Val turned to his aid and began identifying targets through his goggles. The North Spear men were not-so-well equipped and fired blindly down the rocky tunnel, hoping to get lucky more than anything.

Cody saw the muzzle flash of their rifles like beacons every time they pulled the trigger. He could see their eyes reflecting the IR illumination from his laser as he targeted them, giving the appearance of glowing eyes. Their opponents, on the other hand, saw nothing but the occasional dull orange jet of flame emitted from the end of the suppressor.

Half of one man's body was exposed around a corner giving Val a clean shot directly into his right pec. He stumbled backward for a step and fell to the ground. Cody engaged him as well, both lasers dancing over the man's body like fireflies caught up in a dogfight.

Silence returned to the cave as the last piece of brass clanked on the rocky ground and rolled away. After a couple seconds, both Renegades made sure they couldn't see any additional targets that would need to be engaged. After they confirmed they wouldn't, Val took a moment to reload his HK416.

"Val, let me take point with the forty-six. We might be able to gain the initiative if I can knock them on their heels with the belt fed," Tom called.

Val nodded, and Tom moved to take his spot.

"C'mon, let's go. We gotta be getting close if they're setting up defensive positions. If we keep pushing them, maybe they won't get a chance to get dug in."

"Agreed. At least we know we're going the right way," Frank said with a squeeze to Cody's shoulder, giving him the signal to move.

The four-man team continued forward through the underground temple complex toward their objective. They moved at a pace that was just under a run, clearing the empty rooms to their left and right as they came upon them, casting their IR light and looking for anyone hiding in wait.

Ahead, Cody could see some form of light emitting from a room in the distance. The tunnel curved to the right, and Cody signaled Tom to hold his position while he cleared around it.

"Clear."

He moved around, rifle up, Tom right beside him. They had taken a couple steps forward when they each caught the movement in their goggles, but action was faster than reaction. Bullets struck the cave walls all around them, Al and his men exposing themselves from their positions of cover. A bullet from one of the North Spear men impacted Cody's helmet, the force of the impact snapping his head to the rear. Lifeless, he dropped to the ground as Tom returned fire. Val and Frank ran to grab Cody by the vest and pull his body to safety around the bend.

40

Cody found himself standing in a valley with snowcapped peaks all around and a magnificent river flowing in front of him. The sun shone down, cascading beautiful light, a soft breeze blowing the grass back and forth. He felt calm, at peace. A feeling that he hadn't felt in long time.

What is this place? he thought.

He saw something moving in the tall grass on the opposite side of the river. He watched as the same lion from both his dream and the river confidently walked toward him. It stopped just as it reached the water's edge. The lion's eyes locked with Cody's. His face was like lightning, His eyes like a flaming torch; He had the look of a warrior. Cody felt no fear of the animal. Instead he felt its opposite—an overwhelming sense of love. Cody could tell the animal wanted to talk.

"Am I dead?" Cody inquired, though not with his voice. He seemed able to speak with his heart and mind.

"No," the lion replied. His voice rang through Cody's head, enveloping him.

"Who are you?" Cody asked.

"I am the first and the last, the Living One, who is and who was and who is to come. I alone have conquered death and hold the key to Hades, and I have a purpose for you," He answered. The lion's voice was strong and confident. It felt soothing.

"What purpose could I offer? I've done so many horrible things. I've killed, lied, put myself above my family. I'm useless to You."

The lion gazed at him expectantly. "Let me define your worth. All have sinned and fallen short, Cody. Remember, you are fearfully and wonderfully made. You can choose to take up your cross or be crushed by the weight of it. But in the end, the choice is always yours alone."

Cody shook his head. "How do I do that?"

"By placing your trust in Me.

"Our time is up. Your friends and sister need your help."

The lion turned and began to walk away, the tall grass swallowing him.

"Wait, I have so many questions. Wait!" Cody yelled out. But as he tried to follow, the edges of his vision began to blur. The world began to fade.

"Wait, wait, come back," he continued to yell.

When his eyes opened, he was suddenly aware of Val kneeling above him, his voice faint and distant.

"Get it together, bro, we need you. Can you fight?" Val was asking him loudly, tapping his face.

"Yeah . . . yeah, I think so," Cody replied, squinting his eyes.

"How many fingers am I holding up?" Val asked, holding three in his face.

"Three."

"Good. I think you'll be alright, but you're one lucky bastard. Took one right to the dome, knocked you unconscious, but the helmet sure as hell did its job."

Cody sat up, his hand reaching to his head. He had a pounding headache.

"I can't believe you're alive, dude. I thought they blew your head off. You got lucky on this one, somebody was looking out for you," Val said, hand on his shoulder to steady him. Cody could register the sound of bullets still being fired from farther up ahead.

"You could say that again. Remind me to buy some stock in Ops-Core helmets if we get outta here," Cody groaned. "Here, help me up."

Val helped him to his feet. Cody conducted a quick self-check of the rest of his body, which seemed more-or-less unscathed.

Cody managed to fall in behind Val as the North Spear men continued to fire. He retrieved a flashbang from the back panel attached to Val's plate carrier. Cody pulled the pin and reached his arm around Val's shoulder to show him the distraction device. Val nodded in approval and halted their advance. Cody tossed the flashbang around his teammates.

"Bang out!" he yelled.

A blinding flash of light made its way down the tunnel, echoing loudly off the walls around them.

Luckily for Renegade, they were expecting it and could more-or-less anticipate the blast. The North Spear gunmen were not as lucky. Like a jungle cat ready to pounce, the four-man team moved forward effortlessly around the bend, their adversaries momentarily blinded and deaf. Three men stumbled around, unable to gain their wits. Tom went to open up with a burst from the belt fed, emptying what remained of it into one man. He lowered the weapon as Al, now out of ammo, took the opportunity to close the distance and dove into Tom with the force of a professional linebacker.

Tom grunted, taking the full force of Al's large frame and tucking his head to prevent being knocked unconscious. Together they tumbled on the cavern floor, too intertwined for anyone on Renegade to get off a clean shot. Cody, Frank, and Val pushed past them to finish off the guys trying to shake off the effects of the flashbang. Frank turned to address Cody and Val.

"You two go. I'll help Tom!" he yelled, knowing he wouldn't be able to move as fast as they could.

Closely matched in size, Tom realized rather quickly this guy was no stranger to fighting on the ground and must have had some formal training. Al tried breaking free of Tom's legs, fighting completely by feel; his night vision goggles were blurry due to the close distance. Al struck down hard with his elbows into Tom's thighs, causing another grunt and unseen wince.

Thanks to Tom's head tuck, Al's blows were rendered nearly useless as they rained down on his helmet and NVGs. Tom thrust his hips up and to the right in an attempt to knock Al off balance. Al had countered it by sprawling his arms out in front of him. Frank ran to assist and found the pair still too mixed together to get a well-placed shot.

Frank slung his rifle and reached down and took ahold of Al. He planned to pull him off Tom enough to put his pistol to the North Spear man's head and finish him off that way. But in a fury, Al swung his elbows wildly catching Frank directly into the injured ribs. With a grunt, Frank was forced to release his grasp. Though Frank's plan was unsuccessful, it gave Tom the chance he needed.

Tom returned the assault gladly and threw heavy blows into Al's side. Al clawed, desperately searching for anything on Tom's kit to grab on to in the hopes of keeping him down. Feeling Al's attempt, Tom decided it was time to end the fight. He reached into his waistline and pulled his LowVz Colonel blade from his belt. Now armed with a fighting knife, he punched up into the man's neck, the curved nature of the knife acting like a bladed single brass knuckle.

Al was helpless against the onslaught as the treated steel repeatedly pierced his arms and sides. Tom pushed up again with his hips—this time successfully—and took the mount. He continued punching with the Colonel blade, landing strikes into Al's carotid artery, his cheeks, and finally his eye socket. Tom felt his adversary go lifeless, but his fury remained as blood continued to pour onto the rocky ground.

Frank turned to see Tom unleashed, realizing the man underneath was dead.

"Tom! Tom! You got him, ease up!" Frank yelled, grabbing his teammate under the arms and pulling him free.

Tom sucked in air, gasping for breath. The whole exchange lasted less than a minute, but Tom had given everything he had.

"Holy shit, Tom, you went ballistic on that asshole!" Frank exclaimed.

Tom wiped the blood from his face and made his way to his feet.

41

Tessa held the chisel in front of her body out of Bart's sight. She knew that if she simply drove the tool into Bart's thigh all he had to do was pull the trigger and her head would likely explode. He pulled her backward, trying to drag her toward the tomb. She felt his body stop as it pressed against the Nephilim sarcophagus with nowhere to go.

She could tell he was starting to panic at the sound of the gunfire, so she waited for her opportunity. The gunfire subsided for just a moment, just enough for her to hear Bart's tense breathing. They watched the doorway—Tessa with bated breath and Bart with his heavy one.

In a flash, two men entered the room, weapons ready, night vision googles protruding from their helmets. *Cody! Val!* she thought as she recognized their faces even in the dimly lit cavern room. They scanned their areas and focused their attention on Bart and Tessa.

"Not another fucking step, or I'll kill her!" Bart yelled.

Neither said a word as they split directions, hoping to get Bart to expose himself for a shot. Cody flipped up his goggles, the lights in the room too bright to see for a hostage rescue shot. Val did the same.

"Wasn't that your plan to begin with?" Cody asked, trying to draw his attention.

Bart laughed a laugh laced with no humor. "The plan was to open the tomb, and your sister decided she was too noble to make that happen," he said, clutching her even tighter.

Val moved to his left, searching for his angle. Cody saw the movement in his peripheral and did the same to prevent a crossfire. Frank and Tom poured into the room behind them, identifying the threat and orienting their weapons toward it.

"This can end in more ways than one, man. Just drop the gun and let my sister go. Nobody else has to die. We'll figure something out," Cody said.

Bart pondered his options and realized he didn't have any. He was too outgunned and too outmanned.

I haven't come this far to barter for what is rightfully mine. Who are they to tell me how this was going to end? No, if I'm going down, then I'm taking everyone with me.

Tessa flashed the chisel in her hand for Cody to see. He caught the movement and nodded ever so slightly. With all the force she could muster, Tessa drove the edged tool into Bart's groin behind her, twisting it to the side before dropping out of the way.

Bart fired harmlessly while Renegade seized the opportunity and began shooting as soon as Tessa was clear. The North Spear executive's bullet-riddled body fell to the ground in a heap.

Tessa scrambled away from him and then ran and hugged her brother as quickly as she could, tears in her eyes.

"I knew you guys would make it. Thank you," she whispered to him, clutching him tightly, and he squeezed her back in response.

Frank ran up, trying to avoid wincing. "You okay? You hit or anything?" he asked her.

"No, but next time, I'm definitely staying in the back with you," she said, wrapping her arms around his neck.

"Trust me, there ain't gonna be a next time," he replied, enveloping her.

"Even better," she replied before her lips planted a tender kiss on his.

As the team patted one another on the back and prepared to leave the tomb for good, the blood from Bart's wounds began to drain from the body. It slowly ran along the edge where the sarcophagus met the floor. Unseen, it crept underneath hidden channels, which carved into the bottom. Suddenly, the ground shook, like a muted earthquake as the tomb hissed. Pressurized air released from the cracks. Dust kicked up all around, clouding their view through the lights.

The sound of stones dragging across one another filled the air as they readied their weapons, unsure of what to expect. The top of the rectangular burial chamber began to slide open horizontally.

Val was the first to speak. "What the hell is this? Did y'all do anything?" he yelled over the sound of the rock's movement.

"Negative," Cody replied.

"Nuh uh," Frank said.

"I didn't touch shit!" Tom offered.

"Tessa, what's going on here?" Cody called toward her.

"The tomb," she said breathlessly. "It's opening from Bart's blood."

They stood speechless, hands clutching their weapons. Seconds passed as no one was sure what to do. They watched as the burial chamber lid came to a stop with a thud. After what seemed like a lifetime, Val nudged Cody by the elbow.

"We gonna stand here all day or take a look inside this thing?" Val asked.

"You volunteering to go first?" Cody asked.

"I'll go," Tessa said. "I've been wanting to see inside this thing my whole life."

Without waiting for anyone to protest, Tessa ascended the ladder and peered over the edge once she reached the top. Her heart raced as her eyes gazed upon the decayed Nephilim corpse.

Its exposed bones were thick like the trunk of a tree. Tessa's eyes traced down the skeletal structure. She counted six fingers with long pointy nails the size of spear heads. The skull was slightly elongated, complete with a double row of jagged teeth. A chill washed over her body and, somehow, she felt the evil it had once committed. Filled to the brim of the tomb were the skulls of those of who had been sacrificed to it thousands of years ago.

"Tessa, you okay?" Frank called out to her from below.

"Yeah, just taking it all in," she replied.

She could only imagine how many people died at the hands of the giant inside this tomb. Thousands upon thousands of skulls surrounded the ghastly bones. His skeleton was adorned with golden-laced armor, and atop his head laid a crown of jewels. His arms were folded across his chest, his hands still holding something. She couldn't quite make it out. Tessa resisted the temptation to retrieve it and came down the ladder.

"Thank you for that, guys," she said. The men had the good grace to look away and pretend not to notice as she wiped the tear from her cheek.

"So uh, seeing as how we were supposed to have prevented this thing from opening, what are we going to do about closing it up?" Cody asked, turning toward her.

"I . . . I have no idea. Your guess is as good as mine at this point," she admitted.

"What if we blow it? The entrance to the temple," Tom asked, shrugging.

"With what? You got some demo in your back pocket?" Frank asked, eyebrows raised.

"C'mon, dude, I used to be a Ranger. Of *course* I do. I got a few breaching charges in my back panel. All we need is an accelerant, and it should do the trick," Tom said, smiling easily.

42

Renegade and Tessa made their way back to tent city, which was now barren of people. They all joined in Tom's search for suitable homemade explosives to blow up the entrance and hopefully seal the Nephilim skeleton underground forever. Tessa and Frank had just started going from tent to tent looking for anything useful when she heard a muffled noise. She turned quickly in the direction she'd heard it. Frank oriented his rifle in the same direction, weapon light activated.

"I think it came from over here," she said, making her way around the side of the canvas living quarters.

Tessa turned the corner and suddenly realized they were next to Bart's tent. *Jake!* she remembered. She'd forgotten all about her friend and mentor. She tore the flap open and rushed inside to his aid.

Poor Jake was still gagged and bound to the main tent pole, his muffled yells and sounds urging for help. She pulled the rag from his mouth.

"Thank God, Tessa, you're okay!" he immediately said. She laughed, giving him a hug. "What happened?" he asked incredulously.

She looked at Frank. "In short, Jake, the good guys won. We won."

They heard Tom yell from the across the cave. "I think I got it. Come here and give me a hand."

"Who's this guy?" Cody asked once everyone was together.

"Cody, this is Dr. Jake Reynolds, a friend. Jake, this is my brother, Cody. He and his friends are the ones who saved me."

"Looks like I'm in your debt, young man," Jake said, reaching over to shake his hand.

"Don't mention it," Cody said, returning the grip. "It took a team.

"Alright, Tom," Cody called over his shoulder, "whatcha got?"

"I found a few generators lying around with full gas tanks," he said, pointing them out. "All we have to do is put them at the entrance of the temple with the breaching charges. The charges with the fuel from the generators should be enough to close it up or at least block its path."

"Seems good enough to me. Tessa, you good with that?" Val asked, eyebrows raised at her. After all, this *was* her life's work.

But she nodded in reply.

"How much det cord you got? Gonna be enough to make it out of the cave?" Cody asked.

"Eh, not really. It's enough to make it to the tunnel that leads outside. Y'all probably ought to wait outside for me."

Satisfied with that answer, they stacked the remaining generators at the temple entrance along with any additional fuel cans they could find. Tom placed every charge he had at the entrance and worked his way back to the tunnel as everyone else made their way outside.

Soon as he clacked off charges, he ran like hell. Tom had made it to within fifty yards of the massive door when the blast of the explosion caught up with him, sending off a cloud of dust, which covered him as it blew outward. The two scientists and the rest of Renegade watched as Tom finally came out covered in dust, coughing.

"Still got all your fingers?" Cody asked, slapping him on the back when he reached them.

Tom nodded and held them up for good measure.

"I don't suppose there are any North Spear vehicles still around?" Val asked, looking around. They looked to where the vehicles had been parked, but nothing was there.

"I guess everyone left in a hurry and took our rides with them," Cody said.

"Actually, not *all* of our rides, Cody," Frank said. "The car Fren and Juanita got us is still out there just sitting in the jungle not too far away from here. The keys should still be in it."

Cody smiled. "Dr. Reynolds, I hope you don't mind being packed into a car like a sardine."

Epilogue

A week had passed since Renegade had stood inside the heart of the Nephilim temple in Peru. Back at Renegade Ranch, all four members were inside the team room celebrating Cody's official return to Renegade. Tessa and Lucy accompanied them as they reminisced and laughed about past memories. Lucy smiled as she noticed the subtle cues of romance between Frank and Tessa. A soft touch here, a giggle there. Not to mention the twinkle in each other's gaze as they made eye contact.

She pulled a seat next to Val, who was reading a leather-bound journal, flipping the pages back and forth. She tried to peek to see what it was, but Val sighed and closed it.

Lucy rolled her eyes. Never off the clock, that one. No matter. Deciding to deal with the more pressing matter at hand, she nudged him playfully on the shoulder. "Please tell me you're seeing what I'm seeing over there?" but he just frowned.

"Over where?"

"Oh c'mon, Val. You can't be that blind."

"What are you talking about?" he asked, glancing around at their group.

"Frank and Tessa, *hello*."

"What about them?" With a scoff, she realized he was being serious. He was totally unaware of what she was talking about.

"Oh, never mind. You were never any good at gossip. What are you looking at anyway?"

"This? Oh . . ." He shrugged. "Just something Cody brought back with him from Peru."

Lucy peered over his shoulder. She looked at the handwritten words but was unable to make any sense of it.

"What language is that?" she inquired.

"German. This is a journal belonging to none other than Dr. Josef Mengele, the Nazi scientist who experimented on people."

Lucy squinted at him. "Since when can you read German?" she asked, more surprised in Val's skill than who owned the journal.

"I learned in high school. It was something that kept me busy while I was in the army."

"Well," she said. "What does it say?"

"I'm a little rusty, but even then, some of it doesn't really make sense. It seems like one page he's talking about the war and the concentration camps and the next he's talking about an ultimate knowledge and genetic manipulation or something . . . I dunno. I'm out of practice. One thing is certain, he was one weird cat," he said before closing the journal again and laying it in his lap.

Lucy sipped her drink. "You think there will be blowback from y'all's little adventure? With ProCorp, I mean," she asked.

"Undoubtedly, but given everything that's happened, I'm a pretty good bullshitter, if I do say so myself. Besides, I've been in this business a long time, and I'll call in a few favors if I have to." He paused and looked to his boys. "I just got this family back together, I ain't gonna let it split up that easy."

Lucy smiled. "Who knew Val Grayson, Renegade Actual, had such a soft spot."

"Don't go telling everyone. I have a reputation to uphold," he said, looking at her seriously, and she laughed. "I have no doubt Hedgehog and Longbow are gonna shit bricks when they find out how much it cost to get Mike to fly us back and forth to Peru though," he said, running his hand over his head. "Not to mention all the carnage we caused back in Iquitos. At least we got a few more months to figure it out and come up with something."

"Why not tell them the truth?" Lucy asked.

"Because sometimes the truth is stranger than fiction. Would you believe that we stopped a crazed businessman from sacrificing Tessa to open a giant's tomb only to accidentally open it ourselves, forcing us to blow it up so no one finds it ever again?"

She paused to consider it. "Yeah, you're right. A lie sounds much better."

"Say that part again, the part about me being right. I like it when you say things like that. You should do it more often," Val said with a grin.

"Well, Val Grayson, I would, but unfortunately it doesn't happen very often," Lucy shot back with a grin of her own.

"Ouch."

"I will say this though, you were right about picking these men. We've got one heck of a team here. It's really nice to have them all back together," Lucy said, watching them all laugh and joke as though they didn't have a care in the world.

Val nodded in agreement, watching his team while Lucy stood leaning on his shoulder. He made eye contact with Cody, and Val raised his glass in his direction. Cody returned the toast with a glass of his own, filled with jalapeño margarita. The world around him felt at peace for the moment, with everyone in their rightful place.

The off-road trucks splashed through the muddy trail down the somewhat-worn dirt road. It had only been a couple weeks since the last North Spear vehicle had left the jungle and left Azazel in the rearview mirror, but the jungle worked fast to reclaim its property. The shrubs and various tree limbs scratched at the doors as though they were clawing to get inside, hungry for its contents.

The lead Range Rover came to a stop, facing the massive waterfall at the entrance to Azazel. The following SUVs pulled alongside each other, making three in total. The front passenger's side door to the lead car popped open, the thick, humid air rushing to meet the occupant. The well-dressed eighty-year-old man stepped out of the vehicle with his six -foot-nine inch frame. Despite his age, he didn't look a day over fifty and moved just as effectively. He was disgusted he was here in the middle of nowhere having to clean up Bart's mess.

Mr. Adams, chair member of Legion Acquisitions, owner of North Spear, stood there outside the car just staring at the entrance. The remaining doors opened, revealing Adams's personal executive security consisting of mostly former special-operations combat veterans. Mr. Adams's driver came around to his side, standing next to his boss.

"Sir, this is the spot Mr. Cox sent out."

Mr. Adams nodded.

His driver began issuing orders to the rest of the protective detail. Heavily armed and ready for action, they led the way toward the mouth of the cave. Mr. Adams stopped right before they entered and gazed at the angelic statues on either side of it. Since learning the truth about his ancestors, he'd always wanted to see them. Now, he stood before their stone portrayals carved thousands of years ago when they reigned supreme.

Mr. Adams closed his eyes and said a quiet prayer to them in respect. "I honor your strength and wisdom. If you would allow, I ask that you bestow that same power and wisdom in me, that I, Ezeqeel Adams, one of your last descendants, may restore the glory of the Watchers and the Nephilim to the world."

The combat-hardened protective detail made their way through the tunnels that had been well-traveled just two weeks prior following the still-present signs of activity. Inside the main cave chamber, he looked upon the archaeological site that was now a ghost town thanks to the unknown threat. The canvas tents used as offices or sleeping chambers were empty. Equipment boxes were turned over and their contents spilled out. He walked to the steps of Azazel and found the entrance blocked; debris was scattered about everywhere. He took in the ruined ancient structure, his hands outstretched, fingers running along the walls as he studied the remaining carvings and glyphs carefully.

Whoever had done this would pay. Perhaps not today, but Mr. Adams was a patient man. A man who wielded power most men could only dream of obtaining. North Spear was just one of the main companies he owned as a chair member of Legion Acquisitions.

"Sir, best as we can tell from Bart's reports, it's behind all this. Someone wanted to make sure it never saw the light of day," one of his men said next to him.

"How long to get through all this?" Mr. Adams asked quietly, looking at the blocked temple entrance.

"Sir, I don't . . . uh," the man said, stuttering.

"How long?" he inquired louder, but icier, making eye contact with his inferior.

"It shouldn't take too long once we get everyone in here," the man replied lamely.

But Mr. Adams nodded his approval.

Several hours later, the protective detail had moved enough rocks to make a hole large enough for him to fit through. He entered into Azazel and smiled.

"Send the security teams in and let me know when they find it," he told his driver.

The driver nodded and relayed the message to the team. The men moved past them, disappearing into the temple and returning some time later. Mr. Adams's driver appeared from one of the various tunnels that led deeper into the underground temple.

"Mr. Adams, I believe we found it, sir."

"Take me to it."

Together they walked through the damp halls, Mr. Adams's foot scuffing something beneath him with a clank. He paused to see what it was and realized it was a bullet casing. Suddenly he realized they were littered everywhere—evidence of a hostile takeover. The closer they got, the more the tunnels reeked of death. Eventually they came upon the source of the smell, the dead North Spear men rotting on the ground. He continued to follow his driver, paying them no mind.

He walked into the final room and grabbed a flashlight from one of his men. Inside the burial chamber he found Bart's body. *Fool.*

He scanned back and forth with the light, only being able to see what was illuminated. He saw the tomb, his eyes taking in as much detail of the inscriptions as he could. Carefully he continued toward it, hoping what he had been searching for was inside. Mr. Adams walked around the tomb, finding a ladder against the far wall. Quickly he grabbed it and propped it up on the side of the sarcophagus.

He climbed to the top and peered inside. He scanned with the flashlight and observed what was left of the Nephilim skeleton. His eyes took in his glorious size and stature. Mr. Adams imagined how glorious he would have been if he were still alive. He light continued to sweep the bones and steadied on something. Something inside the tomb.

His heart rate quickened. *There, in his hands.*

Bart had been a fool for thinking Mr. Adams had simply wanted a DNA sample from a Nephilim. Then again, Bart didn't know that Mr. Adams's DNA was more than sufficient enough for that purpose. Diluted, of course, but sufficient.

No, the DNA was useless without the understanding, the knowledge, of how to manipulate it. He knew how to gain that knowledge, of course. Before him was one such a piece that would move him closer to that goal: a stone tablet of such ancient origin only a few knew of its existence. One of five total pieces from the Tablet of the Watchers.

All the knowledge of the two-hundred angels who first descended to Earth that eventually gave in to their lust of the daughters of Eve. Finally, he was within arm's reach. He was now in possession of two.

Author's Note

I decided to write this book in April of 2019 while my family and I made our way back home after a quick weekend trip to Galveston, Texas. While we were there, we visited Moody Gardens, a very well-executed rainforest ecosystem attraction contained in a pyramid. While inside, you walk through the various stages of the ecosystem down to the floor where they have some artificial ancient ruins complete with a pool and waterfall.

Howard Thurman once said, "Don't ask yourself what the world needs. Ask yourself what makes you alive, and go do that, because what the world needs is people who have come alive." The scenery inside the glass pyramid of Moody Gardens captivated my imagination and made my soul come alive.

Later, we ate at the Rainforest Café and took part in their jungle river ride. The whole experience awakened something me I never knew was quite there. I thought to myself, *Man, I wish someone made a story in this kind of setting that had a touch more tactical or espionage action to it*. Sure, video games like *Uncharted* and *Tomb Raider* have crept into this space a little more than say *Indiana Jones*, but I wanted something different. This new thing, this idea had made me come alive. Then, at the advice of Thurman, I decided to go and do that, and in the end, it worked out.

When I left home in 2004, I joined with the sole intention of becoming a Navy SEAL. In 2005 I attended BUD/S class 256 and broke my left hip early in training. It was surgically repaired that summer, and I feared my would-be career in special operations was over. With a lot of training and rehab, I returned in 2007 with class 268 to complete my quest, which again was cut short due to a skin infection called cellulitis in my left leg. I restarted from ground zero for a third time and realized something wasn't right. The life I once thought I wanted seemed less desirable. In January of 2008, I cried out to God, asking for His guidance. I can still remember standing in my barracks room when I heard His voice. He told me, "You don't have to do this. I have so much more for you."

It wasn't words like you hear with your ears, but it most definitely wasn't my conscience either. We went to breakfast, and at the end of my meal, I decided to do the one thing I swore I'd never do. I rang the bell three times and quit. I'd seen that same decision destroy a lot of my peers' lives. Because I firmly believe that I listened to His voice, it had the opposite effect. I was relieved of all the baggage I'd been carrying around associated with wanting a life as a Navy SEAL. The desire to be part of a high-performance team of like-minded individuals, however, remained.

Four years later in 2012, I was fortunate enough to be a part of a small tactical team that was responsible for active-shooter response on board of our particular naval base in Florida. We had some unique strategic partnerships, one of which was the local FBI SWAT team. I learned a lot about small-unit operations and team life. This really helped pave the way for my understanding of the small-team dynamic. My experiences here largely provided the framework for my protagonists within the small team, callsign Renegade.

Once I had the who, I needed a McGuffin. Admittedly I panicked initially because I thought I knew absolutely nothing about ancient history. This is where things got interesting. Suddenly I remembered a trip I took with my mom in 2005 to San Diego. She had a ten-disc sermon set about angels that she had brought with her. I recalled one sermon that mentioned the Nephilim and how they were the hybrid offspring of angels and humans. Immediately I said there's no way the bible says anything about that. Genesis 6:4 proved me wrong.

I hope you've enjoyed reading this novel as much as I have enjoyed writing it. Since starting this endeavor, I've found that I'm paying more attention to what historians tell us about specific people, groups, and regions, and it has really engaged my critical thinking. Of course, this is entirely a work of fiction, but I hope that somewhere deep down inside, it might cause you to ask yourself, "Were there really giants? Could they have existed?"

I'll leave that for you to decide.

Acknowledgments

This book exists solely because of my family and friends. I mean that in more ways than one. When I began writing this back in 2019, I decided the best way to write the characters would be to imbue them with certain peculiarities from people I know. The main characters found in these pages represent relationships with the people in my life who have had an immeasurable impact on me.

I would be remiss if I did not thank my beautiful wife first. From the day I told you I wanted to embark on this journey, you were nothing but supportive, from watching the kids to uplifting words when I felt like I couldn't keep going. Without you, this would never have happened. From the bottom of my heart, thank you, my love.

Secondly, I would have to thank Johnny, who helped me build this world from the ground up. We spent hours upon hours drafting the framework for every character, every setting, and every scene. This is just as much yours as it is mine.

Next, I would like to sincerely thank Eric and Ryan, two friends that I would trust with my life. Not having any real background in writing up until this point, I remember being scared to death giving you each an early version of the manuscript as a litmus test of sorts. Your advice and encouragement early on made this book what it is today.

I'm extremely grateful to my sister, Jessi, who I knew would shoot everything to me straight. You've always looked out for me more than I deserve, and thanks for not letting me die on those thousand-plus occasions where you saved my life.

Vaughan and Dave, you both stuck it out there for me without a second thought and didn't even really know me—that is something I'll never forget.

I sincerely appreciate the opportunity provided to me by Tom Reale and to the team at Brown Books who were able to make this all a reality. I love to see professionals do what they do best, and you all exceeded my expectations.

Speaking of professionals, lastly, I cannot begin to express thanks to the real Renegade Actual, JF, who provided the basis for all these characters and situations. When we met over a decade ago, I knew we were developing a friendship that would endure. Thanks for all the laughs, adventures (both real and life harrowing), and for teaching me that family isn't always the people who share the same blood. Sometimes they're chosen.

About the Author

Christopher Clay was born outside of Nashville, Tennessee, and moved to Missouri at the age of twelve. He grew up reading anything he could get his hands on and developed a taste for thrillers, particularly espionage, at some point in high school. At the age of nineteen, he enlisted in the US Navy in 2004 where he served for more than a decade. During his time out at sea and abroad, he found his imagination running wild with fictional adventures in which he wished he could partake. In 2016, he departed active duty service and headed to the great state of Texas to serve his community as a full-time police officer for a large agency. He continues to reside in Texas with his beautiful wife and children. He loves conspiracy theories about the ancient past and spending time outdoors with his family. He loves shooting, hiking, and hunting.